THE
HURRICANE

ALSO BY R. J. PRESCOTT

The Aftermath

THE HURRICANE

R. J. PRESCOTT

FOREVER

New York   Boston

Forever
Hachette Book Group
1290 Avenue of the Americas
New York, NY 10104
hachettebookgroup.com
twitter.com/foreverromance

Printed in the United States of America

RRD-C

First published as an ebook
First trade paperback edition: February 2016
10 9 8 7 6 5 4 3 2 1

Forever is an imprint of Grand Central Publishing.
The Forever name and logo are trademarks of Hachette Book Group, Inc.

The Hachette Speakers Bureau provides a wide range of authors for speaking events. To find out more, go to www.hachettespeakersbureau.com or call (866) 376-6591.

The publisher is not responsible for websites (or their content) that are not owned by the publisher.

Library of Congress Cataloguing-in-Publication Data is available upon request.

ISBN 978-1-4555-9312-5

THE
HURRICANE

PROLOGUE

CORMAC O'CONNELL

I felt like a total fucking creeper as I leaned, with my hands in my pockets, against the lamppost, and stared at her through the cafe window from across the road. For weeks now, I'd found myself in the same spot, wondering when I was going to grow a pair of balls and talk to her. Man, this girl was fucking perfect. At least that was what I'd built her up to be. I wasn't sure I could handle the disappointment if she was anything less.

I tilted my head to the left as she walked from the kitchen with a pot of coffee. I didn't want to lose sight of her. Even in that shitty uniform, she was gorgeous. The first time I saw her, I thought she was hot. Then again, every girl I fucked was hot. But this girl was something else. She was beautiful, and there hadn't ever been much of anything in my life you could call beautiful.

Her blond hair was tied back in one of those messy knots that she always wore to work. Loose, I knew it was long, thick, and curly at the ends. I was getting hard as I imagined her straddling me, that hair cascading down as I fisted my hands into it. Jesus, now I was standing on a street corner at 6:30 a.m. with a hard-on. It was official. I was definitely a creeper.

Just then Danny said something funny, and they shared a laugh. Danny was an old man, and I was still jealous. What I wouldn't have given to have her smile like that for me.

She blushed as she glanced around with those beautiful blue eyes, suddenly self-conscious that someone might have seen her laughing. She never did anything to draw attention to herself, which made her the complete opposite of pretty much every girl I'd ever met. Even from here, I could tell she didn't have any makeup on, but she didn't need it. Her skin was flawless, and her plump, pale, pink lips were edible. I was sure a good kiss would darken them up. If I had my way, I'd find out soon enough.

Her cheekbones were a little hollow, which wasn't surprising given how tiny she was. I had at least a foot, and over a hundred pounds on this girl, and I realized how uneasy my size might make her. She was nervous and skittish, so I was probably going to scare the shite out of her. There was fuck all I could do about it, though. It's not like I could have made myself any smaller. Maybe if I waited until she left then sat down before she came back, I wouldn't seem so big.

Despite her size, she had killer legs that went on for miles, and a little hourglass dip at her waist that made me want to wrap my hands around it as I kissed her.

I shifted my weight to the other foot, willing my erection back down before some arsehole walked by and got the wrong idea. To make matters worse, I was fucking freezing. I'd left my hoodie at the gym, thinking it would help my cause to show off my body. It was pretty much the only thing I had going for me. Instead, I just felt like a fucking eejit, knowing that it was too cold for anyone but a total poser to be walking around in a T-shirt. It was the sort of thing that Kier and I would take the piss over. He'd be laughing his arse off if he could see me now.

Emily.

I whispered her name as I rolled it around on my tongue. I heard it yesterday when one of the other waitresses called out to her. It suited her. I thought once more about bottling it and heading back to the gym when she turned and walked toward the kitchen. This was my chance to sit next to Danny before she came back.

Fuck it.

Shoving my hands in my pockets, I headed across the street. I had no idea how much my life was going to change from the minute I sat down at that table.

CHAPTER ONE

Oh, my God, I am so late! I ran down the street, my heart pounding. The early morning commuters trying to make it into the office were oblivious to my plight as I dodged in and out of people. My thin summer shoes offered nearly no protection against the bitter bite of the frosty morning. By the time I opened the back door to Daisy's Cafe, my teeth were chattering and my fingers were stiff with what I was sure was the onset of frostbite. I had no idea what I was going to do when winter really set in. I was barely scraping together enough money for rent and food, let alone having to worry about gloves and a winter coat.

"Mornin', Em." Mike, the owner, smiled as he turned the bacon over in the pan. For the last few weeks, I'd been pulling extra shifts at the cafe and then studying when I got home. I thought I could handle it, but after waking up at my desk half an hour ago, I knew I was wrong.

I wasn't surprised that Mike didn't seem mad. I'd never been late for a shift before, and more often than not, I was the last to leave. Daisy's had heating, after all. Heating and company. Two of the things I was in need of most at the moment.

"Sorry I'm late," I mumbled to Mike. I avoided making eye contact and raced to hang up my coat and tie my apron. Tapping down the pocket, I made sure I had my pad and pencil and quickly scraped my hair back with one of the elastics kept permanently around my wrist. Wrestling it into a messy bun, I weaved through the kitchen and grabbed a pot of coffee.

I passed Rhona who'd been at Daisy's since the doors first opened.

"Slow down, love," she said with a warm smile. "You just need to do the refills and take the order for table two." She breezed into the kitchen without waiting for a reply.

Daisy's was one of the only cafes around that offered unlimited tea and coffee refills with a meal, which meant the place was usually packed for breakfast. After running around topping up coffees, I said hello to Danny as he sat down at his usual table. We chatted for a bit and, promising him a fresh pot, I headed to the kitchen to pass Mike the order for table two.

As I walked back out, I froze. Sitting next to Danny, and glancing at me over the menu, was hands-down the hottest guy I had ever seen. His nose had a slight crook in it, which made me think it was once broken, but that was the only flaw in his otherwise perfect face. Razor-sharp cheekbones, tanned skin, and dark hair added to the beauty that seemed completely at odds with his stature. If it weren't for the broken nose, he could be a model, but I knew that whatever this man did was dangerous, because everything about him exuded violence. I had no idea who he was, and the fact that he was sitting with Danny should have eased me, but it didn't. My internal alarm was going off big time. From the set of his shoulders, to the sheer size of him, he looked like nothing but trouble. Whoever he was, it looked like Danny was raking him over the coals about something.

Danny was a small, wiry man, who couldn't have been much

younger than seventy-five. The deep grooves in his face and leathery skin spoke of hard living, but he was no frail pensioner. Mike was twice the size of Danny, but even he was a little bit scared of him. From my very first shift at Daisy's, he'd strolled through the door a few minutes past opening, plonked himself in an empty booth in my section, and beckoned me over—which soon became our morning ritual.

But that first day was different; I'd been absolutely petrified of everything and everyone. Most regulars had gravitated toward the other girls' sections, wary of the new girl messing up their order. Danny had no such compunctions, though. He'd sat straight down and called out, "Hey, sunshine, come and get me a cuppa coffee. I don't bite."

Shaking like a leaf, I filled his cup and, by sheer force of will, avoided spilling the scalding liquid all over his lap. If he noticed my nerves, he'd never said anything. He rattled off his order then unfolded a crisp, clean newspaper and read silently until I brought out his breakfast. When he was finished, I removed his plate and refilled his coffee.

"Thank you, sunshine," he said, without smiling and without looking up from his paper.

Things went on that way for a few weeks, and when I finally stopped shaking, he spoke to me. It was never anything too personal, just remarks about the weather, questions about school, and what I thought of my professors. In the beginning, I did my best to find one-word answers, but just over a year later, Danny was the closest thing I had to a friend.

I wanted to run and hide in the kitchen. But hiding wouldn't do me any good, it never did. Ten horrific years of my stepfather, Frank, knocking me around had taught me not to speak unless spoken to and not to make eye contact. Whenever I felt threatened, those were the rules I fell back on.

Moving quickly through the tables, I wiped down a couple,

gathered up a few dirty dishes, and after dropping them off at the kitchen, I could procrastinate no further and headed to Danny's table.

"Two full fried breakfasts please, sunshine," Danny croaked, with his usual scowl. If he ever did smile at me, I was a little worried that his weather-beaten face might crack.

Lowering my eyes, I gave him a small nod but didn't reply. It was our usual routine, and he was familiar with it. Without asking him, I filled up his coffee cup, and my hands trembled. It had been months since that happened, and I knew if I had to ask Danny's companion if he'd like coffee, my voice would crack. I turned toward him with the coffeepot in my hand, and my eye caught on the sleeve of his white T-shirt. The biggest biceps that I'd ever seen strained the seams, and beneath, the edge of a tattoo was visible. It looked like a series of intricately woven Celtic designs. From what I could see, the artwork was beautiful.

"O'Connell, do you want coffee or not?" Danny snapped at him. I flinched at the sharpness of his tone, but he did, at least, save me from speaking.

"Yeah, sure," the guy replied lazily, almost bored. I shook badly again, and I was sure that I'd spill it, but I didn't. Gathering up their menus, I all but whispered, "I'll be back with your order soon," and fled to the kitchen to hide. The guy's eyes were boring a hole in my back as I walked away.

Ten minutes later, their order was done. Taking their warm plates through to the cafe, I placed the identical breakfasts down in front of them and escaped.

"You keep your eyes off that, boyo. That one's not for you," I heard Danny warn quietly.

Danny was born and raised in Killarney, Ireland, and I very much doubted that the forty years he'd spent here in London had softened his accent much.

"Why was she shaking so badly?" the man Danny had called

O'Connell asked in a deep, husky voice with a slight Irish lilt that was just about the sexiest thing that I had ever heard.

Danny sighed deeply before answering. "You probably scare the shite out of her. That one's special, but she ain't for you, so you'd best mind yourself and leave her to her business. Now, stop looking after something you can't have and think about what I said, 'cause if we have one more conversation about you drinkin' and fightin', you eejit, then you and me are gonna have words!"

The rest of the conversation was lost on me. The idea of Danny threatening this mountain of a man with anything would be enough to make me smile, if he hadn't mentioned the fighting. Truth be told, you only had to look at O'Connell to know that he was dangerous. It was hard to tell how tall he was, but by the way he was crammed into that booth, I'd guess he was big. Broad shouldered and ripped, he looked every inch a fighter, but it was that relaxed, almost bored, indifference about him that sold the package. He could take care of himself, and he knew it.

A few more of my regulars made their way over to my section, and after doing my rounds with the coffee and rushing back and forth with orders, I realized that the seat across from Danny was empty. I let out a deep breath and began clearing the table.

"Give my compliments to Mike," Danny told me, as I stacked up the plates.

"Sure, Danny," I replied. "Can I get you another coffee?"

"No, thank you, sunshine. My bladder control is not what it used to be, and I'm gonna find it hard enough to get back to work as it is."

This was more information than I needed to know. I was sure that he threw it out there just to get a rise out of me, and I humored him by rolling my eyes.

"Make sure you wrap up warm, then." I gestured toward his coat and scarf on the bench. "It's bitter out."

I dealt with ringing up his check, and before he'd even closed the door behind him, Katrina Bray was up in my face. With her shirt pulled tight against her impressive cleavage and a skirt rolled higher than her apron, she stomped her way toward me.

"What the hell was Cormac O'Connell doing in your section?"

I gave her the one-shouldered shrug. "I have no friggin' clue, and you're welcome to serve him next time," would be my response of choice, but I kept my mouth shut. Katrina was the last person that I needed to start an argument with.

"You have absolutely no idea who he is, do you?"

She obviously deduced this for herself, given the vacant look on my face. Without waiting for an answer, she flounced off in a cloud of cheap perfume. Rhona, having heard the whole exchange, shoulder bumped me on her way back to the kitchen.

"Go on, girl. 'Bout time that madam had a bit of competition, and once upon a time, I wouldn't have minded a piece of that boy, myself. I wouldn't be turning a blind eye if I was twenty years younger."

"Need some help?" I motioned to the dishes in her hand, trying to change the subject. It had completely escaped her notice that I was neither flirting, nor being flirted with. I was no expert, but I was sure that you actually needed to talk to someone to start a relationship.

"No thanks, love, I've got it. Your section is getting pretty full."

She nodded back toward the cafe. Seeing she was right, I hurried back to take orders. People were pretty slow about coming into my section to begin with, but once they saw me waiting on Danny every day, they slowly started drifting over. The breakfast and lunch shifts flew by, punctuated by evil looks from Katrina. I guessed from her attitude that O'Connell was on her hit list and she hadn't scored with him yet. Which would put him in the minority, from what I heard.

When Katrina wanted a guy, he usually didn't offer much resistance. She had nothing to worry about from me, though. If O'Connell came in here again, she was welcome to him. However good-looking the package, I didn't need that kind of trouble in my life. It wasn't as if he'd ever give me a second look anyway.

By the time my shift ended, I was glad to be heading to class. Waitressing was okay, and it was nice to have some company, but school was where I really lost myself. Getting a place at UCL had been the scariest and most exhilarating thing that had ever happened to me. None of it would have been possible without my former teacher Mrs. Wallis. I had been wriggling around in my seat, trying not to let the chair touch any of the fresh bruises hidden under my sweater when she had approached me. With tears in her eyes, she had told me she knew I had a difficult home life, and as I was nearly eighteen, there was a way of escaping. If I wanted her help, I would have it.

That was the nearest that I ever came to breaking down. Part of me wanted to scream at her that, if she knew, then why didn't she tell social services so they could get me? I think we both knew that would only have made things worse though.

I didn't scream at her or cry, but actually setting out the bare bones of a plan was terrifying. The fear of being caught, and of my stepfather, Frank, discovering what I was doing, had me feeling sick every minute of every day. Using Mrs. Wallis's address, I had applied for university places and identification. When I turned eighteen, I changed my surname legally. I accepted a place studying applied mathematics at University College London, and now, eighteen months later, the only person who could ever connect Emily Thomas from Cardiff, South Wales, with me was Mrs. Wallis, an elderly home economics teacher who was the only person I'd ever trusted.

I'd breezed an access course in accounting over the summer,

but my heart was in math. It was clean and pure, and in my world of gray, it was black and white. If I had any chance at building a future, then I needed qualifications.

The dread of being caught was always ever present though. I guessed that Frank was looking for me but getting my degree was worth the risk. If I committed to staying in one place long enough to finish university, I had to keep a low profile. It was my best chance of evading him. So I did what I'd always done. I made no eye contact and never initiated conversation.

It had worked in high school, but university was a completely different kettle of fish. The guys here were relentless. Politely turning down unwanted advances, without causing offense, had become an art form that I'd perfected. It was the safest way to live, but I was lonely. There were days that I desperately wanted someone, anyone, to call a friend. In lecture room three, on that frosty Tuesday afternoon, I got just that.

"This seat taken?"

I looked down at cherry red leather boots with a killer heel and looked up to see that the voice belonging to them liked to coordinate her cherry red hair with her outfit. Clearly I was more than backward when it came to accessorizing. My hair didn't go with anything.

"Um..." I looked around, desperate to say yes, hoping to remain as anonymous as possible. The lecture theater was only a third full, at best, and there was no reason why this girl would want to sit next to me. She wore a denim miniskirt, a fitted black top, and a leather jacket that I would have given my left arm for. With the killer boots and her glossy hair layered artfully around her face, she looked edgy and hot. No wonder half the man-geeks were drooling. My first thought was that she was in the wrong place.

"No," I replied. Could I have been more socially inept? If she was in the right place, it looked like she'd be beating off the guys with a stick, so what better place to take cover than beside the only other girl in the room.

"Nikki Martin," she said, sliding into the adjoining seat.

"Sorry?" I mumbled.

"I'm Nikki Martin," she stated, expectantly awaiting a response.

"Oh, hi," I replied, as I went back to copying down the equation from the projector.

"Oh, my God, you really are one of them," she laughed, teasingly.

"One of them?" I answered, glancing up in confusion.

"The freaks who only speak in numbers and have no social skills whatsoever."

"Wow, rude much?" Oh, my God! I've never been confrontational, *ever*, but with this girl, it just slipped out.

She laughed again, probably at the look of sheer horror on my face. "So the kitten has claws. You know, you and me are going to get on just fine."

I had no idea what to say to that. This girl was like a beautiful steamroller.

"Okay, a name would be good about now, unless you want me to call you Mathlexy all term."

"Mathlexy?" Yep, I was getting good at repeating everything she said back to her as a question.

"I can tell you're a math fiend by the stack of handwritten notes you've got there, and you're the sexiest thing this lot has probably ever seen."

She gestured around the lecture hall, and I wasn't convinced that the guys would actually wait until the end of class to pounce on her. The wide-eyed looks of disbelief, appreciation, and finally hunger reminded me of starving hyenas, eyeing up their appetizer. I giggled at the image and snorted through my nose at the absurdity of the name. Snorting was neither sexy nor attractive.

"Emily McCarthy," I offered up in return, hopeful of rejecting that ridiculous nickname before anyone heard it. The last name was new. I'd only had it for a year, and I was still getting used to it. But I figured that keeping my first name wouldn't hurt. Emily was a pretty common name, and people got suspicious if you didn't answer to your name when called because you didn't know it.

"Well, it's nice to meet you, Emily McCarthy," she answered.

By the end of the lecture, I had three sides of crisp clean notes, and Nikki had half a page and some lovely heart and floral murals.

"What's your next class?" she asked, as we were stuffing things into our bags.

"I don't have another one for a couple of hours," I replied. "I was just going to the library to study."

"Perfect, I have a couple of hours free. Let's go and grab a coffee. My treat."

She looped her arm through mine and all but dragged me out, clearly not caring about my plans.

Latte, espresso, tall, fat, mocha, grande. The board in front of me laid out the endless possible taste sensations, and I agonized over my decision. I loved coffee, but on my budget, regular coffee at Daisy's was about as good as it got. So if this was my treat for the month, then I was going to make the most of it.

"Come on, Em," Nikki moaned, "I'm growing old here!"

"A cappuccino, please," I ordered quickly. The barista handed me my drink, and I pulled out the chair next to Nikki.

She took a long sip of her coffee, sighed deeply, and turned to me. "So...the whole social hermit thing. Is it just for a term or are you committed for life?"

CHAPTER TWO

I was so grateful to have escaped my former life that living for three years without forming any attachments seemed like a small price to pay for my freedom. The reality was that I had escaped from hell, only to find that fear still incarcerated me in a prison from which there was no escape. I was afraid that the more memorable I became, the more likely it was that I would be found. However irrational that fear was, it made me close myself off from forming any kind of friendship.

Until Nikki sat down next to me, it was the only way I knew. I'd been so caught up in surviving and staying free, that I'd forgotten that freedom was a state of mind. I might have escaped physically, but mentally I was still giving the son of a bitch that power over me. Changing that cycle would need a conscious decision, and making a new friend seemed like a good place to start.

"Why would you think that I'm a social hermit?" I asked, already knowing the answer. I was curious, though, to find out how she saw me.

"Look, I didn't mean to be rude. I've been sitting behind you in class since the start of term. Granted, most of the class seems fairly antisocial, but you don't talk to anyone, and you seem to avoid catching people's eyes so they don't initiate a conversation."

"You've been in that class for a month?" I asked, slightly shocked.

"See, that's what I mean. If you'd looked up from your notes occasionally, you'd have seen me."

"Sorry," I apologized. "I'm not much good at making new friends."

"Neither am I," she admitted, which surprised me. "Well, I'm not much good at making girlfriends, anyway. Most of my friends are guys. I guess my tendency to say things as they are, without filtering, puts girls off. If you ask me how you look, and I think your dress makes your arse look fat, I'll tell you. If you ask me what I think of your boyfriend, and he's a dick, I'll tell you. I think that makes me a pretty awesome friend, but most girls don't agree." She shrugged humorously, and I couldn't help but like her.

"Anyway, I'm sick of not having anyone to talk to in class, so I thought I'd say hello. If you really don't want to talk, though, I can go back to sitting behind you."

"Like that wouldn't be weird," I replied. "I'm glad you sat next to me. It's nice to make a new friend."

"Well, don't get too attached to me. I'm sure I'll say something to piss you off by the weekend."

"I don't have a boyfriend, and I don't wear dresses, so we should be fine."

She grinned at me, and her smile was infectious.

"Look, one of the guys on the rugby team is having a party in a couple of weeks. How about you come with me?" she asked.

I almost choked on my coffee at the thought of dancing around in a tiny skirt and chucking back the shots.

"Um, thanks, Nikki, but I'm kind of working double shifts

waitressing to pay for my course. If it's on a weekend, chances are I'll be working."

"Well, just think on it. You can get ready at my place and borrow some of my clothes and stuff. We'd have a blast."

I had no intention of going, but I was blown away that this girl, who hardly knew me at all, would be so generous. I wasn't used to such random acts of kindness.

"I'll think about it," I replied, knowing my answer wouldn't change. "So how come you're going? Do you know some of the guys on the rugby team?" I asked, taking a sip of my coffee and burning my tongue.

"I'm friends with a few of them, and there's a few going who I wouldn't mind being more than friendly with."

I looked down and blushed as I thought about O'Connell, who was pretty much the only guy I'd thought about like that in a very long time. When I looked back up, Nikki was staring at me as though she was mentally sizing me up for a boyfriend.

"I'm not interested in meeting anyone, Nikki," I warned. "I've got enough on my plate between my job and classes."

"Fine." She sighed dramatically. "You can be my wingman when I'm wearing beer goggles. I have terrible taste in men when I'm drunk. Just pull me away from the ones I'd chew my arm off to get away from in the morning."

I burst out laughing at the image, and it was the first time that I could remember laughing in a very long time.

* * *

I woke up the next morning shaking with fear. It had been a while since I'd dreamed at all, and I'd forgotten just how bad they were. I had no doubt that my conversation with Nikki yesterday had triggered it. New things always did. The nightmare was one of a hundred memories that I'd never be free of.

I had been about fifteen at the time and taking out the rubbish when Noah Rawlinson, a guy from my class, strolled by my house, walking his dog.

"Hey, Em, how are you?"

"Good, thanks. He's gorgeous, what's his name?" I asked, as I bent down to rub the coat of the overenthusiastic golden retriever licking at my hand.

"Umm . . . Barbie," he mumbled, his face coloring with embarrassment.

"Seriously," I replied.

"I know, I know." He laughed, rubbing Barbie's coat along with me. *"I wanted a dog when I was a kid and Mum let me choose the dog, but my little sister got to pick the name."*

I tried not to smile but couldn't help it. "That's pretty tragic. Poor dog."

"Poor dog! You should try yelling after this crazy animal in a park full of people. I'm sure he's disobedient just to make me look stupid."

Noah and I had caught each other's eye a couple of times in class, and I'd been hoping he'd ask me out. He pushed his floppy blond hair out of his eyes and shifted from foot to foot, obviously building up to something. I bit my lip with nervous anticipation.

"So were you planning on going to the end-of-year dance?" he asked. *I carried on patting Barbie's coat. The poor dog would be bald by the time we made a date.*

"I hadn't really thought about it yet," I lied. Hello! *What girl in my year hadn't thought about the dance?*

"Well, would you like to go with me?" Noah asked sheepishly.

"I'd love to. Thank you," I replied, after a slight pause.

"That's great. So I guess I'll see you at school?" he suggested with a happy grin.

At my nod and smile, he pulled Barbie along to continue their stroll, lifting his hand to wave good-bye as I walked inside.

I was still smiling and contemplating what to wear to the dance when the slap came out of nowhere and hit with so much force that the side of my face smashed into the kitchen cabinet. As I landed on the floor, Frank's boot hit me straight in the stomach, and I choked back the bile that would only make him madder.

"You little, fucking slut. You can't even take the rubbish out without lifting your skirt for the nearest pussy-sniffing son of a bitch out there. Have you fucked him already? You have, haven't you?" he screamed, not waiting for an answer as a second boot planted in my gut.

It was a long time before the hits stopped coming. Apart from the one cut to my eye, my clothes would cover the worst of the damage. I didn't make it off the floor that night, and the next day I made it as far as my bed, but as soon as I was well enough, I gave Noah some lame apology and broke our date.

He never asked again, and I stopped looking him in the eye. I stopped looking everyone in the eye. The floor had become my new favorite scenery, and my stepfather's reign of power had begun.

* * *

I had work soon, and I needed to get my head in the right place. Using a technique I'd first read about on the Internet, I grabbed the scented candle on my bedside table, lit it, and inhaled deeply, savoring the candle's sweet vanilla fragrance. Holding my breath, I focused on clearing my mind of everything and exhaled. After a few minutes the panic had receded. I was always afraid, but I could think past the anxiety now.

Looking at my watch, I saw I only had thirty minutes before my shift started. For the second day in a row, I was running to work again.

* * *

"Good mornin', sunshine," Danny croaked in his usual gruff voice. He sounded like he smoked twenty a day, but it was probably more like fifty. The tips of his fingers gave away his habit as much as his voice.

"Morning, Danny. How are you today?" I asked.

Danny looked up from the menu. He always read the menu, and I had no idea why, because he ordered the same thing every day.

"What happened?" he barked at me.

"What do you mean?" I asked, frowning in confusion.

"You asked me a question. Aside from asking me what I want for breakfast, you never do that. So I want to know what's up."

I could feel myself clamming up. I looked down instinctively and bit my lip.

"Now, don't you start cowering on me, girl. Something's happened to you, and I'm nosy enough to want to know what it is. You should know me well enough by now to know that my bark is worse than my bite, so stop looking at the floor and better still, take a seat and talk to me a little bit."

He nodded at the seat across the booth from his. I looked up and met his gaze. You could tell a lot from a person's eyes. I wasn't the world's best judge of character, but I could usually tell when a smile on the face hid meanness behind the eyes.

"I can't, Danny. I don't think Mike would much like me sitting down on the job."

"Don't you get breaks?"

"Danny, you're always my first customer of the day. It's a little early for a break, don't you think?"

"Rhona?" Danny barked, as she headed toward the kitchen.

"Can you spare our girl for five minutes?" He nodded toward me, and I was stunned.

"Course I can. We won't get many in till half past. Just keep an eye out for anyone in your section," she called back, seeming unperturbed. So far Danny was my only customer so, pouring myself a cup of coffee, I sat down in the booth opposite him. He waited patiently.

"Don't you want to order your breakfast while we wait?"

"I've got all day," he said. "You can put my order in when the next table fills up. So?" he barked.

"I made a new friend," I answered. His expression didn't change, but the tone was more inquisitive.

"Boy or girl?" he asked.

"Err, girl," I replied, embarrassed.

"Good. I hope she's got a bit of spunk about her. You need someone to bring you out of yourself."

"How do you know this isn't the extrovert me?"

"Huh," he grunted. "If this is the extrovert you, then the introvert you must be bloody mute."

I didn't know whether to laugh or be offended.

"So this is the reason why you're so cheerful then?" he inquired.

"I guess," I replied, swirling the spoon around my coffee. "She's very different than me, but she seems really nice."

"It's about time you made some new friends and started living a little. Life is for the living, my girl, and anything else is just marking time."

"Well, it's not like I'm going to become a social butterfly overnight. It'll just be nice to have some company at school, that's all. Making friends is fine but going out with friends usually requires money. I need as many shifts as I can get at Daisy's to pay for school. You know that," I explained as I sipped my coffee.

"'Bout that. I've been having a think to myself, and I reckon we could help each other out, you and me."

"How do you mean?" I replied.

"Do you trust me?" Of course, I trusted him. Up until yesterday, he was probably my only friend in the world. But when someone asked if you trusted them, it was usually because they were about to put that trust to the test.

"I trust you, but I'm not sure how you think we can help each other."

"Thing is, I've got a business down on Barking Road here in Canning Town. It's not really all that big, so up until now I've been doing all the books myself. Ain't much work, just a couple of nights a week, but I'm ticking on now and most nights I'm just too tired to take care of it. Now last few years business has been good, so I'm thinking to myself that a bookkeeper is a mighty fine idea. Course, I'm not paying through the nose for it."

I listened politely until his meaning sank in, and I was floored.

"You want me to do your bookkeeping?"

"Well, now that you mention it, girl, I think that would be a grand idea."

"But how do you know if I'm any good, and more importantly, how do you know if I'm trustworthy?"

"You're not much good at interviews, are you, girl?" His question was obviously rhetorical, and before I could say anything else, he continued.

"I've known you for over a year. You're polite, punctual, and smart." Only Danny could bark out my best qualities like he was reading stats off a baseball card.

"I can check on your work, and as for being trustworthy, you'd have to get up early in the morning to get one over on me. So what do you say?"

"Thanks for the offer, Danny, but I don't think I can add another job in with school and the shifts I'm already doing."

It sure was tempting, though. Most days my feet ached and my back hurt. I should be snapping Danny's hand off to take the chance to get paid to sit at a desk and do something that was bread and butter. But Mike had been good to me, and if nothing else, I was loyal.

"I've already had a chat with Mike and Rhona, and they're happy to drop you back to your original two shifts a week if you can finish out weekends until the end of your rota. You can pick up two nights a week with me after school, and I pay forty percent better than Mike for the sort of work you'd be doing."

I did the math in my head, and with that pay, I could drop down to working four evenings a week on better pay than I was making now. More importantly, I'd have three nights a week off and no more dawn starts.

I could have cried with relief. This morning I was stressing over new gloves, and now I felt like doing cartwheels. Danny really was an angel. Then a horrible thought occurred to me, and my face dropped.

"Are you sure the work is there, though? I'd hate to get there and be twiddling my thumbs because you're just trying to help me out."

"The only person I ever help, sunshine, is myself. Rhona and Mike need you Tuesdays and Wednesdays, and if you don't mind, you'll be working for me Thursdays and Fridays. Now . . ." He spit on his hand and held it out to me. "Do we have a deal?"

I grimaced at the spitting, but shook hands firmly with the angel of my salvation. I had a new friend and a new job in twenty-four hours. I was, most definitely, on a roll.

CHAPTER THREE

Un-frickin-believable. There was absolutely no way I was going inside. I tightly clutched the piece of paper on which Danny had written the address of his business, and looked up again at the number above the door in the hope that I was wrong. I felt so stupid. I, who questioned everything, had never asked Danny what sort of business he ran. Apparently my streak of fortuity had come to an end. I was standing outside the heavy oak doors of Driscoll's Boxing Gym.

A thickset arm reached from behind me to pull open a door by the polished brass handle, and I was jolted forward as the biggest man that I had ever seen caught me with the edge of his gym bag. As he walked inside, oblivious to the knock, he turned to hold the door open for me.

"Well then, darlin', are you coming or going?"

I said nothing but swallowed hard. He chuckled at my obvious discomfort, winked, and let the door fall shut behind him. I stood staring at the doors like a zombie. The guy was huge and fiercely intimidating, but I hadn't felt even slightly scared of him. A little overwhelmed, maybe, but not scared.

"Fuck it," I said aloud, pulled the door open, and walked in with more bravado than I actually felt. I passed slowly through a narrow corridor and up a flight of steps as the sounds of the gym grew louder.

On the right was a huge notice board covered in posters promoting fights and handwritten notes advertising equipment for sale. Among all the signs was one that read: FRIDAY IS DUES DAY. IF YOU HAVEN'T PAID YOUR DUES, DON'T EMBARRASS YOURSELF BY HAVING TO BE ASKED FOR THEM.

That explained why Danny wanted me at the end of every week. If that was when dues were paid, chances were that was when he paid bills and wages, too.

Knowing I couldn't stand in the corridor forever, I approached the gym as unobtrusively as I could. The place was much bigger on the inside than you could ever guess from looking at the street entrance, and it was absolutely packed. At the back of the gym was a full-size boxing ring but all around were stations where fighters were training, some with hanging punch bags and others with speedballs or just pads.

Caught like a deer in the headlights, and with a death grip on my shoulder bag, I scanned the room for Danny. One or two of the fighters noticed me and stared inquisitively, but much to my relief, no one stopped training.

My gaze stopped on Cormac O'Connell, and I doubted there was another woman under sixty whose eyes would have drifted any farther. I was right about him being tall. Even from this distance, he looked to be at least six-foot-five.

His back was to me as he tapped fist-to-fist against a speed-ball, and what a view it was from behind. Broad shoulders rippled with definition down to a lean waist.

He was too far away for me to see any detail, but the tattoo that I'd glimpsed beneath his shirt spanned his arm from his elbow all the way to his shoulder and around his upper back. It was as hot as the body it adorned.

As though O'Connell could feel my eyes on him, he stopped punching and turned to meet my stare. Just like that, his face lit up with a smile. Not a cocky throwaway grin, but a genuine smile, like he was really pleased to see me. I felt as though he'd caught me gawking and looked away.

Thankfully, my savior, and the one who'd gotten me into this predicament in the first place, came to my rescue. Despite my fear that he would, Danny didn't shout across the gym at me, but when he spotted me from a door at the back of the room, I had the sense that he wanted to. He stomped my way, and I was amused at the sight of big, burly fighters hurrying to move.

"Found us okay, then?" he asked.

"You run a gym?" I squeaked stupidly, stating the obvious.

He motioned for me to follow him as he plowed another path through the fighters.

"I've had this gym for over thirty years. Don't think I could ever work for anyone else. I live, breathe, and sleep this place. Smells like home to me."

"It smells pretty bad, Danny," I replied, with another squeak.

"It smells like hard work and pride, sunshine."

I felt ashamed. I'd been knocking Danny's livelihood when he'd been kind enough to offer me this job. Not knowing how to dig myself out of this one, I kept quiet.

"Don't worry about it, girl," Danny smirked. "You'll soon get used to it." He led the way to his office. With one last look over my shoulder at O'Connell's curious, smiling face, I followed Danny in.

I didn't know what I expected, but there weren't many signs that Danny spent a great deal of time here. Facing the door was a large walnut desk, which sat in front of a battered leather swivel chair. A much lower, comfier-looking, but equally battered, chair faced it.

Danny pointed to the lower chair with a chuckle. "I make the boys sit there if they have to explain to me why they haven't paid their dues. Does the gobshites good to sit lower than me while they squirm."

I think it amused the secret masochist in Danny to watch big guys feel intimidated. Hell, I felt intimidated just being in the same room as him, and I probably weighed more than he did wet, which was saying something, given my stature.

A blind, thick with dust, covered the large picture window behind the desk. In the little space left in this tiny room, a filing cabinet and small table, on which sat a coffeemaker, were tucked to one side. The desk housed an older-looking computer and a huge stack of papers. I had no idea where he wanted me to start, so I asked him, and he chuckled.

"Start wherever you like. I've been told I should computerize my records for the next tax year, but I haven't got a feckin' clue how those things work," he said, banging hard on the monitor.

"One of the boys sorted me out with the computer. Said it should have all the stuff you need. There's a copy of last year's return in the cabinet. Most of my receipts for the year are on the desk, and entries for dues are in the ledgers, so just see what you can do."

I sat down with a thump in the office chair and looked around dejectedly.

"Too late to back out on me now, sunshine."

I frowned at the mess before me, and he looked at me like he knew I was going to bolt at any second. I probably would have, too, if I hadn't been feeling so guilty about offending him earlier.

"Okay, Danny. I'll give it a go."

He nodded at me then jerked his head in the direction of the coffeemaker.

"Help yourself to coffee. I'll come and see how you're getting on later."

With an audible sigh as he closed the door, I dropped my bag under the desk, draped my coat across the back of the chair, and got to work. By the time Danny returned, I'd given the desk a rudimentary dusting and had sorted the mess of paperwork into some semblance of order.

"So how did you get on?" he inquired.

"Danny, your books are a mess." I beamed.

"If they're such a mess, what's put that grin on your face?" he retorted.

"I had fun making some sense of the chaos, and it's a lot less stressful than waitressing."

"Well, so long as I'm getting my money's worth," he huffed, but I could tell he was pleased that I hadn't bolted. "Tomorrow's sub collection, so the boys will be by through the evening to drop 'em off. That okay with you?" he asked.

I wasn't thrilled with the idea of being alone in a tiny office with some of these guys. But this was part of the job, and Danny was paying me too well to turn my nose up at it. I'd had a great time burying myself in the books, and if any of the boys made me feel uncomfortable, I'd mention it to Danny. That didn't mean that I wasn't going to make myself sick between now and then worrying about it though.

"It's fine," I mumbled quickly, before I could talk myself out of it.

Nodding curtly, he gestured his thumb toward the door. "Come on then, sunshine. You've overstayed your welcome. You get off home now, and I'll see you tomorrow."

I shut down the computer, making a mental note of what I needed to bring tomorrow, threw on my coat, and slung my bag over my shoulder as I headed out of the door. Although the gym had emptied a little since I'd arrived, I was surprised to see people still training. As dedicated as they were, I hoped they didn't notice me skulking toward the door.

Outside the cold, crisp air threatened snow, and I breathed deeply before rocking on my heels and contemplating how long it would take me to walk home.

"Hello, sunshine," a voice spoke softly to me, as warm breath grazed my ear. I jumped and put my hand over my heart, as though that could alleviate the impending cardiac arrest. I turned to see O'Connell behind me. Too late I realized that I'd instinctively cowered away from him, flinching against a blow that never came.

His face dropped, as he understood what I'd done. "Ah shite, I'm sorry. I didn't mean to scare you. I was just trying to be friendly."

He held up his hands in a gesture of innocence, and I was mortified. "No, I'm sorry. I'm a little jumpy, that's all. I wasn't expecting anyone to be behind me."

I could feel my cheeks coloring, making the embarrassment worse. In my defense, it was the first time since high school that I'd had anything resembling a conversation with a good-looking guy.

"So I hear Danny's got you working the books. You go to school around here?" he inquired.

"Um, I'm studying applied math at UCL," I offered reservedly.

He whistled as he raised his eyebrows. "So does that make you out of my league, then?" he asked.

I frowned back in confusion. Even if I hadn't chosen to live a life that would make a nun's seem easy, this man was so far out of my league that we might as well be on different planets. Finally figuring that he must be teasing me, I kept my mouth shut and looked away as my cheeks became even redder.

"Don't worry, princess," O'Connell said softly. "I get the message."

How could this crazy, beautiful man think that I was agreeing with him?

"I'm not really in anyone's league. I don't date."

I adjusted the bag on my shoulder, betraying my nervousness, and looked anywhere but in his eyes. I had good reason for being this way, but it didn't make me feel any less stupid saying it. I wanted O'Connell, but I was completely out of my depth with him.

He didn't move for a few seconds, so I risked a look at his face only to find him grinning down at me. Not the nice smile that he'd given me when I first walked in, but the cocky grin, signaling to women everywhere that they should get ready to drop their knickers. This time I didn't bother looking around and just gazed straight at the floor.

"I'm just messing with you. You have to loosen up if we're gonna be friends."

"Um, I don't really do friends, either," I replied quietly as I glanced back up at him.

"Well, you do now," he answered, as though my opinion on the subject was completely irrelevant.

"Don't look so worried," he reassured me. "I'm a fierce friend to have in your corner." He turned toward the gym to grab his bag, and I saw my chance. Bolting past him, I all but ran back to my flat. Closing the door behind me, I chucked my keys on the table and collapsed onto my bed, throwing my arm over my eyes. I'd had more human interaction in the last couple of days than I'd had in the last six months, and my head hurt. Meeting new people, and talking without fear of reprisal, was hard. I wasn't a natural conversationalist, and any confidence I might have once had, was gone.

As hard as today had been though, and as much of a fool as I'd made of myself, I'd loved the work. It was pretty much a dream job while I was studying. Once the door to Danny's office had closed, I'd lost myself in numbers and everything outside of that office ceased to exist.

The scariest part was those five minutes with O'Connell. I'd been attracted to boys like Noah when I was younger, but once the abuse started, I was sure that part of me had died. Five minutes with the full force of O'Connell's charm was all it took to realize that I was wrong. Everything about him, from his heart-stopping, gorgeous smile, to a body that I could spend days memorizing with my fingertips, screamed sex.

The man was the whole package. But I couldn't become the sort of girl O'Connell was used to in a week, and I was pretty sure that's how long it would take for him to realize that I wasn't worth the effort.

* * *

I squeezed my eyes shut tight and pretended that he'd knocked me out cold. The pain in my side was agonizing, so breathing in and out to make it seem like I was unconscious was excruciating. It felt like he'd broken a rib.

I had no idea whether he usually stopped beating me when I passed out, but I was guessing so. Where was the fun without the fear?

As always, Mum was my Achilles' heel. As soon as I came home from school and saw him whaling on her, I intervened. Not that I thought I'd stop him, just deflect the punishment and hope that he didn't kill us both. She'd never done the same for me; she'd always run and hide when it was my turn, but I had hope.

I could feel the sick fuck standing over me, assessing his handiwork. Frank wasn't the type of guy to beg for forgiveness and plead remorse after a beating. The arsehole took pride in his work. I felt his big sweaty hand squeeze my breast roughly, and I fought my gag reflex to keep pretending.

It wouldn't be long now before the beatings turned to rape. As my body matured, I could sense the change in him. When his tongue licked the path of blood along my cheek, I opened my eyes and sat up with a start.

My cracked ribs, like all my other injuries, had long since healed, but breathing wasn't so easy anymore. I ran a glass of water to calm myself down and reached for my candle. I'd have to get another one soon because the dreams were becoming much more frequent lately. It was like he could sense that I was beginning to live again, and he was letting me know he still had dominion over me. As long as the sick fuck was still in my head, I'd never really be free.

CHAPTER FOUR

"Hey, Em. Are you still rocking the hermit thing or can I park my arse here?"

Nikki, with her weight rested on one hip, held out her food tray and waited for my reply.

"Feel free." I smiled back. As she sat down and started unloading more food than most rugby players could eat in one sitting, I couldn't help but ask her about it. "How come you can eat all that and stay so tiny?"

She grinned back at me. "God has blessed me with a fast metabolism. I can eat pretty much whatever I want without gaining weight. Plus I have low blood sugar, so if I go more than a few hours without food, I get Incredible Hulk cranky."

"Hello, baby. I see you saved a seat for me." A big, burly bear of a man dumped his tray down next to Nikki's and landed a kiss on her head as he reached over to pinch her apple.

"What gave you the impression that I saved a seat for you, arsehat? And are you so hard up for money that you have to come and steal my food?" she retorted sarcastically.

"Ah," he teased, "don't be so mean. You'll have people thinking you don't love me anymore."

I guessed this was banter that they'd shared before, and it was kind of amusing to watch. Nikki seemed to decide that arguing was futile, and with a roll of her eyes, she relinquished her fruit.

A couple more trays landed on our table with a clatter that made me jump, and two more bears joined the company of the first. I ate almost all of my meals in solitude. It was strange that today my table had become a Mecca for the rugby team.

"Hi. I'm Albie," the bear opposite offered with a smile. Its genuine warmth caused me to blush immediately. My inability to control my blushes in any number of situations was as humiliating as it was annoying.

"Um, Emily. Nice to meet you."

"Sorry, Em, I'm a shit friend. Em, this idiot is Ryan, and his much nicer friends are Albie and Max."

The apple thief seemed affronted by the introduction, though Max and Albie were highly amused. I would like to have known the history between Nikki and Ryan, but we didn't know each other nearly well enough for me to ask. They started bickering about the introduction when Albie leaned over and whispered to me conspiratorially. "Ryan knew Nikki back when they were kids. He was always a player, and now she won't give him a chance."

"Are you sure she just doesn't like him that way?" I whispered back.

"Nah," he retorted, "just look at the two of them. They're totally into each other. She's just afraid he'll play her. He doesn't have the best history of following up a first date with a second."

I looked more closely and frowned. They did seem to have chemistry. But with my limited experience, really, what did I know?

"So how do you know Nikki?" he asked.

"We have applied math together," I replied quietly. No matter how much of a gentle giant Albie seemed, I still wasn't all that comfortable with the art of conversation.

"Wow, that's a serious course. I'm impressed. I'm studying history," he offered, and I gathered that he was pleased with his own choice.

"What are you hoping to do with that?" I inquired.

He laughed between bites of his sub. "You sound just like my mum and the careers advisor."

"Sorry." I blushed. "I'm just never really sure what employment people without vocational degrees want to go into. I didn't mean to be rude."

"I know you didn't. I'm just teasing. Truth is, I'm not really sure either. I like playing rugby, and I enjoy history, so that's what I decided to study. I'm hoping that a career choice will become clear before I graduate, but in the meantime, I just want to see how the rugby pans out."

It amazed me that someone could be so nonchalant about their future career. It didn't mean he was spoiled, but that kind of indifference could only come from someone who'd never gone hungry because they couldn't find the money for a meal. Once I graduated I needed to find a decently paid job as soon as I could to get back on my feet. It just went to show how poles apart I was from these people.

A few more trays landed as I picked at my meal, but I lost the thread of everyone's conversations quickly, not having been to any of the parties and not knowing any of the people they were talking about. I was ashamed to say that I started to panic. I understood isolation, but now the void was being filled so quickly, and I felt like I was freaking out.

When I'd decided to start making friends, I had no idea that it would happen so quickly. The domino effect of one introduction leading to another left me suddenly immersed in Nikki's social circle. It was like jumping into the deep end of the pool when you'd planned to wade in slowly. My problem was that, regardless of how I'd landed in the middle, I had no idea how to swim.

Figuring that since I'd held up one end of a short conversation without embarrassing myself, now was as good a time as any to cut my losses before I had a total meltdown. Loading up my tray, I made a dipshit excuse to Nikki about needing to speak with one of my tutors. With a wave to my new acquaintances, I left. As I turned to go, I saw Nikki elbow Ryan swiftly in the ribs and mutter, "Well done, arsehole. You've scared her away."

She had no idea how on the money she actually was.

* * *

My second night at the gym wasn't nearly as traumatic as I'd built it up to be. The first day in a new job had to be the worst, but today I knew exactly where to go and what to do. I was proud of myself that I didn't so much as hesitate when I pulled open the door to Driscoll's. It was worth having to deal with a few thousand pounds of sweaty boys to be working with numbers. Somehow it seemed easier to think of them as boys rather than men, and though all of them were pretty cut, most didn't look that much older than me. I was relieved that no one really stared as I walked through. With a bit of luck, I'd be part of the furniture after a couple of weeks.

Unconsciously I searched out O'Connell, only to find him dancing around the ring, sparring with another fighter. As soon as I caught sight of him, a shiver ran though me that left me with goose bumps. It amazed me that for someone so big, he could be so light on his feet. He bounced around on the canvas like it was a trampoline, and he was full of limitless energy.

As quick as he was, his direction change was so fast it must have been instinctive. Although I didn't think I could stomach seeing him land a punch or take a hit, I had to admit he was pretty fucking beautiful to watch. Adjusting my shoulder bag before I was caught staring, I made my way to the office. O'Connell had finished his round, and I felt his eyes follow me.

I expected the office to be uncomfortably chilly, but as I walked into the room, I found it was as warm as the gym.

"You're back then, sunshine," Danny barked. With a cigarette half burned down and hanging out of his mouth, he shuffled around pouring himself coffee.

"Did you think I'd quit?" I inquired quietly.

"Well, I had my doubts. You're a tough little nut, but I didn't think you'd figured that out yet."

I chuckled at his positive opinion of my good character and wondered how he could come to that conclusion, given how little he knew about me. "Well, I'm back now, so before I get spooked again, how about you put me to work and get your money's worth?"

"Well, well." He laughed with a throaty chuckle that gave away a lifetime addiction to tobacco. "A couple of weeks ago you were afraid of your own shadow, and now you're giving me cheek. Well, you'd best straighten up that backbone, missy, 'cause the boys will be coming to see you soon to pay their dues. Petty cash box is in the top drawer. They'll give you their names, and the amount they owe is in the green ledger. You'll just need to enter the amount they pay. End of the night you give me the names of those who didn't pay, and I'll get to work."

"*You* hound the boys for their dues?" I asked, horrified at the thought of my tiny, frail-looking friend confronting mean-looking fighters who were trained to hurt and who looked pumped up enough to do just that.

Danny cackled at the look of horror on my face. "Sunshine, most of these boys have been men long before they walked through my door, and don't you be worrying about me. If any of 'em are stupid enough to miss dues without talking to me 'bout it first then they get what's coming to 'em. Besides, this lot are more scared of me than I am of them."

When I thought about it, it really wasn't too hard to believe. He terrified me when we first met, and it wasn't a stretch to see him mouthing off to one of his fighters.

Feeling brave, I pointed to the coffee. "May I have some, please?" I asked.

Apparently this amused Danny because he chuckled again.

"What's so funny?" I inquired, slightly confused.

"Just getting used to good manners again, Em. Don't worry about it. It's been a long time since I've seen or used 'em, that's all."

He poured me a large cup of coffee and motioned to a heater that hadn't been there yesterday. "It was feckin' freezing in here earlier, so I got the lads to bring a heater in. You keep that going till you leave."

"Thanks, Danny," I answered, sipping my coffee.

"No thanks needed. You get sick from sitting in a freezing office then you can't work," he muttered at me, cigarette still hanging precariously from his mouth.

It was on the tip of my tongue to say that he was all heart, but despite all his whining to the contrary, I truly believed he was. I thought about how nights spent constantly on my feet for minimum wage had been swapped for nights spent in a warm office, with a comfy chair and a cup of good coffee, doing something that I loved. My half smile became a full-blown grin.

Danny just rolled his eyes at me with an indecipherable noise. He carried his coffee and shuffled out of the office, shutting the door behind him.

Shrugging off my jacket, I hung it on the back of my chair and set to work. Yesterday the office was Danny's. Today I was making it mine. Pre-armed with cleaning products from home, I cleared the desk of papers then scrubbed it until it gleamed. It might have been old, but by the time I finished, the pattern of mug stains, a legacy from yesterday's dusting, had all but gone. Only those stains literally burned into the wood remained.

When the smell of lemon and beeswax finally overpowered the smell of nicotine, I got back to the real work. Booting up the PC took almost as long as cleaning the desk had, but I got there in the end. Pulling up the program I'd set up yesterday, I reached for a stack of invoices and got to work.

Danny, I quickly learned, was used to bookkeeping the old-fashioned way. Neat cursive told the story of his business in a shelf full of green ledgers. When he had attempted to computerize his records—that was when things had gone south. What he had done was horrific, and abandonment was the only way to go. Luckily he'd invested in a decent software package, so I had a good base to work from. Deciding to computerize everything from the beginning of the financial year, I could then keep things up-to-date while working through the backlog.

I worked for half an hour before a hard thump on the office door startled me. If there was ever a time when an unexpected noise didn't put my heart in my mouth then I was anxious to get there.

"Come in," I called though no invitation was necessary. A few more poundings like that and the door was coming through anyway. The guy who entered was huge and just as built as O'Connell. He was sweating profusely and smelled like he'd been in the gym for days, not hours, but he grinned, completely unaffected, as he strode in.

"So for once the rumor mill in this shit hole is true. There's a gorgeous woman in the gym, and Danny's locked you in here to save you from us."

Obviously a heavyweight, he was seriously cut in a way that was hard earned, not gym gifted. His blond buzz-cut hair and chocolate eyes contrasted completely with O'Connell's dark spikes and wolf-like gaze. He lacked O'Connell's intensity, but the gentle eyes and dopey grin were still charming. Grabbing the comfy chair, he swung it out and sank into it in a well-rehearsed move. I could easily imagine him spending a lot of time there, being bawled out by Danny like a naughty school kid. He leaned back with his hands behind his head then thinking better of his manners, held out a hand for me to shake "Kieran Doherty. Nice to meet you," he introduced himself politely.

"I'm Emily," I practically whispered.

He didn't make my spine tingle like O'Connell, and he didn't have that look in his eyes that made me fear him. It didn't matter if a man was short and thin, or tall and built; some men had a stare that gave away a poison behind it. A poison that made them want to hurt and break what most men would protect and cherish. I'd had a *lot* of practice looking at that stare, and all I saw in Kieran's eyes was laughter. If I wasn't comfortable, it was because I'd spent so long avoiding any kind of contact, especially with men.

"Well, darlin', you're a breath of fresh air around here. Handing over my hard-earned cash isn't so painful when you're doing the collecting."

He carried on smiling as he let go of my hand, having given it a solid shake. I guessed that he expected me to make some conversation.

"Um, have you boxed at Danny's for long?" I inquired, searching for his name in the ledger.

"Sure. Since me and Con were kids. Must've been six years old when Danny stopped us from kicking the shite out of each other on the street and put us to work. He was mean, too, but fuck knows we needed a bit of discipline."

"Con?" I asked, wondering who he was talking about.

"Cormac O'Connell," he replied, knowingly. "He's the big, ugly fecker with the tattoos you see me sparring with. Course...

that pretty much describes all of 'em. Con's like my brother, I guess, though I'll deny it if you say anything to the shithead."

I was a little overwhelmed by the cursing and the way Kieran spoke about O'Connell, despite him telling me that they were best friends. I guessed that working here would be an education in roughneck camaraderie.

He pulled out a few notes from the pocket of his shorts and chucked them down on the table as the door flew open and banged against the wall. "Sorry," a gruff voice called out, as the body belonging to it muscled through the door.

"Ever heard of knocking, arsehole? Didn't your ma ever teach you any feckin' manners?" Kieran barked with a scowl.

"Chill out, Kier, I just forgot it wasn't Danny, that's all."

Desperate to diffuse any hostility, I interjected. "It's fine, no harm done. Do you have your dues?"

"Well, hellooooo beautiful. If I knew Danny was hiding something so fine, I'd have hauled arse with my dues an hour ago. But now I'm here, you gonna make my day and let me leave with your number?"

Kieran jerked his thumb toward him. "This tool is Tommy Rierdan. I wouldn't worry about recognizing him by his face. When Con hears he's been hitting on you, he's gonna get it rearranged. That's if me or Danny don't do it first."

Tommy, like most of the other boys, was cut like an underwear model. Of course, his eight-pack abs were about the only part of his body not covered in ink. Both his arms had sleeved tattoos that spanned down to words that I couldn't decipher across the back of his hands. He was much shorter and leaner than the other guys, and unlike their neat marine-like buzz cuts, his shaggy brown hair was just shy of falling into his eyes. What he lacked in size, he certainly made up for in confidence, though.

"Fuck off, Keir. You're just pissed 'cause you know she's feelin' it."

He was so ridiculously cocky that it was hard not to laugh. I honestly wasn't sure whether he was acting this way to make me smile and break the ice or whether he really was this confident. Regardless I could see Kieran losing his temper.

"Ten," I blurted out.

"Huh?" they both grunted at the same time.

"It's my number."

"Come again?" Tommy said, but a slow smile spread across Kieran's face. I tapped the book in front of me.

"The ledger says you owe ten pounds this week. It's lovely to meet you, Tommy, but I'm afraid that the only numbers I'm giving out this week are the ones in the ledger." I spoke quietly and didn't want to sound like a bitch, but I was knocking potential advances on the head, even if he wasn't serious.

"D'you hear that, Kier? I get a new set of numbers next week. Five quid says I'm getting her phone number."

I sighed softly to myself. There really was no stopping this boy.

"Okay, fuckwad, you've got a deal. A fiver says Em's too smart to let you anywhere near her. Either way, you're out of luck next Friday. You'll either be five quid short or your face will be so badly fucked up, she'll have to find your lips before she can kiss them."

"Whatever. She's totally worth it."

It was very flattering, but more overwhelming than lunch, and I was still only two names down in the ledger. Tommy pulled out a ten-pound note and set it down on the desk.

"Same time next week then, sweetheart?" He grinned, with a wink, and was out the door with Kieran following close behind.

"See you later, Em, and if any of those fuckers give you shit, you come and see me."

He shut the door behind him, and I took a deep breath to regain my equilibrium. I needn't have bothered. Not five minutes later, a light knock at the door preceded its opening, and in walked Cormac O'Connell.

CHAPTER FIVE

O'Connell walked into the room holding a large drink bottle and closed the door gently behind him. Without saying a word, he grabbed Kieran's chair and sat down, leaning his elbows on his knees.

"So then, sunshine, why'd you run out on me the other day?"

He'd covered himself with a T-shirt, which was ridiculous. Considering that it was so soaked with sweat that the T-shirt molded to his abdomen like a second skin. I watched the flex and movement of his biceps as he leaned forward. His broad shoulders tapered to lean hips, but every inch between was pure solid muscle. With a body trained to punish and endure, from his deltoids to his abdominals, he looked sculpted by hard work and pain.

It wasn't surprising. He was completely relentless, even sparring. There wasn't an ounce of remorse or mercy in any punch he threw, and inside those ropes, he looked ready to kill. When he wasn't fighting, he was primed and tense with anticipation. It wasn't much of a stretch to imagine that the fuse between his fist and his temper was a short one. His lazy grin, suggesting to the world that he didn't give a shit, was all a front. Only an idiot would turn his back on this man in a fight.

Every fiber of my being should have been screaming at me that being inside four enclosed walls with him was a bad idea, but as soon as he closed that door, I could practically feel the static electricity buzz between us. I feared his attention yet craved it at the same time. I wanted to know that I made him feel as needy and alive as he made me, and yet it scared me because he wouldn't lack the courage to do anything about it. When I finally looked up, I saw his piercing gray-blue eyes assessing me. He didn't frown or scowl but gazed at me in curious amusement, like I was a puzzle that he was trying to figure out. His real smile was slow and rusty as though it hadn't been used in a while, but unlike his usual sexy smirk, it was genuine, and in spite of myself, I relaxed a little in his company.

"I wasn't running away. Not really. I'm just antisocial by nature. I wouldn't take it personally."

His smile became a full-blown grin, making my heart sink. Logically I knew that falling for this guy would break every rule that had ever kept me safe, but where O'Connell was concerned, I felt as though I was standing at the top of a precipice, powerless to stop myself falling into the oblivion.

"Well, you say what you think, sunshine, I'll give you that. But for future reference, friends don't run out on each other."

"Duly noted. Any other guiding principles of friendship I should know about?"

I spoke quietly but with sincerity. At this point, any advice on how not to fuck up the friendships I'd been making would be welcome.

He thought seriously, taking a long, deep drink from his protein shake while I tried not to drool at the bead of perspiration running sexily down his throat, and floored me. "It would be nice if you could assume I'm not going to hit you every time I try to strike up a conversation."

I was mortified. That he had seen my cowardice, or guessed what that could mean, horrified me. This was supposed to be my new start, and I was trying so hard not to be that person anymore, but O'Connell had made me feel that as long as I acted like a victim, I would always be one.

"Look, I'm not saying that you shouldn't be on your guard. Pretty girls like you are always gonna attract predators, but through the front door of this place, there's not one man who would lift a finger to a woman," he rationalized.

"I'm sorry," I mumbled. "I didn't mean to flinch. I guess I was just feeling a little intimidated, with it being my first day. Everyone here seems really nice, especially Kieran."

I thought it would make him happy that I was getting on with his best friend, but this made him frown, hard.

"He's been making moves on you, then?" he asked dangerously.

"Of course not," I replied in confusion. "He just tried to make me feel welcome here."

The scowl didn't really lessen, but it seemed to relax him to know that Kieran hadn't been hitting on me. It was a little heartwarming to have someone act a little protective. It wasn't like it was something I'd ever had before, but the completely irrational part of my brain wondered how it would feel if he were jealous rather than just protective of a new friend.

"So we're good? No more flinching or running off?"

"We're good, O'Connell, but it's pretty terrifying, you know, walking into the middle of a load of guys trying to hit on anything that moves."

He smiled. "So you know my name, then. Most people call me Con."

"You're pretty infamous around here. Would you prefer me to call you Con?"

"Nah, I like the way you say my name." I didn't know how to respond to that.

"I'm Emily," I introduced myself.

"Thanks, sunshine, but I already know your name."

I blushed that he would take the time to find out, and I fussed about with the ledger, embarrassed that I was floundering in my attempt to hold a real conversation with this man.

"Are you all Irish? Only your accents aren't as strong as Danny's," I asked curiously before I could stop myself.

"Danny was born and raised in Ireland. Me, Kieran, Tommy, and Liam were born there, too, but our parents moved over here when we were kids. Most of our mates are Irish. There's a pretty big community here."

The more he spoke, the hotter and more nervous I was getting. I squeezed my thighs together as the heat in my core intensified. His accent only made him more irresistible, and fuck if he didn't know it. He looked like he was about to ask me something, and unwilling to talk about myself, I scrambled to change the subject. "Um, the ledger says that you owe twenty pounds for this week. Is that okay?"

I had no idea how much these boys earned, but we weren't in the most affluent part of town. Despite Danny's attitude toward dues, I hated asking the boys for their money. He handed over the cash as I wrote in the ledger.

"Why does everyone call me 'sunshine'?" I blurted out.

It was the first time I'd seen him exude anything but confidence, and he seemed embarrassed about telling me. He rubbed his hand over the back of his neck, betraying his unease, and finally said, "Danny gave you the nickname, and I guess it kind of stuck with us. You'll have to ask him why he gave it to you."

He was lying. Sure, Danny had called me sunshine first, but there was more to it than that. O'Connell had decided not to share, and that disappointed me. There was a sharp knock on the door, and unlike Tommy, the person on the other side knew better than to just barge in. O'Connell seemed a little pissed at the intrusion but got up to answer the door.

"See you later, then?" he asked, and I nodded with a small smile. He smiled back as he opened the door but gave the death stare to the fighter who entered as he left.

* * *

By the end of the night, all but one of the boys had paid up, and Danny confirmed that the last fighter had cleared it with him that he could carry his dues over for the week. Danny chuckled throatily as he looked through the ledger. A burned-down cigarette hung from his mouth and I wondered how many he'd smoked since I'd started tonight.

"Looks like more of those eejits paid tonight than usual. Means I don't have to go chasing any of 'em. Seems like you're going to be good for business, Em, even if I only have you collecting dues."

I sincerely hoped that wasn't all I'd be doing. I really enjoyed the bookkeeping. In truth, dues collection would have taken half the time tonight, but each of the boys who crossed the threshold seemed inclined to either chat me up or introduce themselves and give me the third degree. I was exhausted. Danny kicked me out, as usual, but to be honest, if he left me to my own devices with the books then I'd have been there all night. Maybe it was because the office had been so warm and cozy, or maybe it was because my jacket felt more threadbare than usual, but the evening chill was bitter. As I stepped out into the night and wondered whether to walk the few miles home or take the bus, I couldn't help but stuff my hands into the pockets of my jacket while trying to wrap it around me. Figuring that the walk would soon warm me up and that I'd need to save my bus fares for winter, I put my head down and started out for home. Mentally calculating the days until payday, I contemplated whether to use the extra in my wages to buy some nice warm gloves or just put it away toward a winter coat. The pounding of feet on the sidewalk grew closer, and I looked around to see who was following me.

"Jesus, you have to be quick on your feet to keep up with you, woman!"

"Maybe I'm running away from you," I replied with a smile, as O'Connell caught up to me.

"Nah," he replied cockily, "I'm irresistible."

"I'm sure," I answered dryly.

He was irresistible, and he knew it. There was no need to inflate his ego any more. It was better to feign indifference.

"So where are you headed?" I asked. If he was walking, I figured he lived fairly locally. "Same place as you are," he replied.

"What do you mean? I'm going home."

He might be hot, but he was starting to freak me out a little.

"I'm walking you home. Danny was the one who agreed to your hours, so he figured he's responsible for you getting home safely."

He said it so matter-of-factly. Like it was common for all female employees to have a personal escort home. I rolled my eyes at Danny's overprotectiveness.

"Look, that's really nice of you, but honestly, I'm fine. I've been walking on my own for a very long time now. I'm a big girl, and I have a rape alarm." I was probably more conscious of my surroundings than anyone else he'd ever met, and I also protected my own privacy.

"Darlin', I bench press more than you weigh, and a rape alarm in this neighborhood won't do shit, trust me. You want to work for Danny then it's his rules. That means that one of us walks you home every night you're here."

He seemed amused by the futility of the exchange, like walking me home was a foregone conclusion.

"Again don't take this personally, but I just met you a few days ago. I'm not telling you where I live."

He had the good grace to look sheepish. "I already know, Danny told me."

I stopped stock-still in the middle of the pavement. O'Connell had gone on a few paces before he realized that I wasn't with him and turned around in surprise. I didn't say anything. Really, what was the point? My fight wasn't with O'Connell; it was with Danny. I'd been a doormat for too long. If Danny wanted to walk all over me, I'd be fucked if I'd lie down and take it. Turning on my heel, I stalked back to the gym, threw open the door, and stomped up the stairs, feeling the indignation fuel my rage.

"Why did you tell O'Connell where I lived?"

Danny, who'd been leaning against the ring ropes watching two guys spar, looked over his shoulder at my question. In fact, pretty much the whole gym had stopped to stare at me. I hated being the center of attention, but right now, I was too buzzed to worry about it.

"How's he supposed to walk you home if he doesn't know where you live?" he asked this like I was stupid.

"You had no right, Danny. I don't need babysitting, and you had no right revealing personal information about me without my permission."

It was obvious that I was unhappy, but I wasn't exactly screaming at him. That kind of disrespect in front of his boys just wasn't me.

"Office," he barked, and I jumped. Duly summoned, I followed him into the office, and he closed the door gently.

"I know you're mad, sunshine, but I trust these boys with my life, and as it happens, with yours, too. I was raised in the old way, meaning you don't allow a lady to walk home alone."

"You mean well, and I get that, Danny, but I don't want anyone knowing where I live. If you wanted to know how I was planning to get home, you should have asked me. You had no right to give out my address without my permission."

I choked back the tears as my voice started to break. The more people who knew where I lived, the easier it would be for Frank to find me. Danny's voice was gentle when he replied.

"You'd never have let me tell Con, and your safety is more important than me pissing you off. Now are you gonna give this old man a break or what? You know if anything happened to you on the way home from the gym, it'd just about break me."

Danny Driscoll was tough as nails, and I doubted that anything could break him, but he was tugging on my heartstrings, and he knew it.

"I don't like it, Danny." I sighed with exasperation.

"You don't have to like it, but humor the old man, okay?"

I'd had my little temper tantrum, but a fat lot of good it had done me. Trust wasn't an easy thing for me to give, but the decision to trust was sort of out of my hands now. Danny was only trying to look out for me. I'd said my piece, so the best thing I could do would be to act graciously about all this.

"Fine." I sighed again, leaving the office. Okay, so not too graciously, but Danny got what he wanted, and I was sure he wasn't too bothered. The only question to ask now was how did I make conversation with a man like O'Connell for twenty minutes, twice a week, without hyperventilating? By the time I made it back downstairs, I found O'Connell leaning against the doors with his hands shoved in the pocket of his hoodie, like he didn't have a care in the world.

"Sorted?" he asked. I answered with a nod, and we walked side by side, all the way home, in awkward silence. I caught him staring at me every now and then, though I pretended not to notice. You could see that he was keen to make conversation, but after today I kind of needed the quiet.

"You don't like me much, do you, sunshine?" he interjected, as we were almost home. I was horrified that he'd misinterpreted my fucked-up issues that way.

"Of course, I do. I warned you that I don't really do friends. I've been on my own for a long time now, so it's going to take me a while to get used to this," I answered, as I gestured between us.

"Well, it makes a nice change," he replied. "Usually it's me who fucks things up. So what're you doing this weekend?"

"Um..." I wasn't sure how to answer. I had a couple of shifts at the diner and then I planned on doing laundry and catching up on some assignments. This was not what most girls my age would be doing on a Saturday night, and too embarrassed to admit my real plans, I floundered for an itinerary packed full of exciting things to present him with. He jumped in before I had anything.

"Me, Kieran, and a few of the boys are going to a party that one of your rugby lot is throwing if you're interested?" I looked up with a start.

"I didn't know you were a student." He laughed aloud, and my cheeks reddened automatically.

"Do we look like fucking students?" he replied, like the whole notion was ridiculous. I wisely said nothing, figuring that any answer I gave would only dig the hole I was in deeper. He stopped at the door to my building and reached out to tug on one of my curls.

"Parties are the best place to pick up pretty little students, happy with a bit of rough for the night."

"Don't you need to be a student to go?" I asked naively. After all, what did I know about college parties?

"Don't sweat it, sunshine. Kieran and I know a few of the

boys. They get us into parties, and we get them fight tickets. It's all good. So you coming or what?"

"Thank you for the invitation, but I don't really do parties, either," I replied softly.

"Can't say I'm surprised, but you know where I'll be if you change your mind," he said, as he pulled on my curl again. I smiled but knew he was only being polite. Not for the first time I wished I were a different sort of girl, one who could let the man she was attracted to touch her without recoiling.

"Well, thank you for walking me home. Will you have far to get home yourself?" I asked.

"Fuck me. It's Friday night. The only place I'm going is to get a few beers in me. You want me to walk you up?" he asked. Of course, he was going out. It was too much to hope that he'd be tucking himself up in bed, safe from the advances of bar sluts all too eager to wrap their legs around him for a night. Swallowing back the bitter taste of disappointment, I looked at the ground again.

"No, I'm fine here. Thanks again for walking me home."

"You're welcome. See you soon."

He watched as I let myself into the door of the building, and once I was safely inside, I locked the handle and made it to the window just in time to see him walking off into the darkness. There was nothing about this man that made us right for each other, but I was deluding myself if I didn't think I'd be counting down every minute of the next six days until I could see him again.

CHAPTER SIX

"Em, God gave you skin like that for a reason, and it wasn't so you could cover it up with plaid flannel."

I looked down at the fitted shirt I wore with a vest and leggings. It wasn't what I was planning to wear to the party, but I loved this shirt. Nikki obviously didn't share my fashion sense, or absence thereof, and her mention of showing skin worried me. God only knew what stripper outfit she'd bring out next. I was beginning to think that letting her talk me into going to this party was a bad idea. Her campaign this week had been subtle, but relentless. I finally caved when the lunch table cottoned on to our discussion. Unable to give them a good enough reason why I wasn't going, they cajoled me into accepting. I promised myself that I'd stay just long enough that people would remember my appearance, but forget what time I left. Despite my reservations, I was secretly thrilled at the prospect of seeing O'Connell outside of work. Thursday and Friday night had been much the same as last week. O'Connell and Kieran stopped by for a chat, and it wasn't long before Danny was shepherding them out of the office. With a cheeky grin and a wink every time I caught his eye,

O'Connell was starting to get to me. Although I was still crap at making conversation as he walked me home, I hadn't completely embarrassed myself yet. Of course, there was always tonight. Having never been to a student party, I had no idea what to wear. I needn't have worried. As soon as Nikki could sense my resolve crumbling, she pounced and dragged me to her dorm to pick out an outfit. If she hadn't, I would have agreed to go then taken one look at my miserable wardrobe and changed my mind again.

"Here we go." She beamed as she pulled more clothes out for me.

"You looked like you were sucking lemons when you saw those dresses, so we'll work up to that. This is much more your style. Now go and try them on," she ordered, as she piled me up then pushed me toward the door to the bathroom. I was as shocked to discover that I had a definable style as I was to find that I liked the outfit. The blue silk strappy top had a cleverly hidden support and was loose enough that it didn't make me feel uncomfortable, but fitted enough to show off my curves. The tight denim hugged my figure and made my legs seem impossibly long. The cute heels, that seemed to tower because I was used to walking in flats, topped off the outfit nicely.

"Perfect," Nikki announced as I made my reveal.

"Add some makeup and jewelry, and you'll look amazing. If we get ready here, I can do your makeup."

I must admit that by the time Nikki was done with me, I did feel pretty awesome. She had chosen a long delicate silver necklace with a small heart charm at the end of it and a pair of beautiful stud earrings. My makeup was natural-looking and not too flamboyant, which was perfect for me. For the first time in a long time, I felt pretty. Not jaw-dropping, stand-out-in-the-crowd attractive, but pretty. Nikki had done a great job, and considering that we hadn't known each other that long, I was touched that she'd done so much for me. Of course, any self-confidence she'd given me with the makeover pretty much evaporated as soon as I walked in the door to the party. The place was absolutely packed. Grabbing my hand tightly, Nikki weaved us through the throng toward the kitchen. The smell of stale beer and over-powering aftershave was nauseating. Heads turned as we walked through, obviously drawn to Nikki's stunning figure. She shared none of my self-doubt or aversion to showing skin. Her killer heels and figure-hugging strapless black dress left little to the imagination. She stood out in a way that I never would, but I was totally fine with that. Hers was a good shadow to stand in. As we reached the kitchen, drinks were flowing.

"What do you drink?" Nikki asked.

"Um, I'm not sure. I've never had a drink before," I replied.

"You're shitting me," Nikki exclaimed slack-jawed.

I shrugged my shoulders and smiled, knowing it was almost unheard of for someone my age.

"Okay, lightweight." She sighed, taking a bottle of Becks from the fridge.

"Rule number one: You never accept a drink from anyone, and I mean *anyone*, who isn't in our group. I'm going to start you off on beer, seeing as shots would probably put your un-trained body into an alcoholic coma. You only take sealed bottles from the fridge and you open them yourself. Rule number two: You don't go off on your own with any of the guys here. Most of them are decent, but it only takes one stupid arsehole to convince himself he's God's gift, and that 'no' is the secret code word for 'yes.'"

These boys had nothing on what I'd seen. I was grateful for Nikki's concern, but I didn't have any interest in drinking, ei-ther. The idea of losing control, especially in a place like this, scared me. I'd never hear the end of it, though, if I didn't at least look like I was drinking. For most of the people here, not drinking meant that you weren't having a good time. Determined to drag out my drink then refill the bottle with water afterward, I tipped back a mouthful of beer. It tasted gassy and heavy, but not as bad as I thought it would. Watching guys chucking back pints, I figured it must be an acquired taste. Grabbing a vodka and soda for herself, she pulled me back into the fray. It was obvious when she saw Ryan because her relaxed posture suddenly stiffened. He was chatting to a girl, and from the way she was pushing out her enormous tits and half rubbing up against him like a cat in heat it was clear what she wanted. Ryan, on the other hand, didn't seem at all receptive and was mildly amused at best. He didn't push her away, but he wasn't interested, either. I didn't think Nikki realized how ambivalent Ryan was. She didn't say anything, but her rage was palpable. Ryan glanced back to see us staring at him, and his face dropped. He knew what Nikki thought she was seeing, and his chances with her went from slim to nonexistent. He practically shoved the slut aside to get to Nikki, but she was already beating a hasty exit.

"I'm just going to the bathroom," she mumbled, "I'll see you in a bit."

"Nikki," I called after her. I wanted to reassure her about Ryan, but she was gone. *Fan-fucking-tastic.* I was alone at a party I didn't really want to be at. I was too scared to drink, and now that Ryan and Nikki had disappeared, I literally knew no one there. The only thing worse than being at a party you weren't actually invited to was turning up and realizing that you didn't know anyone else there. I was seriously contemplating cutting my losses and bailing, when someone touched my elbow.

"So you made it, then." Even though I was in heels Albie dwarfed me, but as he gave me his best cheesy grin, he looked about six years old. I sighed with relief when I realized I'd been rescued.

"Albie. I'm so pleased to see you!"

"Wow. What I wouldn't give for a welcome like that every day."

"It's not like that," I said, knowing he was teasing. "Some girl was rubbing up against Ryan. Nikki got pissed and Ryan's gone after her, so I'm on my own," I explained.

"The usual drama with those two then. Fear not," he said, draping an arm across my shoulders and herding me toward his friends.

"I will be your host with the most tonight. After we gave you so much shit about coming to this party, I will personally make sure you have a good time." I smiled at him and for the first time since I'd left Nikki's door, it wasn't forced. I still didn't completely trust him yet. It wasn't in my nature to give that gift away easily. But I did believe that I was well on my way to making another friend. After watching me struggle with my beer, Albie replaced it with a soft drink, for which I was very grateful. Ironically, without the fear of getting drunk, I relaxed a little more. He didn't bombard me with questions or push me, but chatted about himself and told me funny stories about people he knew at the party. Not having to hold up my end of the conversation made it easier to chip in when I could. Eventually some of Albie's friends joined in, and as talk drifted toward the subject of the last party they'd all been to, I allowed myself to look for O'Connell. He'd mentioned that he was coming, but who knew whether he'd make it, and it was a big party. Even if he was there, he could have been anywhere. When I finally found him, all traces of his cocky smile were gone, and the blank look he always wore to fight was in place. He was shut down, giving his opponent absolutely no warning of the torrent of rage that was to come. Why then was that gaze aimed squarely at me? He sat reclined against the sofa, his posture reeking of boredom, swigging occasionally from a bottle of beer. Although I recognized a couple of guys from the gym, other students mainly made up the group, all seemingly falling over themselves to impress the bad boy fighters. To O'Connell's left sat a girl who was my complete antithesis. A hot pink T-shirt that I suspected was sized for a child was stretched tightly over her fabulously fake breasts. Add in some barely there skintight black shorts and some killer strappy black heels and her outfit, what little there was of it, was complete. Her long raven hair fell across her shoulders like black silk and settled on artificially bronzed skin that made her look voluptuous yet slutty all at the same time. She was every man's ultimate fantasy. She had her legs coyly tucked in beside her on the sofa, and she leaned her head against one hand while twirling another around a strand of her hair. She was leaning so far against O'Connell to whisper in his ear that she'd be sitting in his lap in a minute, and all the while he stared at me. I raised my hand to wave hello. It seemed only polite as we'd caught each other's eye. But he just gave me a quick nod, not even a smile, in acknowledgment. I felt hurt by his indifference. Had Kieran been there I might have been brave enough to go over, but as long as he sat with that girl, I just couldn't. I wondered if he was mad at me for not coming over when I first arrived. The girl had moved from hair twirling to rubbing her hands seductively up and down O'Connell's chest. My stomach turned over as the disappointment built up inside me. I was jealous, and I had no right to be. It was better that way but damn if I hadn't imagined what those granite abs felt like under the gentle touch of my fingertips. Just then Albie placed his hand protectively against my back and bent down to ask me if I was all right. I smiled at him and answered that I was fine but when I glanced back at O'Connell, I was anything but. Any pretense at subtle flirtation had been abandoned, and they were halfway to having sex, right there on the sofa. She was straddling him now, her shorts pulled so tight I half expected them to split at the seams. She was nib-

bling and licking her way up his neck, like some dog who'd just
found an ice cream cone on the pavement and was rushing to
eat it before any other dogs turned up for a lick. He watched
me stare at him in shock. Like a rabbit caught in the headlights,
I couldn't look away as he slid his hand up her thigh to grab
her arse. He whispered something in her ear and didn't look
away from me as she answered him with a nod. My heart plum-
meted and I felt bile rising from my stomach as he gripped her
and stood, so that she wrapped her legs around his waist. This
must be a regular occurrence for O'Connell, because no one in
their group batted an eye at their behavior. He carried her across
the room and down the hall to what I assume was a downstairs
bathroom. It wasn't too much of a stretch to imagine that he was
doing her up against the sink. To say that his actions gutted me
would have been an epic understatement. I was devastated. In
my ridiculous little mind, I'd created the fantasy that he wanted
my legs wrapped around him. Me who he'd giggle and cuddle
with after. I picked at the hem of my top, wishing with all my
heart that right then I was in sweats, curled up on my bed crying and feeling sorry for myself. Instead I was putting on a brave
face and pretending that the first man I'd been attracted to for
years wasn't banging some slut in a bathroom like a street-corner
prostitute.

"You sure you're okay?" Albie asked me again gently. "We can
go if you've had enough?" It was only then that I realized that
Albie had left his hand on my back the whole time.

I forced a smile, and reassured him once again that I was fine.
Call me a glutton for punishment, but I just couldn't bring myself
to leave yet. Ryan came storming back into the room soon after
and his hair looked crazy, like he'd just spent the last half hour
pulling on it.

"Right, boys," he called out, "who's up for shots?"

"Shit," Albie whispered. "Clearly things didn't go well with

Nikki. Shots this early means he's getting shitfaced tonight, which means I'm getting shitfaced. We've got practice tomorrow afternoon so our coach is going to hand me my arse."

"You don't have to get drunk with him," I pointed out.

"Of course, I do." He smiled. "We're mates."

This was where my understanding of the team sport mentality fell short. Just because one of them was doing something stupid, didn't mean they all had to do it. In my mind, that made them seem less like mates and more like lemmings. I probably wasn't being fair. I knew little about friendship, and Albie seemed like a nice guy. Maybe solidarity was part of the mix. I let them herd me into the kitchen, but politely declined the offer of a tequila shot. I was nauseous just thinking about what O'Connell was doing. Any alcohol to hit my stomach would come straight back up, and the bathroom was most definitely occupied. Having finished the shots, the boys busied themselves with lining up the next run, while Ryan leaned against the cabinet drinking something nasty looking. I really did feel for him, getting the blame of his reputation when I knew he'd done nothing wrong. I gave him a small smile of encouragement when he caught my eye, and he gave me a sad smile in return. We were both having our own pity party; only mine was alcohol-free and less hardcore than I feared Ryan's would be. I hoped Nikki wasn't too upset, but I didn't feel quite brave enough to wander around the house looking for her. If people were using the downstairs bathroom for quickies, heaven only knew what they were using the rest of the house for. The hallway called to me, and although I couldn't see the bathroom door from the kitchen, I carried on staring into the abyss. Even the fantasy of the two of us together had been a fucking joke. I knew that being with O'Connell was never seriously a prospect, but when we were alone together, I'd allowed myself to buy into the idea. If there was ever any doubt before, he'd made it clear tonight that a friend was all I'd ever be. Maybe that had been his intention. He'd seen me getting a little starry-eyed and wanted to set me straight before I was disillusioned any further. If so, he'd succeeded. I looked around the kitchen, and I'd never felt so alone. I wanted to be a part of life instead of a spectator. But I was fucking kidding myself, thinking the party had been the way to do it. Even here, where I believed that no one would hurt me, I couldn't help the rising panic when I saw the guys doing shots. Half an hour later and the boys were completely trashed. I figured I'd about paid my dues at this party when Nikki sidled up next to me and gently bumped my hip.

"You okay?" I asked quietly.

"I'm good," she answered. "Ryan just makes it pretty obvious why we shouldn't be together, that's all."

"He didn't do anything, you know. I'm pretty sure he was telling that girl that he wasn't interested," I tried to reassure her.

"I know, he told me. It's just that up until recently, he'd have been all over her and behind her there'd be a girl just like her waiting for a turn. A long time ago, I really liked him, and he turned me down. Now he's decided that I'm it for him, and he's trying to show me that he's a changed man. To be honest, I don't get it. I'm the same girl I always was, but he's treating me like I'm God's gift to men, and I have no idea why. It's easier just to think of him as an arsehole, because the alternative is exhausting. Anyway, how are you doing?" she asked.

"I'm having a great time," I lied, "but I've got an early shift tomorrow, so I'm going to make a move in a few minutes."

"Ah, Em," she whined, "don't go. I know I haven't been great company, but stay and I promise you'll have a better time."

I didn't remind her that for nearly two hours, she'd been no company at all. After all, she didn't hesitate to lend me these beautiful clothes or help me with my hair and makeup, so the least that I could do was try to be more grateful.

"It's fine, Nikki, really. I haven't been to a party in a really long time, and it's been great. But if I don't leave soon, I'll never make it to work tomorrow, and I really need the money."

"You're going?" Albie asked between shots. He threw his arm around Nikki's shoulders, and I suspected it was the only way he could stay standing.

"Aren't you glad you came?" he slurred amusingly.

"I am. You were right to talk me into it."

I thought about how it felt, watching O'Connell walk away with that girl, and a wave of sadness swept over me. Despite that, a bit of me meant what I said. I was happy that I'd been brave enough to try the experience. I just wasn't in a hurry to repeat it. At least now I could say that I'd been to at least one party while I was here.

"I'll see you guys at school," I offered, as I made a move. I worried about the impending showdown I was sure to face with Nikki about how I was getting home, when a deep unmistakable voice behind me said, "I'll walk you home."

CHAPTER SEVEN

It told me a lot about how sad and pathetic I was, that knowing what he'd just done and smelling her perfume still on him, I was pleased that he hadn't forgotten me. I didn't understand why I was so desperate to be the focus of this man's attention, when I'd tried for so long to stay in people's peripheral vision. Nikki and Albie stared at both of us slack-jawed until Nikki recovered herself.

"Well, hello gorgeous. It's very nice of you to offer, but we can take care of our friend." She softened the rejection with a pretty, yet sensual, pout, which I suspected was well rehearsed.

"It's nice of you all to worry, but I can take care of myself," I intervened with finality.

I'd just seen O'Connell cart off some random slut to the bathroom. There was no way that I could handle any more of Nikki flirting with him. I'd had my quota of crazy for the night, and I felt an overwhelming need to crawl back into my shell.

"I'll see you all soon." I smiled tightly. With a small wave, and without meeting anyone's eyes, I turned and made my way toward the front door. Only when it closed behind me could I breathe again. Not stopping, I put my head down and set a brisk pace toward my flat. Seconds later the sound of heavy boots running toward me made me flinch.

"Hello, O'Connell."

"You don't hang around, do you, girl."

"It's late. I really just want a hot drink and to curl up in bed."

I sighed, as I contemplated the safe cocoon of my flat. To call it warm would be an exaggeration, but it was all that I could afford at the moment. It had little insulation, and heating that worked only intermittently. Even then, it only came on after some serious abuse with a frying pan.

"What are you, like ninety? It's not even midnight yet," he mocked.

"Well, then, don't let me stop you from getting any more action. The night is still young."

I was going for sarcastic, but I had the feeling I just sounded tired. I waited for the witty comeback, and when it didn't come, I glanced across at him.

"You saw then," he mumbled quietly.

"I kind of thought you wanted everyone to see by the way you carried her through the party," I whispered.

"Why didn't you come and talk to me?" he asked. Was he fucking kidding?

"You looked kind of intimidating, sitting there with all of your friends," I answered honestly.

"They're not my friends," he replied.

"It doesn't make them any less intimidating."

"I wouldn't have done it if you'd come and talked to me."

"Are you serious?" I stopped walking and stared at him in disbelief. "You had sex with that girl because I didn't come and talk to you?"

He turned around to answer me and, for the first time since

I'd met him, he didn't look cocky or arrogant, just pissed and a little shamed.

"I got pissed, okay! You told me that you didn't do parties. Then I see you laughing like you're having the time of your life, with some fucker all over you. If you wanted to blow me off about the party, you should've just told me straight."

How could I be pissed at him and pleased at the same time? I should, really, be scared. He radiated anger, and, although he wasn't drunk, I got the feeling it would take only one wrong word from the wrong person, and he'd find an outlet for his temper. With everything I'd been through, he should be the last person I'd want near me, but my heart and mind were in two different places.

"You are such an idiot." I sighed.

"I don't go to college, so that makes me a fucking idiot?" he argued.

He was practically shouting at me, but I never raised my voice. It just wasn't in my nature.

"You're an idiot because I only came to the party to see you. My friend ditched me, and Albie was the only other person there I knew."

Just like that I'd taken the wind out of his sails and deflated his temper.

"I didn't fuck her, you know. I was pissed off, and I wanted to make you jealous. But as soon as I couldn't see you anymore, I knew what a huge fucking mistake I'd made. I blew her off to come and find you."

I sighed with relief. He wasn't mine, and I wasn't his. But just knowing that he hadn't been with that girl made everything seem better.

"How did she take it?" I pressed, and he chuckled in response.

"She wasn't happy, but she'll get over it.

"Why didn't you come and talk to me?" he asked gently.

"I already told you how intimidating you looked with them all. I'm not like those other girls you were with, O'Connell. I never will be."

He looked like he was in pain as he stared hard at me. I couldn't take the heat from that stare and dropped my eyes to the ground as I felt my cheeks coloring.

"I know you're not, sunshine," he responded sadly.

I started walking again, and he fell into step beside me. Neither of us said anything for a while, but it was a companionable silence. I liked the way he could share my space without needing to fill it.

"You looked beautiful tonight," he said quietly.

"Really?" I smiled. It was so pathetic how happy the compliment made me, but I didn't think anyone had ever called me beautiful before.

"Yeah," he answered. "You know you should smile more often. It looks good on you." I didn't want to bring us both down by admitting that I hadn't had much to smile about in a while.

"I'm working on it," was all I offered in return.

"How come I didn't see Kieran with you? I thought he was going to the party as well."

"Um...he was there," O'Connell mumbled, as he rubbed the back of his neck, looking a little sheepish.

"I didn't see him."

"He was getting laid upstairs."

"Oh."

Honestly, what could I say? Had I known that the party was going to be one big orgy, I'd have definitely found a better way to spend my Saturday night. Then again, O'Connell and I wouldn't be here now.

"So is this how you guys spend most of your weekends?"

"Pretty much, I guess. I love fighting. The partying and

women just come with it. I used to think it was a pretty good life," he confessed.

"Used to?" I questioned.

"Yeah. Until you. Most of the girls I know will fuck you for a Bacardi and Coke. Taking what they were offering never seemed wrong before, but when I offered to walk you home, you looked at me like shit. Made me see how my life looks to you."

I didn't know what to say. Sure, I hated the way that women threw themselves at him and the partying definitely wasn't me, but who was I to judge? My own life was too fucked up to allow me to judge anyone else's.

"I'm sorry. I didn't mean to be judgmental. I'm not used to it, that's all. It was a shock. But given that half the stuff I saw tonight was a complete eye-opener, I think I'd be better off sticking to what's safe from now on."

"You know safe is boring, sunshine." O'Connell smiled with his trademark sex-appeal grin and not the genuine one that made me tingle.

"Perhaps," I replied sadly. "But boring is still safe."

When we made it to my apartment block, I opened the main entrance door and, without even thinking about it, allowed him to walk me to my door. Letting myself in, I leaned against the doorframe to say good-bye.

"Thanks for walking me home," I told him.

"You're welcome," he replied, tucking one of my curls behind my ear. It was so beautifully intimate that I had to steel myself not to close my eyes as his touch grazed my cheek.

"I'm sorry I fucked up tonight. I would have liked hanging out with you," he told me sadly.

"I would have liked that, too," I replied. "It's probably for the best, though," I admitted painfully. "The drinking and partying isn't me. I couldn't give you what those girls do, not even close. I'd go from a novelty to a bore in the space of one evening."

"You really have no idea, do you?" He chuckled. I said nothing, having no clue what he was talking about.

"You know I'll make it up to you. Turns out that I'm as shit at this whole friends thing as you are, but I'd like to have another crack at it." His swagger was back now with renewed enthusiasm and his optimism that we could ever be friends was infectious.

"You think it's possible then?" I asked.

"What...that we can be friends? Hell yeah, baby. Course that doesn't mean I won't try my best to make you fall in love with me, too," he joked.

"Don't worry, I'm fairly immune to your charm," I quipped.

I could see that he was itching to volley with a sleazy comeback, but he really was reining it in. Maybe he was serious about being friends. I worried that I would spend half my time with O'Connell wanting more, but wouldn't I be doing that anyway, even if he weren't with me? Despite his cocky charm, there was no way I was letting myself fall in love with this man. I really didn't think that my heart could take the beating.

"You working at the cafe tomorrow?" he asked.

"Uh-huh. The early shift," I replied. "Why?"

"No reason. I might develop a sudden urge for a fried breakfast, though."

I grinned at the thought of seeing him tomorrow and cursed myself for being so obvious. I literally had no game face.

"Good night," he murmured, and in the sweetest move ever, leaned forward and gently kissed my cheek.

"Good night," I whispered back. I closed my door as he strode down the hall and banged my head back against it. So much for not falling for him. I was absolutely fucked.

Work the next morning was a double-edged sword. I'd been used to enough late mornings and warm nights hunched over the computer in my office that I'd become spoiled. Having to get up at the crack of dawn and drag myself through the icy streets in my thin shoes was brutal. The double edge to the sword was the delicious anticipation of seeing O'Connell again. I was so busy cleaning my station, I didn't even realize he was there until he was right behind me.

"Good morning, sunshine." I felt his breath, warm against my neck, as he whispered his greeting into my ear. He was so close behind me that a fraction closer and his lips would have been touching my skin. The slightest scent of his aftershave lingered, and my stomach clenched with excitement.

I turned around to face him. "Good morning, yourself."

"You're getting better, you know," he pointed out.

"Better?" I asked.

"Yeah. Not too long ago, you'd have jumped a mile if I'd crept up on you like that, but today you didn't flinch."

"Well, I'm kind of getting used to having you man-giants around," I replied with a grin as O'Connell slid into a booth.

"Boo," a second voice behind me said over my shoulder.

This time I did jump a mile and turned around just in time to smack Kieran on the arm.

"Arsehole," I muttered as I hit him.

"Ow," he moaned, rubbing his arm as he sat across from O'Connell.

"How come he gets the smile, and I'm the arsehole?" he moaned.

"Because he warned me that he was coming," I replied.

It was somewhat true, but I didn't think I was brave enough to confess that I'd been watching and waiting for O'Connell all morning. Even now, the sight of him in worn jeans and a crisp, clean white T-shirt that hugged his biceps like a second skin made me hungry with a craving I wouldn't satisfy. Every woman in the cafe, young or old, looked his way. I saw them surreptitiously stealing glances at him as he watched me, and why wouldn't they?

At six-foot-five inches of solid muscle, he was easily the biggest man in here, but it was more than that. He was the embodiment of everything that women wanted but didn't know they were looking for. He was big enough to protect, but dangerous enough that it was a turn-on. His raw masculinity triggered the release of an unfettered string of pheromones wherever he went. Even just taking his order, I was barely holding it together, and I was betting that there was more than one girl around here whose knickers were wet just from watching him.

That didn't mean Kieran wasn't gorgeous as well. That boy had a killer body, and a great personality to go with it, but it was the danger that drew women to O'Connell. Those beautiful, scarred, and calloused hands could break a man, and the thought that he could do that to protect me made something inside me melt.

It felt like everyone's eyes were on us both, and I began to panic. I didn't want to be invisible anymore, but I couldn't be in O'Connell's limelight, either, and there seemed to be no happy medium. If I couldn't stay a ghost, or at least hidden in the shadows, how long would it be before Frank found me? It was a sobering thought, but just because I couldn't act on my feelings for O'Connell didn't stop me from having them.

I looked up to see both the boys staring at me, and I had the feeling that I'd just missed something.

"What can I get you both for breakfast?" I asked.

"Whatever takes care of this hangover and stops me from feeling like shite." Kieran groaned as he laid his head down across his arms that were resting on the table.

I chuckled. "One coffee coming up."

"I'll have a full fried breakfast with everything, please, sunshine." O'Connell beamed.

"Ah, I think I'm gonna puke," moaned the muffled voice from the table. I smiled as I walked off to put in their order, and when

I returned with their food and coffee, Kieran was still looking green.

"Seriously, mate," he complained to O'Connell. "I'm about two minutes from puking my guts up, and you're gonna eat that shite in front of me?"

"First off, you followed me here. You could've kept your sorry arse in bed. Second, what the fuck did you think I was gonna be eating when I told you we were coming to Daisy's? And third, it's not shite. Daisy's makes the best breakfast in the world. It's not my fault you can't handle your drink."

"Fuck off." Kieran grinned. "You practically dragged me here, and if you'd come back last night instead of leaving me hanging then you'd be feeling like shite, too," he complained.

"You didn't go back to the party?" I asked before I could stop myself.

"I'm turning over a new leaf, sunshine. No more getting wasted, and no more fucking random strangers."

My jaw dropped as Kieran raised his head with a "What. The. Fuck."

"I'm serious, Kier. It makes a nice change to be eating breakfast and training without a raging hangover. I could get used to it."

Kieran looked up at me with a mixture of wonder and disbelief.

"Well, it doesn't take a genius to figure out the reason for this one-eighty, but how far are we talking here? No parties and tee-total?"

"Parties are okay, just not so many of 'em, and I'm not a fucking monk, so a drink now and then is all right. I just don't want to get wasted anymore. Anyway, what are you so pissed for? It's me who'll be doing it."

"What's the point in partying, if you're not gonna do it with me?"

O'Connell just grinned at him as he carried on attacking his breakfast with gusto. Kieran laid his head back down on the table, honestly looking like he was about to be sick at any minute.

"Drink your coffee, Kieran," I urged. "It will make you feel better."

I didn't know if I was smiling because he was endearing or because of O'Connell's resolution, but I was feeling better than I had since before the party.

"Promise?" Kieran asked in his little boy voice.

O'Connell stopped stock-still with his knife and fork suspended in midair and muttered a quiet, "Fuck," as he stared behind me. The slut from last night was strolling bold as brass down the aisle toward my section, like some kind of catwalk model strutting down a runway, wearing exactly the same outfit that she'd had on last night. As she brushed past me, I was the invisible I'd always wanted to be. All the sick feelings from last night came rushing back as sadness and inadequacy pressed down on me.

She slid into the booth next to O'Connell and ran her manicured hand up and down the inside of his thigh. "Hey, baby," she purred. "I was hoping I'd run into you."

"What the fuck do you think you're doing?"

It was Kieran, spluttering with rage, who challenged her. O'Connell looked as sick as a pig and was staring at me like he was waiting for my reaction. The slut completely ignored Kieran as she spoke, still stroking his thigh.

"So . . . you left last night, and I realized that I'd completely forgotten to give you my phone number and email."

As she artfully pulled a slip of paper from shorts that looked vacuum-sealed to her arse, O'Connell seemed to snap out of his trance. "I told you last night I wasn't interested."

She smiled sexily at him, completely unfazed. "After the way we connected, there's no way that you aren't coming back to finish what we started."

"I'm not gonna say this again, so let me make myself perfectly clear. I don't care if you can suck the brass off a doorknob. I'm not interested. If you want more than I was offering, there are plenty of boys out there who'd be happy to help."

Although O'Connell was brushing her off, I still empathized with how sick Kieran was feeling. The slut's expression morphed into one of rage, making her attractive face instantly ugly, and I could sense from the tension that she was spoiling for a fight.

Finally noticing me, she snapped. "What the fuck are you looking at? The service around here is shit, and I have a good mind to complain to your manager that you were eavesdropping on my conversation. Now get your shit together and pour me some coffee."

O'Connell's jaw was grinding in temper, and I could tell from Kieran's body language that he wasn't fairing much better. O'Connell placed his huge hand gently over mine as I poured the coffee shakily. "Do you think you could bring us some more toast, please, sunshine," he asked gently.

I nodded grimly in response, feeling like crap after the way she'd spoken to me. As soon as I was halfway to the kitchen, I heard O'Connell's voice low and menacing.

"Listen, bitch. You don't even get to fucking talk to her. She's worth a thousand of bitches like you, and if you get up in her face like that again, you'll wish we'd never fucking met. Now get fuck off out of my booth so I can finish my breakfast."

"Fine," she sputtered, "but you won't settle for some frumpy little waitress for long. You need someone like me, O'Connell. You'll be back, and you'd just better hope I'm still waiting."

I couldn't hear O'Connell's response as I got to the kitchen and went through the motions of making another round of toast, but his defense touched me. I couldn't remember the last time I'd had anybody in my corner like that, and in the space of one conversation, I'd gone from feeling terrible to being on top of the world. O'Connell had become my emotional roller coaster, and I wasn't ready to get off the ride.

I walked back to their table with the toast, apprehensive of the fallout, but whatever the boys said had worked. She was gone. I placed the toast down on the table as Kieran gave me a tight smile.

"I'm sorry about that," O'Connell apologized.

"No problem. She seemed nice," I replied.

Both boys burst out laughing, probably relieved that I wasn't crying in the corner somewhere, but I was stronger than that. Her insults hurt and damaged my fragile ego, but I'd been abused far worse than that for a long time.

"She's a bitch, and I'm sorry for bringing my shit to your work."

I nodded to let them both know that I was okay, but deep down I knew she was right. O'Connell might be my friend, but I couldn't hold his interest forever. Eventually he'd go back. Maybe not to her, but to someone like her. That was just the way the world worked.

CHAPTER EIGHT

I was walking across campus, with an armful of textbooks, when I heard a crazy voice scream, "Emmmm...wait up!"

Running toward me like a penguin on speed was Nikki.

"Jesus. You can certainly tank it when you want to. I've been chasing you forever."

"Sorry, I was in a world of my own." That was a scary thought in itself. Spatial awareness was usually my specialty.

"Here." She thrust a coffee at me. "It's a peace offering for dumping you the other night."

"You didn't need to do that. I didn't need a babysitter you know," I replied.

"I know, but I talked you into going. I should have been your wingman."

"You're right." I grinned. "You're fired as my chaperone, but, lucky for you, there's a job open as my personal stylist."

"I'll take it," she said, shoulder-bumping me.

"So now we've established that I'm forgiven, it's time to spill the beans on Hottie McTottie."

I laughed at her nickname for O'Connell.

"I don't know what you mean," I teased.

"Girl, you know exactly who I'm talking about. If that boy was any hotter, you could fry eggs on his six-pack," she retorted.

"It's more like an eight-pack really." I sighed, and this did make her stare.

"And you've seen him without his top off how?"

"It's not what you're thinking. He's a boxer at the gym I work at."

"I thought you were a waitress?" she asked, clearly confused.

"I am. The gym is my second job," I replied.

"Well, I'd say you were working too hard, but I can see where you get the motivation."

I grinned and shook my head as we carried on walking, not keen to pursue the subject, but not denying what she said either.

"So what's his name, and how have you not jumped him yet?" she persisted.

"His name is Cormac O'Connell, and even if I wasn't looking to avoid any kind of relationship right now, he's out of my league," I answered reluctantly.

"Em, just because his packaging is pretty doesn't mean that his chocolate tastes any sweeter than yours."

I burst out laughing at her analogy. O'Connell was totally like chocolate. One bite and you were totally addicted, but any more than a little occasionally was bad for you.

"So what happened after he walked you home?" she inquired.

"Nothing," I protested. "He just made sure I got home safely, that's all. He really isn't interested in me like that."

"Oh, my dear Em." She sighed dramatically. "You really are clueless, aren't you? No boy leaves a party where he has hot girls on tap and an unlimited supply of free beer to walk a co-worker home based on a sense of duty and platonic friendship. I'm telling you, that boy wants a slice of your pie."

I was glad that I'd swallowed my sip of coffee or I'd have spat it all over Nikki by now.

"Thanks, Nikki, but I'm pretty sure you're wrong. He almost had sex with another girl at the party."

"Almost?"

"Well . . . he said that he couldn't go through with it and blew her off."

"I see, and where were you when all this was happening?"

"I was talking to Albie and some of his friends."

"Did he see you with Albie?" she inquired.

"Yes, but what does that have to do with anything?"

"Then I'm betting that he was trying to make you jealous but couldn't go through with it."

"That's pretty much what he said," I revealed reluctantly.

"And you still don't think that he's into you?"

"Even if by some miracle he was, you should have seen the girl he was with. There's no competition."

She wrapped her arm around my shoulders and smiled.

"Come, my young Padawan friend. You have a lot to learn, but in time I will show you the ways of the Force."

"Nikki?"

"Yeah?"

"You're a little bit geeky, aren't you?"

"That I am, my friend. A little bit geeky, but mostly a kick-arse, hard-core bitch."

I had to smile at that. What I wouldn't give to be the same.

* * *

If I was truly honest, I didn't really believe that O'Connell would change, but I liked the fact that he wanted to try. Although the incident at Daisy's had changed the dynamic of our relationship, I started to think that maybe he and Kieran really were beginning to consider me a friend.

It was with that thought in mind that I walked into the gym

on Thursday, my step a little bit quicker, and my heart a little bit lighter. I was proud to be making my own way, but more, that I was carving out a real life for myself. My empty heart was filling up with friends, people who cared that they knew me, who could say that they'd been a part of my life.

That was something that Frank couldn't take away from me. If he found me tomorrow, at least I could say that. My life now was more than I'd ever hoped I'd have. I had no doubt that if I'd stayed, I'd be dead by now, or so brutalized that I might as well be. Of course, that was exactly what would happen if he found me again, but I wouldn't go down without a fight. I'd never had a life worth fighting for before, but I had it now.

"Hello, baby. It's been a long, cold, lonely week without you. What say you give me your number, and I'll keep all your nights next week warm for you."

I'd barely even made it through the door before Tommy was throwing his sweaty arm around me and trying his luck. I couldn't help but laugh, but my laughter didn't seem to put a dent in his ego. It was like I'd given him the reaction he was looking for.

"Tommy, get your arm off her right now, or I'm gonna break it in at least three places," O'Connell shouted down from the ring, as Kieran helped him on with his gloves.

"Fuck off, O'Connell." He smiled in good humor. "She's totally into me."

Tommy was clearly just yanking O'Connell's chain, but both O'Connell and Kieran stopped stock-still and turned to face Tommy. Suddenly I wasn't so sure he was joking when he'd threatened Tommy, and from the speed at which he moved his arm, neither was Tommy.

"Chill out, guys. I was only kidding." Tommy turned and gave me a quick peck on the cheek as he said, "I'll come by for that number later, baby," before legging it to the changing room.

"You're doing something about that when you spar later, aren't you?" Kieran questioned O'Connell, as he finished tightening his gloves.

"Oh, yeah." O'Connell smirked. "That cocky fucker's gonna be kissing the canvas before the night is over."

I wasn't worried about Tommy. He was quick and cocky enough that he'd find a way out of a beating later. Besides, none of these guys seemed to need an excuse to whale on each other.

I was still standing there like an idiot when Kieran climbed out of the ring and walked over to me. "Hello, darlin'. You'd best go and say hello to your man before he goes at it with Shane. He's all fired up tonight, and he fights badly when he's in a temper."

"He's not my man, Kieran," I pointed out.

"Well, Em, someone best tell him that, and it ain't gonna be me," he said as he ambled off to start with his own training.

I looked back at O'Connell shadowboxing in the ring, and I could see that Kieran was right. He was always full of energy, wired almost, which was weird to see in a guy his size. But tonight something was wrong. He seemed edgier and darker than usual, like he was boxing to kill, not hurt.

Not knowing if I was entering the lion's den, I walked tentatively up the steps to the ring and rested my arms on the top ropes.

As soon as he saw me, he stopped and walked over. There was no easy grin tonight. "Hey, sunshine," he said, "you okay?"

"I'm fine, thanks. How are you doing?"

"I'm better now that you're here."

He hung his head as he banged his gloves together, and I had the strongest urge to run my hand through his hair, like you'd do to comfort a small child.

"You know a problem shared, is a problem halved," I told him, hoping to lighten things up a little.

"Thanks." He smiled sadly at me. "But sharing my crap just drags you into it. Tell me about your day; that will help."

I hated that he was clearly upset. I wanted him to open up, but our friendship was still too new and fragile to push it too far, so I struggled to think back over my highly uneventful day.

"Nikki gave me a hard time for not jumping your bones, but I got an A on my spot test, so it wasn't all bad."

He wasn't better, but I'd managed to get a smile out of him at least.

"Well, I'm in Nikki's camp there." He spoke softly. "You heading off to the office to work?"

I nodded my head in agreement.

He ran the back of his glove along my cheek gently. "Okay, sunshine. I have to train late tonight, so Kieran's gonna walk you home later, but I'll see you tomorrow, okay?"

He looked so sad that the urge to kiss him, to comfort him, was overwhelming. But I didn't. Of course I didn't. Because guys like him didn't kiss girls like me.

I just gave him a small nod and walked down the steps toward the office. Just as I reached the door, I stopped and turned. Only part of the ring was visible, but it was all I needed to see. He rolled his shoulders and looked up toward Shane. In that instant all trace of sadness and vulnerability was gone, and in its place was pure, unadulterated rage.

The bell rang out, and O'Connell's wrath was unleashed. He bounced up and down on the canvas like he had too much energy to keep contained, ducking and weaving as he did, with a stealth that belied his size. He eyed Shane like a predator sizing up his kill, and as Shane made the first lunge, O'Connell dodged left and slammed into his midsection, with a rib-crushing right hook.

I'd taken a few right hooks in my life, so by all accounts; this show of violence from O'Connell should be freaking me out. But

I was so turned on I couldn't see straight. My heart was beating so loudly that I couldn't hear anything else. Everything just faded into white noise.

Shane was clearly winded and dodged around the canvas, trying to recover his breath. Seeing the weakness, O'Connell went in with a combination. They were supposed to be sparing but he wasn't pulling any punches. The sweat beading around his forehead trickled down his cheek and splashed onto his chest, and damn if I didn't want to follow its path with my tongue. I imagined the feel of those tight, sweaty abs beneath my fingertips and how the silk of his training shorts, encasing all that hard muscle, would feel pressed up against me.

There wasn't a single part of my body that wasn't totally aware of every single part of his, and the more he lost control of himself, the more I lost control with him. By the time he'd knocked Shane out with another killer right hook, I was a mess.

"For fuck's sake, O'Connell, you're supposed to be fucking sparring, not knocking him into next week. I've warned you before. This has got to fucking stop."

Danny was going ballistic, and O'Connell, still breathing hard, dropped his hands to his sides while he tried to control himself. I knew that I couldn't be right in the head to be this turned on when he'd just knocked a man he called a friend into unconsciousness. I was breathing as hard as he was, as though my lust, like his temper, was something we could rein in.

He turned and caught my eye, and he knew I'd seen the whole thing. His mask of indifference was replaced with a frown, and I guessed he was worried that he'd scared me with his performance. Before he decided to come over, I turned and shut myself in the office. I couldn't deal with O'Connell when I was in this state. Christ, even being a foot taller than me, I'd have his back flat against the door the second we were in a confined space. What I needed right now was to pull myself together.

By the time I was ready to leave, O'Connell was nowhere to be seen. Kieran was waiting outside for me just as O'Connell had been that first night. He would know exactly where O'Connell was and how he was doing, but I was too gutless to satisfy my curiosity. He filled the uncomfortable silence with his usual cheerful banter, but it was woefully one-sided as my thoughts were consumed with the well-being of one man.

"Are you going to be okay here?" Kieran asked, eyeing the security of my door with some skepticism.

"I'll be fine, thanks. There are about five locks behind my door."

I paused as I contemplated what to say. *Fuck it.*

"Is O'Connell all right? Will you take care of him?" I spoke so fast that I wasn't even sure he'd heard the question.

He smiled at me, like he was pleased that I cared.

"He'll be fine. He just needs to blow off some steam. Don't worry, Em. I'll make sure he's good."

Of course, he'd be okay, and now Kieran was probably laughing his arse off at my concern over a giant of a man who trained to hurt people.

"You just make sure that you lock this door good and tight behind me, and I'll see you tomorrow, all right?"

I frowned but nodded. He waited on the top of the stairs for me to shut the door and throw the locks before I heard him descend.

Knowing that I was too keyed up to sleep, I took a hot shower and dried my hair before throwing on a pair of yoga pants and a vest top. I'd piled as many blankets and throws on my bed as I could, and, diving under the covers, I shivered as I waited for the cold sheets to warm up around me. It was pointless to turn on the heating. By the time the piece of crap warmed up, I would be ready to go to sleep, and I couldn't afford to run it all night.

The low after my earlier lust-filled adrenaline rush had hit, and the lure of sleep beckoned. Knowing that I could never fulfill the sexual fantasies of my own making, I surrendered to it.

* * *

The series of loud bangs at my door had me bolt upright and out of bed in seconds. My heart beat like a jackhammer as I approached it, knowing that if it were Frank, I'd have seconds to dress and grab my emergency backpack before escaping through the window.

I looked through the spy hole to see O'Connell staring back at me. I had no clue what he was doing at my flat, but I wasn't going to find out on this side of the door. Taking a deep breath, I ran my hands though my hair in a futile attempt at bringing order to the chaos. As the next round of banging began, I opened the door.

"I missed you, sunshine," O'Connell told me with the kind of ridiculous, doe-eyed sad face that a toddler would use to elicit sympathy.

"I can tell by the need you have to break down my door at..." I grabbed his thick wrist to check the time on his watch and dropped it again just as quickly, "...three o'clock in the morning. Do I even want to know how you got through the main entrance door?"

He stood there looking stupid and sheepish.

"It wasn't locked," he slurred. I shivered involuntarily at the lapse in security and tried hard not to think about how easy it was to get to me. My illusion of safety was quickly evaporating.

"You know it's a good thing I'm here to look after you. This is not a safe building, you know."

"And do you have any suggestions as to where I could move that would be cheaper than this place?" I asked sarcastically.

"You could live with me," he suggested hopefully.

I rolled my eyes at his ridiculousness. It would serve him right if I agreed then waited until he woke up sober, with a raging hangover, before announcing my new-found residency status as his housemate.

"Fuck me, O'Connell. Even off your face, you're fast," Kieran piped up from the doorway.

"What are you doing here?" I asked.

"He was already half baked when I found him, and I've been trying to keep him out of trouble all night. He had the bright idea that he wanted to say good night to you, and there was no talking him out of it. He sprinted up here as soon as we got in sight of your building."

"Well, thanks for trying to help. Do you think you'll be able to get him home on your own?"

Kieran looked over my shoulder and chuckled. "Sorry, Em, but I don't think that's going to be an option."

I turned around and sure enough there was O'Connell, passed out on the right side of my bed.

"Great. How the hell am I supposed to move him?"

Kieran rubbed the back of his neck, seeming to ponder the problem while he tried and failed to hold back a smile. "Look, if you really don't want him to crash in your bed, I can try and make up a pallet on the floor and move him there, but I won't get him far. He's out cold."

I felt bad then. I wasn't really selfish enough to roll him onto the floor. This place was so cold at night he'd probably wake up with hypothermia.

"It's all right. Leave him there. I'll think of something."

"Thanks, Em. I'm off then, 'cause no offense, but your place is kind of small and I don't feel like crashing on the floor."

He walked over to my desk and grabbed a pen and sticky note. "Here's my number. If you need me, just call, but if you let him sleep it off for a few hours, he'll be fine."

He closed the door with a wave and I bolted each of the locks in turn.

"Well, I don't have a phone, but the thought was there," I muttered to no one in particular.

Although I'd already done it before I went to sleep, I ran through my security routine again, because the front door had been opened. By the time the adrenaline rush from my late-night visitors had worn off, I was exhausted and freezing cold.

I managed to get O'Connell's boots off, but after that struggle, I gave up with the rest of his clothes. He'd probably be warmer with them on anyway.

In the absence of any alternative, I pried the blankets from under him, which took some doing, and threw them over both of us. His body radiated heat, and I curled up against his side, contemplating all the while how to pass the whole night without jumping him.

CHAPTER NINE

The pain was so excruciating, it burned through the haze of sleep. I had no idea what was happening. Disoriented and confused, my pain receptors were screaming. I had literally been pulled from my bed, from sleep, by my hair. It must have been coming out in handfuls.

Seemingly unimpressed with his progress, Frank stopped to wrap his hand around it, giving him a better grip, and then continued yanking me upward with all his strength. Tears ran down my cheeks uncontrollably. I was helpless to do much of anything, except follow where he was leading. I could hear Mum whimpering in the next room so I knew he'd already warmed up.

I'd like to say that he reeked of booze, but that would be a lie to excuse what he was doing. He was stone-cold sober. Frank did what he did because he liked to hurt people, because he liked to hurt me. He was a monster, and alcohol had nothing to do with it.

We'd reached the utility room off the kitchen when he let go of my hair and shoved me to the floor.

"What the fuck is that?" he screamed.

I looked toward where he had pointed in confusion. Mum hadn't done the washing for a few days, so I'd done a couple of loads and put them out on the drying racks to air. Realizing that I'd be out of comfortable underwear by tomorrow, I'd put a couple of pairs of knickers on the heater to dry.

Frank pushed his screaming, rage-filled face so close to mine that he spat on me as he shouted. "You think that flashing your underwear at me is going to make me want to get inside you, Emily, you filthy little whore! I'm your stepfather for fuck's sake. Do you know how fucking sick it is to put that on display in front of me?"

"I'm sorry," I whimpered in agony, as I fought to control the tears.

With his hand firmly gripped in my hair, he reeled me around and slapped me as hard as he could on the side of my face. The force of his grip held me still so I took the full brunt of the hit. It wasn't the first time I'd tasted blood.

"Little whores like you are never sorry," he sneered. "Don't think I don't know you're out trying to get it whenever you can, because I won't give it to you."

He hit me again so hard that I was dizzy. It was testament to how fucked in the head he was that he equated my drying underwear on a rack in the laundry room to my throwing myself at him. It was a frightening insight as to where these beatings would eventually lead.

* * *

I woke with a start, and as usual after the nightmares, I could barely breathe. Sucking air into my lungs, I tried breathing deeply to gain control before I hyperventilated.

When I caught sight of O'Connell's unconscious form next to

me, I nearly fell out of bed. After a nightmare about Frank, seeing someone in my bed was a sure-fire way to get my heart racing.

He was still lying facedown next to me. With his lips slightly parted and snoring gently, he had gone from looking mean and dangerous to vulnerable and cute. I couldn't help but stare. It was probably the only chance I'd ever have to study him this closely.

His strong jaw held the hint of a five-o'clock shadow, but that only softened the in-your-face sexiness of those sharp cheekbones. He kept the sides of his hair almost military short but the top, usually arranged in messy spikes, was now deliciously rumpled. It only made me want to run my hands through it even more.

Even when he was calm, he was still the most dangerous man I'd ever met. He opened his eyes, and long, inky black eyelashes framed the most hauntingly beautiful eyes I had ever seen. This close, I could see the flecks of silver in the blue that made them so remarkable.

"Good mornin'," he whispered croakily, betraying the amount he'd had to drink the night before.

He looked nervous, and I knew that he was waiting for my reaction to his late night visit. I smiled gently at him, unable to prolong his agony in anticipation of my reaction.

"Good morning. If you're waiting for breakfast in bed, I'm afraid this hotel stopped serving at eight."

He grinned, and his relief that I hadn't balled him out was palpable.

"I totally owe you that," he replied.

"It would be pretty amazing," I said as I rolled over in bed to look at the ceiling. "I've never had breakfast in bed."

"No?" he said in astonishment. "What, never?"

I turned my head to look at him and shook it to answer no, unwilling yet to share the details of my sad and pathetic life.

"What would you have if we were in a fancy hotel now and you could have anything?"

I didn't need a minute to think about this one.

"Deliciously rich, expensive coffee and a selection of fresh Danish pastries," I breathed out on a wistful sigh.

O'Connell chuckled and looked across at me hungrily. Without any warning he sprang up, leaned over the bed to grab his boots, and sat down again to put them on.

"Are you going home?" I asked reluctantly, afraid of the disappointment I'd feel when he answered.

"No." He grinned. "I've got some errands to run, but I'll be back in half an hour."

"Okay," I answered, without asking him where he was going. I moved to get up with the intention of seeing him out.

"Why don't you stay in bed where it's warm, and see if you can't get back to sleep?" he suggested.

"I'm sorry it's so cold in here," I said nervously. "My heating isn't great, and it takes so long to come on that I'm usually on my way out before the room is warm, so I don't bother with it most of the time."

Anger flashed through his eyes, and I could see him biting the inside of his cheeks to refrain from saying something. I didn't think that O'Connell's financial circumstances were much better than mine, but I still felt shamed at the obvious evidence of my poverty. A sure sign of wealth was that rich people never needed to feel cold or hungry.

After a moment that felt like an hour, he leaned forward, grabbed the back of his sweater, and pulling it over his head, passed it to me.

"What are you doing?" I asked him in shock, still staring at the definition of his eight-pack that had been revealed when his T-shirt rose.

"It will keep you warm, and I won't be gone long."

"You'll freeze!" I cried in horror.

"Don't worry," he chuckled, "I tossed my jacket on your chair before I passed out. I'll be fine."

True to his word, he shrugged on his jacket and grabbed my keys off my desk before throwing the locks on my door.

"Don't deadlock the door behind me, okay? I've got your keys, so I'll just let myself in."

I nodded, still grinning like a fool, as I sank further into the warmth of his sweater. He gazed at me intently, like he was trying to memorize something, then with a wink, he let himself out and closed the door behind him. I'd bet good money that he'd used the exit wink more than once before. I didn't for one minute think that he'd come back, but if nothing else, the sweater was a pretty awesome souvenir. I had a spare set of keys, but I'd have to find a way to get my others back from him.

I pulled on the neck of his sweater and inhaled deeply. It was still deliciously warm from the heat of his body, and as I snuggled back into bed, the chill of the room barely bothered me.

The luxurious smell of expensive coffee brought me round, but the beautiful blues staring down at me were enough to keep my eyes open. I sat bolt upright in bed in surprise.

"What are you doing here?" I asked.

"I told you I'd be back," O'Connell answered in confusion. My cheeks colored as he realized I hadn't believed him, but he was nice enough not to call me on it. He reached toward my bedside table and handed me a foam cup. The smell literally made me groan.

I leaned back, wrapped up in O'Connell's sweater and sipping luxury coffee, feeling like this was the best dream I'd ever had. The dream got even better when O'Connell started stripping.

"Umm," I mumbled, sounding like a complete moron, but unwilling to put an end to the free show. When he was down to his jeans and nothing else, he slid into bed next to me and grabbed a box by the side of him.

"As promised . . . breakfast in bed." He grinned, obviously feeling very pleased with himself, and damn if he wasn't holding a box full of warm Danish pastries.

When we'd gorged ourselves completely, I lay back down on my side, full and contented. "That was the most amazing thing anyone's ever done for me, and you're totally forgiven for waking me up in the middle of the night."

He set aside the box and lay down to face me. "I'm sorry about that. Yesterday was kind of a rough day for me," he admitted.

"What happened?" I asked gently. I didn't mean to pry, but O'Connell looked like he needed to talk.

"Ma fell off the wagon again night before last. We got into it, and we both said some things we can't take back."

There was nothing to say that could make him feel any better. I gathered that she was an alcoholic, and reached out and lay my hand over his in a gesture of support.

He stared at it for a really long time and then carried on. "Dad was a twat who was off fucking anything in a skirt for as long as I can remember. Eventually Ma kicked him out, and that's when things got bad. She started drinking and would go on binges for weeks at a time. When she tried to clean herself up, things would get better. There'd be food in the house again, and she'd start giving a shite about me going to school and stuff, but then she'd hear about my dad's latest hookup, or we'd get a final demand on a bill, and I'd come home to find vomit all over the kitchen floor and her passed out on the sofa."

O'Connell looked so nervous telling me, like he thought it would change my opinion of him. I wouldn't pity him. We all had our own sad stories to tell, but now he stood taller in my eyes. Any man who could survive a childhood like that would.

"How did you stay out of care?" I asked.

"I was pretty good at covering for her and taking care of my-self. Kieran's ma knew that something was up, but she never called me on it. When things were really bad, she fed me and let me bunk in Kier's room, which pretty much saved my life."

He closed his eyes like talking about it was too much for him.

"Why did she fall off the wagon this time?" I persisted, poking at his open wound.

Now he'd started, I figured that he needed to let all the poison out before it would heal.

"Who the fuck knows," he admitted. "But I'm so fucking over it. How am I supposed to sort my crap out, when I'm always dealing with hers?"

"You shouldn't drink when you're angry. It probably makes things worse," I whispered. I didn't mean to preach, but it sounded like the drinking was a dangerous path for his mum, and I didn't want him meeting the same fate.

"I'm pretty sure that being a loser is in the blood," he admit-ted, as he opened his eyes to look back at me sadly.

I didn't cuddle him or offer false platitudes that everything would be fine. That was a promise that I couldn't make, for him or me. If he wanted to change his life, then only he could make it happen. I knew that better than anyone.

I reached across to my bedside table and grabbed a black pen. He looked stunned as I started writing across his rock-hard pec. His chest really was worthy of appreciation. All rock-hard muscle beneath my fingertips. When I was done, I looked over my handi-work and smiled.

"What does it say?" O'Connell asked, looking down at his chest.

"It says," I replied throatily, "'*A champion is someone who gets up when they can't*'—Jack Dempsey. I figured you'd ap-preciate the boxing reference, and I think that if you can pick yourself up, even when you think you're rock bottom and can't get any lower, well, then that makes you pretty special."

He swallowed deeply and pulled me down onto his chest. With my head pillowed against his arm, I fell asleep. Just like that, more warm, rested, and peaceful than I'd been in a very long time.

* * *

A week had gone by since that night with O'Connell. As the days passed, I convinced myself that he must have dismissed the weekend as another drunken lapse in judgment. So when I entered the gym on Thursday, it was with a heavy heart.

The atmosphere inside was buzzing. The place was packed, and Kieran and a few other boys were crowded around the ring, chatting with a few of the trainers. I tucked my head down and made a beeline for the sanctuary of the office, but as soon as I walked in the door, Danny grabbed me and landed a smacking great kiss on my cheek. Then bounding away like a jolly little leprechaun, he began pouring us both a coffee. I'd screeched when he grabbed me, but now I just stared at him, my mouth wide open like some stupid fish.

"Um . . . what was that for, Danny?"

"Because you, my girl, are a bloody genius! I've been trying to get that boy to fight seriously for years. He trains with one foot in and one foot out. He lacks commitment and conviction. But I'm telling you, that cocky little shite has something special. It's a gift that, up until now, he's been pissing up the wall.

"Then Monday morning he comes and tells me that he's all in and he wants me to train him to go professional. I don't know what you've done to him, but he's been working out like a machine ever since. Can't say I'm thrilled about what's going on between you two, but I never thought it would lead to this."

He shoved the hot mug of coffee into my hand, but didn't pay any attention to my stunned expression. Never in all the crazy scenarios that I'd thought up did I imagine that this was what had been going on this past week.

"Nothing is going on with me and O'Connell," I stated flatly.

"Really, darlin'," Danny replied with a chuckle. "You must think I'm a right eejit. When he's not training, that boy's walking round with a stupid bloody grin on his face, and he's spent the last half an hour checking the door every time it opens. Now if he's not looking for you, I'm a feckin' monkey's uncle."

I kind of squeaked and looked at the door myself, remembering that I hadn't seen O'Connell on the way in.

"Not you, too, sunshine," Danny snorted. "Don't bother looking for lover boy. I've sent him on a long run. See if that helps with his concentration. Now get to work, wench, and earn your keep."

He laughed again to himself and left the room whistling some tune, in any key but the right one, and in a better mood than I'd ever seen him in.

I sat down hard on the office chair and stayed there for a good five minutes while I processed what was happening. There was no way that I could take any credit for anything that was going on with O'Connell, but I couldn't help the small spark of hope that maybe I hadn't been dismissed as easily as I'd thought.

Determined to get a grip and stop mooning over some nonexistent fictional relationship, I started work. Danny came back about an hour later for a refill on his coffee, and I barely spared him a glance, determined to rise above his needling and prove him wrong.

When the door went again I didn't look up until I felt breath hot against my neck.

"Jesus Christ!" I yelped as my heart jumped into my mouth. I spun my chair around to see O'Connell wearing the biggest shit-eating grin on his face.

He was shirtless, as usual, and wearing the uniform shorts that he always trained in. He leaned his sweaty, ripped torso forward and put his hands on the desk on either side of me, trapping me in the circle of his arms. Even sweaty from training he still smelled good, and I wondered how it would feel to kiss my way down those abdominals. He was so built and hard that being this close made me feel even smaller and more fragile than I usually felt.

I noticed straightaway that my neat black cursive still adorned his chest.

"Shouldn't that have washed off by now?" I asked. I sucked in a breath as a thought occurred to me. "I didn't use permanent ink, did I? I thought it would come off with water."

He grinned even bigger, if that was possible, then grabbed my hand and placed it gently on his pectoral. With my fingertips, I traced the raised bumps of each line.

"Holy shit!" I whispered. "You've had it tattooed on you."

CHAPTER TEN

"You shouldn't curse," he teased.

I ran my fingertips back and forth across his skin in case I was wrong, but sure enough, the ridges of the text were slightly red and scabbed.

"But..." I muttered, at a complete loss for words.

O'Connell seemed to find my reaction highly amusing. "You should see your face, sunshine."

"They weren't even my words," I exclaimed, as though he could still somehow change his mind about the tattoo.

"I know. But you gave them to me."

"But my handwriting is terrible," I replied, horrified yet exhilarated with what he'd done.

"It's perfect and it will give me a good story to tell our kids."

"Holy shit!" I whispered again.

I was sure he took pleasure in leaving me speechless as he laid a gentle kiss on my head and moved toward the door. On his way out he turned back to me. "I have to train late again tonight. Can you wait an extra hour for me, or shall I get Kier to walk you home?"

"I'll wait," I replied, as I felt my cheeks reddening.

He grinned back knowingly, and as he shut the door behind him, I crossed my legs to relieve the ache.

The door tapped a little bit later and in walked Tommy, more subdued than I'd ever seen him.

"Hey, Tommy." I smiled. "What's up?"

"Thought I'd get in while Con's distracted and try for that number," he answered.

"Sorry." I grinned back. "Numbers are tomorrow night, you know that."

He rubbed the back of his neck in a gesture that betrayed his unease.

"About that. Me da's broken his leg which means he can't work, so I'm gonna need to help Ma out with the rent. I've had a word with Danny, and he's knocking my dues down to five quid a week for the next month till I can get my folks back on their feet. Danny wanted me to tell you in case he forgets to mention it."

"Oh no!" I exclaimed. "Is he all right? Is there anything I can do to help?"

"He's okay, thanks, Em. He just feels like a bit of an eejit for falling down the steps drunk. Ma tore him a new one, though."

"Your poor mum. I hope she's all right, but let me know if there's anything I can do," I offered.

"Well," he drawled with his trademark confidence, "maybe I should take your number, you know, just in case I can think of a way you can help."

I laughed at his tenacity and pointed toward the door. "Go and let me get on with some work before Danny catches us skiving. If you need me, you know where to find me."

He left happier than when he'd arrived, and I got to work.

Hours later I was immersed in numbers when O'Connell walked in, drenched with sweat. "Hey, sunshine, I'm just grabbing a shower. You about done here?" he asked.

"Sure." I sighed. "I'll close down here and meet you outside."

"No, stay here where it's warm, and I'll come and get you in a minute."

I shut down the computer and put on my coat and scarf, making sure to turn off the heater and coffee machine. He must have taken the quickest shower in history, but I was ready by the time he came for me. He grabbed my bag without asking and threw it over his shoulder with his training bag. The gym was empty by the time we left, but I assumed that Danny was still here as the lights were all on and someone had to lock up.

"You know, Danny was right. When I first came in here, the smell was disgusting, and now I'm so used to it, I can't smell anything at all."

O'Connell chuckled at that, and then frowned when I buried myself deeper into my coat as we hit the fresh air.

"Is that your only jacket?" he asked softly.

"Yeah," I muttered, embarrassed at my poverty. I knew I needed a better one for winter, but I was trying to save as much as I could for school.

"We'll have snow soon, I can tell. I'll start bringing my car next week. It'll keep you warmer on the way home."

"You drive?" I asked surprised. I'd never seen O'Connell with a car, so I just assumed he didn't have one.

"Yeah," he replied sheepishly. "A Ford Mustang. The boys helped me fix it up a couple of years ago, but I don't drive it much lately."

"Why not?" I asked. This time it was his turn to look embarrassed, though he needn't have.

"I had to give up my job in construction to train with Danny full-time. He's trying to get us some sponsors, but until I win a few decent fights it's gonna be tough. Kier's ma is letting me crash with Kier for a bit, rent free, but I'll probably have to sell the car soon to pay for training. Danny's offered to help me out with expenses, but I don't want to take his money. It's enough to ask him to train me."

I nodded but didn't say anything so he'd keep talking.

"I used to make pretty good money bare-knuckle boxing, but I promised Danny I wouldn't do that anymore. I can't afford to if I try to go pro."

He looked nervous like he was waiting for my reaction.

"Danny told me you were trying to go professional. He seems to think you have a good chance."

"What do you think?" he asked.

His question puzzled me. "I don't know anything about boxing, O'Connell. I think that trying to better yourself at anything is a good thing, especially if it means cutting back on the partying and drinking. But honestly I worry about you getting hurt fighting with professional boxers."

He smiled, looking pleased with my answer.

"What?" I questioned at the look on his face.

"It's kind of nice having someone worry about me."

He grabbed my hand and pulled me to a stop facing him. He moved in so close that our noses were almost touching. "Tell me you can feel this. I need to know I'm not the only one," he spoke gently.

"I feel it," I whispered, staring at the ground. "But I'm not doing anything about it. Everything that you make me feel is completely overwhelming, and I can't give you what you need, not even close. I don't want to talk about why I am this way, but just offering you friendship is a big deal for me right now."

I finished my rant feeling more desperate than ever. This big, strong, beautiful, terrifying man had feelings for me, but seriously how long would they last? I was getting better, but I was afraid of my own shadow most of the time. I was small, weak, and lacked any self-confidence.

O'Connell was dangerous, addictive, and so sexy that I was

consumed by lust every time we were in the same room together. He used his body like a weapon and the danger attracted
women like a magnet. With that many women, all vying for his
attention, what little charm I held for him would fade like mist
in the morning sun. If I let him in, he had the power to break
what little of me was left whole when I couldn't keep him.

Reaching out one giant, scarred, and calloused hand, he
tucked a wayward curl behind my ear. He lifted my chin with
his knuckle forcing me to meet his gentle gaze. He looked so
happy and intense right now that I could feel my eyes welling
up. I never thought that anyone would ever look at me like that.

"I know I'm scary and loud. I'm fucked up, and I'm gonna
fuck up with you a lot because I've never done this before. I
don't date girls, I fuck them and walk away because that's what
they expect. It's all they think I'm good for. I'm not smart like
you, and I know I don't deserve you.

"Right now I'm dirt poor, but one day I'm not gonna be. I will
fight to make something better of myself, to be someone better.
Someone you can be proud of. If you need time, then I'll give
you time. If you need friendship, then I'll give you friendship.
But you're mine, and when the time is right, when you're ready,
I'm coming for you."

I nodded, so close to tears I knew that if I tried to speak,
I'd completely break down. I swallowed hard, and the tears fell
anyway. O'Connell wiped them away with his thumb and gently
pressed his big firm lips to mine.

Just like that my fears were forgotten. The kiss was gentle, but
fireworks exploded all over my body. It was like he had invig-
orated every cell with life. The touch of his lips wasn't enough
to satisfy, only to feed my addiction. I knew in my head that I
wasn't ready for a relationship, but my body wanted to drown
in the revelation that it could feel something other than cold,
hunger, and pain. It was a kiss both chaste and pure and every-

thing I hoped that my first kiss would be, because everything I gave to him, I gave freely.

Slightly out of breath, our lips parted and he rested his forehead against mine.

"I'm gonna give you the fuckin' world, baby," he whispered against my lips.

He kissed me again quickly and, grinning like a kid, threaded his fingers through mine.

"You know friends don't hold hands," I whispered, knowing that there was no way that I was letting go first.

"Huh," he grunted. "Me and Kier hold hands all the time."

I burst out laughing at the thought, and he reveled in my happiness.

"It's a good thing we're sticking to being friends," he explained. "The next couple of months are gonna be really tough. I should be taking you out on dates and buying you flowers and shit, but I'm going to be training every hour I can, and I won't have any money."

"It's not about the money or anything else, you know that, right?" I pressed him.

"I know, Em. One day you'll tell me about the skeletons in your closet, but if I didn't give you at least an idea of how I feel, I'd lose you before you ever gave us a chance. I swear to God though, if Tommy asks for your number one more time, I'm gonna break his fucking face."

He was only half-serious but his possessiveness and intensity turned me on when it should have had me running. I ran my thumb across the back of his knuckles, and I felt him shiver.

"There's not exactly a queue of men trying to date me. Tommy is a nice guy and your friend. He just likes messing with your head, that's all."

O'Connell lifted our joined hands and kissed the back of mine.

"You really have no idea how fuckin' beautiful you are, do

you? I've knocked out guys at the gym already for looking at you the wrong way, and I'll fuck up anyone else who tries."

I rolled my eyes, half wondering if he'd be better off peeing on me to stake his claim, like a dog marking its territory.

"Well, no more fucking anyone up, okay? If I'm ever ready to date anyone, you're at the top of my list, so save all the aggression for your fights. I have a hard enough time dealing with you boxing in the ring where there are rules, let alone out of it."

He squeezed my hand in agreement, though I noticed he didn't make me any promises.

"Baby, I'd better be the only one on that list. I feel like I'm gonna lose you before I even get a chance. I'm fucked-up possessive over you. I know that, and I'm afraid that you'll get sick of all the bullshit that comes with me."

It wasn't like O'Connell to freely admit any of his insecurities. I appreciated knowing that he came with his own baggage, too. We made it to my building all too soon and he turned to face me.

"I'm not gonna rush you, okay? I've never wanted anyone as badly as I want you, but I want you to trust me, too, so I'm gonna kill myself and take this slow. When you're stronger, when you're ready to give me a chance, I'll be here."

I nodded because I was incapable of replying. It was human nature to want to jump his bones. He was the most amazing specimen of man that I'd ever seen. But I needed slow. Time was the only thing that would bring back the pieces of my soul, but I had the feeling that O'Connell might turn out to be the glue that held them all together.

Walking me up to my flat, he unlocked my door and handed me back the keys. He reached his hand around my nape and pulled me to him for another kiss.

The minute I started to appreciate his firm soft lips, I sighed, and his tongue slid into my mouth to caress mine. The ache between my legs intensified until the only thing that I was aware of was the desperate need to have my lips on his skin and find relief from this exquisite torture.

His hand slid into my hair holding me to him more tightly, as if there was anything more than a whisper of air between us anyway. His free hand moved from the small of my back to my arse, pressing my pelvis to his. At the feel of his rock-hardness against me, I couldn't help but moan, and he ate it up, pressing harder.

This wasn't a delicate seduction. O'Connell's actions were deliberate and unapologetic. He didn't try to discreetly work his hand down my back as we kissed in the hope that I didn't notice what he was doing. No, he practically mounted me to him because, despite my protestations of friendship, my body wanted this. If his skills so far were anything to go by, I doubted I would have been sorry to let it go any further.

"Fuck," he muttered, as he pulled his lips from mine. "That was supposed to be me saying good night and taking it slow."

"If you tell me that's how you and Kieran say good night, I'm really going to start worrying."

He chuckled then bowed his head toward me. "One more kiss before we go back to being friends?" he suggested.

"Uh-huh," I murmured. "Good night then," I whispered and pretty much attacked him right back. My hands slid into his hair and pulled his huge frame down until I could trap his lips between mine. He groaned loudly against me, the vibrations rocking through my body and intensifying my craving.

After a few minutes, we were both out of breath, and with his hands still firmly pressed against me, he tucked his head into the crook of my neck and inhaled deeply. "You're like an addiction, sunshine. It's making it difficult for me to do right by you. But I want this too badly to fuck it up."

"You know," I reassured him, "you're pretty addictive yourself. No one's ever made me feel like this."

It killed me to imagine that this could be our last kiss, but despite what my body wanted, I knew that no relationship would ever work until I had time to sort out my head. I could only hope that he would still be willing to give me a chance when that day came, and I needed to know that he would stick around before I gave him any more of myself. There would come a time where I needed to tell him about the monsters under my bed, but not yet. They weren't going anywhere. They never did.

"Do you have a mobile phone?" he asked.

"Sorry. I don't have a mobile or a landline. I've had to try and keep my overhead down as much as I can." I was once more embarrassed about my poverty, but O'Connell had pretty much admitted that his circumstances were the same.

"I had to give mine up when I quit my job. I'm with Kier most of the time, though, so if you ever need me, just call him from a pay phone. He told me he left you his number."

I nodded, but just then I'd never wished for a mobile phone more. The anguish of going days without seeing or hearing from him was pretty depressing.

He smiled, sensing my gloom. "I guess we just do this the old-fashioned way then. Do you have a pen and some paper?" he asked.

I pulled a piece from my notebook and handed it to him with a pen.

Leaning over my desk, I half wondered if the archaic piece of furniture would hold his weight as he wrote out a note, folded it over, and handed it to me. "Don't read it tonight, save it for the morning, okay?" he asked.

"All right," I agreed. "Will I see you tomorrow night?"

"Of course, baby. Kieran's gonna walk you home, but can I come by after training?" he asked hopefully.

"I'd like that," I admitted shyly, hoping that he still felt the same way tomorrow.

He carried on holding me like he couldn't quite bring himself to let me go. "Bye, sunshine," he whispered against my lips.

"Good-bye, O'Connell." I sighed as he pulled back and walked out the door, sporting a look of unadulterated hunger.

I quickly threw on all the bolts then raced to the window. Feeling my eyes on him, he turned around and blew me a kiss before shifting his training bag higher on his back and disappearing into the night.

Collapsing onto my bed, I contemplated waiting until tomorrow to read O'Connell's note, but my curiosity was stronger than my conscience. There was no way that I could sleep tonight if I was wondering what he'd written me.

Hey baby,

I knew you wouldn't make it until morning to read this. I'm shit at this friends thing, but you're worth the wait.

Miss me all night like I'll miss you.

Love OC xxx

P.S. You looked beautiful tonight

Jeez. In six lines, he had turned me to mush. What kind of a man writes notes in this day and age? The freakin' awesome kind, that's who!

I flattened out the note and put it inside my favorite book. Still dazed, I brushed my teeth and changed into my pajamas. Tonight I was walking on air, and for the first time in a long time, I was happy.

CHAPTER ELEVEN

I walked my tray down the lunch queue, contemplating the delicate balance of craptastic culinary experiments on offer, bearing in mind my modest budget. The salad was fresh looking and cheap, even if a little basic, and my stomach grumbled as I thought about Mike's spectacular quarter pounder with cheese, lovingly known as "the Daisy burger." If O'Connell ever took a break from training, then a Daisy burger would be my treat.

"Right, then. Spill. You've been mooning around this canteen for ten minutes looking like you've just won the lottery, and you never smile like this, so what's going on?"

Albie gently butted into the queue and dumped his tray down next to mine. He loaded it with enough food to keep me in lunches for a month, and then followed that with two cartons of milk.

"I have no idea what you're talking about," I answered. "I am merely perusing the canteen's many culinary delights. If I'm smiling more than usual, it's probably because I'm overwhelmed by the overabundance of decadent menu choices on offer today."

Albie looked at me stunned, and then laughed deep and

heartily. "You've just said more words to me in one sentence than you've said to me in the whole time I've known you. Horniness makes you verbose."

Humor gone, I stared at him gobsmacked, my cheeks reddening. "I am not horny. Who told you I was horny?" I spluttered.

"No one. But I can't imagine you floating about like this unless you were hot for some guy. Plus you do have that I'm-thinking-about-a-man-naked look about you," he said laughing.

"No, I do not," I blustered indignantly.

I absentmindedly reached for a piece of carrot cake then put it back again when I realized that I didn't need it and couldn't afford it.

"Em, you're so easy to wind up." He smiled as he carried on loading up his tray.

"I'm glad you're happy," I huffed.

I wasn't used to being teased, and it was hard allowing myself to feel excited about my fledgling friendship with O'Connell. Whenever I'd had anything to feel good about, Frank had taken it away. It gave him a kind of perverse pleasure, but coveting my happiness didn't need to daunt me anymore. I had friends, I was happy, and I needed to stop worrying about hiding the fact.

If anything, I should be grabbing O'Connell by the hand and shouting at the top of my lungs, "Holy shit, can you believe that this unbelievably hot-as-fuck man-mountain actually wants to date me!" Okay, so that might be a little extreme, but sharing a little of my happiness with my friends shouldn't be such a big deal.

We paid for our trays and, as I sat down next to Albie, was cornered by the gang.

"So you hooked up with Hottie McTottie yet then?" Nikki said teasingly.

"Who's Hottie McTottie?" Max asked.

"Only the six-foot-five, dark, built, intense, brooding fighter who's been mooning over Em for the last few weeks," Nikki replied.

"He hasn't been mooning over me, and we're not together," I corrected. "We're friends, that's all."

Nikki grinned, but Albie laughed out loud. "Sweetheart, we've only seen you both together once, and you were setting the place on fire. Seriously, I saw my life flashing before my eyes when I offered to walk you home. It's not a big jump for us to imagine you two together."

"Well, it's a big jump for me," I admitted quietly.

"We know," Nikki said soothingly. "But that boy has it bad for you, and it's only a matter of time before he wears you down. If he fucks it up, though, he'll have to answer to us."

I really wasn't that much of a prize, but it was nice of them to care. I did giggle a little at the thought of Nikki, who was probably only a little bigger than me, pounding on O'Connell for some perceived wrongdoing. I'd bet he'd had splinters that hurt more.

"You do realize who O'Connell is, don't you, Nik?" Ryan volunteered, and I bristled, waiting for the insult.

"Everyone knows who he is, Ry," Albie answered. "But I'm telling you, man, you didn't see the way he looks at her."

"Just be careful, that's all I'm saying," Ryan warned.

I knew more than anyone that my guard should be up, but it had been up my whole life, and it felt good to let it down. If O'Connell was going to trample all over our friendship, then so be it. Every moment that I'd spent with him so far made the risk worth it.

I had finished my salad and contemplated leaving when a plate slid in front of me. Albie grinned as he passed me the carrot cake I'd been eyeing.

"What's this?" I asked.

"That ridiculously big piece of cake you talked yourself out of. It's a celebration," he answered.

"What are we celebrating?"

"Finding something decadent that you know is bad for you and sinking your teeth into it."

I was about to remind him that O'Connell and I were just friends when he winked teasingly at me. Accepting the gesture with a smile for the act of kindness that it was, I plunged my fork into the moist cake, groaning at the first bite.

We chatted about our plans for later, but I already knew what I was doing with my afternoon and Albie had been my inspiration.

* * *

"What is it?" Tommy asked later that night as he stared at the tin like it might be filled with anthrax. I opened the lid as he held it in his hands.

"You've got to be fucking kidding me." He grinned and I was pleased that he looked so impressed.

"What's going on, Em?" Liam, one of the gym's other ridiculously large fighters, asked.

"I've baked Tommy's mum a chocolate fudge cake."

"Seriously?" Tommy asked. "That's fudge in the middle?"

"It sure is, and if you heat it up, the filling should melt so the chocolate fudge sauce will cover the cake."

"Why's Tommy got chocolate cake?" Kieran pitched in.

"Em baked it for the little fucker," Liam told him.

"Sunshine, I'm your boyfriend's best friend. If you should be baking anyone chocolate cake, it should be me."

"It's not for Tommy, it's for his mum," I reminded them. "I'm sure Tommy will get a piece, but his mum's been under a lot of stress lately, so this is to make her feel better, and I'm your best friend's friend not his girlfriend."

None of the guys actually said, "aww," but they did all look at me like I was a cute, little puppy.

"Wait," said Tommy, "you called Con her boyfriend."

"Only a matter of time, my friend," replied Kieran, slapping Tommy on the back.

"Fuck," muttered Tommy, as a few people round the gym groaned or muttered.

"What's wrong with them?" I whispered to Kieran. "Don't they think I'd be good enough for him?"

Kieran laughed at me. "Are you kidding me? You're the sweetest, most innocent thing this bunch of depraved maniacs has ever seen. You're smart, gorgeous, and you bake. They're pissed off that Con wants to take you off the market. He's shown his hand. So if any one of these fuckers wants to ask you out, they need to go through him, and there's no one in this gym who can take Con."

I was thinking that Kieran wildly exaggerated my attributes, but I was still pleased. I wasn't great at cooking, but I could bake a mean chocolate cake. In all of this I did wonder if O'Connell had heard me at all when I told him that we'd only be friends. Maybe I was fighting fate, but I needed to know that I was strong enough to stand alone before I'd fall back on O'Connell for support.

"When me ma sees this, she's gonna be pissed that I didn't bring you home first," Tommy said gloomily. Then after a short pause he smirked. "Still, it's not like she's engaged or married or anything, so there's still plenty of time for her to wise up, blow off O'Connell, and marry me."

"You really are fucking relentless, aren't you, Tom," Kieran told him. "Con's gonna be ten times more protective now that he's staked his claim."

"Tough shit, arsehole," Tommy replied cockily, "'cause right now Danny's dropping medicine balls on Con's stomach, and I'm going home with his girl's chocolate cake."

I laughed as Tommy ducked Kieran's jab, without as much as

tilting the tin. He might not be as tall as the other boys, but he sure was quick.

As the guys went back to their training, I felt a quick, wet peck against my cheek. "Thanks, sunshine," Tommy told me, in possibly the first serious tone that he'd used since I'd known him. "No one's ever done anything that nice for me before. Making it yourself rather than buying it takes work. It's gonna make me ma cry, but in a nice way, you know? So thanks," he said, then kissed me quickly on the cheek again and legged it before Kieran caught him.

"You're welcome," I called back as he fled.

As I turned to go into my office, I saw O'Connell back in the gym. He'd finished with the medicine ball and was pounding on the speedball so hard I was sure it would break. His rhythm was literally seamless, and his face a mask of concentration. He didn't miss a beat, though, as he caught my eye, smiled, and winked at me. This earned him an ear bashing from Danny, which didn't faze O'Connell, but had me fleeing back to the computer.

I didn't see him when Kieran came to take me home, and I suspected that Danny was deliberately scheduling O'Connell's runs to coincide with my arrival and departure. He didn't even come in with dues, but Kieran explained that O'Connell wouldn't be paying them anymore.

"How's he doing?" I probed as we walked out.

"Seriously, he's training like a fucking animal. I've never seen him fight like this. He's like a machine. Danny would be pretty excited if he wasn't waiting for the other shoe to drop," he explained.

"What do you mean?" I asked.

"Con only goes off the rails when his ma falls off the wagon. It's like they're linked. When's she's doing good, he's doing good. Danny's agreed to train him because he left home, and he's never done that before. When she finds out what Con's doing, she's gonna be pissed. Either that or she'll want a piece of the action. That's when Danny thinks the shit will really hit the fan."

"Why wouldn't she be happy that O'Connell is really trying to make something of himself? Unless she's worried about him getting hurt."

"She couldn't give a fuck about him," scoffed Kieran. "The selfish bitch likes Con to come running when she needs him. She likes being the center of his world. I guess fighting takes away from that. Plus he doesn't have any money to help her out now."

The whole relationship sounded toxic to me. My own example of a mum was just as bad, though, so I kept my feelings to myself.

"Do you think he'll go back once she finds out?" I asked.

"No, Em. I think you were the game changer he needed. As long as you don't bail on him, I think he'll see past her bullshit this time."

Kieran was good company on the walk home, keeping me entertained with stories of all the trouble they used to get into. After he made sure that I was safely in my flat, I went straight to bed, happier than I'd been in a long time.

A tapping sound against the window woke me with a start. As usual, my first thought was that Frank had found me. But he'd be breaking down my door like it was his right to come in that way.

The noise continued, and I risked moving back the curtain slightly to see who was out there. O'Connell stood under the streetlamp throwing stones. I looked back at the clock to see that it was gone midnight. Pushing up the window, I could feel the bitter bite of frost creep into the already chilly room. "Hey," I called down.

"Hey, baby. I'm sorry to wake you, but I missed you today. I was hoping to say good night."

"Come up then. I'll buzz you in."

There was no time to change or even check my appearance in the mirror. Seconds after pressing the ancient buzzer to the main entrance, O'Connell was knocking lightly on my door. He must have raced up the stairs.

I opened up for him, bleary-eyed and conscious that I was dressed only in a pair of old boy shorts and a fleecy sweater. Dumping his training bag inside the door, he pulled me toward him, and I became a soft, sleepy puddle in his arms.

He kissed me gently, almost reverently. He kissed me like it was our first kiss, like I was a priceless treasure that could be broken or stolen from him at any moment.

"You know friends don't kiss," I reminded him, and he grinned back at me.

"Fuck that. I kiss Kier all the time." I laughed that this would be his answer every time we blurred the line of friendship.

"Shit, baby. It's freezing in here. Get back into bed."

"Umm," I protested. "I don't want to let you leave yet."

"I'll get in with you for a bit."

Appeased, I turned to look at the door. "Can you lock it up for me? I won't relax until it's locked."

"Nobody's gonna get to you while I'm here."

I gave him a sad smile of agreement, but my heart wasn't in it. I knew rationally that he was right, but phobias were deeply ingrained and not easily dispelled. What if Frank found me with O'Connell and attacked him when his guard was down? A thousand what-ifs ran through my mind and must have shown on my face.

"Okay, sunshine. You get back into bed, and I'll sort out the door."

He didn't realize how much of a big deal it already was for me to let him check the door rather than doing it myself, but I'd never willingly let him know how deep my fears ran.

The sheets were still warm as I slid between them. O'Connell shrugged off his jacket and clothes, leaving them draped over the chair in the corner. In only his jeans, he climbed into my small bed beside me. He didn't give me time to worry about what would happen next.

"Turn on your side away from me, Em."

Doing as he asked, his big hand pulled me back against him, spooning me in the cradle of his chest. My sweater had risen up slightly, and he traced gentle circles over my stomach. I could feel his need hard against me, but it didn't seem to bother him so I ignored it.

"How was training?" I whispered in the darkness.

"Brutal. Danny says he's beating all the pussy out of me." He chuckled. "I'm aching in muscles I didn't know I had."

I was fully aware of every one of his muscles, even if he wasn't. I'd happily rub each one of them better given half the chance.

"Is there anything I can do?" I whispered innocently.

"You're doing it," he said, and I could feel him smiling against my hair. "If I got to feel like this every night, I'd happily take a beating or two."

"You know that cuddles with me do come without the beatings, don't you?" I asked him.

"I know, baby," he mumbled, "but at least this way, I feel like I've spent a bit of every day earning them."

He paused, and I thought he'd fallen asleep.

"I heard what you did for Tommy. That was really nice of you."

"I thought you'd be mad because Tommy's been winding you up about my number."

"I'm pissed that he got to try your chocolate cake before I did, but his ma will love it. It's just another thing that makes you pretty fucking spectacular."

"It wasn't much, but if it makes you feel better, I'll make you a chocolate cake when you win your next fight."

"Oh, so there are conditions attached to my chocolate cake then?" He chuckled sleepily.

"I'm doing my best to keep you in peak physical condition. When we're old and gray I'll feed you chocolate cake every day."

I felt him swallow as he whispered throatily, "I'd like that, sunshine. I'd really like that."

We lay quietly for a while as I rubbed patterns back and forth over the back of his hand.

"Em, it's Liam's birthday this week, and he wants to go to a club Friday night. Will you come after work?"

I hated clubs of any sort. In our own little bubble I could pretend the outside world didn't exist. But being in a club surrounded by half-naked gorgeous girls who all wanted O'Connell and who would be staring like he was crazy for dropping his standards so low seemed like my idea of hell. To me, it would be like standing a daisy in a bouquet of beautiful roses. Who in their right mind would ever pick a daisy over a rose?

"I thought Danny banned all that."

"I'm not drinking, and I'll only stay for a couple of hours, but Liam's my friend so I'll have to show my face. Honestly, though, I don't get to spend much time with you, and I'd really like for you to be there."

How could I say no to that? He absolutely killed me.

"Okay, O'Connell, but when I've had enough I'm leaving," I replied warily.

"Fair enough, baby."

He was so tired that I could sense him falling asleep as he mumbled his answer.

"Sleep now," I whispered, squeezing his biceps.

He kissed the back of my head, and all too soon, the gentle

rise and fall of his chest and the wonderful warmth of his body next to mine lulled me back into a deep and dreamless sleep.

When I woke in the morning, the bed was cold, and O'Connell was gone. A wave of depression washed over me as I realized I was alone. Turning to the clock, I could see that it was barely 7 a.m. But next to it was another note.

Sunshine,

I hate to leave, but I love to watch you sleep. I'm probably already training when you read this but I'm thinking about you right now. I hope you wear those shorts to bed every night. They are sexy as fuck. Miss me like I miss you.

Love OC xxx

Ten seconds ago I was depressed and now I was on top of the world. I wondered why I ever bothered telling O'Connell that I only wanted to be friends, when every day it seemed to be me who wanted more. I rolled over to look at the ceiling, knowing that I was starting to forget all the reasons why we shouldn't be together.

CHAPTER TWELVE

O'Connell had absolutely no intention of letting me dictate the pace of our relationship. Every night that I wasn't at the gym, he'd stop by my flat after training to say good night. The training schedule that Danny had him on was brutal, and by the time he reached my door, he was dead on his feet. He didn't stay long before he ambled back to Kieran's to stockpile the calories and squeeze in as much sleep as he could, but those twenty minutes were the best part of my day. He didn't kiss me again, but every time he touched me or looked at me, it was like he was savoring the moment to remember it later.

Although he only grunted when I asked him how training was going, he devoured details about my day as though he'd missed me for every minute of it. With O'Connell training so much, I still had time to work and study, and the joy of finding his notes in random textbooks was priceless. How he slipped them in without me noticing was a mystery, but I saved each and every one.

His strategy was foolproof when I thought about it. Left to my own devices this week, I would have been filled by now with self-doubt and would have undeniably convinced myself that any attempt at a relationship with him was a car crash waiting to happen. Instead he'd sown the seed of hope between us and had spent every day since watering and nourishing it, so by the time Friday rolled around, I was beginning to think we might have a chance.

I opened the door to a freshly shaved O'Connell, who smelled so incredible that it took all of my willpower not to stand there slack-jawed and gawking. His black shirt molded perfectly to his sculpted torso, and with his sleeves rolled back, even his forearms looked sexy.

"Wow, Em, you look beautiful."

Seeing him look so fine immediately made me question my own appearance, but the look of hunger on his face restored my confidence. Once again Nikki had come to my aid with another outfit. Although I felt slightly shamed to be scrounging from her, she really didn't seem to mind. If anything, she treated me like her dress-up doll.

Although I often balked at some of her outfit choices, in truth I bathed in the affection that I imagined sisters might share. It was an affection I'd never had, and Nikki was unknowingly filling that void. For all intents and purposes I was like an awkward, gangly teenager struggling through the quagmire of adolescence. Most fifteen-year-olds had more figured out about themselves than I did at twenty.

Looking at O'Connell's face, I said a silent prayer of thanks for Nikki's help. My buttery soft skirt ended above my knees but was still a respectable length, but the knee-high boots she'd loaned me made my legs feel ridiculously long. Teamed with a fitted black top, my favorite long, silver heart locket, and understated earrings, I was out of my comfort zone, but a lot more at ease than I would have been in my own clothes.

"Shit, Em, those legs go for miles. I'm gonna be cracking heads left, right, and center tonight."

I smiled at the implication, but I seriously doubted that he had anything to worry about. I still thought that he was being deluded for feeling as he did about me, and I worried about the day he would find enlightenment.

He held my jacket out to me like a true gentleman, and, like that gentleman, he didn't comment on the fact that the jacket clearly belonged to Nikki. Once I locked the door, I tucked the keys into my pocket.

"Aren't you taking a bag?" he asked.

"No. I'd only end up leaving it somewhere. My money is in a hidden pocket in my skirt, and I'll just keep my keys in my jacket."

"Do you want me to carry them?"

"Thanks," I replied. Handing them over, I was bemused that it seemed like such a couple thing to do. He slipped his huge fingers between mine and squeezed gently as we walked down together. His black Ford Mustang sat gleaming outside my building, and he grinned as he rushed round to open my door.

"O'Connell, this is your car? It's gorgeous."

"Thanks. I figure it's mine for another month before I have to sell it. So tonight make the most of having your very own chauffeur."

"You're not drinking then?" I asked, figuring that he'd want at least a couple of beers tonight.

"Nope. I promised Danny I wouldn't. Until I get a few decent wins under my belt, this amusement park is now a temple." He tapped his stomach as he said it, like there was a pinch of anything other than skin on his perfect body.

"Do you have to train in the morning?" I asked, hoping that he'd stay over, knowing how wrong it was for me to lead him on.

"Half day tomorrow. Danny told me to give myself a break and come in at eleven, so we get a lie-in together."

I didn't say anything as I pondered how to deny him what we both so obviously wanted, but even if he had been my boyfriend, in my heart I knew that I wasn't ready for sex. Letting him sleep over was unfair when I knew it wouldn't lead anywhere.

"Hey." He tilted my chin up, getting inside my head again. "Just friends, right."

"We're blurring the lines, O'Connell. We're not together, but I feel like this weird idea of friendship between us has me reaping all of the benefits and you none of the rewards."

"Why don't you let me worry about that, Em."

I looked down at my hands and I couldn't help but feel concerned.

"You stress about this shit far too much, okay? Who's to tell us what friends should or shouldn't do? If someone tells me that holding your hand or being close to you when you sleep at night is wrong because we're just friends, then they can go and fuck themselves. I do it because it makes me feel good, and if you enjoy it, too, then why's it wrong?"

When he put it like that, I couldn't see why the thought had me so worked up. I wanted so very badly to throw my lot in with him and tie my life to his as tightly as I could, but Frank had done his work well. The death and destruction of a child's spirit was not the work of a moment, but a campaign of dedication to that cause.

Whether I liked it or not, a few weeks with O'Connell couldn't repair the kind of damage that Frank had inflicted. I still wasn't sure that what he had broken inside could ever be fixed, but I did know that when I was with O'Connell, every good, clean part left in me felt alive. As long as he treated that as the gift that it was, I didn't see any reason to give up on that feeling.

"Listen. Just because I'm staying over doesn't mean that things are gonna go any further between us. I need to know that you respect me, and that I'm not just a piece of meat to you before we go all the way." He was so sincere and somber-faced that I couldn't help but laugh out loud.

"You're making fun of me," I said, not in the least bit offended.

"No, sunshine, just lightening the mood. I told you that we're gonna take this slow, and I meant it. Now tonight I want you to cut loose and have fun, not borrow worry about what other people think. When things go further between us, there won't be any hesitation because you'll know you're ready. So until then, fuck everyone else." He grinned.

I smiled back at him, just a little bit more smitten than I was before. After a time I started tapping my knee up and down, thinking about who would be there tonight and all the conversation that I'd have to make.

"You okay?" O'Connell asked.

"Sure," I lied.

We parked and walked to the club, my hand clasped firmly in O'Connell's. It was absolutely freezing outside, but my shivering was attributable to more than just the temperature. My stomach clenched at the thought of going into the club.

The last few weeks I'd become quietly confident, and my individual contact with each of the fighters had strangely made the gym a safe place for me. It was rare that I spoke to all the guys as a large group, and now that I'd met everyone, it wasn't often that I saw any new faces around the place. I was never great with crowds and the last party that I'd been to hadn't been the best experience. O'Connell was right, though. Tonight was about having fun and celebrating with Liam, and if I could stay out of my own head long enough, it would be a great night.

The bouncers at the door smiled and did the one-handed backslap shoulder bump with O'Connell that told me he knew them well. They shot the breeze while I stood by silently, contemplating how long it would take hypothermia to set in. After a few minutes we bypassed the large queue and entered the club. The noise inside was deafening. O'Connell turned to speak to me, but it was pretty clear that I couldn't hear him this close to the speakers, so he led me toward the back of the club. I felt a small amount of relief when I spotted our guys already seated there.

"Em!" they all seemed to call out in chorus.

I blushed, but I was happy that they were pleased to see me. It amazed me how many shoulder bumps and backslaps the guys gave O'Connell, given that most of them probably had seen each other only a few hours ago.

"What do you want to drink, baby?" O'Connell spoke into my ear from behind me.

It was easier to hear at this end of the club, but I loved the way that his lips softly skimmed the shell of my ear as he spoke. It sent delicate shivers down my body, and I knew that O'Connell felt it, too, when he squeezed my waist.

"I'll have an orange juice, please."

"You don't want to drink?"

I studied my surroundings and bit my lip. A drink probably would help me relax a little more so that I wasn't so uptight and on edge, but the idea of voluntarily conceding control of my senses in a public space made me shudder. It made me more vulnerable than I was usually, and despite the small army of gladiators around me, I couldn't help but wonder whether they'd notice if I went missing.

From a place like this, it would take Frank only seconds to snatch me, and nobody would be any the wiser. Most of them clearly looked as though they got an early start at the bar, and given the number of women they were attracting, I would soon be lost in the crowd. I knew I was paranoid, but the foundation of my fear was strong, and I had the scars to prove it.

It was scary how O'Connell could read me so well already, enough to sense my insecurity. He hadn't pressed me about my past, but he knew that something had happened. The fact that he didn't push the subject made me fall for him a little deeper.

Strong arms wrapped around my waist, and he pulled me into his embrace, my back tight to his chest. I closed my eyes and breathed deeply as he buried his head in the crook of my neck and everything just fell away. The blaringly loud music, the shouts of drunken men vying to be heard over one another, the high-pitched giggles of flirtation, the chink of glasses, everything. It all fell away until there was only O'Connell and me. There was the tantalizingly sweet aroma of his aftershave, the warmth of his hands spread across my hips, and the strength of conviction in his voice.

"Don't panic, sunshine. I'm here with you, and I'm not going anywhere. If I go to the bar or the bathroom, then one of the other guys will be watching, and I promise that they won't let you out of their sight. You're mine and that means you're un-fucking-touchable, okay, baby?"

I nodded and relaxed against him. I didn't know how he did it, but inside O'Connell's embrace, the rest of the world ceased to exist. None of the bullshit on the outside could touch us. I gave him something to protect, and he gave me something to cherish.

"I'm sorry," I said.

"There's nothing to feel sorry for, sunshine. It's going to take time, but eventually you won't need my touch to know that I'm there. One day you'll know that you never need to be afraid again, but right now you're here, and that's something."

He had no idea the gift that he was giving me. His strength and confidence gave me strength. In simply being here, I was saying "fuck you" to Frank. I just needed O'Connell to remind me that courage isn't the absence of fear, but the will to carry on regardless.

"Thank you," I answered.

"You're welcome. Now show me how grateful you are for lending you this rock-hard body as your protection for the night."

I turned around in his arms and kissed him softly until the whooping and whistling brought us back down to earth.

"Fuck off!" O'Connell called over my shoulder with a grin, and I buried my face into his chest in embarrassment. He nuzzled my neck, then, pulling away, he grabbed my hand and led me over to the sofa where Liam was lounging.

"Liam, look after my girl for me, would you? Nobody fucks with her while I'm gone, understand?"

Liam grinned at him, offering him a two-finger salute. With a wink to me, O'Connell was gone.

"Well, baby girl, you sure look pretty tonight. I guess you're around the gym so much it's hard to remember that you're an honest-to-God woman and not one of the boys."

"That's just the way I like it," I admitted.

"You know you're a good influence on him," Liam told me, nodding toward the bar.

"So I've been told. But I don't think that Danny is crazy about us being friends."

"He's protective of you, that's all. He loves Con like a son, but he's unstable. If things go to shite for Con, he's worried about you getting hurt in the fallout."

"I appreciate his concern, but I think that being O'Connell's friend is worth the risk."

"He's a lucky bastard, Em. I hope he knows how lucky he is."

"He knows, shithead," Kieran retorted as he sank onto the sofa next to me.

Liam grunted at him like he wasn't so sure, but I was glad to let the subject drop. Determined to steer the conversation elsewhere, I pitched in. "We have to find you a girl tonight, Kier," I told him.

"Don't worry, Em. I plan to find at least one tonight."

I frowned back at him in response.

"Not that kind of girl. A nice girl, Kier."

Liam and Kieran laughed. "Sunshine, I'm pretty sure that nice girls don't troll bars like this," Liam told me.

I was slightly affronted that they were laughing at me, but looking around, I could see they were right. Most girls here were rail thin with ridiculously large, and I was guessing mostly fake, tits, too much makeup, and way too much fake tan. Skirts were just below the underwear, and any jeans were air-brushed on.

I tried not to let my insecurities swamp me, but I needed O'Connell back and soon. I missed the bubble that we'd been living in since I met him. I looked up to see two girls walking toward us, and to my horror I realized that one of them was Katrina Bray. Her friend clearly knew Kieran intimately because she didn't stop when she reached our sofa, but climbed onto Kieran and straddled his lap. Okay, so that wasn't at all awkward with him sitting right next to me. The tiny miniskirt around her waist rose to her hips as she did it, giving Kieran, and most of the club, a look at her underwear.

If I had any guts at all, I would have coughed out the word slut, but most of the girls in this club looked ready for a punch up, and I really didn't feel like getting bitch-slapped this early in the evening. If that was the sort of girl that Kieran wanted to hook up with, that was up to him.

Clearly my demeanor of disapproval did little to dampen his horniness anyway. When his hands started moving up her thighs, though, I took that as my cue to find O'Connell. I wasn't lucky enough to make it to the bar before Katrina intercepted me.

Blocking my path with her hands on her hips, she looked me up and down with an expression of disdain that made me feel like mold. "I fucking knew the goody-two-shoes thing was all an act," she sneered. "You walk around with your nose stuck up in the air, lording it over the rest of us, but when it comes down to it, you're not above slumming it on a Saturday night."

It wasn't so much that I wouldn't stand up for myself, although I was naturally nonconfrontational. It was just that I was stunned. I barely knew this girl, and yet it seemed like she hated me. It never occurred to me in all those months of trying to keep my head down that she'd see me this way. Not so long ago I would have stared at the floor and made my escape as apologetically and as unobtrusively as I could. It didn't matter what I said now, though. I was in her territory, and she was pissed.

"I'm not slumming it," I told her quietly but with dignity. "I'm here with friends."

"What friends, bitch? From where I'm standing, the little princess looks all alone."

"Then I suggest you open your eyes, bitch, 'cause her friends are right here."

I looked around in surprise to see Nikki, as fierce as ever and shooting daggers at Katrina. Behind Nikki stood Max, Albie, Ryan, and Nikki's roommate, Lauren. I was stunned, but there was no way that I was going to let Katrina see.

You see, hyenas were essentially pack animals. They bonded together with other scavengers and did the best they could to pick off the easiest prey. But when they were separated from their pack, they became cowardly, especially when confronted. Katrina was definitely a hyena, and as my pack grew bigger, her courage began to crumble.

"Whatever," she sneered and knocked me aggressively as she shoved past me. I couldn't even bring myself to be bothered about it as I turned to greet my friends.

"What are you doing here?" I asked in surprise.

CHAPTER THIRTEEN

"Thank Hottie McTottie!" Nikki grinned.

"Huh?" I grunted, confused.

"O'Connell knew you didn't feel comfortable about going out tonight, and he thought it might cheer you up to see us here."

I looked across the bar to find him ambling cockily toward me, leaving a trail of damp knickers in his wake.

"Look at your face," he told me. "You've got the biggest grin I've ever seen."

"How? I mean how did you even know who they were and how to get a hold of them?" I asked in stunned amazement.

"It wasn't hard, Em. A couple of the guys from the party knew Nikki and gave me her number. I called her from the gym and invited her and a few of your friends out."

I bit the inside of my cheek to stop myself from grinning any wider. Could this guy be any sweeter?

He handed out drinks to everyone, and I looked around at my two very different groups of friends. Albie and Liam seemed to have struck up a conversation, but Max, Ryan, and Lauren stood around awkwardly, clearly out of their element. Well, at least now I wouldn't be the only one.

"Are you sure you're okay with them being here?" I asked warily.

He smiled back then maneuvered me so that I was standing in front of him. As we looked out over the club, he leaned down to speak to me, and I felt his breath warm against my ear. "I wouldn't have invited them if I wasn't. Having them here helps you relax a bit, so it's all good. As long as that kid keeps his hands off you tonight so I don't need to fuck him up."

He nodded over toward Albie, and I couldn't believe that he was still bothered about him looking after me at the party. I rolled my eyes and felt him chuckle behind me.

"I know you're rolling your eyes at me, but I'm serious."

Kieran ambled over without the slut. "Hey, guys. Aren't you going to introduce us to your friends, Em?"

At no point while saying this did he take his eyes off Nikki. If Ryan wasn't careful, he'd have some competition. Most of the guys from the gym had wandered over to us, so I introduced them all.

"I'm thinking shots for the birthday boy. Anyone up for it?" Tommy piped up, rubbing his hands together mischievously. Tommy was determined to get poor Liam trashed, but he went along with everything in that laid-back, mildly amused manner of his.

"I'm in," Nikki volunteered. Ryan groaned, knowing what kind of night he was in for if Nikki was starting on the shots this early. Nearly all of the guys agreed to join in except for O'Connell, and nobody dared call him out over it. If O'Connell said that he wasn't doing something, you didn't argue. I have no doubt that all the boys at the gym respected what he was trying to do.

"Don't worry, peaches. Tonight I *promise* to look after you," Nikki reassured me.

"Really?" I answered with a raised eyebrow and more than a pinch of skepticism. Last time we partied, she hadn't even managed to stay in the same room as me.

"Why does she need looking after?" Kieran asked.

"She'd never had an alcoholic drink until the last party we went to, and I'm pretty sure she's never drunk anything other than beer before."

Honestly! There really wasn't any point in my being part of this conversation, when they talked about me as though I wasn't there.

"Holy shit, Em! Is she fucking with me?"

"I'm serious. Tell him, Em!" Nikki retorted.

I rolled my eyes again at the pair of them. Was my abstinence really that much of a big deal?

O'Connell chuckled as though he wasn't surprised but found the floor show amusing. "Em, drink as much or as little as you like. Just let your hair down and have fun. I've got your back."

"Hell, yeah, she's having fun!" Tommy piped up, having returned from the bar. He passed the shot to me and handed the rest to everyone except O'Connell.

"If you're gonna drink it, don't smell it or sip it, just knock it back in one," O'Connell advised.

Nodding, I watched as Tommy held up his shot glass in a toast.

"To Liam. May I never be as old as you look. Happy Birthday, brother."

I lifted my shot glass to clink against everyone else's then put it to my lips and, as O'Connell recommended, knocked it back in one. I coughed fiercely as the sting hit the back of my throat, and my eyes watered.

"Holy shit! That's like drinking lighter fluid," I gasped between coughs. The whole group burst out laughing, and even O'Connell struggled not to join them.

"Here. Drink a bit of this. It will take the burn away," Nikki told me as she passed me her beer. I might not be the biggest fan of beer in the world, but the sour, foul-smelling beverage was better than this horrible burn.

"Yuck. Why would anyone do that twice?"

"You'll find out, baby girl," assured Kieran.

"Ohh. I love this song. Let's dance," screamed Nikki as she grabbed my hand and dragged me to the dance floor.

"Wait for me," shouted Tommy.

"Tommy, you're worse than a fucking girl, I swear." Kieran shook his head and laughed.

I hadn't danced since I was little, and one shot and a swig of beer wasn't nearly enough Dutch courage. But watching Tommy shake his arse all the way to the dance floor was the funniest thing I think I'd ever seen. Nikki and I laughed so hard we literally doubled over. He didn't stop once he started dancing, either. Throwing shapes and moving around like some seventies disco diva, he did it all with a perfectly straight face.

I looked up at the DJ booth to see Kieran having a word with the DJ. When he started smirking and shaking his head, I knew that he was up to something. Moments later the opening bars to "It's Raining Men" by The Weather Girls sounded out across the club, and the dance floor erupted. Tommy stopped, looked at Nikki and me, grinned, then went absolutely nuts. This was definitely his party trick. I'd never have guessed, but it was attracting women like magnets, and a huge group of girls soon surrounded us.

Laughing together we threw ourselves into the mix. Chucking our limbs around and copying Tommy's moves, I was having so much fun that I forgot to worry about Frank and anyone else who might be around me. I let go of everything and became caught up in the sheer joy of the moment. I couldn't remember a time when I'd had so much fun.

O'Connell promised me that he had my back, and I had absolute faith in him. I didn't need a white knight to swoop in and save me from my crappy life. I was just fine saving myself. Besides, O'Connell wasn't a knight. He was the battle-scarred dragon that would lay waste to armies to protect me.

This mismatched band of people, educated and uneducated, fighters and pacifists, were slowly becoming the family that I'd never had. With them around me, I was young and happy, and for the first time in my life, carefree.

Eventually the diva songs morphed into something a little edgier, and the dance floor became crowded. I couldn't see O'Connell or the other guys, but I knew that they were out there somewhere, keeping an eye on me.

A couple of guys who looked like college students had been dancing near us for a while. One of them leaned down next to me to speak over the loud music. "Do you know what time it is?" he asked.

I clearly wasn't wearing a watch or holding a purse so I frowned as I tried to work out why he thought I'd know. A shiver ran down my spine as strong, big hands skimmed my hips.

"What do you want?" O'Connell asked this guy from behind me.

"Chill out. I was just asking her for the time." The guy smiled, though he looked very nervous. It wasn't hard to work out why. I could feel the anger radiating from O'Connell like heat.

"It's time for you to fuck off. Right. Now," he added unnecessarily.

The guy was already moving off the dance floor, looking like he was going to piss himself at any second.

I turned around to face O'Connell. "That was rude. He was only after the time!" I lectured.

He laughed as he tightened his hold on me. I lay my hands against his chest, trying not to show him how hot his possessiveness made me.

"We've been watching those arseholes eye fuck you and Nikki for ten minutes. I think I deserve a kiss for showing enough restraint to warn him first instead of just walking over and punching him in the face."

"Really?" I exclaimed, pondering whether or not that was a good enough excuse for a platonic kiss.

When Nikki announced that it was time for shots again, I was reluctant to let him go, but desperately in need of another drink. Wanting anything that would quench my thirst, I threw back the shot that Kieran passed me and chased it again with a beer. O'Connell looked at me with an unfathomable expression, probably worried that I couldn't handle the drink.

A couple of hours, and countless dances later, I'd lost track of how many drinks we'd had, and my pleasant buzz now had me feeling a bit sick and dizzy. Liam and Albie were still happily shooting the breeze as they had been all night. Nikki was on the dance floor with Kieran, which meant that Ryan stood, beer in hand, staring daggers at the both of them. I'd seen Tommy a while back sucking face with some random girl, who sat in his lap as the others milled around.

My ongoing euphoria died a death when I spotted Katrina by the bar, looking at me like road kill she'd like to reverse back over. Right then I lost my footing and, to my mortification, realized that I was going to face plant right at her feet. As I fell strong hands lifted me like I was weightless, just long enough for me to regain my footing. I turned around clumsily in O'Connell's arms, and no longer caring about Katrina, kissed him full on the lips. This gorgeous, sexy, lethal man could have as many Katrinas as he wanted, but he'd chosen me. Right now, as drunk as I was, I couldn't see a reason for not showing him how happy that made me.

His firm lips molded to mine in a way so natural and powerful that it was addictive. Every breath made me crave him even more. His kiss ramped up every one of my senses until all I could smell was the whisper of his aftershave and the uniquely addictive scent of his skin.

All I could hear was the rasp of our breathing as we struggled to take in as much oxygen as possible between kisses. All I could feel was the hard strength of his muscles tensing as he hauled me against him, and the gentle shiver that ran through his body when I stroked the soft skin at his lower back.

He broke away from the kiss to whisper in my ear. "Fuck, sunshine. You have no idea how much willpower I'm exercising by not wrapping your legs around my waist and carrying you out of here right now."

Just the idea of wrapping myself around his body filled me with lust. Alcohol had stripped me of all inhibitions, and I stared at him longingly, silently willing him to do it.

He looked pained as he shook his head. "No," he said firmly, and my heart sank at his blatant rejection. The great Cormac O'Connell, who'd fucked countless women, was turning me down.

He tilted my chin up with his finger until I met his eyes. "I take you out now with you wrapped around my waist, and I'm fucking you. Hard. I don't want that for us. Our first time together is something we won't ever forget, and I have some big plans for us. So stop raining on my parade. You deserve all that romantic shit, but I'm so hard it's getting painful. So go easy on me, baby, okay?"

Well, wasn't that the most romantic thing I'd ever heard? O'Connell had made me feel sexy, loved, and wanted all in the same speech as rejecting me. My huge, drunken, sloppy grin told him just how cute I thought that was. I leaned up on my tiptoes and reached my lips up to his ear. Thinking that I was trying to talk to him, he bent his head toward me.

Feeling bold and brave, I sucked the lobe of his ear gently

between my lips and nipped it lightly before I answered him. "Promise me a few more kisses tonight, and I promise to stop trying to wrap myself around you like a pretzel."

He groaned as he touched his forehead to mine. "A pretzel? Fuck, baby, you really are gonna make me come in my jeans. You have no idea how sexy you are, do you?"

I shook my head vigorously as though the question wasn't rhetorical, and O'Connell kissed me quickly on the lips. "Come on. Let's get some water in you."

After drinking at least two pints of water, I felt a pair of floppy arms wrap around my neck.

"See. I soooo promised to take care of you, didn't I?" If I was drunk, then Nikki was completely plastered. Her idea of looking after someone and mine were wildly different, but there was no doubt that my first choice for a friend had been a brilliant one. Nikki was one of the kindest, most generous people that I'd ever met. She loaned me clothes, worried about me, and cared enough to turn up tonight with practically no notice. If she was a little unreliable when drunk, well, it wasn't the worse fault to have. I only hoped that given time I could be as good a friend to her as she'd already been to me.

"Do you know I'm a teensy bit drunk," she told me very matter-of-factly as she held up her thumb and index finger slightly apart to indicate just how fractionally drunk she was.

"Do you know, I think I might be a bit, too," I admitted.

At this point, our arms were wrapped around each other in solidarity as we struggled to hold each other up. O'Connell and Kieran looked amused, but Ryan was pissed.

"What shall we do now, shots or dancing? My vote's on shots," she decided for us, as she pulled me toward the bar.

"Who wants a shot?" she shouted to everyone. Tommy didn't once detach his lips from his slut, but lifted one hand off her tit and raised it in the air to show that he was part of the round. I held my hand up as well and waved it enthusiastically like a little kid, afraid that she'd miss me even though I stood right next to her.

"I'm good, thanks, sweetheart," Liam answered.

"Me, too," agreed Albie, shaking his blond head no.

"Well, count me in, baby," Kieran hollered, looking at Nikki dangerously.

"Arsehat?" Nikki asked Ryan.

"For fuck's sake, Nikki. I have a name, use it!" he grumbled.

She rolled her eyes at him. "Okay, don't get your knickers in a knot."

"Don't you think you've had enough?" he asked her.

"Who are you, my mum? Do you want a shot or not?"

"Fine!" he all but screamed at her.

O'Connell and Kieran grinned openly at the pair of them. You could cut the sexual tension between them with a knife. It was only a matter of time before they either kissed or killed each other.

Nikki brought the tray of shots over and handed them out. Tapping our glasses together, we threw them back like pros. I fought the shiver that ran through me as the liquid hit the back of my throat.

"This has been such an awesome night. Thanks for inviting me, Con," Nikki screeched at O'Connell, while squeezing me like a rag doll. I could feel the bile rising up in my throat as she did it.

"No problem, Nikki. It's been pretty cool hanging out with some of Em's friends. We should do it again sometime," he answered.

Everyone except Ryan seemed pleased at the suggestion. I did feel a little sorry for him. Having his masculinity threatened by all these God-like men might not have been so bad if Nikki was acting a little nicer toward him. Right now, though, I had bigger things to worry about, as the churning in my stomach seemed to get worse.

"O'Connell?" I whispered, tugging gently on his shirt as I clutched my stomach with the other hand. "I don't feel well."

"What's wrong, baby?" he asked with concern.

I opened my mouth to answer him when my stomach rolled over. Losing all control I vomited down the front of his shirt.

CHAPTER FOURTEEN

I tried not to cry as my stomach emptied itself repeatedly. For one brief and glorious moment, I'd feel better, then my stomach would churn, and I'd vomit all over again. Even when there were no fluids left inside me, I was still going, retching so much that my stomach hurt.

"Make it stop, please," I begged O'Connell, as he held back my hair. I wouldn't be surprised to hear amusement in his voice or even censure. It was the least that I deserved, but he seemed genuinely concerned for me.

"Sunshine, if I could take your place, I would. But it will stop soon, I promise."

With his free hand, he rubbed big comforting circles on my back, and I slumped against his enormous frame.

"I don't deserve you. I get blind drunk on my first real taste of alcohol, vomit all over you, then spend the rest of the night showing you exactly what I had to eat yesterday. And you're still here."

He chuckled as he let go of my hair and reached up to wet a washcloth in the sink. Squeezing out the excess water, he placed the cool compress over my eyes.

"Ahh, that feels so good," I moaned in relief, as it shielded my poor retinas from the blinding bathroom light.

"Before I met you this was pretty much my typical weekend morning. I hate that you're feeling shitty, but I kind of like the fact that you felt comfortable enough to get drunk with me. I know you wouldn't have let down those barriers of yours if you didn't think I'd protect you."

"That's important to you?" I asked him curiously.

He removed the compress and looked into my eyes. "When you're with me, you never have to be afraid of anything. I would decimate any fucker who so much as looked at you wrong if you asked me to. Tonight you believed that, and you dropped your guard. You trusted me. Every time you let down another one of those barriers, I know that you're a bit closer to being mine. One day, when the last one falls, you'll be as much mine as I am yours."

With that mind-blowing declaration, he kissed my forehead gently.

"Are you sure you want them down? The stuff behind them isn't pretty," I whispered hoarsely.

"There's not one bit of you, inside or out, that isn't fucking beautiful. Nothing that happened to you before me is gonna change that," he replied.

"I'm scared," I admitted, the tears running tracks down my reddened cheeks.

"Me, too. I'm scared that you'll take my heart and stomp the fuck out of it. But there ain't nothing in this world for me worth fighting for more than you."

O'Connell was literally seeing me at my worst. I was raw and ugly, yet still here he sat, making himself as vulnerable to me as I was to him.

"I'll tell you everything. But not today, okay?" I whispered, and he smiled gently.

"Not today," he agreed.

"I'm sorry about your shirt." I groaned.

"You really will do anything to get my clothes off, won't you?"

I couldn't help but laugh, only to stop suddenly and lurch forward. Instinctively, O'Connell reached for my hair as I retched again, praying that this would all be over soon.

* * *

The pounding sounded like a bass drum next to my ear.

"Is that my head or the door?" I mumbled to O'Connell, my voice muffled by the pillow I'd pressed over my ears.

A few months ago I'd have been in the wardrobe at the first knock. Now I trusted that O'Connell was bigger and badder than anything on the other side of the door. He would never know just how much progress that was for me.

"You've got company, sunshine," O'Connell called out, as a body collapsed on the bed beside me.

"Why'd you disappear last night on me, bitch?" Nikki's voice was hoarse from all the drinking she'd done.

"Don't call me a bitch. It's not nice," I answered, though I was barely audible with my face embedded in the pillow.

"I don't feel nice this morning, but I need credit for being an amazing friend 'cause I bought you a coffee on the way over."

I groaned with appreciation as I inhaled the delicious aroma. Peeling my face gently away from the pillow, I braved the daylight to look at her.

"You look like I feel," I groaned.

"Now you're definitely being a bitch." She grinned.

O'Connell walked toward me with a glass of water and some painkillers, and sat down next to me on the bed.

"How you feeling, baby?" he asked as I gratefully downed both.

"Awful. Why would anyone do that more than once?" I asked.

"Last night was great. Totally worth the hangover," Nikki enthused.

"Maybe you should go a little easier next time," O'Connell cautioned.

"I am NEVER. DRINKING. AGAIN," I replied firmly. He chuckled and pulled me into his chest.

"Considering those abs are rock hard, you give pretty good cuddles," I complimented him, as I snuggled in deeper.

"Yuk. Get a room," Nikki complained.

"We did. You're in it!" O'Connell replied.

I smiled at the two of them, but I knew if Nikki wasn't there, getting closely acquainted with each one of O'Connell's abdominal muscles would have sounded like a pretty good hangover cure.

"You need anything before I go?" O'Connell asked me.

"Do you have to leave?" I groaned, perfectly happy to spend the rest of the morning lying across his chest.

"If I miss training even once, I don't think Danny would have me back. Kier's supposed to be sparring with me today, so if he turns up hungover, Danny's already gonna be on the warpath," he warned.

"Don't worry. I know you have to go."

I glanced up at him, and he looked torn.

"What's wrong?" I asked, alarmed.

"You never ask me to stay, and the one time you do, I really have to go," he replied.

I smiled gently, even though it really made my head hurt to do it. "I'm not asking you to stay. It's important that you don't let Danny down. If you mess this up, he might not give you another shot. Be gentle with Kier, though. I have a feeling he's going to be a bit delicate today, and if you knock him out, you won't have anyone to spar with. Then Danny really will be pissed."

"You're no fun." He grinned. "I've been looking forward to beating on Kier all morning."

I had the feeling that Kieran was really going to regret agreeing to train today. I was guessing that O'Connell kept a change of clothes in his car, because he was carrying his training bag when he bent over to kiss me.

"Bye, baby. I'll see you soon." He spoke softly, as we tried to ignore Nikki's dramatic gagging noises by the side of me.

"Bye, Nikki," he called out, winking at me on his way out. The soft click of the door sounded like a gunshot in my head. In the absence of O'Connell's lovely warm body, I collapsed back into the pillow.

"If your man was a bar of chocolate, I'd be nibbling on that all day."

"Nikki!" I blustered. "If he was a bar of chocolate, I'd never let you open the wrapper."

She giggled at me, and I blushed, both of us knowing that we were picturing O'Connell naked.

"Don't worry." She sighed. "That boy only has eyes for you."

The fact that O'Connell and I were technically just friends, and that Nikki had every right to look as much as she wanted, was something that would have to wait until my hangover had gone.

"I feel like crap," I complained.

"Go back to sleep then. You'll feel better later."

"What are you going to do?" I asked her. It was kind of a weird situation, never having had a friend around just to hang out at home with before.

"I brought my laptop and some movies so I'm going to veg here all day until I feel less like I've been licking the pavement all night."

"You dragged yourself all the way over to my shitty flat to do that? Your place is much nicer," I told her in disbelief.

"What can I say, bitch? Misery loves company," she retorted. Having set up the laptop, she climbed under my covers, and we spent the next couple of hours watching movies. My eyes were begging for sleep, but I loved every minute of just chilling out with Nikki, so I wasn't giving this up. Sleep could wait until later.

By the time she left I was exhausted but less nauseous. After a quick shower that brought me back to life, I climbed into bed and slid my hands under my pillow. The sharp edge of a folded piece of paper jabbed at my fingertip, and I pulled it out with a smile.

Hey baby,

I'm rock hard writing this because I know that right now you're lying in bed in those sexy boy shorts that I love so much. I'm going to spend the whole day pretending that I don't know what your fine arse feels like because if I get hard in front of Danny, he's gonna throw a medicine ball at it. I hope you're feeling better. Fuck I wish we had phones!

I miss you already, OC xxx

Jeez, that boy seriously knew what he was doing. With Nikki gone I was starting to worry about how I could face everyone tomorrow, knowing that I'd completely humiliated myself by puking all over O'Connell. Now all that I could think about was my seriously sweet, hot fighter.

* * *

The rest of the week rolled by quickly. Despite my anxiety, none of the guys made a big deal about "vomit gate," and I think they knew me well enough to guess that I'd retreat back into my shell if they gave me too hard a time about it.

I hadn't seen O'Connell since Sunday morning, but I had a note waiting from him every single day, either waiting underneath my door before I woke or delivered by Kieran. I was beginning to think that the main entrance to my building was less a security door and more an inconvenience to O'Connell because he never asked me to buzz him up to deliver any of these messages. They were so much better than text messages or emails, though, because each word was in his handwriting, and holding them in my hand made them tangible and real.

O'Connell hadn't been able to give me flowers and take me on extravagant dates, but this stack of notes that I kept so carefully was his way of dating me. I loved it. They conveyed so much more than a text ever would have. When his handwriting was messy, I knew that he was tired. When he underlined the word sexy, I knew that he was horny. When he signed with a kiss, I knew that kiss was real. True, I missed his voice, but I really did love these notes.

* * *

I came out of class Thursday to find Kieran leaning against his fire-engine red bike, legs and arms crossed and winking at all the pretty first-years.

"Seriously! Don't you ever get sick of chasing girls?"

"Nope," he replied. "Having a body like this is a gift, and I feel a moral obligation to share it with the world."

I wondered if he was joking, but I doubted that he was. There was no denying that Kieran was sex on a stick, but O'Connell was the only flavor I was interested in.

I grinned as I waited for him to hand me my note. I really was starting to get a little clingy about those.

"Why is he sending me a note? I'm seeing him later," I asked.

"Not soon enough, apparently. He sent me to come and get you because he's having withdrawals." He reached behind him to grab a helmet.

"No note, then?" I was disappointed about the note, but jump-up-and-down excited that he was as eager to see me as I was to see him.

"Fucking hell. You two are getting ridiculous with these notes. I'm not a fucking postman, you know," he grumbled.

"How does this thing do up?" I asked, ignoring him as I fiddled with the strap of my helmet. Instead of a cool biker chick, I suspected that I looked more like a bobble head.

He rolled his eyes and fastened the strap for me.

"Did I ever tell you how awesome you are?" I asked him as I climbed onto the bike behind him.

"Yeah, yeah," he mumbled. "You only love me 'cause I bring you stuff from your man."

"He's not my man, you know," I reminded him.

"Whatever you say, sunshine." He sighed, and we pulled off toward the gym.

* * *

"That was amazing!" I squealed as I climbed off the bike fifteen minutes later.

"Liked that, did you?" Kieran grinned as he took back my helmet.

"You drive like a demon, but it was amazing."

"I was going thirty miles an hour most of the way. Con threatened to cut off my balls if *anything* happened to you. I don't think I could take the pressure of giving you a ride again. Besides, I couldn't breathe anytime we went round a corner. You're stronger than you look, half-pint."

He rubbed his rock-hard stomach as though I'd actually wounded him by clinging so tight.

"I'm totally getting a bike one day," I told him seriously.

He laughed out loud at me. "Unless you can find a way to

ride wrapped in bubble wrap, Con's never gonna let that happen. Do you even know what type of bike this is anyway?"

"Of course, I do. It's the big, shiny, red type. I think I'll get one in black."

He rolled his eyes at me, smiling, but I could tell that he was pleased I'd enjoyed myself.

I practically skipped into the gym because I was so excited to see O'Connell. The atmosphere inside was electric, and the place was packed.

"What's going on?" I asked Kieran who walked in behind me.

"Danny's got Con a fight in two weeks. The guy he's fighting is established, meaning there'll be sponsors there. If he puts on a show, he could get sponsorship, and that's huge. He'll get paid to train, and Danny can get his name out there, get him better fights."

I was so pleased for him but terrified at the same time. An established fighter meant that he'd become established by pounding away at other heavyweights and winning.

Danny didn't usually like me hanging around in the gym when the boys were training. He never said anything to me, just scowled more than usual, which had me scuttling as quickly as I could to get to my office. The clock on the wall at the back of the gym told me that it wasn't even five, and I wasn't due to start work for an hour. Deciding that facing Danny's wrath after a week of O'Connell abstinence was worth the risk, I wandered toward the ring. I found him on the floor doing sit-ups, while Liam was throwing medicine balls on his stomach. He was covered in sweat, but those abs looked like they'd been carved in ice.

I didn't want to interrupt his training, so I hung back, watching my fill. He was so fine that, with every rise and fall of his chest, I was getting more and more turned on. My palms were sweaty, and the heat building between my thighs had me squirming where I stood, giving me away to Danny.

"You're a bit early, aren't you, sunshine?" Danny barked.

"Umm..." I scrambled to explain my presence at the gym. I swear that Danny was like a disapproving parent. He only had to scowl at me in a certain way, and I knew that I was in trouble.

"I thought I'd get an early start tonight, and someone offered me a lift. So..." I felt like I needed to keep talking because, when I stopped he stared at me with his arms crossed while a cigarette dangled precariously from his lips.

"And I'm a feckin' monkey's uncle," he said after what felt like forever. He sighed like I was the biggest pain in the arse in the world.

"Con," he practically shouted, "get your lazy arse up. You two get ten minutes, then I want you back here with your head in the game, understand?"

"Sure, boss," O'Connell agreed happily, as he grabbed me and started walking. I could hear Danny muttering about how he'd never get anything good out of O'Connell now that I was here.

O'Connell pulled me into the office and shut the door behind us. Before I could even say hello, he pressed me up against it, and his lips were on mine. He groaned into my mouth as he moved his hands around to my backside and lifted me to wrap my legs around his hips. His hardness against my achy core had me rubbing up against him, trying to find some relief.

"Fuck!" he hissed out loud, and I flinched at his tone.

"Sorry, baby," he whispered, as he pressed his forehead against mine. "I didn't mean to scare you but having you like this is just about the sexiest fucking thing ever. I'd give anything to be balls deep inside you right now."

"Aww," I replied giggling, "you say the sweetest things."

He didn't reply but pressed against me harder. I stopped giggling and groaned as the ache became worse. If I'd been any other girl, I'd have given him the relief that we both needed, but I wasn't that brave, so this was as much as he was getting. Tommy probably had his ear to the door anyway.

O'Connell bent his head toward me and breathed deeply, as we both tried to calm down. After a minute or two, he released me and walked over to the chair. He sat down and pulled me onto his lap, nuzzling his head into the crook of my neck. "Mmm. You smell beautiful, sunshine."

I sighed, trying to stop myself from squirming around. I was so turned on that the need to ask him to touch me was almost unbearable. "This gets harder every time we see each other, doesn't it?" I asked him.

He groaned. "If it gets any harder, it's likely to snap."

I laughed but immediately felt bad because O'Connell really looked as though he was in pain. "You know, if you were with any other girl, you wouldn't have to wait."

He knew exactly what I meant, and he didn't like it. "If I was with any other girl, baby, it wouldn't be hard."

I frowned. Of course, it wouldn't be hard. Sex with anyone else would be a walk in the park. Most girls probably didn't even wear underwear around O'Connell to emphasize just how easy it was.

"No, sunshine," he chastised, reading my thoughts by the look on my face. He grabbed my hand and, bold as brass, placed it on his cock. "With any other girl, it wouldn't be hard."

"Oh, my God! I can't believe I did that," I squeaked, pulling my hand away and burying my head into his chest with embarrassment.

He chuckled and hugged me against him. "Sorry, love," he apologized. "It just got even harder."

CHAPTER FIFTEEN

The next few weeks at the gym were absolutely crazy. Every day that O'Connell trained, we could feel magic in the air. It was as though we were all part of something really special. O'Connell had so much fight and endless determination that it made us better just to be around him.

For nine hours a day, six days a week, O'Connell trained *relentlessly*. Not once did Danny give him so much as an inch, and not once did O'Connell complain about it. If Danny said ten more sit-ups, then that was exactly what he did. If Danny said that push-ups were to be one-handed, even when O'Connell was dead on his feet, then that was exactly what he did. Danny demanded and O'Connell delivered.

By the time that fight week arrived, O'Connell was sparring for ten rounds then combining half bag with half mitt work. Danny had been tapering that off as the week went on, ostensibly to allow O'Connell's body to recuperate before the fight.

Today was Thursday and weigh-in day. I didn't get to go to the gym where it was taking place. Danny told me that it was because he was paying me good money to be working tonight and not skiving. I thought it was mean, enough that I poked my tongue out at him when he left the room. Still I wasn't brave enough to argue to his face.

Secretly I suspected that he didn't want me somewhere where I would be so deeply out of my element. I couldn't say that being left behind was any better, though. Walking through the gym was creepy. Usually bustling with life and energy, the speed-balls were still and the bags hung lifelessly from the ceiling. Nearly all the guys were at the weigh-in as a show of support for O'Connell. A few of the younger guys, whom Danny wouldn't let follow him, were allocated menial tasks around the place, and Liam had stayed to supervise. It was patently obvious that the bunch of fifteen-year-olds currently cleaning the shower room didn't need Liam's level of supervision. After his fifth time of checking on me in two hours, it became clear who he was really babysitting. Danny's sense of chivalry was working overtime again, it seemed. He was out of luck, though, if he thought he was getting his money's worth from me. I'd been like a cat on a hot tin roof all night, and it was only the weigh-in. There was absolutely no way that he was keeping me away from the fight tomorrow.

A knock on my door pulled me back down to earth. Liam opened it and popped his head around. If he asked me if I needed anything one more time, I was going to throw something at him.

"They're back." He grinned.

I pushed my chair back from the desk, stood up, and raced around the door as he pushed it open farther for me. O'Connell, Kieran, Tommy, and most of the older guys were standing around laughing and shooting the breeze.

"How did it go?" I asked them all, still hyped up from the anticipation of waiting for them for half the night.

"Two hundred and twenty pounds, exactly," O'Connell replied

with a grin, as he wrapped his arm around my shoulders and pulled me into his side.

"Is that good?" I asked. I was a little confused by this new pugilist world that I'd been plunged into.

"Absolutely. Same stats as Foreman in his prime," Kieran replied enthusiastically.

"Mmm. Foreman was the one who made the grills, right?" Literally everyone looked at me and burst out laughing. Great. Halfway through a degree in applied mathematics, and I managed to sound like a complete moron.

"Yes, he's the one with the grills, but he's also one of the greatest fighters who ever lived. He was my height, and two twenty was his weight in the prime of his career. It's a good omen."

I nodded shyly, not wanting to embarrass myself any further.

Danny came barreling through the door at a speed that belied his size. "All right, you lot. I don't know why you're all patting yourselves on the back 'cause he made weight. He still has to win the feckin' fight yet."

The guys chuckled, suitably chastised. But in all honesty they were like kids on Christmas Eve, full of excitement and energy but no patience.

"Right, then. You all know what time it is, so make yourselves presentable and let's get going. That includes you, sunshine. Liam, round up the other boys. Cleaning time is over. Ten minutes and I'm locking this place up."

"Where are we going?" I asked.

"Church," Tommy enlightened me.

I figured that this was a metaphor for something else and having embarrassed myself once already tonight, I decided to keep my mouth shut.

"Go and get your coat and bag, love. I'll walk you home after," O'Connell told me gently. He hadn't called me that many times before, and if it was possible my heart just sighed.

I turned off my computer, grabbed my stuff, and met them outside. Danny turned off the lights and locked the doors behind me. Our ragtag group of misfits ambled down the road to who knew where, with me safely tucked into O'Connell's side. Fifteen minutes later, we were walking up the steps to St. Paul's Catholic Church.

"Shit. You really did mean church. I haven't been to church since I was little," I squeaked.

"No feckin' swearing in church," Danny barked at me, throwing his cigarette away.

I figured that this must be a serious religious occasion because it had only been half smoked. The church was empty as we all went inside, and the guys all sat down in the last two rows at the back of the church. Not knowing what to do, I sat down with them. The sound of a door closing echoed across the cavernous space, and I looked around to see a priest, not much younger than Danny, walking purposefully toward us.

"Hello, Danny," he greeted, shaking Danny's hand vigorously. "Not much longer now till the big day. Is he ready?"

"Of course, he is, Father," Danny replied.

"Good," the priest said, "because I've got a fiver on him with Father Mulvey over at St. Joe's, so he'll be in my prayers tomorrow."

I was slightly scandalized that a priest was betting and, worse still, condoning fighting so that he could capitalize on it, but O'Connell only smiled as he listened to Danny and the priest talk.

"Right then, boys. Who's going first?"

Tommy stood and shook the priest's hand.

"Ah, Tommy. You're usually the longest. You're better off going first."

They walked off together into a room with a thick mahogany door built into the paneling of the wall.

"Where are they going?" I whispered to O'Connell, keeping an eye on Danny for fear of another telling off.

"Confession," he replied.

"Why?"

"Danny figures that to win in the ring you need to go in with a clear heart and a clear head. We tell Father Patrick what's on our mind and all the things we're sorry for, and he gives us absolution. Then we spend all our time after the fight committing more sin ready for the next fight," he explained.

"But it's only you fighting. Why is everyone else here?"

"Doesn't matter who's fighting, even if it's one of the kids. When one of us goes into the ring, everyone from Danny's is with them."

Whether they realized it or not, they were Danny's family, and he was theirs. One by one the guys went in to see Father Patrick. By the time the last of the kids was done, I was more than ready to leave. Don't get me wrong, the church itself was beautiful, but I felt out of place here. I was an intruder eavesdropping on a ritual that I had no part of. This was a part of Danny's relationship with the guys, and I didn't understand why he'd brought me.

"Emily, are you ready?" Father Patrick's accent was broader than Danny's, and I wondered if they were from the same part of Ireland.

"I'm sorry, Father, ready for what?" I asked confused.

"Confession, my dear," he replied with a smile.

I felt the first fluttering of panic, as I was cornered. "But . . . but I'm not a practicing Catholic," I stuttered.

"Never mind, dear, nobody is perfect."

He stood patiently as he waited for me to follow him. I turned to O'Connell who squeezed my hand, clearly expecting me to go through with this. Sensing that I had no other option, I stood and walked with the priest to the side of the church. Behind the door was a small anteroom with two chairs facing each other.

"Have a seat," he invited, as he sat down. "Now don't worry, I won't be asking you for a confession. But I did think that it would be nice for us to have a chat. Now tell me how you ended up tagging along with that lot."

I explained how Danny had given me the job, and he nodded thoughtfully.

"Do you have any family yourself, Emily?" he asked when I'd finished.

Technically I still did, but I'd never think of them as family again. It felt wrong lying to a priest, though, and my cheeks reddened as I became flustered. "No one who means anything to me anymore," I answered at last.

He nodded as though he understood. "Well, now. It seems that God has given you a new family, doesn't it? It must be a difficult adjustment, though, to go from being on your own to having a large, new family, and an Irish one at that."

This wasn't really a question, but he looked at me as though he expected an answer.

"They are lovely. Loud and brash and rude, but lovely. I don't really think I'm considered part of their family, though," I explained.

"You know, I have known Danny for a very long time, and in all that time, no woman has been invited to join them here. That tells me all I need to know about how close to being family you are."

His words warmed me, even if I didn't quite believe them. "I wouldn't exactly say that I was invited," I corrected. "Danny told me to come, and I came."

"Well," he chuckled, "that is Danny's way, isn't it? You can be sure that, for all their talk, they will look after you, you know. It takes time to trust people, and faith is a difficult thing to come by, but you'll get there. And if you need to talk to me about anything, I want you to know that whatever you say will always stay between these four walls."

"I appreciate that, Father."

I liked Father Patrick. I didn't know him well enough to trust him with anything personal about myself, but I appreciated the gesture.

"So are you nervous about the fight, child? You know, with Con being your young man and all?"

Seriously! Even O'Connell's priest thought we were a couple. "He's not my man. Not really. We're just friends."

Father Patrick smiled indulgently at me. "Well, we'll keep that to ourselves, shall we? Con is under the distinct impression that, if you're not now, then you soon will be, and I'd really like to win my bet. Then again, maybe you should belabor the point just before the fight to make him good and mad."

"Father!" I exclaimed, scandalized. "That's terrible!"

He laughed out loud at my reaction and smacked his knee with amusement. "Kieran was right. You're so easy to wind up." He carried on laughing until I couldn't help but smile.

"I've known Cormac O'Connell since he was a lad, wet behind the ears and full of mouth and mischief. Bet or no bet, there's no one in his corner who will be prouder of him than me, save maybe Danny. That's what family is. No matter what, they will always be in your corner as you may choose to stand in theirs. Now, is there anything else troubling you or anything that you want to ask?"

I bit my lip nervously as I contemplated how to ask him.

"Actually Father, I could use your help with something."

* * *

O'Connell walked me home later that night, and he seemed calmer than before, as though the meeting with Father Patrick had settled him down.

"Are you ready for tomorrow?" I asked him.

"I don't think I've ever been more ready for a fight. The hard part is the waiting. Danny doesn't let me train the day before a fight, other than a few warm-up drills a few hours before. You're in uni, and Kieran's working, so I'm just gonna watch a few old fights on tape, maybe listen to some music, and get my head where it needs to be."

"I can skip class tomorrow, if you want me to," I offered, even though I'd never missed a single class since I'd been here.

"I love that you're so smart," he told me. "Your eyes light up when you talk about school. It means to you what boxing means to me, so I don't want you to miss a single class for me. As long as you're at the fight, I'll be good."

"Did Danny say it was okay for me to come?" I asked him worriedly. I didn't want to watch the fight, but after yesterday, I didn't think that I could just sit at home waiting, either.

"Don't you worry about Danny," he told me.

He didn't really answer my question, but I trusted that he'd square it with Danny. We made it to my building and stopped.

"Can I stay here tonight?" he asked sheepishly, as though he thought I'd say no. I assumed that he'd be going back to Kieran's to sleep so I was surprised that he asked. I couldn't help but be excited at the thought of spending another night with him, but I knew it wasn't fair to lead him on.

"Just as friends," I reminded him, and he grinned doing some weird version of the scout's honor sign.

"Just as friends," he agreed.

"I have to get up for class tomorrow, though. Won't I disturb you?" I was reluctant to drive him away, but I also didn't want to ruin his last decent rest before the fight.

"Sunshine, I'm going to be awake at the crack of dawn tomorrow. That's if I get any sleep at all," he explained, as we climbed the stairs to my flat.

"Do you always get nervous before a fight?" I asked curiously, surprised when he scoffed.

"I've never been nervous before. I usually just drink a bit less before a fight, crash, and then wake up and beat the shit out of someone."

"Then why are you nervous now?"

He shrugged his shoulders as we walked into my flat.

"It's different this time," he finally answered. "Danny's invested a lot of time in me, and I'm worried about letting him down. I've given up my job, so without this, I have no income. If I fuck up tomorrow, I could lose my chance at sponsorship and . . ." He trailed off, like he didn't want to carry on.

" . . . and what?" I pressed.

"I promised you that I'd make something of myself. I don't want to fuck this up."

He gestured between us, and for the first time since I'd known him, he didn't look cocky. He looked absolutely terrified. There was no way that he could go in the ring like this; he'd be crushed. All of that training turned his body into a machine, but without his head in the right place, I knew he'd get hurt. And that thought made my insides cramp up.

He sat down dejectedly on my bed, but I stood in front of him until he looked up at me. "Whenever you've lost before, has Danny ever refused to train you?"

He frowned as he contemplated my question. "No, but I've never lost a fight before."

"What, never?" I asked, shocked.

He shook his head. "When we were kids, he used to let the older kids whale on us a bit to toughen us up. But as far as fighting in matches, then no, I've never lost."

I rolled my eyes. Of course, he'd never lost a fight.

"Okay." I sighed. "But you've known Danny nearly your whole life. Do you think he'd give up on you, or any of his boys, if he knew that you tried your best?"

"No, I guess not," he replied honestly.

"There's no guarantee that you would be picked up by sponsors even if you win, and if they're going to be at tomorrow's fight, then they'll be at other fights. Even if you don't make it, fighting isn't your only option, you know. I'm sure that Kieran could get you another construction job, and if that doesn't make you happy, at least it will give you an income. You could always do some night classes while you decide what else you want to do."

He sighed. "I'm no good at book-learning stuff. I don't have any qualifications."

"Don't be afraid of something different. If you need to go back to school to be who you want to be, then I'll help you."

He put his hands around my waist and pulled me toward him as he leaned his head against my stomach. Doing what I had wanted to do to his disheveled spikes since I'd known him, I ran my fingers soothingly through his hair, and he groaned.

"And if I fuck this up between us?" he asked.

"I can't think of anything you could do that would make me want to call time to our friendship. But you and I have absolutely nothing to do with what goes on in that ring tomorrow. There's just him and you and nothing else outside of that, okay? You're in a good place. If nothing else, think about the fact that he's trying to take that away from you, and you know what you said you'd do if anyone tried that, right?"

He lifted his head to look at me and grinned. "I'll decimate them."

I smiled, pleased that he was in the right frame of mind to fight again. I leaned down slightly and kissed the top of his head, though I didn't have to lean far. Even sitting down he was almost as tall as I was. Letting him go, I took off my coat and went to hang it on the back of the door.

"You kissed me," O'Connell called after me. "Friends don't kiss."

"I'm reliably informed that's not the case. Kieran and I kiss all the time," I called back deadpan.

"You're fucking kidding me." He frowned, looking perfectly ready to get in the ring and go a few rounds.

I leaned back and smiled at him to let him know that I was joking.

"Oh, baby. You're in so much trouble if you're gonna start using all my lines."

I giggled when he looked like he was going to come after me. "Please . . . ," I begged. "I'm starving."

He relented at that, and I knew he'd never let me go hungry.

"You get a free pass for now, but any more winding me up about Kieran and I plan on finding out how many parts of that gorgeous body of yours are ticklish."

A shiver ran down my spine at the thought of his hands all over me, but then my stomach growled and ruined the moment.

"Behave," I warned. "Besides, if you're nice to me, I might have a present for you."

At the look of pure shock on his face, I'd almost be willing to bet that he'd never been given a present before.

CHAPTER SIXTEEN

"Baby, it's fucking freezing in here," O'Connell shouted to me, as I was having a shower. As much as we'd wanted to splurge on takeaway, O'Connell had to stock up on carbohydrates before a fight so he'd offered to cook us some pasta while I showered and changed into my pajamas. He said it with his eyes firmly planted on my tits, so I was guessing he hoped that I would change into his favorite pajamas.

"I've turned the heating on. If it's not working, try giving the radiator a bang," I called back.

I was rinsing the conditioner out of my hair and relishing the piping hot water when I heard his voice next to my ear.

"What was that, baby?" he asked, and I screamed, trying to cover up as much as I could with my hands despite being behind an opaque shower screen.

"What are you doing in here? Get out!" I ordered, and he only chuckled.

"Relax, baby. I just couldn't hear what you said," he replied, and I could hear the amusement in his voice.

"I said, bang the radiator to get it going. Now, *get out!*" I ordered.

"I'm not sure," he teased. "This is the warmest place in the flat. Surely you wouldn't let me freeze out there when it's so warm in here. It's not like I can see anything."

No one had ever seen me naked before, and there was no way that this cheeky fucker was getting an invitation. It didn't surprise me that he walked around like he owned the place. He appeared to be railroading my decision that we remain friends, and part of that was stomping around my place and sharing my bathroom, like I suspected a boyfriend might.

I rushed through the rest of my shower, not enjoying it anymore now that I was worried about him coming in again and embarrassing me. I towel dried my crazy mop of hair as best I could then changed into my favorite pajamas, which, fortunately, covered most of my body. The flat did seem cold as I walked out of the steam-filled bathroom.

"I can't believe you did that!" I complained as I hunted around for one of O'Connell's hoodies.

He stood right in front of me and rested both hands on the desk behind me, trapping me against his body. He dipped his head to the crook of my neck and inhaled as he smelled my newly washed hair.

"What are you embarrassed about, baby?" he murmured.

His warm breath against my neck sent heat straight through my body, making me achy and wet. As though he knew exactly how I felt, he pressed his rock-hardness against me, which only made the ache worse. When he ground his pelvis, I moaned, and he captured my bottom lip between his teeth and nipped it. He ran his tongue over the bite to relieve the sting and ground against me again. I gripped his T-shirt in my hands, not sure if I was pulling him toward me or pushing him away.

Letting go of the desk, he reached back and pulled his T-shirt over his head so that my hands were left resting on rock-hard perfection. The sensation of feeling his cock pressed against my core, combined with unbelievably soft skin over steel abs beneath my fingertips, made me even wetter. When I moved against him, he hissed and pulled away from our kiss.

"Fuck, baby," he muttered breathlessly. "Even in those God-awful pajamas you are the sexiest thing I've ever seen. You have nothing to be embarrassed about. I just want you to be more confident in your own body, okay?"

I nodded, though I didn't think that I'd ever be comfortable with him looking over my naked body. Wanting to end the ex-quisite torture building inside me, I pulled his head toward me for more. Our kiss became almost violent, as he lifted me effort-lessly to wrap my legs around his waist and carried me to bed.

As he was laying us down, I cried out in delicious agony as his weight pressing against me had me arching off the bed. I was struggling to remember why I should be panicking about now, or maybe taking this a bit slower. This was O'Connell, and I was safe. He was making me feel amazing. So how could it be any-thing but normal to not want this to end?

The first fluttering of panic only set in when his fingertips crept down inside my pajama bottoms. "What are you doing?" I whimpered.

"Trust me, sunshine." He grinned against my lips. "I've got this."

His huge fingertips brushed gently against my folds, and I al-most came off the bed. O'Connell was a genius to take things as slow as he did. Any quicker and my panic would have ruined it.

After that one touch, he lightly ran his calloused fingertips over the tops of my thighs and around the elastic of my pajamas, anywhere but where I actually needed his touch. All the while we kissed as though we were devouring each other, and the need grew worse with every stroke. He was as hard as a rock against my leg, but I could barely think about anything but what he was doing to me.

"Please, O'Connell," I begged.

"What do you need, baby?" He smiled knowingly.

"Touch me again."

He looked triumphant as he brushed against me gently with his thumb.

"Ahh," I cried out, arching my back and gripping the sheets as I tried to process what he was doing. This time I'd given him permission. Hell, I'd begged him to keep going, and he didn't disappoint. He stroked rhythmically, and I was torn between wanting to pull away from the overwhelming sensations and pleading with him never to stop.

My nipples, hard as buds against his chest, sent darts of pleasure below as they brushed against him. "I can't. I can't...," I whimpered.

"Let go, baby," O'Connell whispered. "I'll catch you."

My spine was a rod of steel, and bright blinding stars burst across the back of my eyelids as I came. It was the most amazingly wonderful thing that I had ever experienced, and I wanted to cry out at the sheer joy of it.

O'Connell looked at me lovingly. I held his jaw reverently in one hand.

"Thank you," I whispered to him. "That was so much more than I ever imagined it would be."

He smiled brightly, and it was like the sun coming out.

"As long as I live, I will never forget how beautiful you look right now."

He cuddled me into his side, but his hard cock wasn't going anywhere any time soon.

"O'Connell?" I paused, not knowing how to say this without sounding like an idiot. "Can I do the same for you?"

I was mortified. Not so much at the thought of doing it. The idea of stroking him in my hand was enough to make me wet all over again. I was embarrassed because I sounded so naively clueless. Any girl my age with a pinch of sexual confidence wouldn't have asked permission; she would have just known exactly what to do.

He didn't answer me so I risked a glance up at him. His eyes were closed, and he looked like he was in pain.

"What's wrong?" I asked concerned.

"I'm trying not to come in my pants," he answered.

I was confused about why he wasn't jumping on me for my help when I'd offered. When he seemed a bit more in control, he explained. "I promised Danny no sex before the fight. It's a golden rule for most of the boys. The banked-up sexual frustration helps with the production of testosterone."

We were both quiet as we wrestled with his promise.

"Fuck!" O'Connell cursed. "I can't believe I just gave up a hand job from you for some miserable, skinny, angry old leprechaun."

"That angry old leprechaun only has your best interests at heart. Besides, I'm not going anywhere. Consider the invitation your reward if you win your fight tomorrow."

He closed his eyes again.

"What are you doing now?" I asked.

"Trying again to focus on not coming."

* * *

An hour later we reheated our pasta and sat cross-legged on my bed enjoying it. My cold, shitty little apartment now felt warm and cozy, and I was so happy that I could burst.

O'Connell had beaten the crap out of the radiator until frostbite was no longer a real threat. He'd lit a ton of candles, ostensibly because we needed all the heat that we could get, but it made the place seem more romantic than it looked in the harsh light of day. O'Connell, shirtless and sitting on my bed, was absolutely drool-worthy, even if he was practically inhaling his meal.

As soon as he'd finished he put the bowl to one side, and in a way that reminded me of a small child, he asked me what had been on his mind. "Can I have my present now?"

I smiled as I always did when he sounded like a little boy. "No. You'll have to wait until I've finished my dinner," I admonished.

"That's not fair," he whined comically, and if he'd been standing, I was sure he would have stomped his foot. "You eat so slowly, we'll be here for months!"

He gave an overexaggerated sigh when he could see that I wasn't going to relent.

"Are you going to eat any more?" he asked after a while. I looked down at the mountain of food that he'd dished up for me, which would be about two of my usual servings. I shook my head no and steadied myself as he bounced off the bed to clear the plates. He washed up the dishes as I dried then turning off the heating, he climbed into bed beside me. It was all so domestic, and I loved it.

I turned on my side to face him, and he did the same.

"Do you want your present now?" I asked.

"Do you want to give it to me?" he answered with a smirk.

"On second thought, it can wait until after your fight," I told him with a straight face, calling his bluff.

"What? No! I didn't mean it. Please, can I have it now?"

I laughed because he really was just too cute.

"It's not very big. Just a token gift," I warned him, worried that I'd built this up into too big of a deal, or that he might not like it after all.

"I don't care. I haven't had a present in years."

"What about your birthday?"

"Danny gives me a week off dues, and the boys buy me a pint," he explained.

"That's awful!" I exclaimed, horrified.

"We're blokes." He laughed. "What did you expect us to do?"

"What about your mum?" I asked.

"I don't remember the last time she bought me anything. But then, coming home to a night when she hadn't passed out in a pool of her own puke was gift enough."

I reached into the drawer of my bedside table and pulled out a box wrapped in brown paper and string. I placed it on the bed in front of him.

"Sorry. They were all out of Good-luck-with-your-big-fight wrapping paper at the shop."

He didn't say anything, which was completely out of character. There were no quips or cocky comebacks. He just stared at it. After a few minutes, he picked it up and pulled the bow on the string, then carefully opened the brown paper to reveal the jewelry box underneath. Still staring he opened it up to find an intricately designed, silver Celtic cross inside on a long, silver chain.

"Do you like it?" I asked worriedly. "I had Father Patrick bless it when we went to church."

He swallowed hard, and when he looked up at me, his eyes were wet.

"You bought this for me?" he asked, and I nodded.

"Sunshine, you can't afford this."

"I'm getting by better with the extra money that I get from Danny, and I did a few extra shifts last month when I finished out my rota."

He carried on just looking at it, and I started to get worried.

"You don't have to wear it or anything. I just wanted to get you something to say good luck and to let you know that I'm behind you."

He launched himself off the bed and threw his arms around me, squeezing me hard.

"I fucking love it. Thank you, baby," he replied.

I grinned, more than a little relieved.

"Father Patrick told me that the ring symbolizes God's eternal love and that the four parts of the cross mean different things to different people, but in your case, he thinks they represent mind, body, heart, and soul. Every one of those parts needs to be ready before you fight, but God will be with you in all of them."

"That sounds like something Father Pat would say. For me, it just reminds me of you."

"I like that, too," I admitted.

He stared at it some more before taking the cross out and handing it to me. I undid the clasp and secured it around his neck as I kissed him gently on the lips.

He pulled me closer until I was straddling him then kissed me hard, touching his tongue against my own. Pulling away, he looked deep into my eyes and asked me to bare my soul. "Will you tell me now about your past?"

I nodded my head although my chest felt so tight it hurt to breathe. Would he see me differently after this? Would this make me unclean and repugnant to him? Unless I told him I'd never know, but I would give a great deal right now to be without the burden of my past.

"My dad died when I was nine. He was the center of my whole world. Then one day I went to school and when I got home, he was gone. Another car skidded on some diesel on the motorway. The other driver lost control and smashed into Dad's car, killing them both instantly. Less than a year later, my mum had met and married Frank," I explained, climbing off O'Connell. I felt dirty just talking about it, and I didn't want to pollute him by touching him as I let this poison seep out of me. Any warmth

I'd felt before was gone, and I fought hard not to let my shaking become noticeable.

"The first time he hit me was for talking to a boy in my class when I took out the rubbish. Mum did absolutely nothing. I was a teenager by then, and I think he'd been beating her for a while. He was nothing like my father, so disapproving and controlling, even from the first time that I met him.

"After the first time he hit me, it was like he got a taste for it. He was never sorry after, either. In his sick head he could justify every punch with a purpose, like he was doing me a favor taking over where my dad should have left off. I wanted to tell people so many times, but my mother never left the house. She was his hostage, and the reason he knew I would never open my mouth."

The tears that I'd kept at bay for so long were running ugly down my face. I couldn't look at O'Connell because, if I saw even a fleeting expression of disgust, what was left inside that was still whole would fracture.

"I was angry that no one around me had worked out what was going on. He was very careful to keep my bruises where my clothes would hide them, but nobody questioned why I had suddenly become withdrawn and why I no longer had any friends. Everyone around us thought that Frank was our salvation. The loving family man doing his best to raise another man's child. I guess they blamed my problems on grief or adolescence, but not one person ever asked me if I was okay."

"What about your mum?" he croaked.

"I think something inside her died when Dad did. Frank must have given her something she needed, I guess, to marry him so quickly. She did my washing and cooked my meals, but in her head, I think she believed that I died when Dad did. When I took a beating, it gave her relief from being beaten herself. By the time I escaped, she'd become a zombie. She never looked at me or spoke to me, but she followed every order he ever gave her. Even when it was to leave me alone with him."

I choked back a sob, and without warning, he reached over and lifted me from the bed to sit in his lap. Yanking the covers, he cocooned them around us and held me so close to his chest that I could barely breathe.

"That's enough now, baby. I shouldn't have pushed you so far."

"You needed to know. There's more, but I'm afraid of how you'll look at me when you hear everything."

He held my face and tilted it until I looked up at him.

"What did I tell you before? Whatever happened before me changes nothing. You are and always will be the most fucking beautiful person that I've ever met, inside and out."

"I've been scared for so long, O'Connell. With you is the safest that I've ever felt, but it won't last. He'll find me eventually and I'm terrified that you'll be caught in the crossfire when he does."

O'Connell held me like he was never letting me go. Swallowing hard, it was almost like he was holding back tears of his own.

"What did I tell you I'd do if anyone tried to take you away from me?" he asked gruffly.

"Decimate them," I whispered.

"Fucking decimate them," he reiterated. "Let him come. It will save me the trouble of looking for him."

CHAPTER SEVENTEEN

I spent the rest of the night wrapped around O'Connell. When I'd climbed back into bed after visiting the bathroom, he'd hauled me against him like he'd missed my warmth. By the time the sun rose and it was time to leave for class, I was dragging my heels.

"I don't want to go," I admitted.

"I don't want to let you leave, brainiac. But I won't let boxing fuck up what you're doing at school. Besides, with you next to me I feel soft and lazy and loving. I need to get my head in the game, and that isn't a side of me that you need to see firsthand."

"I will see you before the fight, though?"

He nodded his head and smiled. "Kieran will pick you up at seven, all right?"

"What do I wear?" I ask nervously.

"Wear whatever you want." He chuckled. "I'm always imagining you naked anyway."

And there was the cocky arrogant bastard that I knew and loved. I raised my eyebrows in mock horror then blew him a kiss and grabbed my bag as I walked through the door. I'd left him my spare set of keys to lock up behind him, which was another huge step for me. O'Connell knew how much of a big deal it was though. He wouldn't abuse the privilege.

* * *

My day went by mercifully quickly, and O'Connell was right to send me to school. I'd have driven him nuts at home. It took me over an hour to choose what to wear. In the end I settled for my best pair of dark jeans, a tank top, and a pretty, off-the-shoulder sweater. I didn't know how smart I'd have to be or how warm it would be there so I figured this would do.

Kieran called for me exactly when he said he would, and my excitement at seeing O'Connell had long since faded under my worry for him.

"You okay?" Kieran asked me, as I was locking up my door.

"Uh-huh," I mumbled, not looking him in the eyes.

"Em. What's going on?" he questioned in a serious tone that was totally at odds with his usual jovial self.

"I'm worried about O'Connell getting hurt," I blurted out.

Kieran grinned big. "Em, he's got this in the bag, lovely. I don't know what you did to him last night, but today, he's electric."

He winked at me knowingly, and I was outraged.

"I didn't do anything to him," I squeaked, and he laughed out loud.

"Whatever you say," he said. As I put on the helmet that he'd given me and climbed on the back of his bike, I breathed a little bit easier. If Kieran was confident that everything would be fine then I would trust that he had good reason for his easy faith.

We arrived at the exhibition center later than I thought, and I was glad that Kier had a bike because we never would have been able to park a car. The place was packed.

"Come on," Kier encouraged, taking my helmet off me.

We wove our way around the maze of cars and bypassed the queue at the main entrance to go around the back. Kieran banged on a door hard and, a few seconds later, flashed two passes at the enormous guy in a black security T-shirt, and we were in. Somehow I thought that the only people back here would be the fighters and their coaches, but I was wrong. People filled the hallways chatting, drinking, and walking around, talking on their mobile phones. Whatever I'd expected, it wasn't this. I was lost in the sea of red doorways when Kier walked into one, dragging me with him. Shutting it behind him, I could see Danny kneeling down and wrapping O'Connell's hands.

"Hey, sunshine." O'Connell grinned, and his face lit up.

"Hi, O'Connell."

Tommy, Liam, and a few of the other guys all filled the room, but no one else looked as nervous as I felt. Not knowing what to do with myself, I sat down on the bench next to him. He clenched and unclenched his fists when Danny finished wrapping them. Jumping up and down like his feet were on springs, he bounced around to warm up and started shadowboxing in the corner. Danny brought out pads, and they practiced a few combinations between them.

With every hit my anxiety got worse. Pretty soon those wouldn't be pads, but another trained fighter whose only mission was to take down and hurt the man that I cared for. I understood why Kieran thought O'Connell had this in the bag. Any sign of last night's nerves were gone. He exuded confidence, and it convinced the guys around him that he was infallible. I couldn't share their euphoria. O'Connell was huge, but so was the guy he was fighting. His sculpted physique was rock hard, but it was still skin and muscle, and the pain when they ripped and bruised over and over would take its toll.

Every time I imagined how the fight would go, I remembered

every punch, slap, and kick I'd ever taken. I imagined Frank beating me, and the snap of bones that would take months to heal. Then I imagined O'Connell in my place, and I couldn't take it anymore. As inconspicuously as I could, I made my way to the bathroom adjoining the changing room, knelt down over the toilet, and vomited. As soon as I could get myself together, I wiped my mouth and cleaned up as best I could. My flushed, red face was a giveaway, and I was a stone's throw away from vomiting again when there was a gentle knock at the door.

"Come in," I croaked quietly, trying not to lose it.

"Hello, sunshine." To my surprise, it wasn't any of the guys, but Danny, who walked in and shut the door gently. He opened his arms for a hug, and I threw mine around him with a sob.

"I don't think I can watch this, Danny. I can't just sit there and watch someone hit him over and over again for twelve rounds."

He rubbed my back like you would do to comfort a child, and when I was a little calmer, he pulled me back and held my shoulders firmly. "Sunshine, do you trust me?"

I nodded my head and sniffed in case I hadn't seemed juvenile enough.

He closed the toilet seat and sat me down on it as he crossed his arms and leaned against the sink. I was about to get "the talk," and our location couldn't have been any less glamorous.

"I've been a boxer my entire life, and that boy of ours has something that you don't see very often in a fighter. You get your brawlers, who will improve their technique over time, and you get the technical boxers who can rack up the points for a win, but O'Connell has something that you can only call magic. When that boy steps between those ropes, it's pure joy. It's like he sees what the other fighter is going to do before they know it themselves.

"He ain't a technical fighter, he's the wild card. It doesn't matter how much punishment he needs to take, he'll take it. He reads them like a book, waits for his opening, and then that's it. It's over. Everything bad that's ever happened to him, everything he can't control, stays out of that ring because, in it, he is master of his fate. For an old fecker like me, that kind of magic in a fighter is the most beautiful feckin' thing I've ever seen.

"Now you need to stop getting yourself all worked up. I ain't worried about that great big eejit, I'm worried about you. You need to trust that I love that boy like my own son, and if I thought he couldn't handle it, then I wouldn't let him in there. But if you don't calm down and watch the fight with a clear head, then you're going to miss the magic. You won't be sitting there for twelve rounds 'cause this thing ain't going to last half that. So do you trust me to get our boy through this?"

He spoke to me calmly, but sharply, and it worked. I was so focused on listening to Danny that I'd stopped flustering and panicking, and I'd started to just breathe.

"Wouldn't it just be better for me to wait here for him?" I asked.

"Nope," he replied. "When one goes into the ring, we all go. He needs to know that you're with him on this, that you have his back like he's got yours. If he's worried that you'll see him differently after he fights, then that will mess with his head. He knows that he has this in the bag, and you need to believe it, too. We're all in this together, no matter what."

"All for one and one for all?" I asked, with a crooked grin.

"We ain't feckin' musketeers, sunshine!" he barked, as though completely offended, and I couldn't help but laugh. It was at that point that O'Connell and Kieran walked in.

"Is this a private party or can anyone come in?" O'Connell asked, but I could hear the edge of worry in his voice.

"Jesus!" Danny exclaimed. "Can't you boys give me five minutes of peace, even in the feckin' loo? What's wrong with knocking? For all you know, Em could have been helping me with my colostomy bag."

"Ohh," and, "Gross," Kier and O'Connell replied together, with a wince.

Danny winked at me then pushed Kieran out the door moaning, "Go on, you fat article, get out of the way," as he closed it behind him.

"You okay, baby?" O'Connell asked worriedly.

"I'm okay," I assured him. "I was worrying about you a little bit, but Danny's given me the pep talk so I'm fine."

"Yep, he's pretty good at those. I had mine when he was doing my wraps." He paused as he looked at me. "I've got this, you know, love."

"I know," I told him. "Just try not to get too battered. I'd hate to have to put some guy on his skinny arse in the car park later because you let him knock you around."

"Skinny arse? He's six-foot-three and two hundred twenty-nine pounds," O'Connell reminded me.

"In my head, he's five-foot-eight and one hundred and fifty pounds soaking wet. That's how I know you're not getting hurt."

He smiled at my freaky imagination then pulled me up toward him. "Come and give your man a good-luck kiss."

"Friends don't kiss each other good luck," I teased.

He smiled, opened the door with the hand that wasn't wrapped around my waist, and shouted through it. "Kier, do friends kiss each other good luck?"

"Hell, yes," he replied in mock seriousness. "I gave Con a good bit of lip-loving this afternoon to cheer him on."

Tommy, who sat next to Kieran, looked at him like he was a sandwich short of a picnic. Without flinching Kier put his left hand on Tommy's jeans-clad thigh. "Don't be jealous, Tom, my feelings for you are still the same. Not even someone as damn sexy as Con can come between us."

"Fuck. Off!" Tommy replied then smacked Kieran a few seconds later when he still hadn't moved his hand.

We were both laughing as O'Connell closed the door, and with a smile still on both of our faces, he kissed me long and hard. The wraps on his hands felt coarse against my skin, as he reached under my sweater and tank top to run his thumb across my ribs. He didn't touch my breasts but brushed so achingly close to them that I arched my back, pressing closer against him and willing him to go farther. Three bangs on the door were enough for me to know that Danny was calling time.

O'Connell rested his forehead against mine. "So does that promise from last night still stand? Do I get my reward tonight if I win?"

"Winning is its own reward," I replied Zen-like, and he groaned.

"If you still have any energy left, then yes, I will make good on my offer last night, but I've never done it before so you need to show me what to do."

"Ah, baby," O'Connell groaned, "how am I supposed to fight now I'm hard?"

"Just imagine what Danny will do to you if you go out there to face him like that."

"All right," O'Connell muttered, "that did it," and with one more quick kiss, we walked out of the door.

Danny laced up O'Connell's gloves, and he shadowboxed a little longer with Danny talking in his ear the whole time. Any trace of my O'Connell was hidden behind the terrifyingly intense gaze of the predator that he'd become.

Music that I'd never heard before pounded through the walls as Danny slipped O'Connell's green silk robe over his shoulders. Banging his gloves together, he turned toward me and bent his head. Grasping his meaning, I unclasped the cross and fastened it around my own neck.

"Keep that safe for me, sunshine. I'll need it as soon as the fight's over."

I nodded in agreement.

As the door of the changing room opened, the noise was unbelievable. Apparently they cranked up the volume when the guys were making their way toward the ring. It seems like it cranked up the crowd as well. Stomping feet pounded along to O'Connell's anthem, and I followed slowly behind his entourage. Tommy directed me toward our seats while Danny and O'Connell climbed into the ring, and Kieran remained in their corner.

"What's up?" said a voice from behind me, and to my surprise the gang was there.

"Why didn't you tell me you were coming?" I asked Nikki.

"Albie sorted it out with Liam," she replied. "We didn't want to miss seeing your man do his thing, and we didn't know we had tickets until yesterday," she told me.

"He's not my man." I sighed, ignoring the number of things that we'd done in the last twenty-four hours to the contrary. "We're just friends."

"And I'm Sugar Ray Leonard," she retorted with a snort.

"Ladies and gentlemen," the booming voice resounded from the middle of the ring, drawing our attention to the front.

"I'd like to introduce you to the main event of the evening. In the blue corner, weighing in at two hundred and twenty-nine pounds, from Calabria, Italy, Benito 'the Hammer' Carmello. In the red corner, from Killarney, Ireland, weighing in at two hundred and twenty pounds, your very own local boy, Cormac 'the Hurricane' O'Connell."

He had barely finished before the crowd erupted. O'Connell might have been born in Ireland, but he lived here now, and that made him their local boy. I turned to Tommy, who was whooping and hollering with the best of them.

"Hurricane?" I asked, and he grinned in reply.

"It's because of the amount of fucking devastation he leaves behind when he's done fighting. He destroys everything in front of him."

Of course that was his name. I felt like I'd been in the path of a hurricane from the day I met him. Only this one wasn't tearing me apart. He was making me whole again.

I watched him bounce up and down and rotate his shoulders to stay warm and ready. Women all over the arena were screaming, "We love you, Hurricane," and other stuff a little more obscene, but they were more than outnumbered in here by the men. Beer was flowing readily, albeit in cheap plastic cups, and I could see why Danny had wanted to keep me away from all of this.

Right then I looked toward O'Connell, who was scanning the crowd for me. When his eyes finally met mine, his face broke into one of the cockiest grins that I'd ever seen, and he winked at me, blowing me a kiss from his boxing glove. He was telling me not to worry, that he had this, and for the first time I really believed that he did.

The bell rang, and the crowd roared. The Hammer was slightly shorter than O'Connell but solidly built. I knew from the boys' gossip that his trademark left hook was like a hammer, giving him five knockouts in his last seven fights. For the first two rounds it seemed like both men were sparring more than fighting. Tommy said that they were sizing each other up.

By round three, just when my nerves were settling themselves down, the Hammer tired of playing cat and mouse. That was when the magic that Danny had been talking about happened. The Hammer went in with a combination that ended with his killer left hook, but it never connected. O'Connell was moving around on that canvas like he was on fire. Every punch that didn't connect wore on his opponent.

By round five the Hammer looked tired and worried, and O'Connell looked ready to close this down. His predatory gaze was frightening, and when he stopped dancing, he didn't stop punching. Left, right, left. Hook, hook, uppercut. With every combination, O'Connell punished. Frank didn't have a fifth of the power that O'Connell had, so I had no idea how the Hammer was still standing.

Seconds from the final bell, O'Connell threw a lethal combination and it was all over. Serving the Hammer with his own signature punch, O'Connell gave him a final left hook that knocked him out cold. The Hammer, arms flaccid at his sides, fell like a tree in the forest, hitting the canvas with an audible smack.

O'Connell went to his corner and waited as the referee called the fight, then the corner men swarmed the ring. Tommy was with them, but I was rooted to my seat, straining to see a glimpse of O'Connell over the crowd.

When the Hammer finally regained consciousness, the look of relief on O'Connell's face was palpable. That was pretty much when the whole arena exploded. The Hammer was undefeated and in line for a title fight later on in the year. I didn't know what that meant for O'Connell, but I knew it was big.

Waves of people pushed down the aisles as O'Connell's music boomed through the speakers, and still I sat. Not knowing what to do next.

After a few minutes, both fighters made their way to the center of the ring and tapped gloves as the announcer's voice boomed through the arena. "Ladies and gentlemen. May I introduce your winner by knockout in the fifth round, Cormac 'the Hurricane' O'Connell."

The seat next to me depressed as Danny sat down and tapped the hand resting on my knee.

"That boy is enough to take years off me," he moaned.

"I thought you said he had this in the bag," I squeaked.

"He did," chuckled Danny, "but watching your kid fight would tie anyone in knots."

I didn't think he realized that he'd referred to O'Connell as one of his own kids, but it didn't matter, that was what they were.

"Well, darlin', speaking of painful experiences, you'd better brace yourself," he told me then disappeared as O'Connell walked toward me. Behind him stood a tired-looking, stern-faced woman.

"Hey, baby, did you see it?" O'Connell grinned then pressed his sweaty lips to mine in a quick kiss.

"I saw it all." I smiled.

Throwing his arm across my shoulders and pulling me into his side, he introduced me.

"Sunshine, this is me ma, Sylvia. Ma, this is my girl, Em."

"Oh shit," was my first thought. *"It's the mother."*

CHAPTER EIGHTEEN

It was clear that his mother had been a very beautiful woman once. How could she not have been? After all, O'Connell had half of her genes. The years of alcohol abuse had obviously taken their toll, and no amount of makeup that she'd troweled on or too-tight clothes could disguise the obvious signs of her aging. When O'Connell looked toward her, she played the doting dutiful mother to perfection. Smiling and gazing at him adoringly, she seemed delighted that her only son had introduced her to the object of his affection. Behind his back she looked at me with nothing less than pure evil, and I had no idea what I'd done to deserve it. I could feel myself withering under the intensity of her animosity. I had been the victim of that look before, and I knew that this meeting would not end well for me. How could I possibly tell that to O'Connell, though? The answer was that I couldn't, so I did the only thing that I could do. I stuck out my hand and said, "I'm pleased to meet you."

"Likewise, dear." She assessed me as she shook my hand.

"Did you enjoy the fight?" I asked her, searching for small talk.

"Of course," she replied, as though that were patently obvious. "I love to see my son win. What about you, did you enjoy it? Cormac tells me that this is your first fight."

I answered her as honestly as I could. "I was proud of him, and I'm glad that he didn't get hurt."

"Well, we're all glad about that, of course," his mum interjected.

"Hello, Sylvia. It's a pleasant surprise to see you sober and upright." Kieran burst into the conversation, and my jaw dropped that he would insult O'Connell's mum, especially in front of him.

"Kieran, I see that age hasn't improved your manners at all. Shouldn't you be out scouting for tonight's STD-infested whore?" she retorted.

I was stunned that they weren't even pretending to like each other. While Kier and Sylvia ignored any kind of social propriety, O'Connell just looked embarrassed. Removing his arm from around my shoulders, he reached for my hand and gripped it hard, as though he was worried that I would run at any moment. I ran my thumb gently across his hand. I didn't know if he'd feel it beneath his wraps, but he squeezed my hand in return, and it was like we were having a silent conversation.

"So are you and my son seeing each other, or are you just tonight's prize?"

"Ma," O'Connell growled. Clearly Sylvia had become bored with playing nice, and O'Connell was beyond pissed. Whether she was saying this to get a rise out of him or me, I wasn't sure, but by the death grip that he had on my hand, I could tell that he needed some reassurance.

"Don't be testy, son," she replied. "It's not like you've ever talked about her before, is it?"

He ground his jaw as he tried not to react to his mother's baiting, and I was beginning to get a sense of how toxic she was.

"I talk about her all the time. You don't know that because I moved out over a month ago."

"Maybe you should move back in, lovely. You'd have your own room, and then perhaps I could get to hear about what's important in your life." She sounded so genuine when she asked him to move back in that it was easy to forget that she was the reason he moved out in the first place. He squeezed my hand again, almost like he was reminding himself that I was still here. I was aware that I'd done nothing to give him the support that she was undermining.

"Thanks, Ma, but I'm fine at Kieran's."

I could see that she was ready to press her case before I jumped in. "In answer to your question, Mrs. O'Connell, yes, Con and I are seeing each other, and I'm sure that we'll get to know each other better now that we've been introduced."

Kieran and O'Connell grinned a mile wide as I admitted for the first time that O'Connell and I were more than just friends. There really wasn't any point in continuing to pretend that our relationship was just friendship. For some crazy reason, O'Connell had chosen me, and like the hurricane that he was, he'd blown into my life whether I was ready for him or not.

"Perhaps we should see how long this lasts before we invest any time in getting to know each other. After all, my son tends to go through girls like they're disposable."

"Ma!" O'Connell admonished in horror.

"I'm sure that was true once, but I'm betting that he's never introduced a girl to you before," I replied.

Sylvia looked as though she was sucking on lemons, and I knew she didn't like me answering back. Frank gave me the same look when I said something in public that I knew I'd pay for in private later. She wouldn't say whatever else she had to say to me in front of O'Connell, but this conversation was far from over.

"Come on, sunshine. We need to leave your boy to talk business." I could practically see the gleam in Sylvia's greedy eyes as Kieran nodded toward the sponsors talking with Danny.

Glad to be away from this conversation, I muttered, "See you soon," and kissed O'Connell briefly on the cheek, which earned me a pulse-racing smile.

"It was nice to meet you, Sylvia," I lied politely. "I'm sure that we'll see each other again soon."

"I'm sure we will," she retorted, as though it were a veiled threat. I had to work hard not to cringe.

Kieran led me back to the changing room, which was packed full. Liam had obviously invited my friends back there, and with the guys from the gym euphoric from the win, it was like a mini-party.

"Oh man, Con rocked! I can't believe that I've never been to a fight before," Nikki enthused, and I grinned. "Em, that man of yours is seriously fucking hot."

She wasn't wrong, and now that I didn't have the fear of him getting hurt hanging over me, the reminder of my promise to-tally turned me on. Hot and sweaty was a look he wore well. The thin sheen of moisture only highlighted a body that I alone would have free rein to explore. Lust made me uncomfortable, and I squirmed in my seat, wondering what delicious things he would do to me later. After so many weeks of hard training, I imagined that he'd want to party a bit first; he'd certainly earned it. With my friends around me, I was relaxed enough to enjoy myself as well. Someone was playing music while we all waited for the guys, and O'Connell's smelly, sweaty changing room was beginning to feel more and more like a nightclub.

"Where's Ryan?" I asked Nikki, looking around.

"Don't know, don't care," she replied in a tone which made it patently obvious that she did care. I didn't want to upset her anymore by pressing for the details. She'd tell me in her own time or not at all, but privacy was a gift that well-meaning friends rarely cherished.

She nudged me with a smile. "I'm good, Em. Buzzed from the

fight and ready to party. Look, I'm going to get us a couple of drinks from the bar, okay? Keep my seat for me."

"Don't worry, it's not going anywhere," I replied.

I was so lost in thoughts about what O'Connell and I might do when he was done with the sponsors that I hadn't even noticed anyone until she sat down in Nikki's seat.

"Well, now would be as good a time as any for us to get to know one another." The malice in Sylvia's eyes was completely unrestrained as she glared at me with contempt. I tried to remember all the rules I lived by when I was around Frank, but it was too late. I wasn't that person anymore. Danny, O'Connell, Kieran, Tommy, Nikki, and all the other guys had changed me. Granted, beneath the surface my insecurities were still there and still deeply ingrained, but my skin was thick enough that I couldn't be bothered by her petty insults.

"What can I do for you, Sylvia?" I asked politely.

"Well, for starters, you can fuck off back to whatever hole you crawled out of before you decided to latch your claws on to my son."

"Wow, we really are foregoing all pleasantries," I baited unwisely.

"Bitch," she sneered as she leaned toward me, "this is me being polite."

I shrank back into my seat. I'd gone from "pleased to meet you" to "bitch" in under ten minutes. I really must secrete some kind of chemical that made people hate me on sight. "Why would you think that I'd want to stick my claws in him? I care about your son, and I believe that he cares about me. I don't understand why you would be concerned about our seeing one another."

"Is it all an act, I wonder, or are you really that naive? My son is on his way to the big time. Some of the promoters were very accommodating and most respectful when they learned that I was Con's mother. It seems to me that he will walk away tonight with a boatload of sponsorship money, and with the fights they have lined up for him, this is only the start."

I tensed in my seat, practically smelling the greed on her.

"Now I'm not disputing that my son clearly has some misplaced affection toward you, but pretty soon his life will be changing dramatically. High-profile fights mean he will be traveling with lots of confident, sexy women who'll be falling over themselves for a chance to be with him. Even if he has the cast-iron willpower to turn away what they're offering, how long do you think it will be before you start feeling insecure? You know you can't compete with any of them, so you'll avoid the fights or hound Con into smoothing over your fears until he realizes that he needs to choose either you or his career. If he chooses his career, you will have spent months falling in love with him, only to have your heart broken. If he chooses you? You'll have ripped him away from a dream that he's had his entire life. Now tell me, if you don't break this off with him tonight, can you live with either ending? Can you make him happy?"

She'd done it. In less than five minutes she'd reminded me of why I should give up the only person that I'd ever loved, and I did love him. Despite my fears, despite my protestations that I wasn't ready for a relationship, despite my anxiety that Frank would one day find me, I loved Cormac O'Connell. Walking away from him now, before he started to feel as strongly as I did, would save him. It would keep him safe from Frank and give him the future that he deserved without the worry of leaving me behind. I would do this for O'Connell but inside my fractured heart was breaking.

"I doubt that we'll see each other again, and I can see by the look on your face that you intend to do the right thing. For your sake I'd suggest that it would be unwise to rethink your decision. Good-bye, Emily."

She lit up a cigarette, put her clutch bag under her arm, and then sauntered out of the changing room on four-inch heels. You'd never be able to tell that she'd just used them to walk all over me. I looked around, and the makeshift party was in full swing. It didn't look as though anyone had even noticed Sylvia.

If I was going to do this, then it had to be tonight. This was the start of the rest of O'Connell's life, and I could make this sacrifice for him, but I had to do it now. If I had to tell him to his face, then I'd break down. The best thing that I could do would be to put a bit of distance between us and let him have his night of celebration. Tomorrow I would set him free, and I was sure that, after a while, he'd move on and write me off as a bad investment. The pain in my chest was so real that it felt like my heart was breaking, but I was sure that I'd never be enough for O'Connell in the long run anyway. My flat would be the first place that he'd go, so it looked like I'd be begging another favor from Nikki. A few minutes later she returned from the bar.

"Nik, I know that everyone's really excited about the fight, but I'm really feeling under the weather. Would you mind if I crashed at your place just for the night? It's just that when the guys get drunk, they have a tendency to show up at my door at all hours of the night."

"You're not staying!" she exclaimed.

"My head really hurts. I just need a couple of painkillers and a good night's sleep, but if I don't leave now, this headache will be a migraine by the morning."

"Sure, no problem," she replied, obviously worried. "My roommate is away for the weekend so you can crash in her bed. Do you want me to come with you?"

She'd been having a ball before she got me a drink, but it was testament to what a good friend she'd become that she'd give up the party for me.

"Don't be silly. I'll be fine," I assured her. "Will you tell

O'Connell that I've gone, but do me a favor and don't tell him that I'm staying at your place. This headache will never go away if he starts banging down my door drunk at three in the morning."

"No problem. I'm not thrilled about the idea of you going home alone, but don't worry about me waking you up. My friend Sarah lives so close to town that I'll probably end up crashing with her. It will save me from getting a taxi home later. Just drop off my key with the night porter if you leave tomorrow before I get home."

"Thanks, Nikki. I owe you one," I told her as she gave me her key.

"Bitch, you owe me like a million, but I intend to collect when I'm struggling with our next assignment."

"Done," I replied, then hugged her and made a hasty exit. If I didn't say good-bye to anyone, with a bit of luck, they wouldn't realize that I had left. The arena was still packed, and I didn't see O'Connell. I kept my head down and didn't look up until I could taste fresh air.

I couldn't afford to hang around waiting for a taxi, so I walked and walked until my feet hurt. Eventually, when I was actually contemplating sitting down and camping on the pavement, I flagged down a passing taxi and made my way to Nikki's place. I was numb. Figuring that I'd imposed on Nikki's kindness so far that she wouldn't mind a little further, I borrowed one of her T-shirts. Washed and changed I climbed into bed and felt the floodgates open. I cried hard and ugly as I grieved for what had been so brief, and what could never be. There was no way that I could go back to the gym now, so on top of losing O'Connell, I was losing Danny, Kieran, and the rest of my new family, and a wave of grief engulfed me again. I'd have to go back to working every shift I could get at the cafe with that bitch Katrina, who'd have ammunition against me for life now that she'd seen me puke all over O'Connell.

I knew that I was free and that was all I'd ever wanted, but was it so wrong now to actually want more? Being strong for so long had left me bone wearily tired, and when the tears finally dried, I was so exhausted and broken that I drifted to sleep, not really caring whether I would ever wake up.

When the dawn arrived I still felt like crap, only now I looked like it, too. In contrast to my own place, Nikki's apartment was warm and had heating that actually worked in the morning. Maybe it was this foreign sensation of being warm as I slept that woke me, but for one brief shining moment, I forgot where I was and what had happened. And then I remembered.

It was so tempting to hide in that lovely, warm room where no one could find me, but I owed O'Connell better than that. Despite having slept, I was still tired. But I needed to get out of there and sort myself out before I faced him. He was probably passed out cold anyway if he'd been partying with Kieran after the fight.

After a brief wash, I dressed and headed home, leaving Nikki's key with the night porter. After flagging down and paying for another taxi that I couldn't afford, I walked with dread up to my apartment, bracing myself against the bitter chill. That the apartment was lovely and warm should have been my first clue, but I had pretty good reason to be distracted. I jumped a mile then when O'Connell spoke to me.

"Hello, Emily."

He spoke firmly, and for all the coldness in his voice, I could have been a complete stranger. As my pulse raced, I saw him sitting on my bed, fully dressed with his arms rested on his knees. He looked beaten up and tired, but more important he was stone-cold sober.

CHAPTER NINETEEN

"Why aren't you in bed?" I asked him, stunned.

"Because you're not with me," he replied. I was tired, defeated, and mostly sad as I planted myself dejectedly down next to him. He looked almost as miserable as I felt.

"I saw you before the fight, and everything was fine. Then less than an hour after you meet my mother, you're gone. What the fuck did she do this time?"

Any semblance of self-control that I'd managed to scrape together crumbled in the face of his pain, and the tears ran uninhibited down my face.

"We never really stood a chance, O'Connell. I thought that what I'd left behind was the worst thing that could ever happen to me, but it's not. This is worse. I'm going to destroy everything that you've worked for if I don't end this now."

He still looked miserable but as he clenched and unclenched his fists, he was eerily calm.

"Why aren't you yelling and going ballistic right now?" I sniffed.

"Because, sunshine, I'm trying to be patient while I find out why you think you're leaving me, and then I'm going to tell you why that just ain't gonna happen."

"You are the most stubborn, obstinate man that I've ever met," I huffed, but he didn't even raise a smile.

"What did she say, Em? I have a right to know," he asked quietly.

I took a deep breath and contemplated the shit storm that I was about to bring down on Sylvia, but O'Connell was right. He had a right to know. I would do right by him, but I wouldn't lie to him.

"She didn't tell me anything that wasn't true. The more fights that you do means more time that you'll spend away from me, while I have to stay here to finish my degree. You'll meet loads of gorgeous women who'll be throwing themselves at you, and even if you don't cheat on me, you'll spend so much time re-assuring me that eventually you'll feel like you need to choose between fighting and me. Either I'll lose you, or I'll end your career before it starts. That and knowing that Frank is looking for me and what he'll do to you to get to me was enough."

He got up and paced before leaning over my chair and grip-ping it so hard that I thought it would break. His jaw locked tight, and I had never seen such pure, restrained rage in all my life. I didn't know how he was controlling it, but if he let go of whatever trigger he was holding on to, I had a feeling that he would lay waste to something. Finally, with a hoarse shout, he gave up and started pounding on the wall until his knuckles bled. I didn't know how to make him stop, but I couldn't watch anymore. I threw my arms around him from behind and held on as tightly as I could. He was so powerful that I doubted that he could even feel me, so I put my lips against his neck and kissed him between reassuring him gently.

"Stop, baby. I'm here, okay? I'm here. Just stop or you're going to hurt yourself."

He stopped punching, but he was still angry, and I saw how much it cost him to rein in all that anger.

"Everything," he muttered. "Everything good in my life. Anything that makes me happy or makes me feel good about myself, she takes it away. You and boxing are the best things I've ever had, so it's pretty ingenious of her to use one to take away the other."

"She didn't want you throwing away your career for me."

"I'm sure she fucking didn't. She found out there were sponsors at the fight, and she got a whiff of money. You threatened her income, and she did what she does best."

I didn't know what to say. Regardless of her motives, her point was still effective. "Are you sure it's just about the money? O'Connell, anyone can tell a mile off how fucked up and insecure I am. Sure, I've come a long way, but to be honest, I wouldn't want anyone like me for my son, either."

He held his hands over mine against his heart, and I rested my head against his huge back. His breathing was evening out, and I could feel that the fight had gone out of him.

"Em, will you lie down with me? Right now I need to hold you and this is a conversation you need to get comfortable for."

I nodded my agreement, and he must have felt me because he turned around and used his thumb to wipe away the tears under my eyes. The knuckles of his hand were grazed and bloody, but he didn't seem to notice. "Wash away your tears, baby. I'll make you a cuppa."

In less than five minutes, he'd gone from beating down my walls to making me tea. The pair of us couldn't be any more messed up. Even the thought of the conversation we were about to have exhausted me, but I knew that it was overdue. Taking O'Connell's advice, I grabbed a quick shower while he pottered about. The blistering hot water soothed me. Craving comfort, I changed into my pajamas then gratefully accepted the hot cup of tea he gave me as I sat cross-legged beside him on my bed.

"What are you smiling about?" I asked him.

"I like that you've changed into your pj's. It makes it harder for you to run from me."

He took a deep breath and really seemed to contemplate what he was about to say. "I'm sure that Kieran, the gobshite, has told you about my pathetic upbringing, and I've told you a bit about how it was. The things I went through are things that I never want my own kids to know about. I mean, what eight-year-old should have to wake up and clean vomit off the floor before they get themselves ready for school and scrounge for something to eat? The times when she would stay clean and sober became more and more infrequent, but the older I got, the angrier it made me to have to live like that. I mean, she was the parent and I was the child, but it's like the relationship was reversed.

"By the time I was a teenager, I was already pretty big and pissed off most of the time, with no idea how to deal with it. Every time she'd get sober, she'd promise me faithfully that she'd try and be a good parent this time around. You know, actually be there for me like a ma should. One Christmas she got me this secondhand computer console. It was old, but it came with a load of games, and Kier and I fucking loved it. When I came home from school two months later, she'd pawned it then vomited half of what she'd bought with the money over the sofa. I was so angry, and I wanted to hit her so badly, but she was still my ma, you know? She was a shite parent, but she was the only one that I had, and when she was sober, she acted like she loved me so much. So I dealt with my temper the only way I knew how. I picked fights with anyone who crossed me, pretty much anyone who wasn't her.

"Danny caught me and Kier getting rowdy with each other, and after a supreme bollocking, he invited us to the gym. It gave me an outlet for my rage, and for the first time, I had a bit of focus. I'm pretty sure that I'd be in a very dark place now if it wasn't for Danny.

"The first time she realized I was disappearing, probably because she woke up alone in a pool of her own puke, she asked around until she found me at the gym. She was blind drunk and fucking humiliated me in front of my friends and Danny.

"That night I was supposed to be sparring with Liam, and I literally beat the crap out of him. Danny banned me from the ring for two weeks, and I think that's when he understood why I am the way I am. He could have tossed me out, but he put me back in the ring and learned to read my moods. It gave me a coping mechanism, but my temper is still always on a knife's edge. If I lose it when Danny isn't around and I've been drinking, then it isn't pretty.

"Then I met you, and I can see from a mile away how different you are, we all can. It's like you're the calm in a storm, and just being around you gives me peace. Instead of just coping with this shite, you make me feel like I have something better to look forward to. Making it as a professional boxer isn't the only thing I want out of life. Don't get me wrong, it would be cool if it happens, but I want more than that. I want a home and a family. I want to know that if I lose or if it's been a crappy day that I'm coming home to someone who loves me, no matter what. I want a reason that makes me believe that there's something more than what I have now. I want you, sunshine. The rest of the shite just doesn't matter."

"And if Frank finds us?" I asked, tears streaming down my face.

"If he's stupid enough to show his face here, then I'll deal with him. That's if I don't find him first."

"I don't want that, O'Connell. Promise me that you won't go looking for him."

"Then promise me that you won't give up on me."

"It was never about giving up on you. It was about helping you to succeed."

"The only way I can do that is with you behind me. It's okay if you need reassurance that I'm not going to cheat on you. In case you haven't worked it out, I'm pretty fucking needy, too. I'm gonna need more reassurance than you do." He comforted me with a smile.

"I'm scared, O'Connell," I admitted.

"I'm scared, too, baby," he replied, opening his arms for me to climb into.

We moved under the covers, and the tension left my body as I melted into his warmth.

"We're family now, Em. I'm yours and you're mine, and no one can take that away from us unless we let them."

I swallowed against the pain in my throat. All that crying had made my voice raspy. "I love you, O'Connell."

He kissed my temple as he whispered back, "No one's ever said that to me before. I love you, too, sunshine, and I can't lose you. So promise me that you won't run again. Even if Frank becomes a threat, I need you to promise that you'll believe in me, in us, and not run. I can't fight for us alone."

"You're pretty relentless, you know that, don't you?" I tasked him.

"You have no idea."

"I promise not to run. I'll fight for us as hard as you will. You realize that this isn't going to be easy, though. There's so much that we don't know about each other, and there are plenty of people who don't want us to make it."

He reached for my hand, threading his fingers back and forth between mine. "We have the rest of our lives to get to know each other, the good and the shite. As for the fuckers who want to try to keep us apart, let them try. They don't call me the Hurricane for nothing."

I smiled with happiness for the first time in what felt like weeks. There never had been any real chance of convincing him this was for the best, but after learning what kind of a shitty start he'd had at the hands of that bitch, I no longer wanted to try. His dream was the same as mine—a home, a family, love, and trust. If I was lucky enough that I was what he truly wanted, then I was going to grab on to this dream with both hands and fight for it.

"This is my world in a grain of sand," I whispered.

"What does that mean?" he asked.

"It's from a poem by William Blake.

'To see a world in a grain of sand
And a heaven in a wild flower,
Hold infinity in the palm of your hand
And eternity in an hour.'

"To me it means that this one moment where we choose each other, it's as tiny as a grain of sand, but it will change our lives forever, and there is nothing closer to heaven than the two of us here together."

He grinned as he rolled over on top of me, resting his weight on his elbows. "My girl is so fucking smart. Keep talking, 'cause I feel another tattoo coming on."

Wrapping my arms around his neck, I grinned back. "Yeah? Well, my boy is smarter. Who figured out that we were meant to be together first?"

"I did," he answered proudly. "I'm gonna drive you nuts, sunshine. You'll spend a lifetime cursing at me, but I'm gonna make sure that there isn't a single day that goes by where, deep down, you aren't thankful you picked me."

"Is that right?" I smiled between his kisses.

"Yep. Even when you're pregnant with baby number four, and

you're cursing me to high heaven for knocking you up, you're still gonna love me."

"Four!" I exclaimed. The thought of being a mother, of having to protect such a tiny, helpless, little life, filled me with fear, and he wanted four of them.

"Yep," he replied. "I want four big, strapping boys that I can play sports and do stuff with. Then I'm going to teach them how to box and beat the shite out of Kieran and all their other uncles."

"What if we have girls?" I asked, trying not to laugh at his horrified expression.

"Fuck me, no. There's no way. The minute my girl introduces a guy to me, if he even so much as looks at her wrong, I'd bury him. There's no way I'm having girls."

"I'm sorry, Con." I smiled. "I'm pretty sure that gender is a potluck surprise."

"No way. I have very manly sperm. It's gonna be all boys."

"Well, how about you keep that manly sperm to yourself for a while. There is no way I want kids my second year into uni."

"Sorry, baby," he joked. "I'm very virile. I have a feeling that I only need to cough, and you're gonna get knocked up."

I stared at him hard. "You're absolutely right. Why take the risk? I always thought that abstinence before marriage was an admirable goal."

His face dropped comically, and it was really hard not to laugh.

"You're joking, right? I was just kidding about knocking you up. Honestly, I can feel my balls getting bluer by the minute."

He genuinely looked worried, and I wondered what he'd say if I wasn't ready.

"What if I told you that I wasn't ready for that, or that I really did believe in abstinence before marriage?"

He stared into my eyes and answered me seriously. "Em, I

want to grow old with you. I'd be lying if I said that you weren't hotter than hell, and that I wasn't hard as a nail every time I touch you, but even if we only ever have what we have right now, it's enough. Having sex, whenever you're ready, will just make what we have even more beautiful, and that's worth waiting for."

Wow. If it was even possible, this boy just got sexier. I lifted my lips up to his and kissed him gently. It was pure and beautiful and without doubt or skepticism, because I knew in my heart that he loved me. Slowly his hand crept beneath my shirt, and his thumb gently stroked my ribs. It was so close to my breast without actually touching it that it wasn't long before I became fired up and needy. I swore that O'Connell was the king of getting me all hot and bothered.

"How banged up from the fight are you?" I mumbled between kisses that were becoming more and more intense.

"What fight?" he mumbled back. Clearly lust had scrambled more brain cells than his opponent repeatedly smacking him in the head.

"This isn't hurting you, then?" I asked as he moved between my legs to kiss the skin that he'd just been stroking.

"I'm good," he replied. He'd slowly been edging my top upward, and he was so talented with his lips that I barely paused when he pulled it over my head to drop it on the floor. When he gently held my breast in his rough, calloused hand and sucked the turgid peak of my nipple into his mouth, I couldn't help arching off the bed and deeper into his touch.

"O'Connell," I moaned, as spasms of white-hot lust shot right to my core. My skin was on fire, and I wanted so badly to climb out of it and into his. He repeated the action with my other breast, and when he gently blew over my hard nipples, I was so close to coming that I cried out.

"Not yet, baby." He grinned with that cocky smile that I loved so much. "You're gonna have to beg before I let you come." With both hands, he pulled my pajama bottoms down my legs achingly slowly, until I was left in simple white underwear. He kissed the tiny daisy at the top of my panties, still grinning.

"These are so you." He smiled.

"Plain and boring?" I replied, slightly hurt.

"Pure and sweet. It's fucking sexy," he answered. "It makes me want to corrupt you."

"I'm not so pure," I whispered turning my head away from his gaze, more than a little ashamed. He cupped my face to look up at him.

"You are pure and innocent. I don't care what that sick fuck said or did. To me you'll always be this way, and everything that happens between us is fucking beautiful. So don't let him make you think any different."

I nodded in agreement, knowing that he was right, but I wasn't sure that I'd ever see myself the way he saw me. It was hard to dwell on my worries as he resumed the path of his lips down my body. When he got to my panties, he peeled them down my legs as he kissed me lower and the tingling only became more intense. I couldn't take anymore. I couldn't remember any of my anxieties, I couldn't remember why I had any self-doubt, and I was having a bit of trouble remembering my own name. All I could think about was this god between my legs, and how at any minute now, he'd make me see stars.

"Are you ready, baby?" He grinned.

I nodded my head, completely incapable of speech, as he pinched my clit between his lips and sucked. My back was taut as a bow, and I gripped the sheets so tightly I felt like either they were going to rip, or something inside me would. I didn't think I could last one more second when he licked me gently, and tremors ripped through my body. Whenever I thought of sex before, I imagined pain and embarrassment. Never in a million years could I have believed such intimacy to be so heartachingly wonderful. As consciousness crept back in tiny increments, my body was weightless, like I was immersed in water. O'Connell collapsed onto his back next to me.

"Watching you come was the most fucking beautiful thing I've ever seen," he said.

"Mmmm…" I mumbled back, still unable even to open my eyes.

Flipping over onto his stomach, with a speed that belied the fact that he'd not long ago fought five hard rounds, he told me, "I'm gonna have to make you come again, sunshine. I forgot to make you beg."

CHAPTER TWENTY

"Are you kidding me?" I whispered. "If you do that again, you're going to snap my spine in half."

"I seem to remember you telling me once that you could bend like a pretzel."

"I was blind drunk. You should never listen to anything a girl says when she's blind drunk."

He chuckled as he kissed me long and hard. It was so intense, so amazing, that I honestly believed that he would have made good on his word if I hadn't decided to repeat the favor. Running my fingers down the washboard abs that I'd admired for so long, I didn't stop when I reached his jeans and brushed my hand gently across the rock-hard denim.

"Fuck, baby, we've got to stop," he muttered harshly, resting his forehead against mine.

"Why?" I asked timidly, worried that I was doing something wrong.

"Sunshine, I'm hanging on by a thread here. If you touch me like that again, I'm gonna come in my jeans like some horny fifteen-year-old."

I loved that I had the same power over his body that he had over mine. I didn't feel ashamed of what he'd made me feel. I felt beautiful and loved and so completely satisfied that I wanted to share that feeling with him. So I offered him something that I'd never offered anyone before.

"O'Connell," I whispered, and he looked up into my eyes. "I don't want you to stop."

His gaze softened as he comprehended my meaning. "Baby, it's too soon. I don't want to push you into something that you're going to regret tomorrow. I don't think I could handle that."

Once upon a time, I would have taken his rejection as a valuation of my self-worth, but I was stronger than that now. This man could have taken whatever he wanted without my consent, or even with it, knowing that I wasn't truly ready. But he didn't want my body if it didn't come with my heart. This giant among giants had never used his strength to intimidate me. His power lay in making me fall in love with him, and to do that, he'd laid himself at my feet, offering all that he had and all of himself without asking for anything in return, except my heart.

"It's not too soon. It's exactly the right time. I love you, and you love me."

O'Connell really looked pained. "Baby, you're ruining this for me. I had it all planned out. There was supposed to be expensive wine and a really nice dinner, followed by a night in a posh hotel room..."

He lost his chain of thought as I nibbled on his neck and resumed stroking his abs, which had quickly become my favorite pastime.

"I'm never drinking again," I reminded him.

"I would have worn a really nice suit and taken you on a great date..." He carried on as I distracted him, until I finally left him speechless.

"It's okay if you have performance anxiety, you know," I joked.

He flipped me over and started tickling me as I erupted with laughter.

"I'll give you fucking performance anxiety," he said, then grabbing my hands he threaded his fingers between mine and held them above my head.

"Are you sure?" he asked seriously. "I wanted this to be special."

"It is special," I reassured him. "It will always be special."

He nodded as though I'd convinced him and released my hands. Stripping at the speed of light, he rescued a condom from his wallet as he chucked his clothes over the side of the bed. Slipping it on quickly, it was clear that he'd practiced this many times before.

I could feel my self-confidence wavering again until he stopped and stared at me, like he was trying to memorize every inch of my face. Leaning forward gently he kissed me like it was the last time he'd ever see me. That was what this felt like. When you loved someone, every kiss was your first kiss and your last, and I hoped to be giving my last kisses to O'Connell forever.

His clever, calloused hands cupped my calf then purposely slid their way up my leg. His plump, pink lips, swollen with our kisses, captured my bottom lip between them and nipped gently as he cupped my arse and rubbed me against him. All traces of languidness were gone, and as if my body was his to command, I was on fire again. We devoured each other with our kisses, and I knew that I'd never be the same after this. He knew exactly what he was doing when he reached around to stroke me tenderly. Slipping a finger inside me, he moved slowly in and out, timing each thrust with a gentle rub of his thumb.

"O'Connell, I can't," I panted. "It's too much."

"Shall I stop then?" He chuckled.

"No! More please."

"Ah, now there's the begging that I was looking for."

I was too turned on to be pissed at him for gloating. He moved his fingers away to settle the tip of his cock against me, and I inhaled sharply. Sliding his fingers through mine, he held our hands above my head and looked deeply into my eyes.

"Are you sure, baby? It's not too late to stop," he reassured gently.

I loved him even more for asking me, even though I was pretty sure that his balls would explode if I stopped now. I kissed his bruised lips gently in answer to his question and tilted my pelvis to slide the tip of him into me. Groaning, he closed his eyes as the ecstasy of the moment hit him. He slid home slowly, letting me get used to his size. He was so huge that it was uncomfortable at first, but a few thrusts later he was hitting every right spot that I'd ever read about. He looked so much like he was in pain that I whispered, "You okay?"

He chuckled nervously. "You're so tight, baby. I don't think I'm going to last."

As my pleasure built, he moved faster inside me. When he let go of my hands, I ran them over his muscled back, relishing the fact that someone so strong and fierce could be so gentle with me. Every movement intensified the sensations between us, and I felt like I was climbing some invisible wall without being able to see the top. His tender touch skimmed my hip then he reached between us to stroke me. Right at that moment, he sucked gently on the lobe of my ear and whispered, "I fucking love you, baby."

His words lifted me over the wall, and I came hard, seeing bright and brilliant stars all around me. With a hoarse shout, O'Connell came straight after, my orgasm tipping him over the edge. Covered with a thin sheen of sweat, he was shaking hard as he looked deeply into my eyes.

"I never knew it could be like that," he admitted. "I've never made love before. Now I know the difference."

He laid his head down on my chest and fell asleep to the beating of my heart as I ran my fingers softly through his hair. His breathing, deep and even in the empty room, gave me more peace than I'd ever known.

* * *

The house was eerily quiet as I let myself in from school. Mum was always home. She never left the house. Frank wasn't due back for another couple of hours so I could breathe easily until then. In that precious time between my finishing school and his getting home from work, I showered and washed my hair. I always did anything that necessitated taking my clothes off when he was gone. If I could have gotten away with only showering at the swimming pool, I would have.

It wouldn't be for long now. Acceptance letters to different universities had started arriving at Mrs. Wallis's house, and by September I would have figured it out.

Mum and I didn't exactly see eye to eye. In fact, I'd be hard-pressed to remember the last time we'd had an actual conversation. Not since Dad died had she made any effort to engage with me. If it weren't for the fact that she plated a meal for me every night and washed my clothes, I would have sworn she thought that I'd died with him. Maybe it would have been better if I had. Still, she was my mum, and indifference was better than abuse so I wasn't leaving her behind. When the time came, Frank would come home from work to find that we'd disappeared. I'd take Mum with me to the farthest university that I'd been accepted to, get a student flat, and hide her away with me until I graduated. Maybe I could even convince her to get a part-time job to help with the bills. It would do her good to mix with people again.

I dropped my messenger bag by the front door and kicked off my shoes as I wandered into the kitchen to get a drink. I didn't even bother looking for Mum. She'd be around here somewhere. I looked out of the patio doors into the garden, and the shock of seeing the rage-filled reflection in the window was enough to make me drop the glass, before I felt the burning pain from being yanked backward. The glass of juice shattered spectacularly against the tile of the kitchen floor, but that was the least of my worries. Frank had bent my arm back at an unnatural angle and was frog-marching me to my room. When we got there, he threw me roughly to the floor and slapped me hard across the face on the way down for good measure. I cried out at the slap but held back the tears; they only spurred him on. He relished my pain. He stood over me, madder than I've ever seen him, just staring.

I kept my head bent, praying that my beating would be over quickly. Eventually he leaned over and slapped me again as he turned away. Frank liked to slap. It was humiliating and demeaning. Personally I think that he just liked the satisfying sound it made when his palm cracked against my skin. It seemed too good to be true that this was all the punishment that he had to give out today.

He stalked over to my bed and grabbed a piece of paper. "What the fuck is this?" he screamed, as he threw it at me.

With shaking hands, I tried to focus on the paper. Fuck. It was an acceptance letter to the University of Edinburgh. So far it was the farthest university away from here that I'd been accepted to. I meant to leave it with Mrs. Wallis, but I'd been so excited that I'd forgotten. Knowing Frank's tendency to search my bag, I'd stuffed it under my pillow in a panic last night and had forgotten to take it with me this morning.

"I'm sorry, Frank. I wanted to surprise you if I got in." I thought on my feet.

"Surprise me?" He screamed and punched me in the face this

time. Now he didn't care about humiliation; he just wanted to hurt me.

"You think that coming home to find that you're fucking off to the other side of the country would be a nice surprise? You're a liar and a slut and staying under my roof is the only thing that keeps you in line. You're lucky that your mother found this and brought it to my attention, because if I had to come looking for you, I'd kill you. Do you understand?"

Knowing that Mum had shown him the letter made my chest hurt, but I nodded still looking down. If he thought that I was challenging him, this would be so much worse.

"Answer me!" He spat in my face as he painfully grabbed my jaw to make me look at him. The pain of my mother's betrayal was so much worse than enduring Frank, though.

"You never learn, do you, little bitch? No matter how many times I teach you this lesson, no matter how much I've done to replace your father, you repay my kindness with shit like this."

He grabbed me by my shirt and slapped me around the face again. My eye felt like it was going to explode, and I was pretty sure that my cheekbone was fractured. There was blood running from the side of my head, and I knew this time it was going to be really bad, because he usually avoided my face. That he no longer cared whether my injuries could be covered up made me more afraid. He was staring at my chest and breathing hard through his nose, and I realized that in pulling me about he'd ripped my shirt open completely.

"You think I don't know why you're really trying to leave? For years you've been throwing yourself at me, and because I wouldn't give you what you want, you're going to whore yourself out like all those other bitches, letting college boys crawl up inside you."

I didn't get a chance to disagree before the boot went into my stomach, and I coughed out blood. I was trying really hard to *stay conscious, but I'd taken so many hits to the head that it was becoming difficult not to pass out. Maybe it was better to be out of it right now, and God knows I wished for it, but unconscious meant vulnerable, and I was vulnerable enough already.*

Yanking the sides of my shirt, he ripped it open completely and grabbed one of my breasts, squeezing painfully. I couldn't help but cry out, and he smiled with satisfaction.

"If you're so hell-bent on getting fucked, then by all means I'll give you what you want. Maybe you won't be so quick to slut yourself out when you see how a real man and not a boy fucks."

"No, Frank!" I screamed, shimmying backward on my elbows away from him as quickly as I could. The pain was forgotten with the dawning of understanding of what would happen next. "Please, no, Frank," I begged. "I'm still a virgin. You're my step-father."

"Like fuck you are, princess." He roared with laughter. He'd unbuttoned his trousers and was pulling them down when I rose and tried to make a run for it. Another punch to my stomach landed me straight back on the carpet. I was so winded that I could barely breathe. He was holding down both my wrists with his full weight pressed on top of me when he bit down hard on my bra-covered nipple.

"Look at you, you little whore. I can tell you're getting off on this."

"No, no, no," I begged as the tears ran down my face unin-hibited.

I was terrified, more afraid than I've ever been before. Bruises fade, cuts heal, but what he was about to do would stay with me forever. With one last burst of adrenaline, I screamed at the top of my voice then yelled, "Mum, help me!"

This made Frank laugh even harder, and he looked at my bedroom door waiting for her to answer. As she appeared in the doorframe, she had a complete view of my room, and it was clear that Frank was about to rape her daughter. There was still nothing in those eyes, though. It was like she was a ghost.

"Mum, please help me," I begged. "Please, please." I kept begging, but I was pleading with an empty shell. Finally she bowed her head and closed the door quietly with an audible click. I heard her shuffling footsteps as she walked away. That was the moment that changed everything. What mother would knowingly abandon her child to be raped by a monster? Maybe something in Mum really did break when Dad died, but I no longer cared. The second that she shut the door behind me, we were done. As far as I was concerned, I no longer had a mother.

"See, even your own mother agrees that you need to be taught a lesson," he mocked as he punched me again. As soon as I was winded, he reached under my skirt and ripped off my panties. Then he pinned down my thighs as he moved between them.

Coming around enough to fight him, I screamed as loudly as I could as I bucked and squirmed against him. If there was anything that I could do to get away, I did it. I slapped him, punched him, and even dug my nails into his face until they started to break off. It only enraged him further and earned me more of a beating. My face was a bloody mess, but I didn't care about anything but what he was about to do.

"You little, fucking bitch," he screamed as he pinned down my arms.

"Please, Frank. Don't do this. I won't try to leave again, I promise. My dad wouldn't do this," I begged one last time.

"Well, he's not fucking here, is he?"

He looked at me with such pure evil malice that I was sure he was going to kill me when he was done. He pushed himself roughly inside me, and I screamed as I ripped beyond repair. He buried his nose in the crook of my neck and grunted with every thrust. I felt the pain and burn of each one, and it was excruci-

ating. This sick fuck was taking away something that I'd never get back, and he was getting off on it. A few groans later he collapsed on top of me, done.

"You enjoyed that, didn't you?" he asked me, licking my neck. "Maybe this is a lesson you need to learn more than once."

The doorbell rang, and I heard my mum's voice as she answered whoever was at the door. He pulled out of me sharply, and it hurt just as much as it did going in. He used my skirt to wipe the blood off his cock, before zipping himself up.

"Just remember to keep your fucking mouth shut," he reminded me and punched me again. Five minutes too late, I got my wish, and everything went black.

* * *

I opened my eyes and tried to scream when I felt a hard body next to me. Nothing came out because I couldn't breathe. When I realized that it was O'Connell, I stopped trying to scream, but it didn't help with my breathing. I was hyperventilating, and I didn't know what to do about it. Searching around for my candles, I panicked when I remembered that they were all gone. My lungs were sucking in oxygen too quickly.

I knew that I was going to pass out soon when O'Connell lifted me onto his lap and wrapped himself around me. His Irish lilt soothed as he held me close and gently whispered, "Breathe, baby. Just listen to me breathing in and out and do the same. I'm the scariest motherfucker you've ever met, and nothing is going to get to you without getting to me first."

He did this for five minutes. Just reassuring me how brutal and bad he was and how he'd destroy anything and anyone who tried to hurt me again, and I believed him. As soon as my breathing was under control, I collapsed in his embrace with a sob.

"I'm so sorry," I cried into his chest.

He wiped away my tears with his big hands and a sad smile.

"It was making love that triggered it, wasn't it?" he asked sadly.

"That, the fight, your mum. They're all triggers, and I guess it just caught up with me."

He didn't say anything, but he didn't stop kissing or rocking me, either. His touch worked so much better than anything else had because everything that he said was right. He was the scariest person that I'd ever met, and there was no way that Frank would stand a chance against him. O'Connell loved me, but I knew that for him to really love me then he had to know all of me. That included my last deep, dark, dirty secret. If he still stayed after knowing the ugly truth, then I could finally believe that this was forever.

CHAPTER TWENTY-ONE

Taking a deep breath I told my horrible ugly story, dreading the look of revulsion on his face I feared I'd see when I was done.

"What happened afterward? How did you escape?" he asked quietly.

He was still stroking my hair, so I took comfort in that.

"It was the police at the door. A neighbor heard me screaming and called them. They told me they were suspicious when they saw the gouges on Frank's cheek. They arrested him and took me to the hospital. My face was banged up. He'd fractured my cheekbone, cracked two of my ribs, and tore me up so badly between my legs that I needed stitches. The hospital gave me STD tests and the morning-after pill, but there was nothing else they could do except give me pain relief while I healed.

"I turned eighteen while I was still in hospital so I was able to discharge myself without being turned over to social services. I already had an escape plan set up with one of my teachers, so I took it and never went back. I stayed with Mrs. Wallis recovering for a couple of months, then when my student loan came through, I used enough to buy some cheap clothes and left for university."

"Why didn't you press charges?" he asked, but I couldn't detect any rebuke in his voice.

"I gave the police my statement and told them truthfully what had happened, and they had the results of the rape kit with Frank's DNA. I guess I didn't trust the system anymore, though. If I stuck around I knew he'd find a way out of the charges. Either that or he'd kill me first. I never told the police where I was going because I couldn't risk him finding me. Frank was in the police force years ago, and he must still have connections.

"They took the university acceptance letter with her address on as evidence, and apart from Mrs. Wallis, that's the only thing tying me to this place. For the first couple of weeks I was terrified that he'd memorized the address on the letter, but he never showed up at her house. Mrs. Wallis found out a little later that he'd been remanded into custody for a while, but she doesn't know any more than that."

"Do you still speak to her?" he asked.

"Not often, but she likes it that way. She thinks the less contact we have with each other, the less chance there is of Frank finding me."

"Do you think he's still looking for you?"

"If he's free, then I'm sure of it. Frank was obsessed with controlling me. If he can't be free, then there's no way that he'd want me to be, either."

"You can't live the rest of your life waiting for that day to come, baby. Either you let me find him and take care of this, or we put it behind us. Because if he ever does come here, I'm not the only one who'll make him pay. I can't live with you going through life afraid. I'd rather take care of him once and for all than have you scared."

"I won't let him hurt you, O'Connell. I'll run first."

"You promised me that you wouldn't run again. Besides, there's no place that you could go that I wouldn't find you. You want to take care of me? Then don't ever fucking leave me, even if you think it's for my own good, because that will hurt me more than anything that happens in the ring."

I nodded in agreement and rested my head back against his chest, exhausted. "I hate these dreams. Everything in my life is going great but then I have these dreams and it's like he's reminding me that it's all temporary and it will be all over when he finds me."

"I don't think that at all," O'Connell told me. "Do you know what I think, sunshine? A person has room inside them for only so much. Last night was the best night of my life. Good stuff like that takes up a fair bit of space in your head and your heart. So this is just your body's way of getting rid of all that poison to make room for the good stuff."

I tilted my head and kissed his neck. "I've never thought about it like that before. Thank you, baby."

"Don't get mad at me, but have you ever seen anyone about this stuff? You know, to talk about it? It might help you to work through everything."

"You think I need fixing?" I whispered.

He detected the difference in my tone and turned my head to face him. "There ain't nothing about you that's broken and needs fixing. I just want you to see yourself the way I see you, and maybe seeing a counselor about this stuff will help you to do that."

I paused, comprehending what he had to say. In O'Connell's arms, I felt safe and protected, but I needed to be strong independently, to not let all of my phobias and self-doubt shape the person that I was becoming. Besides, if letting out all of Frank's dirty secrets was my body's way of getting rid of them for good, then I was happy to speed up the process of draining out the poison.

"Would you come with me if I did this?" I asked him earnestly.

"Try stopping me," he replied.

I kissed him gently, feeling more love for him at this moment than I'd ever felt before. Instead of feeling ugly and dirty enough that I wanted to shower off a layer of skin, he'd given me another way of looking at this horrific legacy.

"How come you're not flipping out? Usually you'd be losing your temper by now," I said.

"Don't get me wrong. If that scumbag ever does show up, I will lose my shit, and I can't promise you that I won't kill the fucker. But I'm just coming to realize that me losing my temper is about me. Making sure that you're okay, taking care of you, is more important to me right now than anything else. I love you, sunshine. There's nothing more important to me than you."

Not since my real dad was alive had anyone said that to me, and a tear rolled down my cheek as I realized how important it was for me to hear it.

"I love you, too, O'Connell. So much."

He turned my face toward him and kissed me deeply, twisting us both around so that my body was underneath him. "I'm never letting you go. You know that, right?" he reminded me fiercely.

"Forever," I whispered.

"Forever," he agreed with a grin and went back to kissing me.

The way that man used his lips should be illegal. It was so hard to think about, let alone worry about, anything else when he was rubbing that talented tongue of his against my own.

Pulling away from me, he rested his forehead against mine. "Stop, baby. I'm rock-hard here, and I don't want to make love to you when I should be comforting you."

I loved his concern, but ran my hand over his rock-hard cock, knowing that he had no idea how much I wanted this.

"Ahh," he groaned, planting his head into the pillow beside me. "You're killing me."

I carried on rubbing his length gently without saying anything, knowing that he'd give into me eventually.

He levered himself back up to look down at me. "Are you sure, love?" he asked.

I smiled and nodded as he bent down to kiss me. The moment was so beautiful because O'Connell didn't see me any differently, knowing what Frank had done. I didn't want his pity; I wanted his love. I wanted to be normal and sexy, and I wanted him to want me as much as I wanted him.

He ran his hand up and down my thigh as he rubbed himself against me, making me moan. I felt his tip at my entrance when he muttered, "Shit. Condom."

I groaned with him. Glad that he at least had some common sense, because I was so keyed up right now that I couldn't think of anything but him being inside of me.

He leaned over the bed to grab another condom from his jeans pocket and quickly rolled it on. He ran his calloused fingertips across me, and I cried out as my body begged for more. Wrapping his hand around my breast, he teased the whole of my nipple with his warm, sweet tongue before sucking hard and pressing his delicious weight against me.

O'Connell had me so hot, so fast, that I didn't know how I could last more than five minutes without coming, once he put those talented hands of his to good use. He kissed his way up my neck, and when our lips met, the kiss was wild and almost feral.

Maybe, after what had happened between us, the sex should have been gentle and loving, but this was exactly what I needed. O'Connell was showing me that nothing had changed, that I was as desirable to him now as I'd always been, and it's what made this frenzied coupling so loving.

Our lips collided, and we struggled to breathe as our hands roamed freely over each other's bodies. He reached between us to touch me, and I was so close that when he eased himself gently inside me, I came immediately, clenching and throbbing as he thrust in and out as hard as he could.

The look on his face was fierce as he tried to hold out, but seconds later he erupted inside me and every muscle and tendon in his body strained as he rode the waves of his orgasm. He collapsed down next to me and effortlessly lifted my languid, weightless body to lie on his.

"Love you, baby," I mumbled, but I didn't hear his response as I drifted happily into a deep and dreamless sleep.

I woke the next morning feeling totally at peace. We had slept away a whole day and night, but we'd both been exhausted. The sun was streaming through the window, and the usual discomfort of waking up in an apartment colder than Alaska was deliciously absent, warded off by the big, warm body wrapped around all of mine. O'Connell was twisting one of my curls between his fingers so I knew he was awake.

"Good morning. I've been waiting for you to wake up for ages."

"Sorry. You should have just woken me up." I yawned.

"You needed the rest. How do you fancy a day of fun today?"

"Fun?" I asked sleepily, as though it was a foreign concept.

"Yeah, fun. I've just won my fight, things between us are back where they should be, and I've got one more day off before I go back to training. So today we're going to forget our shit and our drama and just cut loose."

"What did you have in mind?" I asked.

"Well, I thought we could go to a movie then maybe meet up with all the guys for ten-pin bowling."

"That sounds great!" I said, but I bit my lip as I contemplated the first stumbling block. "I'm not sure that I can afford it, though," I admitted truthfully.

"Don't worry, sunshine, it's on me," he answered.

"And how come you're feeling so flush?" I asked.

"Because," he said while rolling over on top of me. "I have a new sponsor, which means that I finally get paid to train full-time. It's not much, but it's enough to take my girl out on."

"That's fantastic news! So when's your next fight?"

"It should be in about six weeks, just after Christmas. I don't know who it will be against yet, but it'll put me on the radar of title contenders. I'll have to pay my dues for a long time yet, but the better I do in fights like this, the better chance I have of attracting other sponsors."

"I'm so proud of you, O'Connell," I told him, and his grin was enormous.

"No one's ever said that to me before, either."

"I love you, and I'm proud of you," I reminded him, and he kissed me fiercely.

"I'm gonna make it my mission to make sure you always feel the same way, baby. Now go and get that sexy arse of yours dressed so that we can start this date."

I kissed him quickly then hopped out of bed, wrapping the sheet around me. O'Connell might know my body intimately, but that didn't mean that I was comfortable flaunting it in front of him in the cold light of day.

He slapped my backside and watched me jump. I could tell that he didn't have any such reservations about my naked body. The gleam in his eyes told me I'd better be quick, or I'd find myself naked and in bed again.

I couldn't even remember what the movie we saw was about. What I remembered was cuddling into O'Connell's side to share a bucket of popcorn and being late for bowling because we couldn't stop holding hands and kissing in the car park.

"Fuck me, the lovebirds finally made it," welcomed Tommy, where we found him in a lane already loading everyone's names into the computer.

"Don't get jealous, Tom. Con might be taken, but I'm still free." Kieran reassured him by patting his thigh, as Tommy carried on loading names.

Tommy dropped the cocky look and stared at Kieran. "I'm fucking worried about you, ya know," he responded, tipping his beer toward Kieran. "For the millionth fucking time, I am *not* gay, and if you pat my leg or squeeze my knee one more time, you're gonna be pulling back a stump!"

O'Connell sat down and pulled me onto his lap. He was grinning broadly, and I had to stifle a giggle.

Kieran stopped typing, turned to see that Tommy wasn't joking, and then, quick as a flash, leaned over and kissed Tommy on the cheek.

"That's it! You're fucking dead!" Tommy screamed. Shoving his beer onto the table, he launched himself at Kieran, who was laughing so hard that he made only a halfhearted attempt to defend himself.

Liam and the other guys whooped and hollered at Tommy trying to give Kieran a hiding, throwing bits of their popcorn at them by way of encouragement. I looked around us, worried that the boys might be getting a little too rowdy for the other patrons, but the lanes on either side of us were empty, with most of the families down at the other end. I guessed the staff had taken one look at my boys and decided to separate us from the general population.

After their little scuffle, the guys settled down and got serious about their bowling. I thought this was a Saturday afternoon pastime for kids and elderly people—but wisely kept my opinion to myself. With how competitive they all were, you'd think they were contenders for an Olympic gold. When Tommy won with a final strike, I thought he was going to pee himself.

As I sat there cuddled into O'Connell and watching the boys laughing and messing with each other, I realized that this motley band of brothers were my brothers now. From the outside people viewed them as I once did—big, loud, and intimidating. They were all of that, but they were also mine, and there wasn't one of these boys, whether I was O'Connell's girl or not, who wouldn't stand between Frank and me. That wasn't friendship; it was family. That was what my mum should have done for me.

"You okay?" O'Connell whispered as he rubbed my back in gentle circles.

I turned to kiss him on the cheek. "I'm fine, baby. Just contemplating how much I love this bunch of misfits." I laughed as O'Connell actually scowled. "I love them like brothers, you idiot, not like I love you."

"This is one of those insecure moments I was telling you about. I need you to wrap yourself around me and kiss me until I'm feeling better," he pouted.

Giggling, I wrapped my arms around his neck and proceeded to cover him in silly, sloppy kisses. He grinned back, knowing this wasn't what he meant, but loving it anyway.

"Get a room," the guys all shouted, throwing popcorn at us.

"Fuck off." O'Connell grinned and hugged me closer.

We went from the bowling alley to the arcade, where O'Connell helped me play all the games I never played as a teenager. When the guys all gravitated toward the "shoot-'em-up" games, O'Connell gave me his little boy face. I rolled my eyes and told him to join them.

Armed with a pocketful of change, courtesy of my boyfriend, I went exploring. The guys found me half an hour later going head-to-head with thirteen-year-old Lily on the dance machine. She was absolutely flipping awesome at that thing. She'd spotted me milling about with a fistful of change and challenged me. I quickly realized that I'd been suckered, when I noticed the name "Lily M." appeared seven times on the top scorer's board. We were burning through the change pretty quickly, but my score for Shakira's "Hips Don't Lie" wasn't too shabby at all, and before the boys even got there, we'd drawn quite a teen crowd. As good as my score was, it wasn't enough to beat her, but I accepted my defeat with good grace and a little bow to the crowd.

A year ago I would never even have gone into a place like this, and here I was dancing in public and playing to a crowd.

My boys gave me the biggest cheer of all. I smiled but I knew my cheeks were burning red.

The rest of the day flew by in a myriad of happy memories, and it was a day that will stay with me for the rest of my life. It was the first day that I'd ever woken up happy and gone to bed the same way. We finally left the boys at the Royal Oak pub where the drinks were flowing as well as the women. I walked home hand in hand with the man I loved, and when he made me a cup of tea to take to bed after fixing my heating, I fell in love with him a little more.

* * *

I wouldn't say that from then on we spent every waking moment together, because we didn't. The very next day O'Connell was long gone before my alarm went off, back to Danny's brutal schedule. His next big fight was January, and he was taking this seriously.

We were talking about both our futures now. I had end of term exams before Christmas so my time was divided between class and the library, but it wasn't really that much of a hardship, given my love of math. Nikki struggled a little with some of the course material, but she was a quick study and a hard worker so, after a few study sessions, she clicked with some of the concepts that she didn't have the hang of in class.

I think we were both good influences on Max, Albie, and Ryan, who spent as many nights in the warm library as we did. I suspected that O'Connell or Liam had said something to Albie because none of the guys ever let me walk home alone. I was still cautious and had good reason to be, but the fear didn't own me anymore. I had a life, and I was busy living it, but those four days until the weekend were worth the wait.

O'Connell was so exhausted that sometimes he'd only make it

through the door long enough to shower and scarf down a meal before falling asleep with his head in my lap while I stroked my fingers through his hair. We were building a future together and our foundation was a million stolen, wondrous moments like this, and it was a foundation stronger than rock. Every love letter, every kiss, every laugh and shared memory—they were all tiny bricks that paved the road on which we walked. One day I would look back on the journey, and I'd know there wasn't a single one of those memories that I'd regret making.

That wasn't to say that we never argued though. There were days that he'd finish training and pick me up to see me chatting with one of the math geeks, and he'd lose his temper, until I reassured him that I wasn't going to leave him for a civil engineer or a physicist. There were other times when I'd see girls eyeing him up as though his clothes were made of edible chocolate spread, and I'd be grumpy, not wanting to admit why.

We were yet to have an argument, though, that didn't end up with one of us laughing. O'Connell loved it when I argued back. Bit by bit the timid little mouse who flinched before him was disappearing. When I raised my voice, which admittedly didn't happen often, it reminded him of how strong I'd become. That was the thing about love, I'd discovered. It wasn't about having a blissfully wonderful relationship where everything was always sunshine and roses. No matter how pure and beautiful your love was, life could be cruel and ugly. It would throw things at your relationship when you were tired and broke. It would be strained and tested through the worst of storms. Real love, though, the kind that saw couples live through sixty years of World Wars and recessions and still let them stare at each other on their deathbed with the same devotion that they felt on their wedding day, love like that, well, it lasted forever.

CHAPTER TWENTY-TWO

"Are you kidding me? Danny will absolutely feckin' kill us. There's no way you're dragging me into this," Kieran whined as I laid out my plan to the boys.

I turned toward O'Connell, giving him my best puppy eyes, knowing that, if I could rope him in, I'd have Kieran.

"I don't know, love. I'm not sure he's gonna like this. He's never mentioned his birthday before. I'm not convinced he wouldn't just tell us to feck off."

I grinned, knowing that O'Connell wouldn't tell me no. "Look guys, I'm not saying that we throw him a huge surprise party. The shock would probably give him a heart attack anyway. I'm just saying that it wouldn't kill you to put up a few balloons, sing 'Happy Birthday,' and give him a cake."

My suggestion was met with stony silence, and even the sight of them standing to attention with their arms folded was an emphatic no.

"Come on, pleeeeease," I begged.

"How did you even find out it was the old codger's birthday?" Liam asked.

"He needs to give his date of birth on his tax returns," I answered, ignoring the fact that I was completely abusing privileged information.

"Fine!" O'Connell surrendered at last. "We'll put up the balloons when he's out for dinner. You make the cake and meet us here at six. Kieran will pick you up in my car and give you a hand. You can sing 'Happy Birthday' while we stand behind you mumbling then we'll go straight back to training when Danny explodes and shouts at us for wasting his fucking time."

"Perfect." I smiled, and they all groaned.

I was sure O'Connell thought he'd put me off with that little rant about how much Danny would hate my plans, but I was tenacious, and all I heard him say was, "No problem, baby. What a fantastic idea. We'd love to help."

"Thanks, guys," I told them, knowing it was wrong to just let Danny's birthday pass us by.

"You are soft as shite with her, ya know," Liam chuckled to O'Connell.

"Like you could tell her no," he snorted.

"Fuck me, no." Liam carried on, as though I wasn't even in the room. "Especially when she does that doe-eyed thing. I don't know why they call you the Hurricane. The way she tramples all over us, she's more like one than you are."

"What the feckin' hell is going on here?" Danny barked as he walked in the office. "If you lot ain't got nothing better to do than stand round here gossiping like a bunch of old ladies, then you can all give me twenty-five burpees. I want every one of you sorry fat articles out in the gym now!" Danny barked, as he stomped out of the office with the boys following single file.

"I've changed my mind. I say we let the evil bugger's birthday ride," Liam groaned.

"Told you." Kieran pouted grumpily as he marched off to take his punishment.

"This better be a friggin' awesome cake, babe. Danny's gonna have me doin' burpees for a month for this," O'Connell warned.

He didn't look all that concerned, though. He could do twenty-five burpees in his sleep, even after the four hours of training that he'd already done. Yep, my man was a machine.

As it turned out my cake was friggin' awesome, and I should have received some sort of award for producing such a masterpiece in my little kitchenette. I'd made a square cake into a boxing ring and had used boxes of precolored fondant to make the figure of Danny sitting in an armchair in the middle of the ring, cigarette hanging from his mouth and reading a newspaper while a boxer was doing push-ups on the floor next to him.

The boys had loved it, and their gushing enthusiasm for the cake far outweighed mine for their effort with the balloons. About twenty of the smallest, saddest, most pathetic-looking balloons that I'd ever seen decorated the entrance to the office.

"Seriously! That's the best you could do?" I complained.

"He picked 'em," blamed Tommy, pointing at Kieran.

"It's not my fault," protested Kieran. "I didn't blow 'em up like that!"

They started squabbling among themselves, and I rolled my eyes, knowing that it was a pointless endeavor to complain anymore. There was nothing that we could do about it now, anyway. Popping the birthday candles into the cake, I waited for O'Connell, the only one who wasn't arguing, to give me the signal to light them.

"What the feckin' hell is going on in here?" Danny asked without his usual bark.

I burst into a joyful rendition of "Happy Birthday" with the guys mumbling along behind me as promised. When I was done I thrust the cake toward Danny and told him to make a wish. He looked at me hard, and I could practically hear the guys sucking in air as they held their breath, waiting to see which way he would go.

Very slowly Danny reached up to remove the half-burned cigarette that was hanging from his lips, blew out the candles, and replaced the cigarette. Everyone was eerily quiet, and Kieran filled the silence with his solitary party popper. It was all really quite tragic, and I could see the corners of Danny's mouth twitch, but he held back a smile and quietly said, "Back to training." The boys didn't need telling twice, and they legged it from the office like it was on fire.

"Seriously, you made them put up balloons?" Danny asked me when they were gone. Putting down the cake I gave him a great big hug, which he definitely wasn't expecting.

"It does them good to remember that birthdays are for celebrating," I told him. "Now sit down and open your present, and I'll make you coffee to go with your cake."

Sensing that he was about as used to receiving gifts as I was, I didn't want to embarrass him by watching, and set about making his coffee while he opened his gift. When I placed it down in front of him with a slice of birthday cake, he was still palming the butter soft leather tobacco pouch that I'd bought him.

"You're something else, you know that, sunshine?" He spoke quietly.

Standing up he gave me a quick kiss and no more was said. He sat down and tucked into his cake and coffee before putting the boys through their paces. I smiled to myself, knowing that we'd done the right thing.

* * *

Taking the time to bake Danny's cake had messed with my study schedule so I hit the books pretty hard after that. The long walks home from the gym or the library weren't quite so painful now that I had my gorgeous new winter coat. With his first signing bonus O'Connell had bought me a new dark gray fitted woolen coat along with a bright red cashmere scarf and matching gloves. He called them an early Christmas present but admitted there was no way he was letting me go any longer with just my thin summer jacket. I wanted to protest, but I was so grateful that I could have cried. There weren't any jewels or flowers in the world that could mean the same to me as that gift did.

The exams came and went, and I was relieved that the marathon study sessions had paid off because nothing in the tests came as a great surprise. Even Max, Albie, and Ryan seemed unusually happy that we'd made them study so much.

Unfortunately, as all of the gang went off to party, celebrating Christmas and the end of term, I had a shift at Daisy's. I spent so little time there now compared with my old shift rota that I was looking forward to catching up with Rhona and Mike. Unlike the Em of old, I actually engaged them in conversation, and I knew they'd be on tenterhooks waiting to hear how I did on my exams.

Half an hour after me, and ten minutes late for her shift, Katrina flounced in without a single apology for her tardiness and proceeded to take over all of the tables I'd been covering for her. So far I seemed to have gotten away with the whole vomiting-all-over-my-boyfriend incident relatively unscathed, so either Katrina had been so drunk herself that she didn't remember or she was saving up her ammunition for a day when she could really embarrass me.

As it was, I found myself caring less and less. All she could do was humiliate me and it wasn't as if I hadn't experienced worse. Feeling relaxed and happy that my exams were over and life was good, I hummed gently as I wiped down the tables then went to take an order from one of my customers.

"What can I get you?" I asked.

"Well, I believe you know what I wanted but thought better of giving it to me," O'Connell's mum replied.

"I mean, what would you like from the menu?"

"Let's cut the shite, shall we? I wouldn't put anything from this greasy spoon inside me. I'm here to talk about why my son has cut me off."

I refrained from pointing out that eating one of Mike's awesome Daisy burgers would be far less detrimental to her body than constantly plying it with alcohol. Sylvia was scary and intimidating, and she knew it, but my way of dealing with scary and intimidating was about to change. I wouldn't engage in a no-holds-barred slanging match with her. For a start I had far too much respect for Rhona and Mike for that, but above all else, it just wasn't me. My stand would be dignified but firm.

"Sylvia, I respect the fact that you're Con's mum, and we've discussed your concerns, but the bottom line is that we love each other and we want to be together. I understand that you have reservations about our relationship, but I really think that you should discuss those with Con and not me."

I was as polite and respectful as I could be, which, in the circumstances, was probably more than she deserved, but venom filled her face, and I didn't think this would end well.

"What do you know about love, you money-grabbing little whore? You saw an easy mark in my son, and you thought you'd jump along for the free ride!"

None of this was true, but that didn't matter to Sylvia. Despite my initial defense of her, O'Connell was right. I was the only thing standing between her and her meal ticket. This time, though, she was out of luck if she thought she could scare me off, because now I saw her for the cruel and evil bitch she really was, and when I thought about how the man I loved had been treated as a scared, hungry, innocent child, I was enraged.

"I love him enough to want to take care of him and, despite what you'd hoped for, your son and I are in this for the long haul. If you want to salvage whatever relationship you have left, then I suggest you come to terms with the idea. And please don't come to my place of work again. You aren't welcome here," I replied, shaking.

"What's wrong, Ma? Didn't get the message the first time we talked?" O'Connell spoke gently from behind me, making me jump a mile. Mike stood right behind him, and I was mortified by all of the attention.

"Cormac, what are you doing here?" his mum asked, genuinely shocked to see him.

"More to the point, what are you doing here? I was very clear when I told you not to go anywhere near Em and yet here we are."

"I was worried about you, Con. You're much too young to tie yourself down. At your age, you should be playing the field and enjoying yourself. You wouldn't listen to reason, and it's clear that lust has fogged up your brain so I've come in the hope that Emily has a little more common sense."

Everyone in the diner was openly staring at our little scene, and I really didn't want to be part of this train wreck.

"That's it, Ma. We're done. I've told you how I feel about Em. Even after you tried to chase away the only thing that's good and pure in my life, the only person who makes me happy. I gave you a chance to stay in touch with me if you just backed off. I don't make empty threats, so we're done. I've cleared the last of my stuff out of the house, and from now on there will be zero contact between us, so don't even bother asking for food or booze money. You've had the last penny out of me that you're ever gonna get. Everything I make from now on is going toward my and Em's future together.

"I can't stop you turning up to my fights, but you're barred from the gym, and I'll have you thrown out on sight if you come there. And if I ever find out you've so much as blinked in Em's direction again, you'll be sorry. Am I clear?"

O'Connell wasn't shouting, but he was so wound up by this

point that I could see him struggling to keep it together. As much as I loved that he'd defended me, this must be absolutely killing him. Sure, his mum was a complete bitch, but she was still his mum. To have to cut your only parent out of your life, just to have a chance at a happy future, was such a tragic thing.

He was cutting Sylvia out in the same way that I'd done with my own mother. We'd made our stand and decided that from now on our family would be of our own making, and it started with the two of us. O'Connell needed to remember that he wasn't alone anymore. Walking closer I said nothing but slipped my hand gently into his. As always I could feel the anger drain out of him. He looked down at me with love and gratitude in his eyes that told me everything he couldn't.

"Please, baby. I'm sorry for coming here, but don't cut me off like this," Sylvia pleaded. "You've got no idea how hard it is to raise a child as a single parent. You don't know what I've been through to put a meal on the table when you were growing up. I depend on the money you give me now for food. Please don't abandon me now just because you've met someone new."

It amazed me how mercurial she could be. In an instant she could swing from being nasty to playing the aggrieved, impoverished single mother perfectly.

"Fuck off, Ma. You didn't put food on the table when I was a kid. I did. You didn't raise me. I raised myself with a little help from Danny and Kieran's ma. I've been the fucking single parent, not you. If you want money, sell your house. You don't need a three-bedroom place to yourself. But whatever you're gonna do, fuck off and do it so that I can get on with the rest of my fucking life."

Even with my touch to ground him, Sylvia had pushed him pretty close to the edge. Her little play on the heartstrings was like Frank telling me that he was raping me for my own good. She'd played her last hand as far as O'Connell was concerned.

"Fine. If that's the way you feel, perhaps we'll talk again when you've calmed down," Sylvia said stiffly as she got out of the booth.

"No, Ma. There won't be any more talking. Go away and don't come back."

"You don't mean that. Without you I don't have anything to live for," she pleaded.

"Bullshit! I've lost count of the number of times you've threatened me with suicide. You do what you want, but that's your choice, not mine. And if you think that some halfhearted attempt will work like last time, you're wrong. I'll have you institutionalized for psychiatric problems and put on suicide watch."

Sylvia paled, and I wondered if that was exactly what she'd planned to do next. O'Connell had her flustered, and I guessed that didn't happen often. She smoothed down her skirt that was far too short for someone her age, picked up her handbag and, with one more death stare at me, walked out of the door.

"You okay?" Mike asked me. I nodded, and with a small sympathetic smile he headed back to the kitchen.

O'Connell looked around at the cafe's noisy patrons and all but growled as people hurried to divert their attention back to their own meals and away from our drama. O'Connell turned toward me and, in an unusual display of vulnerability, rested his forehead on my shoulder wearily.

"How did you know she was here?" I asked.

"Tommy said she was sniffing round the gym, looking for you, when I was running. I didn't know that she knew where you worked, but I just wanted to make sure you were all right."

He was quiet for a moment. Then, resting his hands on my waist, he looked me hard in the eyes. "You didn't run," he said quietly, almost to himself.

"I promised, didn't I?" I smiled.

CHAPTER TWENTY-THREE

A few days had passed since the exams, and I was pretty sure that Nikki and the gang had been partying for every one of them. I'd managed to pick up a few extra shifts at Daisy's with some of the other girls going home for the holidays. Christmas was only two weeks away, and the extra money would pay for a bit of Christmas shopping. I'd also promised Nikki, after a fair amount of arm bending, that I'd go for a night out with the guys before they headed home.

Walking home from my breakfast shift, I was feeling quite festive for once and looking forward to having someone to spend it with. By noon, the cafe had become pretty quiet, so after treating me to a delicious jacket potato, which Mike assured me I didn't need to pay for, as a customer had changed his mind about an order and it was going spare, sent me home half an hour early.

Although we hadn't actually had snow yet, the frost was brutal and the pavements were pretty treacherous, but I made it home without slipping and breaking anything. I collected my mail at the entrance and hummed Christmas carols all the way up to my flat. Shutting the door behind me, I chucked the keys on my desk and decided to have a cup of tea before checking my bills and attacking my heating.

Seven hours later O'Connell walked in through my door to find me sitting on my bed, the flat freezing cold, and my full cup of stone-cold tea on the table beside me. I was shaking, having held the letter in my icy fingers for so long, but I couldn't let it go.

"Shit!" he muttered, slamming the door behind him. He dumped his training bag and grabbed my face.

"What's wrong, baby? What happened?" he asked urgently. I couldn't let go of the letter so I told him what was in it.

"Mrs. Wallis wrote to me," I turned to look at him, "my old teacher."

"I remember who she is, sunshine," he encouraged.

"She said that her house was broken into. There was nothing in there with my address on it because she keeps that in her diary which she had with her."

"But she thinks it might be Frank, doesn't she? Looking for evidence of where you've gone," he guessed, seeing quickly where I was going with this.

I nodded my head and swallowed. "The thing is, she said that she filed away all my university acceptance letters but forgot to destroy them when I left. If it was Frank, he could have my full name now and a shortlist of universities where I might be. How long do you think it would take him to find me with that?"

"So change your name again and make it more difficult for him, but you're not running."

"I won't run," I whispered. "I promised you I wouldn't. But changing my name will take time and even then I don't know if it will stop him from finding me."

He gave me his most adorable grin as he offered me his solution. "Then use a different way to change your name and marry me."

The shock that had me clutching the letter now made me

drop it to the floor. "Thank you, but I don't want to get married just to change my name. It's kind of you to offer, but I can't," I protested.

"Then don't marry me to change your name. Marry me because there will never be another man in this world who loves you as much as I do. You're my best friend, my missing piece, and the only person who can make my world amazing just by being in it. Marry me because I promise you a lifetime of love and laughter and happiness."

He carried on seamlessly, as though he'd thought about this and wanted to get it out before he forgot any of it.

"I want to be your husband, sunshine. I want to know that you are, and always will be, the other half of me for the rest of my life. I know that people will say we're too young and that we have the rest of our lives, but people don't know shit about who we are and what we've been through. Give me one good reason why you don't think we should get married, and I'll give you a million reasons why I know we should."

He knew that he needed to stop if he ever wanted to hear my answer, but it was as if he was afraid to in case my answer was no.

"You are absolutely certifiable, you know that." I smiled at him.

"I know," he said, tucking one of my curls behind my ear.

"I love you, Em. I will always love you. Will you marry me?" he asked gently.

Leaning forward, I held his face reverently in my hands and kissed him softly. With tears running down my cheeks, I whispered, "Yes, I'll marry you."

O'Connell launched himself at me, smothering me with sloppy kisses. I couldn't help but laugh at his reaction. This strong, beautiful, crazy man adored me and wanted to be with me for the rest of my life. Should I have worried about what the world would think of our getting married so young and so quickly? Probably, but then most people had family and had never been truly alone like we had. Now we would be each other's family, and I know that the caveman in O'Connell wanted me to share his name.

"How quickly do you think we can pull this together?"

"You don't waste any time, do you?" I laughed.

"You have the most beautiful laugh in the world. It makes me sad that you've spent more time since I've known you crying than laughing. I promise you that I'm gonna change that. I promise to put a smile on your face every day that we're married. Even when I make you kick-me-in-the-balls mad, I'll make you smile again before you sleep. I know that I don't deserve you, but I'll work every day to try to be the man that you deserve."

"You're going to make me cry again," I admitted, choked up.

I couldn't believe he didn't think he deserved me, but then maybe the key to success in any relationship was to always be with someone you thought was better than you deserved.

He kissed me again until I pointed out something fairly obvious. "We don't have any money to get married. If we want to do this soon, it will have to be a quick Registry Office wedding."

Crawling onto the bed, he pushed me backward and climbed over me to nuzzle the side of my neck, making me laugh again.

"I'm not marrying you in some quick Registry Office ceremony. I want to get married in church."

"Then we'll set a date for early in the New Year and get married in church."

"Yeah, we're not waiting till New Year either."

"O'Connell, you can't have everything," I said exasperated.

"Watch me." He grinned. "Just leave it to me. I'll sort everything out."

"What are we going to do about Frank?" I asked worriedly.

"Nothing," he told me. "If it's okay with you, I'll move in here until we can afford a bigger place, and if that fucker comes after me or my wife, I'll make him wish he'd never been born."

"You shouldn't underestimate him," I warned. "He doesn't fight fair like you do."

"Baby, I only fight fair in the ring. If he has the balls to come, then let him come. You're not alone anymore."

I cuddled in close to my fiancé until I realized something. "Um, O'Connell. Do you want to jump in the shower?"

He laughed out loud. "You're not very subtle about telling me I stink."

"It's not that," I lied. "I just don't want you to catch cold because you're sitting round my flat in your sweaty training gear."

"I ran home from training to get in a few extra miles, and it's our flat now."

"Not until after the wedding it isn't," I told him. "I'm not living with you in sin."

"Whatever, sunshine. I'm pretty sure I can get you to sin even without the living." With that, he pushed my top up and kissed my belly, slowly working his way up to my breasts as he proceeded to show me just how sinful I could be.

* * *

O'Connell might not have officially moved in, but I was barely alone for a moment anymore. Until we were sure that Frank hadn't found me, one of the boys took me everywhere. It was like they'd organized some kind of rota, which was pretty spectacular for them as I was pretty sure they couldn't organize a piss-up in a brewery.

I have absolutely no idea what O'Connell said to Danny, and forever more it would stay between them. I knew that Danny did a fair bit of cursing and door slamming for a couple of days, but I didn't know whether that was because he wasn't happy about the wedding or because O'Connell had told him about

Frank. But nothing was said to me until O'Connell passed on the message that Danny wanted to see me in the gym on Saturday morning at 9 a.m.

"What, why?" I asked in a panic.

I didn't mind getting the talk about how irresponsible we were being, but I'd prefer to have O'Connell by my side when it happened. The gym was surprisingly busy when I got there, and O'Connell winked at me from across the room as he carried on with his hanging sit-ups.

"I've made you coffee," Danny told me as I walked into the office.

"Are you mad at me?" I blurted out. I couldn't care less what anyone else thought, but Danny mattered to me.

"Why the feck would you think that?" he asked, as he sat down in his chair and lit up a cigarette.

"Because you think we're too young, and it's too rushed," I answered truthfully.

"Do you think that, sunshine?" he asked, carefully.

"No," I replied without hesitation. "I love him. Time and age won't change that."

By now Danny must have known the full story so I didn't pull any punches. "He doesn't see me as a victim; he sees me as strong and empowered. In his eyes he's not good enough for me, when in reality, I'm not good enough for him. I want to marry him because he's the man I want to grow old with. Before him I didn't even have hope that I'd get to grow old. This shitty life takes away far more than it gives us, and if I've got a chance of happiness, I'm taking it."

"Well, then," he replied, "doesn't look like you need my blessin', does it?"

"I don't need it, Danny, but I'd like it. We both would. You might not know it, but you're important to both of us."

"Well, sunshine, you're important to me, too. You both are.

O'Connell told me that he was gonna marry you the first time he saw you at Daisy's. Stubborn fecker was right."

"He did?" I squeaked in amazement.

"I warned him off, but I knew he wouldn't listen. When he wants something, he barrels in like a bull in a china shop until he finds a way to get it. When that didn't work with you, he was lost. You threw him for six, and he had to change his ways to become the sort of person you needed. As soon as I saw that, I decided that I wouldn't come between you. You both make each other want to be better people, and that's a feckin' rare thing. Far too many couples drown each other in their own selfishness these days.

"Now I ain't sayin' things between you are gonna be easy. Con's got a promising career ahead of him, which means that you're gonna learn the ins and outs of this business, no matter what. Lord knows, girl, that there's gonna be enough obstacles trying to trip you up in the next few years so I sure as shite won't be one of 'em. You just remember that this is for life. When he pisses you off, you slap him upside the head and pull him back in line. You yell, you scream, you do what you need to do, but you stay and fight for each other and your marriage."

"I'm not going anywhere, Danny. Thank you," I told him and gave him a big, squeezy hug.

"Now why the feck are you getting all touchy-feely again?" he grumbled, although I noticed that he'd hugged me back.

"Oh, stop your moaning," I admonished and let him go with a kiss on his cheek. He muttered a curse, as though kissing and hugging me was some great hardship, and went back to drinking his coffee.

"So why did you want me to come in this morning?" I asked as I sat back down in the dues chair.

"If you promise not to get free with the hugs again, I'll tell you." He eyed me suspiciously.

"Promise." I smiled, drinking my coffee. He shifted around in his seat as though he was uncomfortable and didn't want to tell me something.

"It ain't right for you to walk down the aisle without a proper wedding dress. So Tommy and Kieran are taking you shopping today, and I'm paying."

"Danny," I choked, "thank you. It's very generous of you, but I can't accept. I've never been wedding dress shopping before, but I can't imagine that it's cheap."

"Huh," Danny huffed. "What do I need all the money I've got saved for? Now no more arguments. Drink your coffee 'cause them lazy feckers are gonna be here in a minute."

Speaking of which I could hear them arguing outside the door.

"Danny, it's only going to be a little wedding. I don't need a big, expensive wedding dress."

He laughed at that.

"You didn't really think that boy was gonna marry you in a Registry Office, did you? Christmas Eve in St. Paul's, you're walking down a proper aisle, in a proper church, so you need a proper wedding dress."

"What the fuck, Danny?" moaned Kieran, barreling in through the door. "That was supposed to be a surprise."

"Well, now it feckin' ain't," boomed Danny, and both the guys shrank back. It still made me smile to see how intimidated they were by him, given how tiny he was. I respected him and still thought him formidable, but to me he was like an armadillo now, hard on the outside, soft and squidgy on the inside.

St. Paul's was a beautiful church, and a Christmas wedding sounded so magical. I couldn't believe this was happening to me. How in the hell O'Connell pulled this off was a mystery and where had he found the time? His fight was three weeks away, and he was training relentlessly every day.

Despite Danny's worst fears, I hugged him again on the way out. "Thanks, Danny," I murmured. I accepted my gift graciously, knowing that there was little point in arguing. Between my new coat and my wedding dress, I was feeling majorly overwhelmed, but so very grateful.

"You're welcome, sunshine," he replied, giving my arms that were wrapped around him a quick pat. I left the office with Kieran and Tommy arguing about who was in charge of Danny's credit card, and went to find O'Connell. He was still doing hanging sit-ups, and it made me feel tired just to look at him.

"What?" he asked, when I stared but said nothing.

I couldn't watch him train without wanting him in the worst way. As though he could see where my thoughts were going, he hauled himself up to the top bar, unhooked his legs, and jumped down. With a quick look to make sure that we weren't being watched, he grabbed my hand and pulled me into the changing room. Without giving me time to protest, his firm, but gentle lips locked onto mine, and I was in heaven. He kissed me like he hadn't seen me in a month, and I was practically climbing up his body to get closer to him.

If I thought he had the body of a Greek god when I met him, it was nothing to the way he looked now. Day after day, week after week, and month after month of relentless training and clean living had sculpted his body to perfection. Since I'd begun cooking for the both of us, he taught me about what different foods would do to my body, about carbohydrates, proteins, fats, and vitamins. Now I looked at the nutritional information on foods before I bought them and stopped at the farmer's market for home-grown fruit and veg. It wasn't like I hadn't cared about what I was eating, but before Danny had given me a job, I was more concerned about the food that I could afford and how I would store it, rather than what it did to my body.

O'Connell's need was as urgent as mine. He picked me up

922

so that my legs wrapped around his waist and backed me up against the lockers with a bang.

"I wanna fuck you right now against my locker, baby," he growled. "I feel like I haven't been inside you for a month."

I moaned as he slid his tongue deeper into my mouth. When he talked like this, it used to shock me. Now I knew that he just liked to tell me how he was feeling, as he was feeling it. It took all I had not to take him up on his suggestion.

"You've probably got less than two minutes before Danny tells the boys to fuck off and comes to see why you're not training," I replied.

"I'm that hard I don't think I'll last two minutes," he moaned, and I giggled.

"Cormac O'Connell," Danny shouted from the gym, and I giggled again.

"I fucking love that sound." He smiled at my joy and carried on kissing me, his rock-hard cock pressed up against me.

"Cormac fuckin' O'Connell. I want twenty-five press-ups for every feckin' minute I have to spend looking for you."

"Go, love. He'll have you training all night, and I'd like to see my fiancé before I sleep tonight if it's all the same to you."

He let me down gently until my feet touched the floor, but carried on holding me in his arms.

"I like being called your fiancé," he said between kisses.

"Well, don't get too used to it. You'll be my husband in a week."

"You bet your arse I will be. Now go and blow some of that tight arse's money and get a dress that takes my breath away."

He kissed me long and hard enough to make me moan and for both of us to hear Danny mumble, "I'm too old for this shite," as he walked into the changing room. I guessed my fiancé wouldn't be making it home for dinner after all.

CHAPTER TWENTY-FOUR

It was an education to learn that you needed an appointment to get a wedding dress. Apparently you were supposed to get one months before the wedding, not days, to allow time for it to be made and fitted. Within an hour of being turned away or laughed out of no less than four dress shops, my earlier euphoria had dwindled, and the boys were getting more and more pissed. It wasn't so much that we couldn't get a dress, but more the attitude of some of the women in these places that was upsetting me and making them mad.

I was all ready to jack in the shopping trip and get married in my jeans when Kieran sensibly suggested a time-out. When the boys had each put away a full English fry-up, and I'd enjoyed a nice cup of tea, Tommy, who was feeling much better, phoned his mum. He explained what had happened, as she apparently knew all about the engagement, and ten minutes later she had gotten us an appointment in an hour at the Fairytale Boutique in Crouch End.

As soon as we walked in I knew that I would get my dress here. There was no word to describe the shop but magical.

Whereas most bridal boutiques that we'd been to were pristine, modern, and sterile, this place was enchanting. The solid oak floors had been lovingly treated and the cream walls, backlit with gentle lighting, were barely visible behind the elegant arrangements of pussy willow branches interspersed with fairy lights and baby's breath.

"Hello. You must be Emily." A beautiful young woman walked toward me and shook my hand. She was dressed smartly but simply, in a fitted gray shift dress with black heels, complemented by a diamond pendant necklace and studs. All in all, she couldn't have been much older than I was, but she had warm eyes and a really welcoming smile.

"Thank you for seeing us on such short notice."

"It's not a problem at all. I had a cancellation, so your timing is perfect."

I turned to introduce the guys, only to find Tommy hopping about from foot to foot like some kid hyped up on sugar who desperately needed the toilet and Kieran staring at the woman with his mouth open.

"This is Kieran and Tommy," I introduced. Tommy nodded his head toward her and gave a "what's up?" which made me roll my eyes. Kieran, as poleaxed as he appeared to be, stuck out his hand.

"It's nice to meet you both. I'm Marie."

"Urr...I'm Kieran," Kieran replied, and kept shaking her hand. I'd never seen Kieran so affected by a girl, and one who worked in a wedding dress shop no less. Usually that alone would be enough to give him hives. By Marie's blush, it seemed that Kieran's attraction wasn't one-sided.

"Do you think that it's too late for us to get a dress?" I asked after a while. They jumped back guiltily, and Marie clasped both of her hands together.

"Oh, usually I would be worried, but to be honest all my

dresses for the Christmas and New Year weddings have been delivered and I make and do the alterations on a lot of the dresses myself, so I'm sure we can find something for you. You might not get it until the afternoon before the wedding, but I'm sure I can help you out."

"Thank you so much." I sighed deeply, relieved beyond words that I wouldn't have to marry the man of my dreams without a dress.

"I'm so sorry, gentlemen. You'll have to sort yourselves out for suits. I only stock ladies' dresses in here."

"Don't need suits. We're the bridesmaids," Tommy deadpanned.

To give her professional credit, Marie didn't laugh at him but eyed him as though she were mentally sizing him up for a bridesmaid dress.

Kieran elbowed Tommy in the stomach, hard. "He's kidding. We're fine, thanks."

Marie smiled as though she wasn't quite sure of them both but guided them to a plump, inviting-looking sofa at the back of the shop. "If you gentlemen would like to take a seat, I'll get Emily ready. Can I offer you anything to drink?" she asked.

Tommy opened his trap, ready to give her his order when Kieran elbowed him again and mumbled, "We're fine, thanks."

With a small smile and a nod of acknowledgment to Kieran, Marie guided me to the dressing room at the back of the shop. "I'm not sure if you have anything in mind that you'd like, but I took the liberty of racking up some dresses that I know I can make or adjust on short notice."

All of the dresses were absolutely amazing. "These are gorgeous," I told her, stunned.

"Thanks." She smiled. "These are all my designs. We'd have to send away for a dress by any other designer and there just isn't the time."

"Wow. You're very talented," I mused, completely truthful.

Each dress was delicate and ethereal and fit in with the theme of the shop beautifully. I tried a couple on, and Marie pinned them at the back to give me an indication of how I'd look when they were fitted to my size. I loved them all, and I knew it was going to be a tough decision.

"Emmmm . . ." Tommy whined as he walked bold as brass into the fitting room. "You've been ages."

Marie looked shocked at his behavior, but to be honest, I was surprised that Kieran had kept Tom out for as long as he had.

"Fuck me, Em, you're gorgeous. If I knew how you looked in a wedding dress, I'd have got in there first."

"For fuck's sake, Tom, what if you'd walked in and seen her in her underwear? Con would have blackened up your eyes so bad that you'd still be blind at the wedding," Kieran said, walking in behind him.

"Sorry, Marie," Kieran apologized, red-faced at seeing her expression.

"It would have been worth it," said Tommy dreamily, obviously imagining what I looked like in my underwear.

Recovering her composure, Marie pulled back the heavy brocade curtain that separated the fitting room from the main shop and pointed. "Out!" she ordered them, and Kieran went immediately back to his seat without argument.

"But she's taking ages," Tommy moaned again.

"This is the most important day of her entire life, and you're making her feel bad. She's going to pick any old dress in a minute rather than the dress of her dreams, just to please you. Is that what you want?"

"No," he admitted shamefully. "Sorry, Em. Take as long as you like," he apologized and left.

"How did you do that?" I asked. This woman could have been a nursery teacher if she wasn't so awesome at making dresses.

"I have three younger brothers," she explained. "Now let's find you that dream dress."

Five dresses in, and I found it. The dress was sheer chiffon over a silk-satin dress. Delicate antique lace was sewn entirely over the straps and bodice of the gown, and a long panel of lace ran down the back of the dress, trailing around the full skirt of the train. The fitted silk satin that could be seen beneath the chiffon was strapless, with a sweetheart neckline, and with some alterations it would be fitted to my body until it flared out from the thigh. The back of the dress was cut quite low beneath the chiffon so that you could see the full effect of the lace across my back, and the whole dress was a soft ivory color making it classy but sexy at the same time. I loved it and knew that O'Connell would, too.

"Please tell me that you love this one as much as I do," Marie told me. "This is perfect for you."

This was the one. "I love it," I whispered, and I would have given anything right now to have a mother who I could share this moment with. I didn't know whether most brides got emotional or whether Marie could sense how I was feeling, but she turned and gave me a big hug.

"You're going to be a wonderful bride, and your fiancé is a very lucky man," she comforted.

"Thanks," I sniffed. This poor girl didn't know me at all, but a hug was exactly what I needed.

"Wait here. We need a glass of something to celebrate the occasion, and I think the boys need a treat for their patience."

She left me in front of the mirror turning from side to side as I admired the dress and returned a few minutes later with a delicious glass of champagne. I'd never tasted it before, but once you got used to the bubbles going up your nose, it was wonderful.

"Now let's get you fitted properly," Marie announced. I looked around the dress for a price tag.

"What's wrong?" she asked.

"Um. I was just looking to see how much it was," I admitted.

I was embarrassed, but still, I needed to know. The dress really didn't look cheap, and although Danny had offered to buy one for me, I didn't want to abuse his generosity.

"It's already paid for, lovely. I spoke to the guys when I got them a drink. They phoned Mr. Driscoll with the price of the dress, fitting, and a budget for accessories, and he approved payment on the condition that I wasn't to disclose the cost to you."

With the new tears that sprang up, it took two more glasses of champagne and a bunch of tissues before we actually got round to the fitting. I didn't think that any of the veils suited me, so in the end I settled on a small antique comb to wear with my hair up. The selection of shoes Marie kept in stock were as beautiful as the dresses, but having spent my life in flats, I didn't think that the aisle was the best place to learn how to walk in heels. Luckily, I wasn't the only bride to have ever felt this way, and adding magic to her other talents, Marie produced the perfect pair of off-white Converse. I'd have no problem dancing the night away in these, and I'd still get to wear them after the wedding.

"By the time I've finished your dress, no one will even know you're wearing them," she reassured me. I drew the line at jewelry. I could only imagine that Danny had shelled out over a thousand pounds already, and the dress alone was more than I could ever have hoped for.

"What's your favorite color?" Kieran asked me.

"Blue," I replied automatically. "Why?" I asked.

"Because Con wants to know," he replied as if this explained everything, and wandered off to talk some more on his phone. Tommy was rooting through all the racked bridesmaid dresses.

"What are you doing, Tom?" I asked.

He didn't pause as he answered, "I'm looking to see which one of the dresses suits my color palette best."

"Why?" I asked, trying really hard not to laugh.

"Because I'm bored," he admitted.

"You're so gay," Kieran told him, apparently having finished his own conversation and catching the tail end of ours.

"Fuck off. You're gay for saying I'm gay."

"Now children," I admonished, "it doesn't matter if you're gay or straight. Being gay isn't an insult, so grow up and play nice."

Kieran turned toward Tommy. "Sorry, Tom. I know you're not gay. You're just very effeminate, and I support you in your life choices."

"I'm gonna fuck you up," Tommy warned him until Marie interceded again.

"You land one punch inside my shop, Tommy, and I'm calling your mother."

I have never seen Tommy jump to apologize so quickly. I really needed to meet Tommy's mum. She must be quite formidable to have this effect on him.

"So are you coming to the party then?" Kieran asked Marie.

"What party?" I asked him, wondering if asking her along to a house party was such a good idea. My first house party experience had been less than stellar.

"Your wedding party," Kieran explained. "You wouldn't mind Marie coming, would you?"

Marie looked completely mortified, and I was too stunned myself to reassure her. "I'm having a wedding party?" I squeaked at him, while trying really hard not to jump up and down.

"Yes, but I'm not telling you anything else. Con would kick my arse."

"I don't want to know." I put my hands up. "You guys have done a fantastic job so far, and given that I thought I'd be having just a quick Registry Office wedding, I'm happy to go along with everything."

Letting the groom organize everything would be most brides' idea of hell. But the thing was, Con always wanted better for me than I wanted for myself.

"Marie, I hardly know anyone here, and it would be great to get to know you better. So if you'd like to come, you're more than welcome. I have no idea where or when the party is, but if you give Kieran your number, he can let you know."

"I'd like that," she replied genuinely. Handing him a business card, she said that the boutique's number and email address were on the card if he'd like to let her know when and where. It gave Kieran a way to get in touch while still keeping it cool and professional.

For someone who was used to women hanging all over him and trying to tattoo him with their numbers, Keiran seemed baffled by her cool indifference. He knew that she was as attracted to him as he was to her, but kudos to her for not giving in to him. Kieran needed the chase until he got to know her better. He was O'Connell's best friend and brother. I wanted for him the same happiness that we'd found.

"Not that this hasn't been really fun, but can we go now?" Tommy whined.

Marie looked at her diary and booked me in another dress fitting for the day before the wedding so she could do any on-the-spot alterations at that time.

"Come on then, Tommy. Let's go," I told him, which earned me a resounding, "Yes!" and him a frown from Marie.

We all told her good-bye, and after a few more minutes' procrastination from Kieran, left the shop.

* * *

"Did you get a great dress, babe?" O'Connell mumbled sleepily as he fell into bed next to me and hauled me up against him.

"I got a beautiful dress. But I feel bad putting Danny to all that expense for a dress I'll only wear once," I admitted.

"You bet your arse you'll only wear it once," he told me as he rubbed his hands on the outside of my thigh making me smile.

"I thought you were tired," I told him.

"Sunshine, the day I'm too tired to get hard around you is the day you get to put me in the ground."

He pulled me back even harder as he pushed against me, and I groaned. As tired as I was, I couldn't get enough of this man. Shocking the hell out of him, I flipped over, pushed him on his back, and threw my legs over his hips to straddle him. My confidence with sex was growing every day that we were together.

He picked me up by the waist, like I weighed nothing at all, and adjusted me so that I was pressed hard against his cock. Sitting up, his mouth latched on to mine, and he speared his hand in my hair, pulling me toward him. With his free hand, he pushed up his T-shirt that I'd commandeered for bed and palmed my breast, scraping the pad of his thumb against my nipple and making me groan.

"Naked. Now," he commanded caveman style. Flipping me onto the bed, he dragged the T-shirt over my head and my panties down my legs until I was naked and exposed beneath his huge, cut torso. His eyes traveled their way down my body, and like every time we made love, no matter how hot and heavy, his gaze was so reverent I felt like he was worshipping me.

I committed every angle and curve of his body to memory, counting my blessings anew that we'd found each other. His dark skin against my pale, his hard body against my softness, his straight, dark hair against my wild, blond curls, he was my complete opposite in every way, but his soul was the other half of mine. He was the loud to my quiet, the confidence to my shyness, the rage to my pain. Separately we were broken and alone. Together we were blissfully happy and complete, and every time that we made love was a celebration of that. Right now, and every time that we were together, I felt like I could take on the world.

His lust-filled eyes raked themselves over me as he pulled down his boxers. The instant that he was naked and protected, he was inside me. His thumb gently stroked my nipple as he thrust slowly in and out. The combined sensation sent tremors shooting straight to my core. His dark head replaced his hand, and he pulled my hardened nipple into the warmth of his mouth and tenderly teased it with his tongue.

I was so close that I arched my back, pushing my breast deeper into his mouth. I was desperately close to release when he abruptly pulled out and effortlessly flipped me onto my stomach. We've never made love like this, and I was nervous but excited. Not being able to see his face added to the anticipation of what he might do next, but I didn't have to wait long to find out. His touch gently skimmed my thighs, and he parted my legs carefully as he encouraged me up onto my knees.

"I love your arse," he told me, smoothing his hand over it.

His hand was so close to touching me where I needed it most that a little shiver ran through my body. The anticipation heightened everything, and I felt like I was standing on the edge of the abyss, waiting for O'Connell to grab my hand and pull me in.

Sensing my need, he pushed two fingers gently in and out of me, and I cried out. His other hand reached around and thumbed my clit in small circles. It was too much and too deep, and I felt myself climbing that invisible wall, desperately chasing my orgasm. I was almost there when he pulled out his fingers and replaced them with his cock, thrusting hard until he was fully seated inside me. It was too much and I whimpered, pleading with him to let me come. He pounded into me relentlessly, and I pushed back with every thrust, wanting this as much as he did. I begged that I couldn't take any more, when he rubbed one last gentle circle around my clit, and I was done. My orgasm crashed over me in waves that seemed to go on forever, and as though my release had triggered something in O'Connell, he covered my breasts with his dark, calloused hands and pulled my body hard against his, riding the crest of his own orgasm and filling me with his heat. I collapsed onto the bed, boneless and sated, and he did the same, pulling me into his body.

"I can't believe I get to do this forever," he admitted. "Sometimes I wake up and I see your beautiful hair spread across the pillow and I think I've dreamed you. I'm too scared to go back to sleep, or leave for training, in case you disappear and then I remember that you're mine, and suddenly it's a brand-new day."

I didn't have the words to tell him that I felt the same. If only math was a language you could speak, I'd be a poet.

"I love you, O'Connell," I told him.

"I love you, too, baby."

CHAPTER TWENTY-FIVE

O'Connell's friends seemed to take the news of our engagement a lot more calmly than mine did. Nikki was the only one whom I told in person, relying on the fact that within ten minutes of telling her, all our friends would know anyway. That girl could get out an alert on social media faster than the CIA could get information out of the Pentagon. Military communications were missing out if they didn't snap her up straight from university.

"What the fuck!" she was still screaming at me, and jumping up and down. "Ohmygod, Ohmygod, Ohmygod," she carried on screaming.

Her completely over-the-top reaction made me smile, and it was heartwarming to share all my excitement with someone.

"How is it possible to organize a wedding in less than two weeks?" she asked.

"To be honest I haven't had to do much other than pick my dress and stuff. O'Connell has organized the rest," I explained to her.

"Oh, dear God," she moaned dramatically.

"Yep," I replied happily. "I have none of the stress and hassle that goes with organizing a wedding."

"Well, at least you're not a bridezilla. Seriously, some people lose their minds when they get married. Still I can't believe you're not waiting longer. I didn't even know that you were engaged until five minutes ago."

"Nikki, neither of us has very much money, you know that. Waiting another year isn't going to change our situation, and I wouldn't spend a year's worth of savings on a wedding anyway. I love him, and he loves me. We want to make a commitment to each other, and all the rest of the wedding stuff, as lovely as it is, to me it's just trimmings." I shrugged.

I wasn't at all flippant about the commitment that I was making, but as long as O'Connell was waiting at the end of the aisle for me, I knew I'd be fine. But Nikki clearly had something on her mind. I really hoped that she wasn't going to try to talk me out of this.

"What's wrong?" I asked.

"I know it's stupid, and it's only a small wedding, but can I be your bridesmaid?" she asked me sheepishly.

"I would love you to be, but I can't afford a dress or anything. Besides, won't you be going home for Christmas?"

"Girl, if you think I'm missing this wedding, you're crazy!" She smiled, pleased to have gotten her own way. "I can get my own dress. Now what color is your bouquet so I can get a dress to match?" she asked.

"I have no idea. O'Connell asked me my favorite color the other day and I told him it was blue, but you're better off asking Kieran if you want to know the details."

It was fortuitous timing that Nikki's phone buzzed with a text message. After a few seconds she started bouncing around happily again.

"Kieran just texted me an invite. Apparently they've all gone out by text, but Con wanted Kieran to wait before texting me so that you could tell me yourself."

"Did he tell you anything about what they've organized?" I asked curiously.

"Yep. But I'm sworn to secrecy. Now get your arse up and get ready. Tonight's your hen night."

I groaned because I hardly knew any girls and I *really* didn't want to do the whole cheesy hen night thing.

"Relax. The guys have organized a combined stag and hen night because O'Connell can't drink and is refusing strippers, and Tommy wants to let his hair down with the girls."

I rolled my eyes, but the memory of Tommy shaking his thing to The Weather Girls still made me smile.

* * *

We made it to O'Donnell's pub to find all our friends in great spirits and downing pints like it was the night before Prohibition went into effect. My man was sitting in the middle of the guys with a pint of orange juice and lemonade and looking fine. His intense gaze held mine as I walked the length of the bar, and as soon as I was in touching distance, he had me in his lap, his soft lips pressed hard against mine.

His kiss was wild and electric. It was a reminder of everything he made my body feel and a promise of everything he was still going to do to me. The slide of his tongue across mine made me moan into his mouth and instantly he was hard beneath me. Our lips parted and he rested his forehead against mine.

"Why does it feel like I haven't seen you for a week?" he complained.

"Because Danny makes a day's training seem like it goes on for a week?" I chuckled.

"Can we go home yet?" he whispered.

"Yes, please," I agreed.

"Seriously, how soon do you reckon we can slip out of here unnoticed?"

"No way!" Kieran grinned, placing a drink down in front of me. "You two are off the market for good, and this is your last send-off before you commit to a life sentence. Now it's bad enough that Danny's bitch here is banned from drinking, the least you can do is watch us all get pissed in your honor while I tell Em every story and dirty little secret I know about you."

"Don't listen to a fucking word he says." O'Connell grinned.

Tommy looked at us a little drunk, a little shocked, and a lot bewildered. "I still can't believe you guys are doing this. I mean, in theory, Em, I would marry you in a heartbeat, but fuck! Sex with only one person for the rest of your life! It sounds a little extreme, don't you think?"

"Did anyone ever tell you you're about as shallow as a puddle," Nikki told him.

"Hey," replied Tommy, looking all wounded. "There's no need to be a bitch. I was just saying, that's all."

"What are we talking about?" Albie asked as he and Ryan walked over from the bar. Liam immediately shifted over to make room for them at the table.

"Only being able to shag one bird for the rest of your life," updated Tommy.

"And being a bitch," Nikki chimed in.

"There we have it. That's our toast then," added Kieran.

"To bitching and hitching," Kieran called out and held up his glass.

"To bitching and hitching," everyone else chimed in and slammed back their drinks.

"Fuck me," O'Connell mumbled, burying his head in the crook of my neck. "Remind me not to let any of these arseholes do a speech at our wedding, especially not Kier," he told me, and I smiled at the craziness of thinking that we'd have any degree of control over these boys at the wedding.

Despite my reticence it was a pretty awesome night. O'Connell was happier than I'd ever seen him, and Kieran was right to make us come out like this, even if O'Connell couldn't drink. Perhaps this was why stag and hen nights were thought up in the first place. To be surrounded by our friends who celebrated the commitment that we were about to make, who supported us in our decision, even if they didn't understand it, was pretty special.

A few hours later we were at a club, and my feet were killing me from all the dancing we'd done. Desperate for a drink I was about to abandon Nikki when a strong pair of hands grabbed my hips and pulled them back so that my rear was pressed against a rock-hard erection. I smiled, smelling O'Connell's aftershave and the delicious scent of his skin. Tipping my head back against his shoulder, I let him guide our hips to the rhythm of the song. He pushed aside my hair with his nose and laid tiny, little nibbling kisses along my neck that make me damp and needy. When he reached my ear, he nipped lightly at the lobe and whispered to me as he spread one huge hand across my stomach, making the ache even worse.

"Three days, baby, and you're all mine."

His deep voice whispering to me in the dark was so erotic. I couldn't wait to get home so that he could give me what I wanted. He knew exactly what he did to me, but two could play at that game, and I had the same power over him that he had over me.

"I'm already yours," I replied, knowing it was true.

"Yeah, but in three days, you'll have my name forever. Do you know how fucking hard that makes me, knowing you'll be my wife?"

"Mrs. O'Connell," I mused happily.

"Babe, get used to saying it, 'cause on our wedding night I'm gonna make you scream it."

The anticipation of knowing he meant everything he said had me imagining everything that he was going to do tonight. As the tempo of the music increased, he ground his pelvis against me to the beat, and I did the same. The whole evening had been foreplay for what was to come, and my skin was on fire.

This virile mountain of a man exuded confidence and self-assurance. He was the toughest, most dangerous man in here, and he knew it. That self-confidence was like a pheromone to women who all wanted to be owned by him. Those amazing, wolf-like eyes found me wherever I was and told me that I was his and he was mine. It didn't help that his intense stare made me instantly wet. He used this to his advantage, often.

"Let's go, baby. If I don't get to sink myself into that gorgeous body of yours soon, then I'm gonna take you inside this club."

The thought of doing something so personal, in such a public place, was horrifying. O'Connell had given me confidence in my sexuality, but there was a limit as to how far that confidence extended. I turned to face him and wound my arms around his neck. "Just let me go to the toilet and grab my jacket and we'll go," I promised.

His hungry lips found mine, and he kissed me like it was the last time he'd ever see me. His huge body wrapped around mine made me feel tiny and cherished, and I kissed him harder, knowing that it made us both hungrier. His hands never left my hips as he guided me back to our table, where I left him with the boys to go and find the bathroom.

"I'll come with you," Nikki volunteered.

Tradition dictated that we'd make friends with the small posse of women in the toilets, and tonight was no different. It was packed with women fighting each other, like territorial jungle animals, for the tiniest scrap of mirror to refresh their makeup.

They made us smile as they recounted, with enthusiasm, their relative successes or failures of the night.

I'd had such a wonderful time I figured nothing could sour my good mood. Fate often reminded me that I was wrong, and it was at that point that I ran straight into Katrina. It was patently clear from the way that she was staggering around that she was absolutely out of her mind drunk. I really shouldn't judge. It wasn't too long ago that I was in her shoes, publically vomiting on my boyfriend, no less.

"Well, look who it is," Katrina slurred. "Miss hoity fucking toity, out celebrating her engagement."

"Hello, Katrina. How are you?" Relishing the fact that my relative sobriety gave me the moral high ground, I made a conscious decision not to sink to her level.

"Why are you getting married then?" she asked me, completely ignoring my question.

"Not that it's anyone's business but ours, but we're getting married for the reason that people usually marry. We love each other, and we want to spend the rest of our lives together."

"Oh, fuck off," she scoffed loudly, looking completely unbalanced. "Everyone knows you're up the duff. Getting knocked up is the only way you could trap a man like O'Connell. So as far as I'm concerned, he's fair game."

Nikki lunged forward as she got ready to put her in her place, but I put my arm out to stop her. I wasn't just O'Connell's girlfriend anymore. In three days I would be his wife so it was about time I stood up for myself and showed everyone what that meant.

"I'm not pregnant, Katrina. Con hasn't been trapped into anything. He's marrying me because he wants to. If you want to know why he's with someone like me and not you, look in the mirror. You're so full of hate and envy it makes you ugly on the outside. Take my advice. Stop being a bitch and find your own man. That having been said, if you insist on coming after mine . . . bring it on."

I didn't shout or scream at her. I just laid it all on the line with as much dignity as I could muster. What she did with it was up to her, but I was done being a doormat. I would fight for O'Connell, but I didn't need to. If he ever found out about all of the attitude she'd been swinging my way, he'd shoot her down in seconds.

"Fuck off," she yelled back at me again. "You might think your shit doesn't stink, but you're no better than I am. Cormac might be all about you now, but he won't stay away from girls like me for long. I can give him what he needs. So the next time he goes out with the boys and comes home smelling of my perfume, you won't need to wonder what happened, because I'll be happy to fill in the details."

"Good-bye, Katrina," I said.

"That's it?" Nikki questioned as we walked off. "That's all you're going to say to her after the shit she just said to you?"

"What's this?" O'Connell asked, hearing the tail end of our conversation as we reached the table. He pulled me onto his lap by the belt loops of my jeans and listened intently as Nikki recounted the whole conversation.

"Who the fuck does she think she is?" O'Connell roared and tried to move me to stand up. Winding my arms around his neck, I kissed him hard and forced him back down.

"Are you with me because you feel trapped?" I asked.

"No, baby, you know I'm not," he pouted.

"Are you going to get bored with me in a few years?"

"No, I . . ." I cut him off again with a kiss.

"And are you going to be sleeping around with anyone else when I'm not there?"

"Fuck, no. You know it's me and you for life," he replied angrily.

"Then what difference does it make what she says about us? I'm yours and you're mine . . ."

"And fuck everyone else, right?" he finished with a smile.

"Exactly," I replied.

"I fucking love you," he mumbled, kissing me.

"Shit. I'm shocked that Danny lets you anywhere near Con on fight day. You kiss the fight right out of him," chuckled Liam. He and Albie seemed to be getting on really well, and I liked seeing the guys bonding.

O'Connell was getting impatient, and I could feel the evidence of his desire growing beneath me.

"Okay, baby, let's go," I told him with a kiss. He practically jumped out of his seat in his eagerness to get me home. After an emotional good-bye to everyone and a promise to see them all at the wedding, we left.

"I am so sick of being cold," O'Connell moaned, as we walked into the freezing cold flat. "Why don't you jump in the shower, love, and get warm, and I'll warm up the bed?" he suggested, waggling his eyebrows. I laughed at his playfulness, pleased that he hadn't let Katrina sour our good mood.

"Are you sure you don't want the shower first?" I asked.

"Nah, I'm good," he replied.

I grabbed one of his T-shirts off the chair, some clean underwear from the drawer, and headed to the bathroom. The shower was tiny, but the blistering heat of the pounding water felt almost luxurious. I tied back my hair to avoid washing it, knowing that there was no way it would be dry before I fell asleep. The T-shirt came to mid-thigh and held the slight scent that was purely O'Connell. I marveled at how lucky I felt, knowing he belonged to me. I was secure and happy and looking forward to a future that was worlds away from the life I had led a year ago. It felt like a gift that I would happily spend the rest of my life earning.

Knocking off the bathroom light I opened the door to a run-way of candles. Nightlights lined the hallway on either side, leading to the main room, which was all lit up. On every available surface were pillar church candles of different sizes, burning their pure white wax. Every space between was filled with tea lights. They made my crappy flat beautiful and roman-tic. In the middle of the room O'Connell stood in only a pair of half-unbuttoned jeans and holding the biggest bouquet of sun-flowers that I'd ever seen. Where he got sunflowers at Christmas I'll never know. Gone was the self-assured cocky fighter, and in his place was a scared little boy, opening his heart to me.

"This is amazing," I whispered and covered my mouth with my hands in shock. I walked toward him, and he handed me the bouquet, which was almost bigger than me.

"How . . . ?" I asked.

"I paid one of the kids at the gym to drop off the flowers and candles while we were out."

He tucked a wayward curl behind my ear, pulled out a small wooden box from his pocket, and sank to one knee.

"I wish I knew the words to tell you how much I love you and how much you've changed my life. Meeting you was like seeing the sun for the first time after a lifetime of living in the dark. I know you can do so much better than me, but if you'll have me, I promise to spend the rest of our lives fighting to deserve you. Emily Maria McCarthy, will you marry me?"

He opened the box, and inside was the most amazing ring that I had ever seen. Instead of the traditional solitaire diamond, he held a beautiful antique-looking sapphire surrounded by smaller diamonds.

"Blue," I whispered to myself. "My favorite color is blue."

I was rooted to the spot, wondering if this was all some cruel dream where I'd wake to find I'd imagined the whole thing. I'd already agreed to marry him so I had no idea why he looked so nervous. Dropping to my knees in front of him, I held his strong, handsome face between my hands.

"I didn't know that it was possible to love or trust a person as much as I do you. You make me happier than I have any right to be, but now that I've found you, I'm not letting you go. I'd be honored to be your wife."

"Thank fuck for that," he replied, in the way that was so typically him. He grabbed me by the waist and kissed me hard, pulling us to the floor and almost catching my hair on fire. I yelped and giggled at the same time, giddy with happiness. Taking the ring from the box, he slid it onto my finger, and it was a perfect fit.

"How could you possibly afford this?" I asked, in awe.

"I sold my car," he admitted sheepishly.

"O'Connell, no," I cried, feeling horribly guilty.

"It's okay," he reassured me. "There'll be other cars, but I'll only have one wife. Besides, we can put what I've got left toward the deposit on our own place someday."

"Thank you," I told him with tears in my eyes, admiring how the ring sparkled in the candlelight.

"You're welcome." He beamed, and his huge grin was infectious.

"Now get to bed, wench," he yelled, throwing me over his shoulder and carrying me effortlessly to bed. "I've got plans for this gorgeous body."

CHAPTER TWENTY-SIX

The morning of my wedding I woke up completely disoriented. It didn't help that my fiancé, whose great hulking presence took up most of the room in my bed, wasn't with me. I'd grown used to waking up next to him so quickly that I'd almost forgotten the immediate sense of panic when he wasn't there. O'Connell was so concerned about my safety that I just didn't worry about it as much when he was around. The front door slammed shut with a loud bang, just as I remembered that I'd spent the night at Nikki's. Loudly and proudly the sound of her voice filled the room as she la-la-la'd her way through "Here Comes the Bride."

"Wake up, bitch. The bestest, most awesome bridesmaid in the world has brought you breakfast in bed."

I salivated as I inhaled the aroma of expensive coffee and could have kissed Nikki as she handed me a cup along with a fresh Danish pastry.

"This is my favorite breakfast." I beamed.

"Well, you can thank your husband-to-be for the heads-up. Now move your butt across. I'm freezing."

She climbed fully clothed into bed next to me and switched

on the television. We had an amazing breakfast watching *The Goonies*, and it couldn't have been a better start to my day.

"Are you nervous?" she asked me.

"A little," I admitted, "but mostly I'm just excited."

"Well then, princess." She grinned. "Let's get this show on the road."

Three hours later I'd been buffed, exfoliated, plucked, and curled. My makeup was delicate and simple looking, giving me that natural, ethereal look that most brides wanted. Nikki had fastened my hair into a beautiful loose knot at the back of my head and inserted the antique comb above it.

A huge bang sounded on the door, making me jump.

"I'll get it." Nikki smiled.

She returned with a beautiful bouquet of royal blue and white flowers for me and a smaller version of the same bouquet for herself.

"Liam just dropped them off," she explained, setting them down. "I take it all back about letting a man organize your wedding. Con is totally hired as my wedding planner when I finally pick a victim."

I start taking deep breaths, knowing that I was seconds away from bawling like a baby. I really didn't want to ruin Nikki's makeup job.

"Here," Nikki said, thrusting some tissues at me. "If you're losing it over some flowers, you've got no chance of holding out for the rest of the day."

Nikki left me a glass of champagne and a bunch of tissues while she went to get ready. An hour later she came out of the bathroom wearing a gorgeous, knee-length royal blue halter dress. The skirt was floaty and delicate, but the ruched bodice fit her every curve. It showed off her figure perfectly.

"Nikki, you look stunning!" I exclaimed in awe.

She'd ditched her traditional red hair earlier in the week in favor of a rich chocolate brown, which curled down her back in waves. Simple silver jewelry complemented her delicate silver strappy heels perfectly, and I was floored by how beautiful she looked.

"I don't scrub up badly, do I?" She grinned, admiring her figure in the mirror.

"Kieran and Tommy are going to bust something when they see you in that dress." I smiled.

"Well, they have to catch me first," she said with a wink. "Now let's get you into that dress."

Marie, being the absolute superstar that she was, had spent nearly all yesterday making alterations to my dress so that it fit perfectly. Unlike most customers who were fitted in the shop, I spent nearly the whole day camped out in her back sewing room so that we could get the dress finished in time. I made myself as useful as I could, making lots of cups of tea and running out to grab her some lunch. By the end of the day, I had a perfectly fitted and absolutely stunning wedding dress and a new friend. I was thankful for both in equal measures.

Nikki fastened the last of the silk buttons just as her phone vibrated. Checking her message, she looked out of the window and yelled, "Taxi's here."

I was excited that it was finally time. But at that moment I couldn't help but feel a little sad, too. My dad should be the one walking me out to the car, and I wondered if he'd be proud of me, if somewhere, somehow he could see me now. As we walked down the stairs, the freezing cold shocked me out of my melancholy.

Nikki held the main door open, as my hands were full with my bouquet and dress, but I nearly dropped them both as I looked up. At the curb stood Danny, looking resplendent in a dark gray suit, in front of a vintage black Bentley adorned with white wedding ribbons.

"Oh Danny, how . . . ," I cried, at a total loss for words.

For all intents and purposes, Danny was the nearest thing that I had to a dad since my own father had passed away. Having him here to take me to the church made the day complete.

"Sunshine." He sighed, looking as though he was fighting back the tears. "You look beautiful." He opened up the car door for me and helped me climb in with my dress. The driver held the door open for Nikki to sit up front, and Danny sat next to me.

"Thanks, Danny. Not just for this, but for everything. You'll never know just how much you and the boys mean to me."

"Go 'way witt cha'. S'not like you've never done anything for me. Can't say I was over the moon with you fallin' for a fighter. I wanted an easier life for you than the one you picked. But Con's my boy, and he'll protect you with his life. That having been said, if the little fecker ever hurts you, come and see me, sunshine," he told me and squeezed my hand.

I swallowed hard, fighting back the tears. "I love you, Danny," I told him.

"Huh," he grunted, rolling his eyes, but he squeezed my hand again, and I knew he felt the same.

When we arrived at the church, Nikki whipped out her phone and insisted on taking a ton of photos of Danny and me. Even the driver jumped in on the action, playing photographer so that Nikki could get into the pictures with us.

Danny didn't complain once. He puffed out his chest like a proud father in every photo, but when the driver started getting a little too arty, we politely rescued the phone and made our way into the church.

"You're walking me down the aisle, right?" I whispered to Danny, suddenly nervous and holding on to his arm with a death grip.

"Sunshine," he replied calmly, "just try and stop me."

The doors to the church opened, and the beautiful sound of

a choir singing assailed us as it echoed throughout the church. Nikki spread my train around the back of my dress then moved to stand in front of me. Looking back over her shoulder, she winked at me then whispered, "Fucking hell, Em, your boy looks hot."

"No swearing in church," Danny scolded in the same mock whisper, and I giggled.

I didn't think it was possible to feel happier than I did right then.

Nikki, completely undaunted, poked her tongue out at Danny and began walking down the aisle. A few seconds later, we followed slowly behind her. Despite it being Christmas Eve the church was packed. People whom I didn't recognize were interspersed with people whom I did. I was overwhelmed to see all of my friends from university and the girls from Daisy's, though I couldn't see Katrina among them, thank goodness. Rhona and Mike were both there, all dressed up, and I was blown away when I realized they must have closed the cafe to be there.

The altar on both sides was surrounded by huge arrangements of candles, and in front of it stood Father Patrick, sporting a big, beaming smile. Kieran and O'Connell stood in front again wearing matching dark suits. They were both clean-shaven and heart-stoppingly gorgeous.

When I met O'Connell's gaze, I welled up with tears again. He looked at me the way that every man should look at his bride on his wedding day, like I was an angel, like I was the answer to every prayer that he'd ever said.

He looked at me like he loved me more than anyone else in the whole world and that he couldn't believe that I had chosen him. It was exactly the same way that I was looking at him.

"Who gives this woman to wed this man?" Father Pat asked. I'd been so captivated by O'Connell that we were already at the altar.

"I do," replied Danny gruffly and placed my hand in O'Connell's as he stepped back.

"You came," O'Connell whispered, swallowing hard.

"Did you think I wouldn't?" I asked, and he nodded, looking vulnerable.

"You look so beautiful," he told me.

"Dearly beloved..." Father Pat began, and I gave myself, heart and soul, to the man whom I wanted to spend the rest of my life with, and in return, he gave his heart and soul to me.

* * *

"Ladies and gentlemen," yelled Kieran, "may I present to you the bride and groom, Mr. and Mrs. O'Connell."

The entire room at St. Paul's Sports and Social Club stood up and applauded. I held on to my husband's arm, who incidentally had been grinning from ear to ear since that ludicrously passionate kiss at the altar. He'd forewarned me on the way over that he and the boys had done the best they could with the wedding but, with little money and no notice, they'd come unstuck with the reception, especially with it being Christmas Eve. Father Patrick and Tommy's mum had, once again, come to the rescue and had leaned on the committee to open up the social club for the evening. The local fish and chip shop served their fare in paper cones for the wedding feast. Personally I thought it was a fantastic idea, and I still couldn't believe they'd pulled it all off. With everyone promising to email us wedding photos from their cameras, there was a good chance that we might even have a proper wedding album one day as well.

Curtains of fairy lights adorned the walls, and in the cold light of day I was sure the club was more than a little shabby looking, but to my romantic love-struck eyes, it was wonderful. We hadn't arrived more than two minutes earlier when a robust-looking woman with red hair came barreling toward us. She crossed the entire room with arms wide open, then threw them around me as she reached us and squeezed.

"You are just as beautiful as Tommy said you were, darlin'. Not that I don't love you like me own son, Con, but if my Tommy had a bit more sense about him, I'd be hugging my daughter-in-law now. You are pretty as a picture in that beautiful dress. I cried when you said your vows, didn't I, John? I cried."

She turned around to poor John as she asked him, hand on heart, but as he opened his mouth to reply, the lady started talking again ten to the dozen. Apparently the question was rhetorical.

"And, Con, you are so handsome. So handsome," she said, as she reached up on her tiptoes to squeeze his cheeks like you might with a chubby toddler.

"Mary, you're looking gorgeous, as usual. If I wasn't a happily married man, John would be in trouble now," charmed O'Connell.

John didn't look as though he'd mind anyone running away with Mary. He grinned up at O'Connell and shook his hand, but before he could congratulate us, Mary started again.

"Get away, you charmer. You'll have to watch out for this one, lovely. He'll charm the birds from the trees and virgins out of their knickers. Now my Tommy, he's a good boy and loyal to a fault. You'd never catch Tommy drinking or flirtin' with other girls."

Tommy would flirt with a nun if she were half decent looking. In fact, as I thought back on some of the train wrecks that he'd hooked up with since I'd known him, I didn't think that good looks were even on Tommy's list of prerequisites. Being a woman, having a pulse, and being over eighteen were probably the only attributes on that list.

"Feckin' hell, Mary. Are you seriously trying to poach my girl for Tommy on our wedding day?"

"Best place to meet a girl is at a wedding." She beamed.

"Not when the girl is the one getting married," reminded O'Connell, who started looking a little irate.

"Ah, stop your moaning," crooned Mary, patting his cheek. "She's only got eyes for you, boyo. Now if I could find a girl like that, who'd bake a cake for people she doesn't even know, I'd be a happy woman. You don't have any sisters do you?" she asked me.

"No. Sorry." I apologized while I could get a word in.

"Nikki is single and she's lovely," O'Connell told Mary, pointing Nikki out across the room.

"What does she do?"

"She's a student at university like Em. They do math together."

"Ohh, an educated woman! Now that would do for Tom, someone to give him a bit of sophistication. Does she bake?"

"I don't think so," I admitted hesitantly.

"Well, never mind. I can teach her. Right, then. See you later, lovelies."

With another pat to O'Connell's cheek and a bear hug to me, she went storming off toward Nikki. Poor John, his leg still in a cast, went trailing behind her.

"Why did you say that?" I asked him. "Nikki and Tommy are a terrible match. Even if you could get them on a date, I'm pretty sure that one of them would come back missing a limb."

"If it keeps Mary away from my wife, she can do her worst."

"I'm getting the feeling that you like calling me that." I smiled at him.

"I like that you're mine, Mrs. O'Connell," he said, cupping my cheek with his hand as he leaned in to kiss me.

"Back at you, Mr. O'Connell." His lips touched mine, oh so briefly, before the entire room started catcalling and wolf-whistling.

"Save it for the honeymoon," someone yelled. I was bright red and absolutely mortified, but O'Connell grinned proudly.

"I never thought I'd see you married, and even more unbelievable, you're dry on your wedding day. That alone is fuckin' shockin'. Are you sure you're Irish?"

"Em, this is my uncle Killian." O'Connell introduced us.

"Pleased to be makin' your acquaintance." Killian bowed with a flourish before kissing the back of my hand.

"Unlike my sister, Sylvia, who is a mean and evil drunk, I am a happy drunk," he slurred, grinning.

"Nice to meet you," I offered back, liking this man immediately.

He had none of Sylvia's malice or artifice, and O'Connell didn't seem to have any reservations about him.

"Right, then, boyo," he addressed O'Connell. "I'm stealing your girl for a dance."

I looked at my husband in horror. As likeable as Killian seemed, O'Connell knew that I didn't often dance. So to have to do it with a man I didn't know, in front of a room full of people, made me panic.

Even if O'Connell sensed my distress, he didn't get the chance to intervene before I was pulled onto the dance floor. I needn't have worried about being able to dance because my feet barely touched the ground. As soon as one song, and my dance with Killian, had finished, I was pulled away to dance with one man after another. By the time I made it back to my husband, I was exhausted and had probably danced with every man in the room.

"Could use a drink, could you, love?" Killian grinned as he handed me a pint of beer.

It wasn't the most feminine of drinks to be sipping in my wedding dress, but I was gasping. O'Connell pulled me to his side and kissed the top of my head affectionately.

"No more dancing with other men," he whispered into my ear and nibbled the lobe, making me shiver.

"That possessive streak making you twitchy?" I teased.

"Baby, you didn't see the look on their faces when they had you in their arms. I'm the only one allowed to get that look around you."

I reached up to my enormous husband and stroked his cheek as I gently kissed his lips. "Only yours, O'Connell," I reassured him.

"Then how about a dance with your husband?" he asked, and I nodded with a smile.

As he walked me to the dance floor, it cleared, leaving us alone. Our song rang out through the speakers, and holding my hand gently in his, O'Connell pulled me in close. We danced as though we were completely alone. He spread his other large hand across the bare skin of my back, stroking me with his thumb and triggering my automatic arousal.

"Do you know how hard it is for me not to throw you over my shoulder and carry you home right now?" he asked me.

"I can feel how hard it is," I teased him.

"I'm going to undo those tiny, little buttons one by one and kiss my way down that beautiful back as I peel off your dress . . ." he whispered.

"O'Connell, stop it." I squirmed in nervous anticipation of my wedding night. I hadn't seen him since the day before yesterday and it felt like forever since we'd made love. I'd gone years without the slightest attraction to any man, and now I was completely addicted to sex with O'Connell. I wasn't sure there would ever come a time when the slightest whisper of his voice in my ear wouldn't make me want to jump him.

"There's only an hour or two left," I whined. "Can't we skip out now?"

O'Connell chuckled as he replied, "You've never been to an Irish wedding, have you, love?"

I shook my head no, confused as to where he was going with this.

"One night," he replied. "Then I get you for the rest of my life."

I rested my head against his chest and breathed in the smell that was uniquely his; the smell that I would go to sleep with forever.

CHAPTER TWENTY-SEVEN

I realized what he meant when the taxi arrived for us at 6 a.m. on Christmas morning. The boys were gutted at not having been able to get a real band, but the disco went on until 2 a.m., which was when I figured the party would break up. You could imagine how shocked I was when a few of the older people whipped out their instruments and carried on playing. I'd never heard any of their songs, but the room sang out in chorus, and the more drink that flowed, the louder our makeshift choir became. During a brief intermission in the early hours, Kieran decided to make his best man speech.

"Hello, hello," he called out, tapping a knife dangerously against his pint glass. Whether it was the alcohol or being around their family, I didn't know, but all of the boys' accents seemed stronger tonight.

"Ladies and gentlemen, my name is Kieran Doherty, and I'm Cormac's best friend. We've known each other pretty much our entire lives, so when the first two people said no, you could imagine how honored I was to be his third choice for best man.

"I'd like to take a moment to mention how gorgeous Em,

our lovely bride, looks. She truly deserves someone handsome, loving, and intelligent so we're really pleased for Con that he managed to get her down the aisle before that guy came along. It's not always been easy for Con being the smaller, less charming, and witty friend, so the fact that you've managed to get a real woman to pick you over me is a massive achievement, and we're all very proud of you. If Em wises up in a few months, remind her that it's too late. You've got the certificate, so she can't back out.

"What that does mean for you, lucky ladies, is that I'm still on the market, and if you'd like to submit your phone number and a brief résumé, I'll be holding auditions for the next Mrs. Doherty all night."

Kieran stopped talking as the room erupted with laughter. O'Connell was taking turns groaning at Kieran's jokes and laughing with the crowd.

"Seriously, though." Kieran chuckled. "I can say, hand on heart, that I never thought Con would ever settle down, but when he met Em, she absolutely knocked him for six. Even before Danny warned him, on pain of death, to stay away from her, it was too late. One look at Con and anyone could see that he was so far gone for our little sunshine; it was love for life.

"Em, you really have no idea how much sunshine you bring into the life of everyone you touch. You are good and gentle, caring and kind, and the fact that you don't see any of these things in yourself makes you more beautiful. There's a great many men here tonight who love you like a sister and a daughter, and as long as you have all of us, you will never want for anything.

"I look at you both together and I see hope. Hope that one day we all might be fortunate enough to fall in love with someone who doesn't want or need to change you, but who makes you want to be a better person. I wish you both a long and happy life together, but if it doesn't work out, Em, you know where to find me.

"Ladies and gentlemen, please raise your glasses. May green be the grass you walk on. May blue be the skies above you. May pure be the joys that surround you. May true be the hearts that love you. To the bride and groom!"

"To the bride and groom!" the room toasted.

O'Connell stood up to embrace Kieran, and they said a few words to each other quietly. Kieran and O'Connell were closer than brothers, and tonight that bond couldn't have been clearer.

As Kieran sat down, Danny stood. Boots were stomped and tables were slammed as applause rang out across the room until, eventually, he waved everyone down.

"All right, you feckers, back in your seats. I'd like to thank you all for coming, especially given that it's Christmas morning now. I've been told I should tell the bridesmaids how beautiful they looked. Em only had the one, so gobshite, where are you?"

Nikki gave Danny the finger from across the room, which made everyone laugh.

"Lovely. Very ladylike. Till you opened your gob, you looked lovely." He grinned drunkenly.

"Where's sunshine?" I was sitting on my husband's lap a few tables away, but I waved so that he could see me. After he had called Nikki a gobshite, I was a little afraid for my turn.

"The very first time I saw you, the sun was shining on that beautiful blond hair of yours, and you looked like an angel. Course you also looked like a gust of wind would blow you over, and you were scared stiff of me, but the more I got to know you, the more I realized that you were exactly like the other little scrappers I can't get rid of. You're a fighter, girl. You've fought for a better life, and with Con, I hope that you find all the love and happiness you deserve. That having been said, if the stupid eejit upsets you or gets out of line, you come and tell me, darlin'.

There's always room in his training for a couple hundred more planks and burpees." He paused for the laughter to die down.

"Walking you down the aisle today has been one of the proudest moments of my life. You are the sun that shines in the dark and the most beautiful part of my day. You've become for me the daughter I never had, and it's no secret that I wasn't the biggest fan of you and Con gettin' together. I'm a little protective of you."

"A little?" Kieran scoffed. Danny stared at him for interrupting, but everyone was chuckling, knowing just how right Kieran was.

"But there was no stopping Con once he made up his mind that you were his girl, so I did what any father would do. I let you both find your own way and hoped for the best." He paused to shift about a bit, clearly uncomfortable.

"Con, when you and Kieran first came into my gym, I knew you'd give me trouble and grief. In fact, I'm pretty sure I didn't have a single gray hair before I met you. What I didn't realize then was that you'd both give me far more than you took. You cocky little gobshites are my kin, and I'm proud to have been there to watch you grow into the men you've become.

"Con, you've surprised me since meeting Em. I do believe that you will spend every day of your marriage trying to be the man she deserves, and that's all I can ask. I mean it about the feckin' burpees mind," he warned with a pointed finger.

Mary was wiping her eyes furiously, clearly touched by Danny's speech. I was barely keeping it together, and my throat hurt from swallowing back the tears.

"Training you and seeing the dedication and commitment you give makes me so proud, and I believe it in my heart that one day you will be world champion. You've given this old man hope for the future, and I wish you both love and happiness, today and forever more."

He raised his glass of single malt in the air. "Sláinte."

"Sláinte!" the room called out, my husband included.

Walking over to Danny, I threw my arms around him and gave him the biggest hug. I kissed him on the cheek and wiped my eyes. I didn't say anything, and truthfully I didn't think I could without sobbing like a baby. Danny knew how much I loved him, and now I knew how much he loved me.

Sniffing a bit, I left him sipping his single malt with Father Pat. Although Father Pat had declined any more to drink after his fourth whiskey, claiming that he had to be sober enough to conduct midnight mass, he wasn't gone two hours before he was back toasting and giggling with Danny like a pair of schoolboys. I had a sneaking suspicion that he had a 9 a.m. Christmas morning service, which would be interesting for the congregation.

"Come on, sunshine. Wrap your arms round me and let me show you what you're missing," teased Kieran, as he pulled me onto the dance floor for a slow dance.

"If that's how you ask nice girls to dance, Kier, you need to work on your lines."

"Baby, Con got the best girl there is." He smiled, twirling me around.

"Ah, someday, Kieran, you're going to make some lucky girl very happy."

"Well, until then I'll keep the good lines to myself and give the bad girls a taste of what they'll be missing."

I rolled my eyes and secretly looked forward to the day that Kieran had what O'Connell and I had found. "Speaking of good girls, where's Marie? I haven't had a chance to chat with her yet."

"She's over by the bar talking to Tommy," Kieran told me without having to look. Any man who automatically knew where a woman was in a room without looking had it bad. I kept my thoughts to myself, deciding not to meddle too much. I had the feeling tonight wasn't the last night that they'd be seeing each other, though.

"You should probably go and rescue her then," I said, nodding toward Tommy.

"In a minute," he answered. "I'm getting a dance with my best girl first."

I looked across to see O'Connell dancing with an elegant older lady. Her hair was pinned in a neat chignon, and her beautiful silver-gray dress was understated and elegant.

"Who's O'Connell dancing with?" I asked curiously.

"Me ma. I think she loves him more than me sometimes," he huffed indignantly, but I could tell he didn't mean it.

"No, she doesn't." I smiled, and he returned my grin full force.

"He really loves you, you know?" Kieran told me seriously.

"I know, Kier. I wouldn't have married him otherwise," I replied jokingly.

"No, Em," he said seriously, "like lay down in traffic for you, forsaking all others, the only one for him for the rest of his life—kind of loves you."

"Before O'Connell, I didn't think it was possible for two people to love each other like that," I admitted.

"Me, either," he replied, and we danced in wistful silence until the song ended. As he relinquished me to O'Connell, he looked as though he'd made up his mind about something and purposefully walked off toward the bar.

"I think Kieran's got a thing for Marie," I told him.

"Who?"

"Marie. The girl who designed and made my wedding dress. I think he's taking Tommy out for chatting her up as we speak."

"Huh. That will last long enough for Kier to get her knickers off," he scoffed.

"I'll bet he said the same thing about you once," I pointed out.

"Fair point, Mrs. O'Connell, and I would pay good money to see the little fucker whipped."

"You have such a way with words," I teased.

"Baby, I don't believe that my way with words was why you married me. I seem to recall I had other skills with my mouth that sealed the deal."

His cheek brushed gently against mine as he whispered softly into my ear, instantly making me damp and weak-kneed. I pressed myself closer against him as we danced; the crackle of electricity potent between us.

Suddenly I caught sight of Liam striding purposefully toward us.

"Hey, Em," he greeted me sternly as he reached us then turned to address O'Connell. "You'd best come outside, Con. We've got trouble."

"You stay with Danny, love. We'll be right back."

"I'm coming with you," I informed him determinedly.

I could see his jaw ticking as he became impatient to meet the trouble head on. "I don't want you getting hurt," he admitted.

"And I don't want you throwing away your whole career because some arsehole is causing trouble," I retorted.

He grabbed his messy spikes and pulled at them absently as he mulled over what to do. "Fuck it," he said, grabbing my hand as he hauled me protectively to his side. "You stay behind me, and you don't move," he warned.

I nodded in agreement, as we went to see who could be trying to ruin our wedding day. We were halfway down the hallway when I didn't have to guess anymore. I knew.

"Get your filthy hands off me. Do you have any idea who my son is? He'll break your neck if he finds out you restrained his own mother!" Sylvia screamed to anyone listening.

Tank stood at the entrance to the hallway. He never really talked much as he trained, but the boys called him Tank because, well, he was built like a tank. He stood in front of the door with his arms crossed, an immoveable obstacle between us and the doorway. For all of Tank's size and strength, I'd never actually seen him throw a punch in anger. His intimidating presence seemed to deter conflict and, although he enjoyed training, I didn't think he had the temperament to be a fighter.

"Oh, thank God, Con," Sylvia cried dramatically, placing her hand over her heart as though she feared for her own safety. "He hit me. All I wanted was to see my own son on his wedding day, and he told me to fuck off and hit me."

Tank looked at O'Connell and raised an eyebrow in amusement. I could cheerfully see him telling Sylvia where to go, but we all knew he would never raise his hand to her.

Con rolled his eyes at Sylvia's antics and sighed wearily. "What do you want, Ma?" he asked.

"That's no way to talk to your mother, son," warned the guy standing next to her.

It was only then I noticed that Sylvia had company. He was a big guy, though nowhere near as big as O'Connell. His dark hair was greased back, and his too-tight trousers made his beer belly hang over the top. He had probably been quite fit and good looking once, but those years had long since passed. From his tired eyes and saggy blotched skin, I would bet good money that he was an alcoholic like Sylvia.

"I'm not your son," snarled O'Connell, looking at his mother. "Now tell me what the fuck you're doing here, so we can go back to enjoying our wedding."

"Baby, please. You're my only son. I'm sorry for the misunderstanding with Emily. I didn't realize how serious it was between you, and I just didn't want you hurt. I've already missed your wedding. Haven't I been punished enough? Please, Con, I just want to be part of your celebration with you."

She pleaded so convincingly that it was hard not to see her as the repentant mother. But I had seen the real Sylvia behind the facade.

"What, so you thought you'd bring this fucktard to my wedding!" O'Connell shouted.

"Who the fuck do you think you're calling a fucktard, arse-hole?" the man screamed.

"Richard, it's fine. Please let me handle this," cautioned Sylvia, standing as a buffer between Richard and her son.

O'Connell looked murderous, but to give him credit, he was keeping his temper under control.

"Con, Richard means well, I promise. Baby boy, it's Christmas. We always spend Christmas together, don't we?" she said, holding Con's face in her hands like he really was a little boy.

For a moment I saw the flicker of longing that explained why he always forgave her behavior in the past. He wasn't just a fighter; he was also a boy craving his mother's love. As O'Connell looked between Sylvia and Richard, the longing faded to resolve and back to anger. In the past it was moments like this when his temper would get the best of him, and if Richard carried on baiting O'Connell, he'd be lucky to leave without repercussion.

O'Connell looked back for me and, when he saw me, reached out his hand and entwined my fingers with his. As always my touch calmed him.

"Go home, Ma. Or go to a bar. Or go to Richard's house. I really don't care. You've burned your bridges with me for good this time. Continually fucking up and going back on your word is one thing. I can even forgive a lifetime of you being a shite mother. But you knowingly tried to take away the one person I love more than anything else in the world, and I'll never forgive that. Em, Danny, Kier, and the boys are my family now, and I take care of what's mine. Now turn around and fuck off so that my wife and I can go back to enjoying our wedding."

He directed this last remark at Richard, whose face was so red that I knew something was about to kick off. Sylvia was stunned that O'Connell had stood up to her. When she realized

O'Connell was serious, she stared at me maliciously, and it was clear that I was apparently to blame for her lot in life.

"What the fuck, Sylvia. You said this was gonna be an easy mark!" shouted Richard.

I could feel the fingers of O'Connell's hand flexing and relaxing gently as he prepared to fight.

"You misunderstood, Richard," Sylvia stuttered. "I would never say anything like that."

"Look, boyo." An increasingly belligerent Richard was getting up in O'Connell's face, and it was like watching a stupid monkey baiting a lion. "I'm getting inside this shithole whether I have to go through you or not. Your stupid bitch of a mother promised me free booze if I drove her here, and I expect payment."

He shoved O'Connell hard, but my man was a six-foot-five mountain of solid muscle who'd been training his body to fight for most of his life. Richard wouldn't know what hit him, but I wouldn't put it past him to try to press charges for assault. After that O'Connell's career would be well and truly over.

"Don't," I warned him. "You're in training."

"Don't worry, love," he reassured me. "I've got it under control. But four weeks from tomorrow I won't need to rein it in, fucker," snarled O'Connell menacingly.

"Surprise, surprise," drawled Richard. "I always took you for a jumped-up little pussy. You don't have the balls to fight me. But I'll tell you what. I'm a reasonable man. Give me two free pints of lager and a shot and I'll leave you and your good-for-nothing dried-up mother to it. Call it my wedding present."

It happened so fast that it barely registered, but in seconds Richard was little more than a heap on the floor in front of me. In unison we all turned to see where the punch had come from.

Tommy wore a beaming smile and shrugged his shoulders as he said, "I'm not in training."

O'Connell and the guys all man-hugged each other then he turned to address his mum one last time. "Go home," he told her forcefully. "It's over." With that, O'Connell led me back inside without throwing a single punch, and we went back to our happy ever after.

CHAPTER TWENTY-EIGHT

"I think you're just supposed to carry me over the threshold," I told O'Connell.

"As far as I'm concerned, the main door to the building is the threshold. I want to do everything right, and it starts with this."

I sighed, knowing there was no arguing with him, and let him carry me up flight after flight of stairs until we got to the flat. The box of wedding cards that I held on to tightly only added to the burden. He paused to juggle between my weight and getting the keys out of his pocket, then let us in and kicked the door behind him.

"Bed, Mrs. O'Connell," he ordered.

"Yes, Mr. O'Connell," I answered, nuzzling into the side of his neck as he carried me the short distance to the bed. As he did I registered that something felt not quite right. It took me a moment to realize what it was.

"O'Connell. Why's the flat warm?"

He grinned as he turned me around and began undoing the row of tiny buttons running down the back of my dress.

"Our wedding present," he told me. "Tommy's dad's a

plumber, so with a bit of help from Tommy, he came in yester-day morning and fixed the heating."

"Ah, I love John." I sighed. It really was the best present in the world to have warmth on tap again.

"Hey, I'm the only one who gets to hear that from now on . . . and maybe Danny, but no one else, so behave, wife," he retorted jokingly.

"I see." I smiled. "Married for five minutes, and you're already possessive."

I could barely breathe as O'Connell bared my back and, with one hand splayed across my stomach, kissed his way down my spine.

"Mrs. O, you have no idea," he said seductively.

My heart raced as he shimmied my dress down my hips. I'd toed off my Converse and was now standing before him, my back to his hard, waiting body. His tanned calloused hand covered my pale naked breast and I shivered, overwhelmed by the way that he made me feel.

He knew my body intimately, knew how to inflame and arouse me and how to make me beg. His thumb teased my nipple, and I whimpered as I started to breathe hard.

The air between us was charged with anticipation, and although I just wanted him inside me, it was clear he wanted to take his time. His kisses peppered my neck and back intimately until he'd worked his way around my body and was standing in front of me. He was so tall that barefoot I had to strain my neck to look up at him. Those jaw-dropping, heart-stopping, wolf-like eyes told me that he was just as far gone as I was.

He held my gaze with a smug, knowing grin as he slowly undressed, unveiling a washboard stomach that still made me salivate. When he was down to his boxers, he slid them down his legs and teased his finger along the lace edge of my panties.

I ached for him, and this teasing only made the need a hundred times worse. "Please, baby," I begged, willing him to stop this torment and take me.

"Turned on, are we?" he asked huskily, and I nodded in reply. "I've been hard for hours, watching you walk around in that dress. I've had all night to plan how many times I'm going to take you, and in what position. But now that I have you nearly naked and all alone, I just want to bend you over and fuck you hard until I can remember my own name again." His deep voice was thick with lust, and I was too turned on to reply.

"Open your legs, baby." I did as he asked, and with effortless strength that made me seem weightless, he lifted me up and wrapped my legs around him. I groaned as his cock pressed up against me. "Fuck, I love that sound," he told me.

He set me down on the bed hard and ground against me in the best, most torturous way. Threading my hands into his hair, I pulled him toward me for a kiss. Nothing about it was gentle. His soft touch had now become a carnal hunger, and he kissed me like he wanted to devour me.

The hard-sculpted muscles of his back flexed beneath my fingertips as I tried to press him closer. My skin was on fire, and I wanted him inside me so badly it hurt.

"Turn over," I demanded between kisses. I was impatient and ready to take control, and he seemed mildly amused at my efforts. O'Connell didn't have a submissive bone in his body. If he didn't have control, it was because he relinquished it freely.

I pushed against his chest, knowing that I had no way of flipping him. His size made me feel delicate and tiny, and I knew that I was more likely to hurt myself than him, trying to put him on his back. Indulgently he rolled over and lifted me to sit astride him. I moved my hands to the waistband of my panties.

"No," he ordered. "I won't last if you do. They are my last line of defense, and I don't want tonight to end."

I smiled, feeling the same way. Sitting over this loving, possessive, sculpted, gorgeous man, I was overwhelmed that he was mine. I didn't question why he'd chosen me or how long it would be before he tired of us. At that moment I saw myself as he saw me, and I was empowered. I felt sexy and emboldened, and I realized that O'Connell hadn't given me this power. It was mine all along.

What Frank had done was horrific and for the longest time I lost myself. But this was who I was, and O'Connell loved me for it. Was I sexy because I was confident or was I confident because I was sexy? I didn't know. But knowing that his body, his release, was mine to control, excited me.

"Tonight ended hours ago. Today is the first day of the rest of our lives."

I leaned forward, allowing my bare breasts to graze his chest, kissing and nibbling a torturous path from one nipple to the next. He breathed hard but didn't try to stop me. Rolling my pelvis, I sat up and leaned back against his cock. I pulled pin after pin out of my hair until it cascaded down my shoulders.

"Do you have any fucking idea how beautiful you look right now?" he asked me.

He reached up to rub my nipples with the pads of his thumbs, but his touch was fleeting as I pulled away to ease myself down his body, kissing a painfully slow path down his washboard abdominals. He groaned when my breasts brushed against his rock-hard erection and closed his eyes when my warm breath blew across him. I licked my way along the length of his cock and took him deep into my mouth.

"Jesus," he whispered as his hips lifted off the bed.

He ran his fingers through my hair but didn't force my head down or make me feel uncomfortable. If it was possible he grew even harder as he moved closer and closer to orgasm, but his stamina wasn't limitless. "Come here, baby," he urged.

I complied, crawling up his body to wrap my tongue around his hungrily.

He slid my panties down my legs and tossed them aside. Moving me beneath him, he slid inside me, all the way to the hilt. Holding each of my hands in his own, our fingers intertwined, he stopped to look me deep in the eyes.

"I love you, sunshine. Forever," he whispered.

"And I love you," I answered contentedly.

I closed my eyes as he moved inside me and trapped my bottom lip between his teeth. Our slow, gentle rhythm quickly became frantic, but I wanted him harder and faster.

As though he heard my silent wish, he complied, pounding into me relentlessly. I was so close that I held my breath, feeling the tremors work their way through my body at the edge of my orgasm. I lifted my hips to meet O'Connell thrust for thrust, and when he unexpectedly leaned down to take my nipple in his hot, wet mouth, I was there. With my husband deep inside me, I came hard, exploding into a million pieces before falling back down to earth.

His body tensed, and he gave a hoarse shout as I took O'Connell with me over the edge. It was beautiful and perfect and the best end to our wedding. He collapsed on top of me, and I welcomed the familiar weight of his body against mine. "I don't want to go to sleep in case I wake up and this was all a dream."

"And what would you do if it was?" I smiled.

"Fuck something up until I found you and made you do it all over again for real," he admitted.

"Sleep, O'Connell. I'll still be here when you wake up."

I never got an answer. He was fast asleep on my chest, and moments later I was, too.

* * *

I got out of the shower the next morning to find O'Connell wearing nothing but tight black boxer briefs and a frilly blue apron, cooking a fried breakfast and singing off-key to the radio. He looked effortlessly sexy, but it was the look of pure joy and happiness on his face that made my heart ache.

Leaving him to it I threw on some underwear, leggings, and one of his oversize hooded sweaters and joined him as he set down our breakfasts.

"I could get used to this." I grinned.

"Sunshine, fuck me every day like you did last night, and I'm at your beck and call."

I choked on my bacon as I registered what he'd said, and he laughed as he slapped my back, helping me cough it back up again.

"Maybe you've had enough meat in your mouth for one day. I don't want you to choke on it."

"Very funny," I said sarcastically. "But try not to say stuff like that when I'm eating. You almost became a widower less than twenty-four hours after becoming a groom."

He frowned, not liking that idea at all. "Sorry, love. It's so easy to make you blush, I can't help myself."

We polished off breakfast and I reached for our box of wedding cards as I sipped my tea. The radio was still playing Christmas songs in the background. The flat was deliciously warm and sitting here with O'Connell felt so domestic and intimate that I wanted to cry with happiness that this was my life now. I wasn't alone anymore, and neither was he.

"What you doin', sunshine?" he asked, licking the last of the bacon off his fingers.

"I was just going to read our wedding cards."

We both picked up a handful of cards and started plowing through them. As I opened the first one, a pile of notes fell out, and I counted up thirty pounds.

"There's money in here!" I exclaimed, shocked.

O'Connell didn't seem at all surprised. If he knew that some people had given us money, why was he so casual about leaving the box of cards lying around at the reception?

"A few people asked me what we wanted for a wedding present, and I couldn't think of anything so I just said money."

We worked our way through the huge pile, and by the time we got to the bottom, we had over fifteen hundred pounds.

"I can't believe people have been so generous."

"They just wanted us to have a good start," he told me, looking more than a little stunned himself. This was more money than I'd ever had in my life, and my first thought was that we needed to get it to the bank, quick.

"Can we put it with the money I have left from the car toward a deposit on buying our own place?" he asked.

"It will be a while before we'll qualify for a mortgage," I warned him.

"I know. But at least we'll have a deposit saved when we do. I just like the idea of having a home that's ours, not someplace that we rent. I learned a lot working in construction. Maybe we can get somewhere run-down for a good price, and me and the boys can fix it up between fights."

He had that little boy lost look about him again, the one that just wanted his own home and family. I climbed onto his lap and wrapped my arms around his neck.

"That sounds like a fantastic idea. How about we go down to the bank tomorrow and open up a joint account? Maybe they can give us some advice about setting up a savings account to put the money into."

He looked at me with his eyes at half-mast, and I knew exactly how we'd be spending the rest of Boxing Day.

"I fucking love you getting domestic, and I especially love it when you start talking numbers."

"You fucking love everything about me," I teased, knowing that he and the boys swore more than anyone I had ever met.

"Well, I'm only gonna have one life, so I might as well spend it with someone I love everything about."

With his lightning-fast reflexes he lifted me up and laid me down so that I was underneath him. Using his nose to push up my sweater, he held one hand on my arse and ran the other up and down my leg.

"Now let me tell you why, for the next few days, all knickers are surplus to requirements," he explained, and being as totally hot for my husband that I was, I didn't wear any underwear for the next forty-eight hours.

* * *

"I can't believe I went into a bank without underwear," I complained, knowing that my cheeks were bright red.

I was back in my office catching up on Danny's paperwork and O'Connell was leaning over the desk behind me and nuzzling my neck.

"You were soaked by the time we got home. I reckon it was all that talk of numbers and interest rates turning you on. It's not the last time you're doing that, either. Only next time I'm going to tell you all the way home exactly what I'm going to do to that gorgeous body of yours. If you're lucky and I'm feeling patient, I'll drop your jeans, knowing there's nothing there to stop me, and I'll take you from behind."

His deep voice purred seductively in my ear, and I squirmed in my seat, feeling desperate and aroused. I wondered how it was possible for my body to develop this Pavlov's dog reaction to his voice so quickly. He went back to his nuzzling, knowing full well that I was seconds away from turning around and jumping him, when the door banged open.

"Jesus Christ, are you two still at it? I thought you were supposed to stop having sex when you got hitched."

"Nope," said O'Connell with a grin.

It was the grin I don't think had left his face since our wedding day. Tommy rolled his eyes and sat in the chair opposite.

"So have you realized yet what a loser you married? 'Cause I'm still single."

"Careful," O'Connell warned, all traces of humor gone. O'Connell loved Tommy like a brother, but Tommy did have an uncanny ability to push his buttons.

I rolled my eyes at the both of them. "You stay single, Tommy. It's not fair to the female population to give all of yourself to just one woman. I'm happy enough sticking with the love of my life," I told him, which made Tommy huff and O'Connell grin.

My husband wasn't wrong before when he warned me he'd need reassurance. We both did from time to time. But that was the joy of being in love. It was no effort to give that reassurance to each other.

"Good morning, Mr. and Mrs. O, and to you, fucktard." Kieran greeted O'Connell and me, and finally Tommy.

"You're in a good mood this morning. Get laid at my wedding, did we?" O'Connell teased.

"As it happens, no I didn't. But it's only a matter of time, my friend." Kieran grinned, and I presumed he was referring to Marie.

"That was an arsehole move at the bar when I was chatting her up. You know that, right?" grumbled Tommy.

Kieran laughed, obviously happy that he'd been successful in prying Tommy away from Marie.

"Listen," explained Kieran, with his hands up in surrender. "It had absolutely nothing to do with my awesome chat-up lines. One look at you dancing to 'Sex Bomb' and belting out Tom Jones, and she was dust."

"What-the-fuck-ever," grumbled Tommy. "I do an awesome Tom Jones," he told me under his breath.

One by one all of the boys filed into the office. O'Connell stopped kissing my neck but was never very far away from me. They were all shooting the breeze about what they'd been up to over Christmas. Danny went to stay with his sister for a couple of days, and the gym had been closed, so most of the boys were now itching to get back into training.

Danny shuffled in as he clocked who was here and who wasn't. His customary cigarette was hanging out of his mouth, and I frowned, wondering how much of a toll this chain-smoking was taking on his health. He poured himself a cup of coffee then looked at Tommy sitting in his chair. When Tommy failed to take the hint, Danny barked, "Move," and Tommy jumped a mile.

Settling himself down, Danny took a puff of his cigarette, then put it out and addressed the boys. "Right, lads, we have our-selves a dilemma," he told us. "In two weeks Con is fighting Roberto Calvari. It's a good fight with a good payday. I set it up because Calvari is a solid fighter. Con won't just be a stepping-stone. If he beats Calvari, he'll be in the spotlight for fights leading to title contention."

"What's wrong? Calvari hasn't pulled out, has he?" asked Kieran seriously.

"Quite the opposite, boyo. Quite the opposite. He's as up for it as ever. And there's no doubt about it, it's a big fight and a big opportunity for Con and the gym."

"So what's the problem?" asked O'Connell, impatient to know what Danny was leading up to.

"Felix Ramos has offered you a title fight."

"Holy shit," whispered Tommy.

I looked around at all the lads who were stunned and slightly awed. "Who's Felix Ramos?" I asked.

"It was a few years ago," explained O'Connell, "but he was World Heavyweight Champion. He's won a few fights and lost a few fights since then, and it's a much smaller title, but it would be the biggest fight of my career, by far."

"So what's the catch?" asked Kieran, who went straight to the point.

"This time Con is a stepping-stone. Ramos's career is on the decline and he wants to fight an up-and-comer. He underestimates Con, and I think it'll be a barnburner but he's rigged it. If we turn it down, we won't get offered another fight again."

"How's he rigged it?" Liam asked.

"Well, there's the rub," replied Danny. "It's in six weeks' time."

"Fuck!" pretty much all of them muttered.

"How is that possible?" I asked.

"That's how he's rigged it, sunshine. It's long enough between fights for surface bruises to heal. On the outside I'll look fight ready, but my body won't have fully recovered from the last fight," O'Connell explained. He looked as grim and thoughtful as the rest of the room.

"So what are you going to do?" I asked.

CHAPTER TWENTY-NINE

I had just plated up a small mountain–size portion of pasta when O'Connell got on my last nerve. Walking over to him, I put both hands on his chest. "Baby, stop," I told him.

He'd been training relentlessly since the meeting this morning and, after the few days we had off together, one day of hard-core training wasn't nearly enough to calm the torrent raging inside him. Since he'd come home half an hour ago, he'd dumped his training bag and jumped into the shower. He'd then spent the last ten minutes pacing the length of our tiny flat.

"What do you think I should do, Em?" he asked me.

"I think you should sit down and eat your dinner. Then we're going to climb into bed and talk about it."

He nodded his head and relaxed his shoulders. After a long day of questioning whether or not to take the fight, he seemed relieved to have someone take a decision out of his hands, even if it was a minor one.

An hour later, after he'd wolfed down his meal and we'd washed the dishes side by side in the tiny little kitchenette, I lay on his chest as he ran his fingers absentmindedly through my hair. At least now he seemed calmer and a little more centered.

"What does Danny think?" I asked him.

"I had a word with him after the boys left. He thinks I can do it; he just wants me to change my game plan. Instead of wearing Calvari down, he wants me to go for the knockout. Calvari's had losses before, but he's never been knocked out. It's a big gamble. If I go at him all guns blazing and I don't knock him out, I might not have enough left in the tank for a win at all. But if I do, then I'll be in much better shape for the second fight."

"What does Kier think?" I asked him, knowing that he valued Kieran's opinion almost as much as Danny's.

"He doesn't want me to take the Ramos fight. He thinks that the purse and the exposure aren't worth the risk of me losing the fight and fucking up my stats. It would probably make more sense for me to cancel the Calvari fight, but I'm under contract. Even if I could get out of it, I'd get a bad rep if I tried to pull from the fight last-minute."

"What do *you* want to do?" I asked.

"Honestly? I want a crack at them both. I've seen them fight, and I think I can do it, too."

"Then take both fights. Train like you've never trained before and take both fights."

"You don't mind? We're only just married, and I'd be training every waking hour of the day. We'll barely see each other."

"Look, I'll start helping out more at the gym, maybe do a bit of cleaning to help Danny out before I go back to school. We won't be together, but at least I'll get to see you during the day. Besides, it's only for six weeks. It will only be a few weeks after the last fight until half-term, so maybe we can go away for a few days together then. Sort of like a mini-honeymoon."

"I like the sound of that. Not the cleaning part, though.

Those lazy bastards can clean up after themselves. But I like the rest of it."

"Then get some sleep and stop worrying about it, love. You've decided what you're going to do, so stop questioning yourself."

"Kieran won't be happy," he told me.

"He might not agree with you, but he'll support your decision. He'll always be your corner man, you know that."

We lay together trying to sleep, but ten minutes later I could still feel the tension radiating off him. Propping myself up on my elbows to peer down at him in the darkness, I kissed his abs gently.

"What's wrong?"

"Frank hasn't surfaced yet."

"Did you think he would?" I asked.

"I sort of hoped. I have a lot of pent-up rage I'd like to direct his way."

"If he'd gotten my address from the burglary, we'd have seen him by now. We just have to assume I'm safe and move on. You're going to have to direct all that rage into your fights. Just pretend that Calvari and Ramos are Frank."

"That will work for the knockout," he snorted.

"Don't borrow worry. Just focus on one thing at a time. You know you can do this. Just be the cocky bastard that I married."

"You're right, sunshine. I do have this in the bag. As long as you're watching I can't lose."

He couldn't see my face in the dark, but I made a good show of convincing him with confidence that I didn't feel. The truth was that he took my heart with him every time he climbed into the ring, and he didn't give it back until he climbed out again safely. I wouldn't rest until his last fight was over, but until then I would keep my fears to myself and hold on to my faith that everything would turn out for the best.

* * *

Danny found me the next day cleaning out the bathrooms at the gym. To be fair they weren't quite as disgusting as I'd feared they'd be, but they were still pretty grim. I'd always been able to use the bathroom next to the office, which wasn't nearly as much of a health hazard.

"What the feckin' hell do you think you're doing?" shouted Danny.

I turned back to look at him but didn't stop scrubbing.

"Cleaning the bathroom," I explained, though I would have thought it was patently obvious from the bucket of hot, soapy water and scrubbing brush.

"Yes, I can see that. But why?" he growled.

I leaned back on my heels and dropped the scrubbing brush back into the water. "Look, O'Connell has training every day for the next six weeks. He's already getting nervous and jumpy about not seeing me for so long, let alone about the fights. I don't have any uni work until I go back after the Calvari fight, so I told him I'd hang around the gym more so we could at least see each other."

"And you think he's gonna be happy when he knows you're in here cleaning the jacks?"

"Well, he wasn't over the moon when I mentioned the idea of cleaning to him, but, Danny, I can't sit around and do nothing," I moaned.

"This shit is for the kids to do. All my boys paid their dues with cleaning over the years, and their chores subsidize their fees. If you want to be useful, you can help me train Con."

"How? I don't know anything about boxing. Besides, wouldn't I be a distraction?"

"You're not a distraction, sunshine, you're motivation. Before you he wasn't interested in turning professional. Now he's giving it everything he's got. To impress you he'll train longer and harder than for any of the other lads. You're the fuel to his fire, so I reckon it's time that we start putting that to good use."

I was gobsmacked. How could I motivate him to go harder? It seemed like he was pushing his body to the absolute limit as it was.

"I don't like it, but I'll do whatever you think is best," I told Danny. "But I'm finishing these toilets first. I hate seeing a job half done."

Danny rolled his eyes and mumbled something about how strange I was. At first helping to train O'Connell meant sitting by the side of the ring watching Danny bark orders. On one particularly strained afternoon, Danny challenged them all to see who could bench-press me.

"No one else is touching my fucking wife," O'Connell growled back at Danny. Instead he lifted me up and, with a very girly yelp and squeal from me, he bench-pressed me until I got a cramp.

As the days wore on, I would learn how to massage and rub him down after training. Even when he was so tired that he could barely keep his eyes open, we didn't dare do the rub-downs unsupervised. Danny had imposed the sex ban again, and the minute that my oily hands would touch his slick, hard body, we would both be on fire. The only thing that killed the feeling was having Danny standing over us and barking out everything that I was doing wrong.

Day after day of seeing each other and night after night without touching was taking its toll. We didn't dare do more than kiss because, once we opened Pandora's box, there would be no closing it. O'Connell thought the sex ban was a joke now that we were married, but he didn't see what I saw. His testosterone levels were through the roof. I only had to walk past him now and his nostrils flared like a bull in heat. If Calvari so much as looked at me before the fight, O'Connell would knock him out in the first round.

As Danny suspected, O'Connell trained harder and longer around me, possibly because I spent most of my time and energy willing him on. After twenty-five one-handed press-ups, I'd push him to change hands and do another set. After thirty minutes on the bag, I'd tell him that he had at least another ten minutes still left in him. I'd encourage and push him in any way that I could. By the time the rest day before the fight rolled around, I was as tired as he was restless.

I woke up to a string of tiny kisses along my spine. "Mmm... don't stop," I begged as he moved away and lowered my T-shirt back down. I'd taken to wearing his T-shirts to bed with sleep shorts because they were huge and much more comfortable than mine. He never let me sleep without holding on to some part of me, but it still wasn't the same as sleeping with all of his body pressed against all of mine.

"I have to stop, sunshine, or I won't stop at all."

I was tempted to say that it was fine with me, but it wouldn't be fair to test his resolve this close to the fight. I rolled over groggily, not fully awake yet.

O'Connell sat next to me, looking insanely hot in just a pair of half-buttoned jeans. It didn't escape my notice just how much his body had changed and hardened in the last two weeks. He didn't look like he had an ounce of fat on him. Only once did I make the mistake of telling him that. What followed was a detailed explanation of his exact body fat index and how it was affected by his training.

I could totally appreciate his hotness without understanding the science behind it. He knew that I couldn't walk past his half-naked body without running my fingertips down his washboard abs, so he made every effort to walk around that way as much as possible.

"I made you breakfast in bed," he told me proudly.

"Why are you spoiling me?"

"Because I can, and technically we're still on our honeymoon. Besides," he said, kissing me soundly on the lips, "I can't eat any of this stuff for another three weeks so I'm eating it through you."

I made short work of breakfast, and as I watched him cleaning up after his efforts, I was struck by how monumentally lucky I was. To wake up warm, with a full belly, and a heart bursting with love was the way I wanted to wake up for the rest of my life.

"So what are we going to do today?" I asked him.

"No idea," he admitted. "My body clock had me up at five a.m., and we've got hours to kill that don't involve sex. Tomorrow, though, I'll need to get my head on straight so we'll need to be apart for that."

I didn't take offense at his wanting some distance. Around me he felt soft and loving, which was not the best frame of mind to fight.

"Okay, we'll have an easy day today then tomorrow I've picked up an extra shift at Daisy's so I'll be there for most of the day anyway."

"I sort of had a couple ideas about today. I thought we could do kid stuff."

I looked at him quizzically, having absolutely no idea what he meant.

"I brought the rest of my stuff round from Kier's, and while you were out for the count, I borrowed his laptop. How do you fancy a *Star Wars* marathon and a couple of board games? I've got Jenga and Monopoly," he suggested hopefully.

"You really are bored, aren't you?" I commented.

"Out of my fucking mind," he groaned, running his hands through his messy spikes in frustration. "I just want to get on with it. I can't train, and I can't touch you. I've been listening to music for hours, and we've got hours left to fill."

"Okay, *Star Wars* it is," I agreed.

He grinned big, slipped the DVD into the laptop, and climbed into bed next to me. It was a wonderfully relaxing day, and after so many stolen moments over the last few weeks, it was great to have this time together. O'Connell was a little pissed when I kicked his arse at Monopoly, and I tried to be pissed when he realized he was beaten and used my weakness to kiss me into submission. I sold him Park Lane and Mayfair for a steal and didn't give a shit that we abandoned the game to kiss some more.

My shift at Daisy's the next day dragged interminably. Since our last showdown Katrina had kept out of my way, but I guessed that was the way with bullies. They're all about confrontation as long as it was on their terms.

"Hey, hun. How are you holding up?" Rhona asked me as I was cleaning cutlery. We were at a lull between customers, and I really needed to keep busy.

"I'm nervous," I admitted. "In my head I know he's ready for this fight, but I guess I'll just never get used to seeing him take a punch."

"Well, there are plenty of ringside junkies who get off on watching men fight. I'll bet he appreciates you worrying about him," she replied.

"Don't get me wrong; watching him train is hotter than hell. It's just that when I think about what can happen to him in the ring..." I couldn't finish, but Rhona knew what I meant.

"He knows the risks, love. He always has," she told me, as she wrapped her arm around my shoulders and squeezed.

"I just have a bad feeling about tonight," I admitted.

"You're a fighter's wife now, which means that on fight day he needs to believe that you've got as much faith in him as he has in himself. So you've got . . ." she paused to look at the clock, "two hours to stop looking like someone ran over your cat and get your game face on."

I smiled grimly, knowing she was right. It was time to stop letting my stupid fears control me. After tonight it would be one down, and one to go. I needed to take one fight at a time and put this stupid, irrational sense of foreboding to the back of my mind. Two hours later my shift finished, and I was ready. As I left the diner, completely bundled up against the cold, I found Kieran leaning against his bike waiting for me.

"Kieran, what are you doing standing out here? You must be freezing!" I exclaimed.

"As it happens, I am a bit feckin' cold, so if you could move your pretty little arse, Mrs. O'Connell, we can get back to your lovely warm flat," he said sarcastically.

I rolled my eyes but climbed onto the back of his bike.

"Where's O'Connell?" I asked.

"He's been hanging about my place for a bit listening to music and playing video games, but he doesn't want to see you until the fight."

"Why?" I asked alarmed, and Kieran turned around to give me a huge grin.

"He's pretty evil right now, and he's looking to fuck someone up. He doesn't like you seeing him like that." I nodded, knowing that O'Connell didn't like showing me the person he needed to become.

If Kieran was that happy, though, he must have thought the fight was in the bag. I was more than ready to watch O'Connell close this down and have him back into my bed. We got back to the flat, and I made quick work of changing and applying my makeup before we were back out on Kieran's bike.

"Hold on to your knickers, baby, and let's get this show on the road," he told me as I grabbed him around the waist and braced myself. It was hard not to be infected by Kieran's enthusiasm. He was so wired with excited, nervous energy he looked ready to burst. The closer we got to the venue, the more my anxiety fell away. Unlike the last time, I was now conditioned to watch O'Connell take punch after punch in training, and I had a better understanding of just how prepared he was. Unlike my soft, bruisable flesh, his abs, his core, every part of his body was rock hard. He told me that he was in the best shape of his life, and it was easy to believe. It wasn't a matter of whether he took Calvari down, but in what round, and how he would do it.

We wound our way through the backstage corridors and then into the main venue.

"Why aren't we going to see O'Connell?" I asked unhappily.

"Because he hasn't seen you all day, so he'll want to kiss the fuck out of you. If I keep you out here, it will make him mad, and tonight mad is good."

I followed him as he led, but I didn't like it. "Kier, you're an evil corner man, you know that?"

He looked back and smiled, waggling his eyebrows and making me laugh. I was slightly mollified when he led me to my front-row seat and I found the gang waiting for me.

"Em," Nikki screamed, hugging me hard. She was already a little tipsy, but obviously pleased to see me.

"Good Christmas?" I asked, and she nodded, regaling me with tales of her many nights out over the past few weeks. Big hugs followed from Albie, Ryan, Max, and a few of the girls I knew in passing as Nikki's friends.

Before I knew it the lights dimmed, and the music started pounding. It was time.

CHAPTER THIRTY

As it was a home fight, Calvari sauntered out first. It was clear this was so much more high-profile than the last fight by the fancy strobe lighting and the legion of entourage following Calvari to the ring. Rap music pounded through the speakers as he climbed through the ropes and walked around wearing a cocky smirk, his hands in the air.

"Jesus, he's huge," I murmured to Nikki.

"So is your boy," she pointed out.

O'Connell's music came on, and my breath hitched. I'd only gone a day without seeing him, but this was the power he had over me.

Kieran, Danny, Tommy, and Liam followed him to the ring, and I smiled when I saw Tommy high-fiving the crowd like he was fighting tonight. Men were slapping O'Connell on the back and shouting words of encouragement as though they were best of friends, but he only had eyes for me. I knew this look. He was focused and in the zone.

He stopped in front of me and bent his head. Hanging from the chain next to his cross was his wedding ring. Taking them both, I held on to them tightly, not wanting to part with them even to tie them around my neck.

"Sunshine," he said gently until I looked him in the eyes, "I got this."

I nodded in agreement as he gave me a quick, hard kiss, but I couldn't help the sense of foreboding that gave me goose bumps.

O'Connell climbed into the ring and looked calm as he bounced up and down, rolling his shoulders to warm up. His gaze remained firmly on Calvari. I could see Calvari baiting him with insults, but my boy remained stoic. Although Calvari was acting more like the underdog than O'Connell, something still didn't feel right.

"Ladies and gentlemen. Thank you for your support this evening and welcome to tonight's main event. Introducing, in the blue corner, from Palermo, Italy, weighing in at two hundred and twenty-seven pounds, Roberto "the Destroyer" Calvari."

The crowd erupted, but there were as many boos as there were cheers.

"In the red corner, from Killarney, Ireland, and weighing in at two hundred and twenty pounds, please welcome, Cormac "the Hurricane" O'Connell."

The noise in the arena was deafening as the crowd stomped and chanted, "Hurricane, Hurricane, Hurricane," in unison. The rows were scattered with slutty-dressed girls blowing kisses and shoving their breasts at my husband, but tonight I couldn't bring myself to be worked up about it. As long as he walked out of that ring under his own steam, everything would be all right.

The referee ushered both fighters to the center for their prefight warning and glove tap. Calvari chose that moment to wink at me and blow a kiss my way. If he was hoping for a reaction from O'Connell, he was out of luck. In the ring he was a machine.

The bell rang, and my boy ducked and weaved as Calvari came out of his corner swinging. O'Connell looked relaxed as he moved around. He could almost be training. When he didn't throw a punch for a little while, I figured he was trying to wear Calvari down and go the distance. It was the safest game plan for winning the fight, but it would take its toll. Calvari was a huge fighter, but he was fit and well-trained to last the twelve rounds and then some.

It was clear "the Destroyer" had come to win, and he wasn't about to hand over an easy victory. Calvari threw a series of punches to the body that were easily blocked, but he kept going with combination after combination. For nearly three minutes Calvari attacked relentlessly, with barely any retaliation from O'Connell. Even as he blocked the attacks, the power behind Calvari's hits looked devastating.

O'Connell threw the odd jab, but it was almost like he was baiting instead of fighting back. We were still only in the first round, but the crowd was already getting restless.

"Just fucking hit him, Hurricane," a guy behind me screamed, and my pulse raced, waiting for the bell to ring. We were seconds away from the end of the first round. Calvari looked smug, like he already had the fight sewn up. O'Connell threw two left jabs that looked like a desperate attempt at scoring a couple of last-minute points, and they were easily blocked.

When the magic happened, it was so fast that I almost missed it. So did everyone else. The jabs to the face were to make Calvari raise his guard and expose his core. With all of his power the Hurricane delivered a bone-shattering right hook to the body. As Calvari dropped his guard in shock, O'Connell was already there with a second right hook that knocked the Destroyer out cold.

O'Connell's hands dropped weightlessly to his side, and the bell rang out loud and clear as Calvari's jaw slapped painfully against the canvas. The whole round had been a ploy to convince him to relax in the dying seconds. The strategy was perfect, and by the end of the first round of the biggest fight of O'Connell's career, he was the winner by knockout.

Danny closed his eyes in silent prayer as the entire arena exploded. People were overrunning the ring to get to O'Connell. Grown men were hollering and backslapping each other in the aisles, and I breathed for the first time in three minutes.

As was becoming tradition, Danny climbed down and made his way over to me as I collapsed back in my seat. He plonked himself down on the seat next to me, which had emptied, and with tears in his eyes, reached over to grip my hand in his own. "He did it, sunshine. He bloody did it."

I'd never heard Danny so emotional, and I wished O'Connell could see how proud he was of him.

"He didn't do it alone," I reminded him.

"No, he didn't." He grinned and squeezed my hand.

Giving in to the emotion of the moment, I leaned across and hugged him. For the first time, without a hint of surliness or sarcasm, he hugged me back. Sniffing a bit as he pulled away, he kissed me on the cheek, got up, and left.

I was desperate to see O'Connell, but he was still caught up in the crowd. I hugged Nikki and all of the guys when I felt someone behind me.

"Got one of those for me, Mrs. O'Connell?"

Grinning his cocky grin, sweat dripping down that perfect inked-up body, my husband stood before me in all his glory. Without thinking I jumped on him and held the sides of his face as I kissed him like I hadn't seen him in a month.

Slipping his tongue into my mouth, he used one arm to hoist me up higher and wrapped my legs around his waist. He was so hungry he could devour me, and I knew that he still had eleven rounds left inside him. Bound by the wraps, his thick fingers speared themselves into my hair as he pressed me closer. We were both short of breath when the kiss ended and he rested his forehead against mine.

"I wanna fuck you in the middle of the ring," he murmured to me. I could feel his strong heart pulse inside his powerful chest.

"Do you think you can wait until we don't have an audience? That might be a little more entertainment than these people paid for."

"Well, at least I'd make it last more than one round." He grinned.

"I certainly hope so." I smiled, kissing him again.

The arena was full of people, but we were all alone as I poured everything into that kiss, showing him exactly how I felt about him. Without warning two arms wrapped themselves around us, and wet lips landed on my cheek.

"Happy, Kier?" I asked him.

"Absolutely fucking ecstatic." He grinned, and his euphoria was infectious.

There was magic in the air, and it was going to take everyone a long time to come down from this high. It wasn't just that he'd won; it was the way he did it.

"This is it, my friend! It's the big leagues now," Kieran screamed, jumping up and down with us in his arms.

The place was still packed, as though nobody could believe it was all over. Danny caught my eye and pointed like he wanted me to grab Kier's attention. Following my gaze, Danny gave him some weird hand signals, and Kieran nodded.

"He's telling me he's got more sponsors on the hook. Come on, fucker, time to show them what to do with their money," he said, backslapping O'Connell.

He bent his head to whisper in my ear so that Kieran couldn't hear us. "Two weeks, baby girl. Two weeks of no sex. Wait for me in my changing room, 'cause as soon as I get done with these sponsors I'm taking you long and hard in that shower, and I don't give a fuck who hears us."

"Yes, sir."

I sighed, as though getting fucked by my husband was any hardship. I knew from experience that I'd be waiting awhile. With how the fight went down, there were probably loads of sponsors waiting to talk with him. O'Connell bent his head, and with shaking fingers, I refastened the chain around his neck.

"I love you, Mrs. O'Connell," he whispered in my ear, before kissing me gently on the lips.

I didn't know why, perhaps it was the emotion of the moment, but it brought tears to my eyes. "Love you, too, O'Connell."

"Kier, can you show her where the changing room is and make sure she gets there safely? I'll keep the sponsors happy till you get back and do your thing."

"No problem." Kier grinned.

He looked so happy, and I knew he'd worked just as hard as Danny to get his best friend to this point. O'Connell disappeared into the crowd, and Kieran looped his arm around my neck to guide me to the changing rooms.

"What about the guys?" I asked him.

"Hey," Kier called out, "you lot fancy meeting us at Murphy's in an hour? Con wants some alone time with his girl before the party," he said suggestively, as I turned bright red.

He'd basically just announced to all of our friends that I was having sex before I met up with them.

"Sounds good," shouted Albie. "See you there."

I didn't get a chance to chat with Nikki before Kier pulled me away, keen to get back to the sponsors, I guessed. My earlier sense of unease had returned, and I figured that I'd be feeling that way at least until the next fight was over.

"Why's there no security?" I asked as we approached the main door to the back of the arena. Last time there'd been a beefy guard outside.

"I guess they only hang around until the fight is over. People lost a fair bit of money betting against Con tonight, so they're probably pretty busy breaking up a few fights of their own."

"Fucking smug, the pair of you, ain'tcha?" Sylvia was absolutely plastered as she slurred and staggered toward us. "I fucking birthed that boy, dragged him up, and fed him. I deserve a cut of his pay now," she screamed.

"Fuck off, Sylvia. You did fuck all for Con from the day he was born. You know what he said. He's done. You ain't getting another penny out of him," Kieran said.

"You're such a cocky little shit. Always whispering in his ear and turnin' him against me. Well, you ain't doin' it this time. If he won't listen to me, then I'm having a word with them sponsors."

She staggered off as Kieran muttered a "Fuck," his earlier excitement gone. "I'm gonna have to get her out of here before she fucks things up with his sponsors. You okay to go ahead on your own? Just go straight down the corridor to the end, then turn left and it's the red door with the number seven on it."

I nodded in agreement. "Just go," I urged him, and he disappeared after Sylvia.

The corridors were empty and slightly creepy as they echoed dully with the noise of the crowd. The chilled, windowless space was a complete contrast to the heat of the arena, and I hurried to find the right changing room, knowing that I'd find one of O'Connell's big thick hoodies in his changing bag.

The door was indistinguishable from all of the others, save for the number. It opened easily, and I wondered, as it shut behind me, why the boys didn't worry about people letting themselves in and nicking their stuff.

"Hello, Emily. It's been a long time."

I swung around to find the object of my nightmares standing

between me and my only exit. I opened my mouth to scream, but I never got the chance. Raising up his fist, Frank punched me hard in the face, smacking me into the wall, and everything went black.

* * *

When I came to I quickly wished I hadn't. Thick nylon rope bound my hands and feet to the bars of a dirty metal-framed bed. I had no idea where I was, but the tiny room was filthy. Dark, moth-eaten curtains blocked out most of the natural light.

My mouth was as dry as sandpaper, and the left side of my face hurt so much that I couldn't lie on it. Frank always did prefer the left. He'd fractured the same cheekbone last time.

A few doors opened and closed close by, and my heart pounded, fearing what I knew was coming. I couldn't believe that I'd let my guard down. How stupid was I to think that he'd ever stop looking for me?

The door opened and there stood the vile, perverted man who haunted me.

"Awake at last." He grinned maliciously.

"Why are you here?" I croaked at him, my voice rusty from thirst and disuse.

"I've come to take you back, of course. You've drifted off the rails somewhat. But with a bit of discipline, there's no reason why we can't all be a family again. In fact, seeing how you've been living, it's fair to say I've come to save you from yourself."

He was delusional if he thought I was ever going back with him. At the first sign of life, I was going to scream as loud as I could. My eyes darted around the room, and I guessed that we were in a flat of some sort. I contemplated screaming now, but if no one heard I couldn't risk Frank gagging me.

"I can see what you're thinking, princess, but let me give you a little warning."

He reached down the back of his trousers and pulled out a knife. I recognized it instantly as his fishing knife. Although he'd never used it on me, he'd threatened me with it plenty of times. It was ridiculously big for a fishing knife and looked new. He liked to keep it sharp and shiny, although rusty and covered in blood would have equally terrified me.

Walking over to me, he took his time looking me up and down. Not in a sexual way, but in the way a butcher might eye a piece of meat as he worked out the best place to make a cut.

As he sat down next to me on the bed, I squirmed against my bindings as I tried to move as far away from him as possible. He chuckled at my fruitless efforts and stopped me, stock-still, when he used the tip of the knife to push up my top and expose my midriff. When I woke up tied to the bed, my first worry was rape. Now my fear ran much deeper.

Lifting up his left hand, he ran his fingertips across my ribs and belly. "Such beautiful skin," he mumbled under his breath.

Then with a sigh of almost remorse, he pierced the skin with the blade of the knife and ran it across my torso. I cried out hopelessly as blood pooled around the cut. I thought it was quite shallow, but it was long, and hurt like you wouldn't believe.

"Now it's a shame to cut that lovely skin, but I'm used to teaching you lessons you don't want to learn. So you scream as long and as loud as you like, but I cut with every scream. The longer and louder the scream, the deeper and longer the cut. Now let's see who quits first."

He smiled that knowing, smug look of a man who'd gotten his way. I wouldn't scream unless I knew it would save me. My only objective at this point was to make it back to O'Connell. Whether I was battered, bruised, or raped, I needed to stay alive.

That wouldn't happen if I baited Frank. He was obsessed with control, and when that control was challenged or taken away from him, it sent him over the edge.

"I won't scream," I reassured him.

He sat back, relaxing his shoulders. "Of course, you won't." Standing back up, he placed the knife on the bedside table, unbuttoned his sleeves, and began rolling them up. Sitting back down again, he picked up the knife and, after wiping the blood-stained blade on my jeans to clean it, ran the tip up and down the inside of my forearm, perilously close to my wrist. The subtle threat wasn't lost on me.

"If you're taking me home, why are we here?" I asked croakily, not sure if I wanted to hear the answer.

"Impatient, are you?" He chuckled.

I'd never really seen this side of Frank. His violent temper usually manifested itself in quick, angry beatings and screaming insults, usually about what a useless slut he thought I was. This cold, calculating stranger had the luxury of time and privacy, and he was enjoying it.

Personally I'd have preferred a beating to one of his cozy chats. I kept my mouth shut, knowing his question was rhetorical.

"Before we leave, I need to be sure you won't run again. Then we have a few loose ends to tie up so that bunch of lowlifes don't follow you," he explained.

I swallowed as I stupidly pointed out the obvious. "I'm twenty now, Frank. I can't stay at home forever."

Dropping the knife with lightning speed, he punched me in the ribs so hard I swore I heard one crack.

"You'll leave me when I say you can leave," he screamed, his spit raining down on my face.

I wheezed and pulled against my bindings as I fought to pull the air into my damaged body.

"You know I just can't work out whether you're too fucking stupid to learn or you like taking a beating."

I couldn't answer him, even if I wanted to. I could barely breathe, let alone talk.

He looked down at me with a kind of morbid curiosity as he assessed his handiwork. If I looked how I felt, I guessed that my body must be a mess of bruises and dried blood. Placing the knife down again, he wrenched my wedding and engagement rings from my finger.

I cried out, though it sounded little more than a whimper, as he stole my only connection to O'Connell.

"You won't be needing these anymore. I've had the paperwork applying for your annulment since before you were stupid enough to get married."

With that little parting gift he left me to wallow in a pool of my own blood.

CHAPTER THIRTY-ONE

I have no idea how long I was bound in that room. It could have been hours, it could have been days. I think I wet myself a couple of times, though I was so out of it I couldn't really be sure. The whole room stank to high heaven so I probably fit right in.

Either Frank had drugged me or he'd hit me a *lot* harder than I thought. I'd taken enough beatings to know that this didn't feel normal. The periods between consciousness, though, were blissful. My mind ran hazily through memories of O'Connell and our time together.

Before when I'd been beaten, I'd never had any of this. O'Connell had given me so many happy moments and a safe place in my mind to hide. He would never know how thankful I was for that. Frank could do whatever he wanted to my body, but he'd never be able to take that away. His increasing sense of desperation during the times I was awake told me that he knew it, too.

When I next opened my eyes, beams of light shone through the mothball holes in the curtains, and I figured it must be morning.

"I said wake up, bitch," Franked shouted, kicking me hard

with his boot in my thigh. I whimpered but opened my eyes to face him. If he stopped hitting me, I'd probably stop passing out.

He paced up and down the room with his hands in his hair. Gone was the cool demeanor of a man unhurried and in its place was a desperate, unhinged psychopath. I guessed that something happened to set him off. He was losing control.

"Tell me you're not going to leave again," he told me, still pacing.

"I promise I won't leave again," I wheezed flatly and without meaning. Yep, that rib was definitely broken.

"I'll fucking gut him if you do. You know that, right?" he asked menacingly.

"I know," I answered.

I wasn't worried about O'Connell. He'd never get near the man I loved because I was putting a knife in Frank's back the minute I got free. I didn't care about going to prison. It was a price I'd happily pay to keep O'Connell safe.

"There isn't enough time. I wanted more time than this," Frank mumbled under his breath. I didn't know what had upset him, but I was glad for it.

He sat back down next to me again and stared at my body. Without warning, he leaned over and cupped me roughly between the legs and bit down hard on my bra-covered nipple.

It was so painful, and so invasive, that I cried out, which hurt my chest. I willed myself to pass out. If this sick fuck was going to rape me, then I didn't want to remember a minute of it.

Gripping my jaw roughly in his hand, he looked me straight in the eye. "We're finishing this when we get home," he promised.

"*Fuck. You,*" I enunciated slowly.

I was expecting another blow, but it never came. He seemed a little less frantic, though. Maybe contemplating all the ways he was going to punish me later had calmed him down.

"You've changed," he pointed out, before leaning over and whispering in my ear. "You have no idea how many different ways I'm going to break you until you learn to do what I say, when I say it."

"If you think you're turning me into my mother, you've got another think coming, you sick fuck," I wheezed but stood my ground.

If I were smart, I would have shut the fuck up. Instead I paid for my stupidity. He didn't hit or molest me again. He just laid his palm on my chest and pressed down. My broken rib screamed in protest.

"All you bitches are the same," he taunted. "It's just a case of learning how to tame you."

I couldn't focus on what he was saying. The pain was too excruciating to hold on anymore. With what little clarity I had left, I imagined that I was lying in O'Connell's arms and closed my eyes. It was only as I hovered on the precipice of consciousness that I could almost smell him and believe that he was really here.

"Oh, no, you don't," Frank laughed, throwing water in my face. "You don't get to pass out on me yet. We've got work to do before we blow this shithole."

Despair and pain made me want to sob, but I refused to give Frank that last victory. "Even if I never make it out of here, you're still going to prison. The police have my statement and the rape kit."

If I died in this hellhole my parting shot would be to remind him he was looking at a lifetime in prison. By this stage I was pretty convinced that he was never going to let me live long enough to see O'Connell again, anyway, so I had nothing left to lose.

"I'm not going to prison, princess. All sorts of things can happen before a rape trial, and this country is all about innocent until proven guilty. You were just an out-of-control kid, and I am the upstanding member of society who did his best to father you through some troubled times." He relayed his ridiculous story with maniacal grandeur, and I could do little more than grunt at him.

"And the rape? How're you going to make that disappear?" I panted.

"Oh, you were raped all right... but by some boy you'd been hooking up with. Understandable, really, given the slutty way you were dressed when you left. You tried pinning it on me because you were pissed at my efforts to instill some discipline. At least that's the account your mother gave to the police."

"You should walk away, Frank. I'm not a minor anymore. I'm a married woman. Any power you had over me is long gone."

I could tell from the look on his face that I was making a mistake. That didn't stop me from doing it. Every time I mouthed back or stood up for myself, I was wrestling a little more control away from Frank. The only way he knew to take it back was to punish me.

"So you'd leave your mother to take your punishment, would you?" he sneered.

"My mother died the day she walked away and let you rape me."

"You fucking bitch," he roared, rearing up and kicking me in the thigh again. It bloody hurt but another hit in the torso would have knocked me out, maybe even killed me. "It wasn't rape. It was you being taught a lesson, and we both know you wanted it."

"Yeah, you just keep telling yourself that," I mumbled.

He lifted up the knife again and held it up to my face.

"Let me tell you how this is going to go. You and I are going to that stinkhole of a gym you've been whoring yourself at. I've been watching it for days, and they haven't opened it since you left. You're going to clear out your stuff and leave a letter explaining that you were never cut out to live in such shitty circumstances. You'll ask everyone to respect your wishes and leave you alone. When we get back, you'll admit to the police that you cried wolf, and you'll move back home."

"If I don't?" I taunted back.

The knife was right under my nose, and from the look in his eyes, I could see he was itching to use it.

"Then I'll stick this in Cormac O'Connell, then Danny Driscoll, and I'll keep going until I find someone who makes you listen."

That woke me up. I had no problem using the knife on Frank, but I couldn't have him touching the people I had loved before I had a chance to do it.

"Okay," I said quietly, trying to feign defeat. "Let's just get this over with."

"Patience, princess. We'll wait until this evening. Then we're gone. I thought I'd have more time, but those little shits are relentless. I need to shut this down now and get you home."

He'd be lucky if I was still conscious by then. I was in a pretty bad way, and I needed a hospital, not that he'd noticed.

He seemed to keep himself busy for the rest of the day. Occasionally I could hear him on the phone in another room, though I couldn't make out what he was saying. From time to time he brought me water. The first time I was so parched I gulped it down thirstily. Then cried out in agony when it hit my stomach, and I vomited violently. After that I learned to sip it. The relief it brought was tempered by the pain I endured every time I swallowed.

As soon as Frank left the room, I allowed my delirious mind to drift back to O'Connell. I turned my face on the pillow, which was stained with my blood. I could see him lying next to me, grinning his cocky, panty-dropping grin.

"Hey, baby," he said.

Silent tears ran down my cheeks as I answered him. "You're here," I whispered.

"Never left, sunshine. I need you to do something, okay? This is really important." His grin gone, he looked at me earnestly. "You need to hold on. I know it hurts, but I'm coming for you. I just need you to hold on a little longer for me. Can you do that?"

"It hurts really bad," I answered through my tears.

"I know it does. Remember, I've taken a hit or too meself." He paused to wipe away a tear with his thumb, sounding a little more Irish than usual. "But you promised me you wouldn't run again. You promised you'd stay and fight for me."

"I don't think this counts as running," I answered.

"It does in my book. You die on me, and I'll be fucking pissed. So you stay and fight for me. Promise me."

"I promise." I smiled as I tried to reassure him.

I was absolutely petrified, but everything was better having him here with me. His face was the most beautiful face I'd ever seen, and it gave me a little bit of peace.

"You have pretty eyes," I mumbled randomly.

"Well, I promise to pass them to our kids. You just make sure you live long enough to give me some."

"I'll do my best," I whispered.

"Good girl. Now sleep, baby. I'll see you soon."

Frank came for me when the sun had set. When I opened my eyes, that beautiful face was gone.

* * *

I protested when Frank raised my sleeve, wrapped something around my arm, and tapped for a vein.

"No. I don't want it. Stop," I groaned, but he was too strong, and I was still tied down.

"It's just a little something to get you up and moving. It's only a small dose. I don't need a zombie. You still have a letter to write," he told me, as the injection went in my arm.

After about ten minutes, the pain had faded enough for me to stand when he cut my restraints. We shuffled out of the door, and I saw I'd been held in a basement flat. I could see why he'd warned me not to scream. Houses along the street were packed closely together. If I screamed long enough, chances were that someone would have heard me.

The street was empty as he pushed me toward his car, the knife still threateningly at my back. I contemplated making my stand now, but I couldn't risk him getting pissed and going after my boys. I just needed to keep my eyes out for a weapon and make a move when I saw an opportunity.

The drive to the gym was mercifully short, and it broke my heart to think about how close to O'Connell I'd been the whole time. Knowing my husband he'd probably torn London apart looking for me.

Frank double-parked in the alley behind the gym. He blocked the other garages, but he wasn't likely to get any bother at night. Most of the businesses around here were only open during the day.

All the lights were out at Driscoll's gym. Frank produced a set of keys, presumably swiped from my bag, and unlocked the back door that I never used because the alleyway was so creepy. The gym looked different in the dark, but the familiar smell felt like home. There was no time to reminisce, though. Frank was shoving me toward the office, knife in hand, and he was in a hurry. When we got there he turned on the desk lamp and pushed me roughly into the chair.

"Now write this fucking thing and let's get out of here," he ordered, slapping some paper and a pen down on the desk in front of me.

I picked up the pen shakily and contemplated what to write. The dirt and dried blood on my hand left smears on the pristine white paper. I pressed the pen down when a noise from the gym had us both looking up. None of the lights went on, but a shuffling sound preceded the door opening and in walked Danny. I was devastated. There was no way that Frank would let Danny walk away from this.

Danny took in the scene and spoke to me softly. "All right there, sunshine. What's happening here then?"

"Nothing much, Danny," I answered softly, as I slowly stood. "Just catching up on some paperwork."

Danny nodded, as though this was a perfectly reasonable explanation for what I was doing and the state that I was in. Frank's grip tightened painfully on my shoulder, but he let go when I stood.

"Haven't seen you for a while. Why don't you come over and give me a hug?"

I moved slowly, not looking anywhere but straight ahead.

"That's enough, Emily. We won't need the letter anymore."

I turned around as Frank rushed toward us. He side-stepped me and went for Danny.

I stepped in front of him and raised my hands to push him away. Danny was the nearest thing I had to a dad, and there was no way that Frank was taking him from me.

"No!" Danny screamed.

I stumbled and fell backward onto the floor. Frank fell on top of me.

As quickly as it happened, Frank muttered, "Fuck," and staggered to his feet. Shoving Danny hard, he ran out of the door. I couldn't believe how fast he was, given the amount of blood he'd lost. It felt like I was bathed in it.

"You okay, Danny?" I asked.

"I'm fine, baby girl. How 'bout yourself?"

"I've been better." I chuckled, relieved beyond measure that Frank was gone and that Danny appeared to be unharmed.

"You just stay with me, darlin'. Con is on his way."

He scrambled toward the desk, grabbed the phone, and dialed frantically.

"It's Danny Driscoll. She's at the gym. I need an ambulance here now and get someone to tell Cormac O'Connell," he barked.

Slamming down the phone, he raced back to me. He couldn't have been gone more than thirty seconds. I'd have waited a lot longer to hear the comfort of his voice.

"Be careful," I warned Danny. "Frank's lost a lot of blood. He can't be far. He's still dangerous."

"It weren't his blood, sunshine," Danny told me grimly, his eyes wet with unshed tears. I followed his gaze downward and saw the knife sticking out of my chest. He held my hand between his two, and I marveled at how warm those weathered hands felt.

"Meeting you was the best thing that ever happened to me," I told him.

"Not sure about that, darlin'. I don't think you'd be lying here now if it weren't for me."

I tutted in admonishment. "Frank would have found me anyway. You gave me a family. I haven't had that in a really long time."

The cold had crept into every part of my body, but the pain seemed to be lessening.

"Me, either," he admitted, crying proper tears now.

"Love you," I whispered.

"I love you, too, sunshine," he replied, squeezing my hand.

As I drifted off into the darkness, it reminded me that I wasn't alone.

CHAPTER THIRTY-TWO

The incessant beeping hurt my ears, and I wanted it to stop, but I couldn't keep my eyes open. The pain in my chest throbbed, and everything felt like an effort, even the tiny action of opening my eyes. The room around me was silent but for the beeping.

After a minute or two, I felt the drugs pulling me back under, though I could still feel Danny's gentle hand, warm in mine.

* * *

The second time I came around, things were much clearer, and the pain was much worse.

O'Connell's head rested on his arms beside me as he slept. Dark circles rimmed his eyes, and he was in desperate need of a good shave, but I was so glad to see him I could have wept.

My hand felt heavy and sluggish, and raising it was like swimming through treacle. I did it anyway and ran my fingers slowly and comfortingly through his unkempt hair. After a few seconds, he woke and, looking up at me, raised a smile.

"You're awake," he said in awe, and I nodded.

"Water," I begged croakily.

With shaking hands, he poured me a glass of water from the jug beside my bed and raised the straw to my parched lips. The cool, clear liquid was a balm to my burning throat, and I lay back on my pillow after a few sips, exhausted from the effort.

"Danny?" I asked him, trying to talk as little as possible.

"He's fine, baby. We're all fine."

He paused, looking pained. Staring at my face, he looked desperately sad, and as he started talking, I realized how much misplaced guilt he had been carrying while I was asleep.

"I'm sorry, Em. I'm so fucking sorry. I should never have sent you off on your own to wait for me. I should have stayed by your side and protected you. My only job is to make sure you're happy and protected, and I fucked it up."

It killed me to see him beat himself up like this, and in truth I was in too much pain to say much. "Not your fault or mine. Just Frank's. He would have killed you as soon as he saw you. Where is he?"

"Police got him," he said with contempt. "They're remanding him into custody so they can add rape to the charges. He's fucking lucky they got to him before I did."

I closed my eyes briefly, silently giving thanks that I wouldn't have to worry about O'Connell being locked up.

I tried hard to open my eyes when he called out my name, but I was already falling back into the darkness, and as I did I could swear that he was crying.

* * *

"What's wrong, doc? Why won't she wake up?"

"Mr. O'Connell, your wife has only just been moved from intensive care. The fact that she has come around once is a good sign, but keeping her asleep is her body's way of taking care of her while it repairs itself. The knife pierced her lung and only just missed the main artery. It's likely that she'll have respiratory problems for the rest of her life, and the road to recovery will be a long one. You're very lucky that she's still alive."

"I fucking know that, doc. What I want to know is when she'll wake up!"

"Con! For fuck's sake, rein it in," I heard Danny chastise him, and I could feel the anger radiating from O'Connell. I desperately wanted to calm him down, but I was trapped once again inside my own body.

"I'm sorry, doc," O'Connell apologized. "I can't thank you enough for saving Em's life. I'm just worried, that's all. I need to hear her voice and feel her touch to know that everything's okay."

"You will, Mr. O'Connell, but right now our biggest concern is the risk of infection. I know it's crass to say, but you need to learn to be patient, and I mean it about the visitors. No more than two at any one time. I've lost count of how many times my nurses have evicted people from this young lady's room."

Their conversation faded away. *Be patient, baby, I'll be there soon.*

* * *

Danny was reading *Moby-Dick* to me when I finally came around. I didn't disturb him, content to let his raspy voice narrate the story for me. I imagined him as an old Irish Captain Ahab.

He glanced up to find me watching him and slammed the book shut. "Thank fuck for that." He snorted. "I thought I was gonna be reading this shite for days."

"*Moby-Dick* isn't shite," I whispered.

"Whatever," he mumbled. "It was in the waiting room, and they told us to keep talking to you in case you could hear, so I picked this shite to read so you'd wake up and tell me to stop."

I smiled at him and reached out my tired hand. He held it in his own, and I remembered his touch as one that kept me warm in the dark.

"O'Connell?" I asked.

"I convinced him to go and have a shower and a shave and something to eat. Course now he'll be pissed that you woke up and he wasn't here."

"How long have I been here?"

"'Bout a week, darlin'. The knife punctured your lung, and they had to operate. He missed your heart and a major artery, but your lung is in pretty bad shape. You got an infection straight off the back of the surgery, so it was touch and go for a while."

I lay there and just tried to process everything. I was in pain, confused, overwhelmed, and tired but, above all else, I was glad to be alive. Frank was behind bars now, and between this and the rape, I doubted he'd get out of prison any time soon.

"I knew you'd make it," Danny mumbled, as he stared at the cover of the book. "I always said you were a fighter, and I wasn't wrong. Besides, it wouldn't be fair. You're not supposed to out-live your kids, especially when they go trying to save your life. It wasn't your time yet, sunshine, not with all of us keeping you here. We need you too much to let you go."

He continued to stare at the book with watery eyes, as he contemplated what could have happened. There was little I could say to console him, but I was alive, and that was all that mattered. Besides, my throat was burned up again from all the talking, and I needed to rest. Tapping his hand, I asked him, "Read to me until I fall asleep?"

He rolled his eyes and sniffed, as he turned back the crinkled cover.

"Call me Ishmael..."

* * *

Over the next week I was never alone. Almost every time I woke up, O'Connell was there. On the rare occasions that he wasn't, one or more of the boys would be there with me.

Danny continued to read to me, and I knew he was secretly enjoying the book because I caught him still reading when he thought I was asleep. I'd already asked Nikki to bring me a copy of *The Color Purple* for when we'd finished. If he didn't like it, I'd let him pick the next one.

Visiting hours didn't apply to me, and sensing that they were fighting a losing battle, the staff at the hospital gave me a private room so that we didn't disturb the other patients. It was the same room that was currently staging poker night. Having no idea how to play and no interest in learning, I flicked through one of the stacks of magazines I'd been given and amused the guys by reading them all their horoscopes.

The hospital's set-in-steel rule of only offering patients, and not visitors, tea or coffee hadn't gone down well with Danny. He'd taken to charming the rounded, stern-faced trolley lady into giving him his regular caffeine shot. Pushing the door open with his butt, he walked in carrying two coffees. Of course I was still too sick to drink anything with caffeine, but the trolley lady didn't know that. So he snagged an extra one for himself.

O'Connell played cards with one hand, as he insisted on holding mine with his other one. He couldn't bear to be in the same room and not touch me, like he was constantly reminding himself that I was still there.

Watching everyone getting comfy, a thought occurred to me. "What's happening about the Ramos fight?"

The whole room stopped as all the boys turned to look at me.

"Um...the fight is gonna be cancelled, Em. With everything that's happened, there's no way that Con will be in good enough shape to fight."

O'Connell had gone back to studying his cards, clearly unaffected by the conversation.

"But if you cancel the fight, will he reschedule?" I asked.

"Will he, fuck," Danny huffed. "He wants a stepping-stone, and they're two a penny. If Con doesn't fight him, he'll find someone who will."

"It doesn't matter. There'll be other fights. I'm not leaving Em," O'Connell said with indifference, as though the fight meant nothing to him. But I knew better.

"What do you think?" I asked Danny.

"The amount of training he's already done for the Calvari fight counts for something. If he puts his nose to the grindstone for the next two weeks, it'll be close, but I think he can go the distance. No fucking point, though, if he can't get his head in the game."

"I've told you I'm not fighting," O'Connell said quietly. "My wife is laid up in the hospital after nearly dying. Quite frankly, I'm fucking stunned you think I would."

Danny seemed guilty and resigned. I looked carefully at his face and realized how dejected he was. Frank had nearly killed me, but he'd also taken away O'Connell's big shot at a title. I couldn't live with that. I wouldn't live with that.

"Guys," I said quietly, "could you give us a minute?"

O'Connell, sensing an argument, put his cards down with a sigh. To their credit the boys filed out of the room without a single word of complaint.

"I'm not fighting," he argued as soon as the door closed behind them.

"Why?"

"I don't want to," he retorted.

"That's crap. Why?"

He crossed his arms and looked everywhere around the room except at me.

"O'Connell," I warned, "why?"

With another sigh, he unfolded his arms and looked up at me.

"You know why, sunshine. I was so caught up in the fight and the sponsors last time that I left you unprotected, and you nearly died because of it. I'm not doing it again. I don't need to fight. I can always go back to working in construction."

"Is that what you want?" I asked.

"I don't want to leave you, and honestly I don't think I could get back in the ring again without being reminded of what happened. Danny's right. My head's too fucked to go back."

"Then we fix it," I told him, running my hand through his hair. It had become my favorite way to comfort him.

He turned his face into my hand. "I'm afraid, sunshine," he admitted.

"Of losing the fight?" I asked.

"Of losing you."

"How much do I need to survive to prove to you that I'm not going anywhere?"

He looked me deep in the eyes, and I could see all of his pain and fear, but he needed to get over this. Even if he lost the fight, if he didn't face his fears and get back into the ring, then he'd have to live with that fear forever.

"I can't do it, Em. It's over."

I rubbed my fingertips over his T-shirt-covered chest, right where I knew his tattoo was. "A champion is someone who gets up when they can't."

"You don't fight fair, you know that, right?" He choked out his words, but I could see him wavering.

"I fight. That's all that matters, and you need to do the same. If you need to picture Frank on every bag or at the end of every fist then that's what you do. This guy is a has-been. He's had his shot in the spotlight, and now it's your turn."

"And if I lose?" he asked me.

"Then you go down fighting. But when you walk out of that

ring, you do it with your head held high because you gave it everything."

"I think they'd be better off calling *you* the bloody Hurricane," he grumbled, but I knew I had him.

"You'll fight?" I asked hopefully.

"I have conditions," he warned.

"Okay," I agreed warily.

"I'm not leaving you on your own until the fight is over and I can look after you. The boys and I will take turns visiting, but you'll never be alone."

"You know that, with Frank in prison, I'm in absolutely no danger, right?"

"Hey, is it my head we're fixing or yours?"

I rolled my eyes at the suggestion but relented. "Fine. Next condition?"

"I get to sleep here when I'm not training."

"No deal. There's no way you can train hard and sleep in a crappy chair. If you're going to do this, then do it right. That means sleeping in a proper bed and getting some rest. You eat right and stick to Danny's training program or there's no point in bothering."

"Jesus, woman, you drive a hard bargain." He scowled. "Fine, but the boys take it in turns to sleep in the chair."

"That's not fair. You can't expect them to do that. Especially when I'm in no danger."

"Non-fucking-negotiable," he growled.

"Anything else?" I sulked.

"Yeah," he said gently, leaning forward. "Win or lose, after this there's no more fighting until you're better. I get to spoil and take care of you and drive you mad, but the fighting stops until you're healthy."

"Deal," I agreed easily, looking forward to it. Standing up, he kissed me lovingly then opened the door to let the boys in.

Kieran had looked at the both of us before he guessed. "You're fighting, aren't 'cha?" Danny grinned broadly as he glanced at me knowingly.

"Seriously, do you even own a set of balls, 'cause I'm pretty sure you gave them to Em when you got hitched," Tommy joked, although he was seriously taking his life in his own hands baiting O'Connell while I was still laid up.

"Laugh it up, fuck bag. You're sleeping in the chair till I fight."

"No way," exclaimed Tommy. "That chair is fucking uncomfortable, and no offense, Em, but I won't sleep for shit."

O'Connell stared at him hard until he relented.

"Fine. I might just lie down next to you, Em, if I get too uncomfy."

"Not if you want to keep your fucking legs," warned my husband.

"Finish your game," I admonished, smiling at Danny. "O'Connell's having an early night."

* * *

The next two weeks dragged on monotonously. Every day meant more pills, more observations, and more tests. I missed O'Connell terribly, even though he used Kieran's phone to call me on Tommy's number four or five times a day. I could hear the excitement in his voice, and I knew that training was going well.

Despite all his initial protests, Tommy didn't moan once about babysitting me and often split duties with Liam or my friends from university. But he was always the one asleep by my bed in the morning.

Tommy's whole family came to visit frequently, and although they didn't have much money, they supplied a steady stream of baked goods to keep me and the boys going. Even Father Pat stopped by a few times.

O'Connell broke tradition and spent the entire rest day before the fight with me, watching movies and listening to music. This time he didn't need the day to prepare. His head had been in the game for two weeks.

As he left me for the final time before the fight to head off to Father Pat's, he sat down on my bed. Undoing the chain around his neck holding his cross and wedding ring, he refastened it around mine. "You know I've got this, right?" he told me cockily.

"I know, baby." I smiled, truly believing he did.

"I wish you were with me," he admitted.

"I will be," I replied. "Now put your big girl pants on and go get a title. The flat's looking kind of bare, and we could use a big, gaudy-looking belt to brighten up the place."

"I love you, Mrs. O'Connell," he told me.

"Love you, too, O'Connell," I replied, and after kissing me the way that every woman should be kissed at least once in her life, he was out of the door.

* * *

Nine hours later he walked back in again with an eye so black he could barely see out of it, a split lip, and a very serious face.

"Well?" I asked impatiently, frustrated that I'd been on tenterhooks for hours and that no one had been answering my calls.

Suddenly his face lit up like the morning sun, and the heart-stopping smile that I loved so much spread across his face.

"Winner by knockout in the seventh round and new IBF Heavyweight Champion," he announced.

"That's my boy," I said leaning back against my pillow.

EPILOGUE

CORMAC O'CONNELL

Jab, jab, cross. Jab, jab, cross.

"If Tommy doesn't get his hands off my wife, I'm gonna fuck him up."

Jab, jab, cross. Jab, jab, cross.

"He's fucking with you, Con. Now concentrate. My nan could hit harder than you are." Kieran took the piss as he held the heavy bag steady.

"Your nan is hard as nails. Even Danny's scared of her," I joked, but threw an extra bit of weight behind the combination, which made him grunt.

"Besides, you owe him for taking care of your girl while you trained," he reminded me. I looked over at Tommy and reminded myself why he was getting a free pass. There were only a few men in this world who I would trust my wife's safety to, and all kidding aside, Tommy was one of them.

Today was the first day I'd let her out of the apartment, and I was not entirely comfortable with her being anywhere but resting in bed. It'd been two months since that bastard took her and my life nearly ended. That was the truth of it because, without Em, there was nothing else. My hollow, meaningless life had been filled by this woman. I didn't deserve her, but there was nothing I wouldn't do, no line I wouldn't cross, to keep her safe.

There was a festering hate burning inside me for the bastard who took what was mine. Believe me, there was a day of reckoning coming when Frank was going to get what was coming to him.

For now I kept my rage contained. Em needed me to grow a pair of balls and deal with my shit, and I'd be whatever she needed me to be so she could heal from this. Of all of us, she seemed the least fucked up. Danny, me, Kieran, we all had guilt. If we'd done things differently, protected her better, she would never have been taken. That was on us, and we had to live with it.

Em didn't see it that way, though. She felt free, like she'd gotten a new lease on life because Frank was behind bars. She made me promise I wouldn't do anything while he was in there. I never made any promises about when he gets out.

"Seriously, Con. Focus. Danny sees you punching like an old lady, he's gonna think you're out of shape."

"Fuck you." I grinned.

Kieran wasn't entirely wrong. I hadn't put on the gloves since I'd won the IBF belt, but as usual, my wife had been kicking my arse. She announced this morning that she was coming to Danny's and that I could join her or leave my lazy, overprotective arse at home. Turns out, she was more of a hardarse when it came to training than Danny.

I wasn't in fighting shape, but with my muscle memory and hard work, I soon would be. Besides, I was hungry for it. I'd had a taste of winning, and I wanted more. With everyone behind me, there was no reason I couldn't have it, too. I never used to think like that, but Em changed me.

She still thought that breakfast at Daisy's was the first time we met. It was true, but I first saw her months before that. My hang-over had been raging, and I'd had bad news to break to Danny. He'd arranged a fight between Liam and a local guy from an-other gym. The cocky little shit had been mouthing off in Brady's the night before. It was amusing till the gobshite turned on me. I couldn't be arsed-mouthing back, so I floored him and broke his jaw. Pretty safe to say that Friday's fight was cancelled after that.

"Danny's gonna put my balls in a blender when he finds out," I had told Kieran, who looked highly amused.

"Tell him now while he's having his breakfast."

"We haven't been home yet. I stink of booze and birds," I had reminded him.

"Listen, Liam told me he's friendly with some waitress down at Daisy's. The old fucker's happiest when he's eating, and if you're in a public place, he can't bollock you so bad."

The man had a point so I decided to risk it. Danny wasn't there when I'd arrived so I waited across the street. I needed Danny to get comfy before I spilled the beans. Round the corner came a gorgeous pair of legs and an arse fine enough to make a grown man beg. She was pretty, in a wholesome good-girl sort of way, but good girls weren't really my type. There was nothing wrong with the legs of the bad girl who'd been wrapped around me last night.

No, it wasn't her looks or her body that caught my attention. It was what she did next. This girl didn't look like she had a quid to her name. Her jacket was threadbare, and she had it wrapped around her like it was the most expensive possession she had. A few yards away from me, a guy was sleeping rough in a doorway. It was a pretty common sight in this part of Lon-don, especially this early in the morning. I barely noticed the homeless anymore. This girl saw him and stopped. It wasn't like she was embarrassed at having to walk past him. She literally had to cross the street to get to him. But when she did, she laid her hand on his arm and asked if there was anything she could do to help. He smiled and thanked her but told her he was fine. Then she emptied her pockets and gave him everything she had. In this day and age, who did that?

That's what made this girl so special. Twenty minutes later she came back over, shivering in her waitress uniform, and handed the guy a hot cup of coffee as he was packing up his sleeping bag. That act of kindness probably made his day, because it sure as hell made mine. It was the first bit of faith in humanity I'd had since Kieran's ma stepped up for me.

I didn't wait for Danny after that. I wasn't ready to face her, but I emptied my pockets to the homeless guy as I walked home. Already she was making me want to be a better person. I turned up at the cafe a few times after that, but never made it inside. When my day had been hard and shitty, I'd watch her from across the street. Seeing how she was with people and how she'd smile shyly when she thought no one was looking instantly made my day better.

Every girl I'd ever met acted like they were performing for me. Everything they did or said invited me to look at them or touch them. It was the rare exception when they didn't want me to fuck them. This girl just wanted to be invisible. I didn't really know her, and I worried that I'd built her up in my head to be something she wasn't, but by the time I grew enough balls to muscle in on Danny's breakfast and actually meet her, I was already half in love. It was probably why I acted like a total tool that first time, too tongue-tied to even open my mouth.

Em knew I loved her, but I didn't think she'd ever know just how much. She was my peace, my inspiration, my motivation, and my reward. She was my salvation. The center of my fucking universe. I was going to conquer the whole world and lay it at her feet. It was the least she deserved. People thought the IBF

Championship fight was the hardest thing I've ever fought for. It wasn't. Getting that girl to fall in love and marry me was the hardest fight of my life.

I hit the bag Kieran was still holding harder and harder until he was grunting with every punch. I could feel Em watching me, and I smiled, knowing that my need to impress her fueled each hit. Now that she had me here, my appetite for training was relentless. Until Frank was gone for good and I knew my girl would get the happy ever after she deserved, this fight wasn't over. It was only just beginning.

Dear Reader,

Thank you so much for reading *The Hurricane*. When I started writing this story, I had absolutely no idea that anyone would read it. I had two strong characters and the opening scenes which kept playing themselves out in my head like a movie. So I wrote them down as chapters and casually mentioned my scribbling to my best friend. She asked to see them and then kept begging me for more and more chapters. Before I knew it, I had a book!

Em's story is a difficult one, and I needed to write it from her perspective so that you could fully understand the journey that she went through to become the strong woman that she is. Although the prologue and epilogue to *The Hurricane* give you an insight into Cormac, his personality is so strong that I wanted you to be able to read more in his own words. So I'm so pleased to be able to give you this bonus chapter. One of the most gut-wrenching scenes in *The Hurricane* is when Em is kidnapped and tortured by Frank. This chapter will let you into O'Connell's head as he lives through those painful few days until she is found.

I am overwhelmed that so many people connected with Em and Cormac, and to finally see their story in print means more than you will ever know. Thank you once again for reading *The Hurricane* and for helping to make my dream of being an author come true.

Happy Reading,

R.J. Prescott

BONUS CHAPTER

I warned my girl once that I was fucked-up possessive. She didn't understand. Or if she did, she didn't call me on it. When you've got nothing, you covet the good shit. I never had much of anything to speak of worth hoarding until Em. Through the window of that cafe, with the sun shining down on that gorgeous blond hair, she looked like a fucking angel. I didn't think she'd ever give me the time of day, but she did.

She was crazy-smart and beautiful inside and out. Her tiny frame made her seem fragile and breakable but that wasn't who she was at all. She was the strongest person I'd ever met. I wasn't good enough for her, and I never would be. But I fought for her, the only thing I'd ever wanted, and now she was mine. So yeah, I was possessive, selfishly wanting as much of her as I could get. Pretty soon someone would figure out that she could do better than me. My job was to make sure that person wasn't her.

I would love her, cherish her, and protect her until the day I died. That was my vow, and if my possessiveness in keeping that promise pissed her off, she wouldn't bawl me out. That wasn't her way. She'd throw her tiny arms around me and hug me until the rage and fear passed, until I could breathe again. That's why I knew she'd be okay with me watching over her like I always did.

"Why aren't you with Em?" I asked Kieran, confused to see him here.

"Listen, Con. Your ma's on the warpath. I don't think she's drunk, but after tonight's win, she's got a sniff of the sponsors, and she wants a cut. Me and Em ran into her a few minutes ago, and she was gunning for you."

"Fuck!" I muttered, searching unsuccessfully through the crowd for my bitch of a mother. "Can you get rid of her?" I asked.

"Sure, but it won't be pretty. She'll cause a big enough scene that it'll spook the sponsors."

His face was as bleak as mine as we quickly considered our options.

"I hate to say it, Con," he said, "but you're probably best paying her off."

"If I chuck that bitch any more money, she'll know how to get to me, and she'll be back for more. That's Em's money, too, now and I'm not taking from my wife so my mother can piss it up the wall."

I'd have Em think I was indifferent, but every time my ma tried to sabotage something good in my life for her own end, I felt the pain of it. That craving for a mother's love had me forgiving more sins that I'd ever confessed to Father Pat, but no more. I'd cleaned up her mess for the last time. Now I was done. Her love was cruel, so mine would be too.

"Fuck it," I told Kieran decisively. "If she finds me, she'll be expecting me to try and pull her aside, so I'll do the opposite. I'll introduce her to all the sponsors and play son of the year. Then when I get her alone, she's out on her arse. Next fight we post our own boys on the door, and she doesn't get inside no matter what."

Kieran nodded in agreement, still searching the crowd. Just then I saw a guy wearing a black-and-red security jacket breaking up a fight.

"Why is security on the floor?" Kieran's gaze turned to follow mine.

"Drunken brawls are breaking out all over the arena. I guess they need to put a lid on it before anyone gets seriously hurt. Find Em for me?" I asked him. He rolled his eyes, knowing I was overreacting as usual.

"She'll be fine in your changing room, but if you get back to kissing arse with those sponsors, I'll go keep your girl company."

The cheeky fucker winked at me and narrowly avoided a smack. If I wasn't so tired, he'd be wearing a nice bruise on that arm of his.

Leaving the bastard to go and take care of Em, I turned back to chat with Danny and the sponsors. This was the part of fighting I hated. If I hadn't needed Kieran to take care of my girl, he'd be the one here selling rainbows and unicorns. Shit, that boy could sell ice to the Eskimos.

I nodded when appropriate and tried not to grunt when they asked me a question. It's like the worst form of torture to step out of the ring, after repeatedly having your head punched, and then have to sell yourself. Danny didn't look any more comfortable than I did, but at least the sponsors seemed to be listening to him.

Despite Kieran's warning Ma hadn't shown up, and with a bit of luck we'd be done soon and I'd be back in the changing room with my wife. My cock hardened as I thought of sinking into that lush body of hers. After weeks of dealing with Danny's mandatory prefight sex ban, I'd need to fuck her against the wall of the shower just to take the edge off us both.

My tiredness forgotten, I looked for some sign that Danny would be wrapping this up soon. Ten minutes and several handshakes later, the happy sponsors wandered off, and I had enough backing to let me train comfortably for another year.

Danny slapped me on the back, looking as pleased as he ever did. "You did it, Con. Your first title! Now don't go getting all complacent. One little title won't make your career. I'll give you a couple of days off, then it's back to training."

"Two whole days off? Wow, thanks, Danny," I mumbled sarcastically.

"Listen, lard arse, you want to sit around getting fat and lazy, that's up to you. There's plenty of young, hungry fighters out there waiting for their shot. Don't waste my time if your head's not in the game."

I knew he worried that my marriage to Em would make me weak and soft. He was wrong. Being with her made me stronger.

I held my hands up in surrender. "I'm joking." I laughed. "You tell me when to train, and I'll be there. You know that."

I'd told him I was in for the long haul, and I meant it.

"Hummf," Danny grunted, noncommittally. "I need a smoke," was all I got by way of a good-bye as he shuffled off, but I could tell by the little quirk of his lips that he was happy.

Making my way to the changing rooms, I seemed to get way-laid by people trying to hug or high-five me like I was their best friend. I didn't mind spending time with them. Half of 'em were three sheets to the wind, courtesy of the arena bar, but they'd spend their hard-earned cash to come out and support me.

By the time I reached my changing room, it was empty. Frowning, I headed out as Kieran came running back in, his hair sticking up like he'd been combing his hands through it. I knew from the look on his face something was wrong.

"Where's Em?" I barked at him.

The frightened look on his face made my stomach drop. Kieran wasn't scared of anything.

"Where the fuck is she, Kier?" I shouted.

"She's gone. The door was wide open but she wasn't there. I've asked around but no one's seen her."

I grabbed a hoodie from my training bag and pulled it over my head as I ran out the door. "Get the boys together and call the police. I'll meet you back here," I ordered.

"Where are you going?" he responded.

"Security has CCTV everywhere. I want to know if they caught the fucker on camera."

I bolted out the door, trusting that Kieran would move as fast as I was. The security room was at the end of the corridor. Banging on the heavy black door, it was opened by a mean fucker looking for trouble.

"I need your help. My wife's been taken from my changing room. Can you check the security feeds for me?"

Waving me in the security guard went straight to a complicated bank of monitors.

"How long ago?" he asked.

"Fifteen, twenty minutes maybe," I guessed.

I was so hyped up on adrenaline that I couldn't stand still. Every minute I wasted was another that my girl was moving farther away from me.

"What was she wearing?" he demanded.

"A red top with dark blue jeans," I responded instantly.

My mind flashed back to how she looked after the fight. Her cheeks all flushed, Em looked beautiful and perfect and so out of place in the crowd of drinkers and fighters and hecklers that it made my heart hurt to think I hadn't protected her. We weren't married five minutes and I'd failed her already.

There's no way she would have left me. If she wasn't in that changing room, she was in the wind. God help the fucker who'd taken what was mine. Wherever Em was, she had my heart with her. All that was left behind was a rage-fueled machine, hell-bent on vengeance.

"There," the guard said, pointing to a monitor on the far left. The picture was grainy and fuzzy but you could clearly see a tall, well-built guy with a dark baseball cap pulled down over his eyes. It was what he was carrying that made my blood boil. On camera it looked like he was helping a drunken girl home, but I'd recognize Em anywhere, and she was unconscious.

"Motherfucker," I snarled. I'd never seen a picture of Frank, but I instinctively knew it was him. "What about the car park feeds? Tell me you got something with his license plate." Five agonizing minutes later, the security guard shook his head.

"Sorry, mate, looks like he got lucky. He carries her around the corner of the building and out of sight of the cameras. I'm guessing he parked across the road. We've got eyes on the gate clocking cars coming in and out, but there's only a low-level perimeter around the building. Makes it easier for people to park across the road and hop the barrier when the car park is full."

I stared at the guy as my fury built. It wasn't his fault the cameras didn't pick up more, but I was pissed at him anyway.

"What do you want me to do?" he asked. "The police should be here soon."

"Make sure this footage stays safe for them to collect and keep looking for anything else. I'm in DR7."

He nodded, probably relieved I was leaving. Running back to the changing room, I opened the door to see the guys all there. Liam, Tommy, Kieran, and half a dozen guys from the gym stood with Ryan, Albie, Nikki, and the rest of Em's friends. Each of them looked as bleak as the other, which only ramped up my anger and fear.

Danny, no doubt sensing my desperation, came forward and pushed me onto the bench. "What do you know, Con?" he asked me solemnly.

I swallowed before I told him. Em would hate for everyone to know her past. She worried that people would look at her differently. But everyone here loved her, and they needed to know what they were up against.

"Em's been hiding from her stepfather, Frank," I said quietly. "He knocked her about for years, but she only left when he raped her and her ma did nothing to stop it. She's convinced he's trying to find her. It's why she was so nervous."

Danny nodded gravely but didn't look surprised.

"You knew?" I asked him.

"I suspected from the first time I met her that someone had treated her badly. Me da knocked me and me sister about, too. She was so much like Em."

I wanted to think he said "was" because she was better now, not because she was dead. I wasn't brave enough to ask.

"When will the police be here?" I asked Kieran hoarsely.

"Should be in the next fifteen minutes. They said they were sending officers straightaway."

I put my head in my hands and said a silent prayer that they'd find her, that she was safe, that he wasn't hurting her.

A firm hand squeezed my shoulder, and I looked up to see Danny in front of me. "We've all lost her, Con, and we're all going to get her back."

I looked up and stared him right in the eye. If there's one person in the world who would tell it to me straight, who wouldn't lie to me, it was Danny.

"Promise?" I asked him.

The face in front of me was hard and unwavering. There was no doubt in his eyes when he answered me. "I promise," he vowed. "Now get in the shower and change. You'll need to give your statement and be ready for what happens next."

It was a relief to be given instructions. Danny knew what to do. I nodded and walked into the adjoining bathroom. When I pushed the door shut, it didn't click, and I caught the end of the conversation next door.

"He's not going to keep it together for long," Liam warned Danny.

"I know," Danny replied gravely. "Till I find her, no one lets Con out of their sight unless he's in the bathroom."

"You think we'll get her back?" Tommy asked, as his voice cracked slightly.

I held my breath, waiting for his answer.

"Of course we're getting her back. She's one of ours. We all need to just stay focused until we do."

Having heard enough, I stripped, pulled off my dirty wraps, and walked under the blistering hot shower. There was no relief, just the paralyzing numbness of knowing I wouldn't last long with my heart walking around outside my body.

Ten minutes later I was dressed and back in the changing room just as the police walked in.

"I'm PC Kent," he introduced himself. "Which one of you is Cormac O'Connell?"

"I am," I replied.

"Can you tell me what happened?" he asked, as he pulled out a notebook and pen.

As quickly as I could, I relayed the whole story.

As PC Kent scribbled furiously, his partner, who hadn't introduced himself, spoke into the radio. "Control, could we have an ID check on Mr. Frank Thomas, believed to be a resident in Cardiff. We should have a rape complaint on file from two years ago from Miss Emily Thomas listing his home address. Can I also have the license plates of any vehicles in his name?"

I carried on giving my statement, including as much information as I could about Frank.

Ten minutes later the partner's radio crackled into life, though I didn't hear what was said before he turned it down. When he finished writing he put his pen away and looked me in the eye. "Mr. O'Connell, your wife will now be officially reported missing. I'm going to ask an officer from the South Wales police force to visit the address of Mr. Thomas to ascertain his whereabouts. In the meantime, we'll search for any vehicles which may be registered or rented to her mother or stepfather. An alert will go out on all of those cars, and if Frank's spotted driving any of them, he'll be immediately stopped and called in for questioning.

"If we have any news, we'll let you know straightaway. Mr. Doherty and Mr. Driscoll have both given me contact numbers, but if you hear from either Frank or Emily, you need to let me know immediately."

I nodded and shook his hand but didn't really notice when he left.

"It's not enough," I told Danny. "Em told me Frank's ex-police. He knows everything they'll be doing, and he won't use a car in his name. I can't sit on my arse and do nothing."

"Then we go door to door," Kieran suggested. "We split up and ask as many people as we can whether anyone saw anything. You never know, we might get lucky, and at least we'd be doing something. We should ask around by the gym too. It's a good bet he's been staking that out as well. You can't even fart outside Danny's without one of the locals seeing something."

I agreed, grasping on to anything I could. "You don't just go door to door," I told them. "We tear this fucking city apart. Speak to any contact you have, no matter how dirty. Find someone who saw something."

They nodded gravely before splitting up and heading out.

"Liam, can you give me a lift back to Canning Town?" I asked him, and he nodded in agreement as he grabbed his keys.

Kieran looked devastated that I hadn't asked him. He probably blamed himself for leaving Em on her own, and now he knew that part of me blamed him, too.

For the first few hours, I tried my best to keep it together for Em's sake. After forty-eight hours, I'd completely lost the fucking plot. The police were feeding us bullshit. They hadn't located Frank, and according to his lying bitch of a wife, he was on a fishing trip and out of contact. The only car registered in his name was in the drive of their house, and according to his employers he was on annual leave, giving the same bullshit fishing trip story.

The police had fuck-all to go on, and neither did we. In two days we'd spoken to every contact we had but nobody had seen or heard anything. It's like he'd taken Em and dropped off the face of the earth.

I hadn't eaten, showered, or slept since she'd been gone, and knowing that my chances of getting her back alive were decreasing by the second was killing me. Em was elemental. She was my sunshine and my air. Without her I was alone in the dark unable to breathe.

Danny had dropped by the gym to check that it was all secure, since none of us had the stomach to go there without Em. For now the guys all took turns hanging out with me at Em's apartment. I guess it was ours now but it didn't feel like that without her.

Kieran walked in and sat down in the chair, looking as weary and desperate as I did. I didn't care. I'd trusted the most important thing in my world to him, and he'd left her alone when she needed him most. Now she was gone, and I had no idea how to get her back.

"Fuck, I'm tired," he mumbled.

Tired? I was consumed with all the evil things that fucker could have done to Em in forty-eight hours, and he was tired? It was my last thought before what little control I had left snapped, and I dived at him. Knocking him to the ground, I got in two bruising body shots before Tommy and Liam pulled me off.

"Fuck off," I shouted as I fought against them. "It's his fucking fault she's gone. He was supposed to stay with her."

"That's not fair, Con," Liam replied. "You could have told us about her stepfather, and we all would have made sure she was safe. We just thought you were being overprotective."

I couldn't listen to him. The weight of any more guilt would crush me. I couldn't breathe as it was. Needing to escape the reality that I might never get Em back safely, I grabbed my jacket and ran.

"Where are you going?" Liam shouted.

"Out," I replied, and slammed the door behind me.

* * *

"Knew I'd find you here," Kieran told me, as he sat down on the pew next to me, clutching his bruised ribs.

"Did you now," I replied.

"Of course! It was the first place I thought of looking after the gym, the cafe, the police station, and pretty much every place you went on a date with Em."

I didn't say anything for a while. Kier was used to my brooding silences. We sat quietly for a few minutes at the front of the church, watching as the altar boys lit the candles for mass.

"I think you broke one of my ribs, you know," he told me, rubbing his side as he panted pathetically.

"What, do you want a hug?" I asked.

"I'm sorry, Con. I know it's my fault she's gone," he apologized.

"The fuck it is," I acknowledged. "I should have told you all about her old man. It's my fault she's gone. Blaming you was just easier."

It was as close to an apology as he was going to get. But for Kieran, I knew it would be enough.

"I can't live without her, Kier," I admitted, my voice cracking as I buried my head in my hands.

"You won't, Con. I promise. Just have a little faith. She'll come back to you."

"I fell asleep last night for half an hour. I didn't mean to. Her pillow smelled like her, and I only closed my eyes for a minute. But how can I sleep when she's gone? I dreamed she was lying on the bed next to me, covered in fucking blood. She was in so much pain, and I could see it in her eyes that she wanted to give up. I made her promise not to leave me. Told her I'd be fucking pissed if she did. What if it was real? Is it selfish that, no matter how much pain she was in, I couldn't let her go?"

Kieran thought about what I'd said for a minute. He looked as devastated as I did at the picture of Em I'd painted.

"I think if it was the other way around, if it was you in the dark, Em wouldn't tell you what you wanted to hear. She'd say what was needed to keep you alive. It doesn't matter what state she comes back in as long as she makes it back," he told me.

"I have to believe that she's okay because, if I let myself imagine that dream was real, even for a minute, I wanna set the fucking world on fire."

He had no response because there was nothing left to say. So my best friend sat next to me and waited while I prayed. There was nothing else left to do.

After about an hour, Kieran's phone buzzed. I didn't think anything of it. His phone had been going off constantly over the last few days as the guys checked in with each other. Out of respect for Father Pat he went outside to answer it. Minutes later he came rushing in and grabbed my arm. "They've found her, but she's in a bad way," he said urgently.

I raced out of the church with him.

"She's at Newham," he told me, which was the nearest hospital.

"Shit, we need to get a cab!" I said.

"No need. Liam's on his way," he replied.

Sure enough, Liam drove around the corner minutes later and screeched to a stop. We piled into his truck in record time, and I held on tight as he broke the sound barrier getting us there.

"What happened?" I asked Liam.

"Danny interrupted Frank at the gym. Don't know what they were doing there, but there was a struggle and Em got hurt. She's alive, but that's all I know."

She was alive. Hurt, but alive. I willed her, with every fiber of my fucking being, to stay that way.

Liam dropped us off at the emergency entrance, and a nurse directed us to the waiting area.

"I need to see my wife. Can you tell me how she's doing?" I begged, having just reeled off her identity and why we were here.

"Mr. O'Connell, if you take a seat, I will try and find out what's happening."

Being so close to Em and having to park my arse in a plastic chair was killing me. But if I didn't cooperate with these people, security would kick me out, and there's no way that was happening.

Reluctantly we did as we were told. A few minutes later it was Danny who found us. When I saw him standing there, covered in my wife's blood, I wanted to puke.

"What the fuck is going on, Danny? Where is she?" I screamed at him.

"Calm the fuck down," he ordered. "You're going to get us kicked out!"

I stopped yelling, but I was far from fucking calm.

"She's in surgery," Danny said as he sat down next to me. "Her stepfather was making her leave a note telling us she'd gone back to live with her family and not to look for her. I interrupted them, and when he went for me, she stepped in and took a knife in the chest." It felt like me who'd been stabbed, the pain of hearing that was so bad.

"Is she going to be all right?" I asked, scared to know the answer.

"I'm feckin' praying for it, son. It's all we can do," he replied.

"Did he rape her again?" I asked.

Danny wiped his hand wearily down his face. "I honestly don't know," he answered. "He sliced her and knocked her about a fair bit. Poor kid was a mess. After all that, she still took a knife for me. I ain't ever seen anyone fight as hard as that girl does."

I was heartbroken to think what she went through. If I ever got my hands on Frank, I'd tear him limb from fucking limb. "Where is he?" I asked Danny.

He knew exactly what I was talking about. "One of the coppers told me he's been arrested. They're not saying anything else," he told me.

"How long until we know about Em?" I said.

"Few hours at least. They took her straight into surgery. We won't know anything till she's out."

Those few hours were worse than all the others before them. I couldn't have her this close only to lose her now. Nearly twenty-four hours went by before they let me see her, and when they did, I cried. I wasn't afraid to admit it either.

Her hair was matted, her face badly beaten, and there were wires and tubes everywhere. She was the most beautiful thing I'd ever fucking seen. The nurses had cleaned her up the best they could, and I fussed around, tucking her in and making sure she was comfortable.

Every few hours Danny or one of the guys would check on me. They tried convincing me to go home for a bit, and when that didn't work, they took pity and brought me bottles of water and sandwiches instead. I wasn't going anywhere until my girl opened her eyes. Even the nurses had stopped asking me to leave. Eventually, when the ward finally went quiet, the beeping of the monitors lulled me to sleep.

When I woke, Em was running her hand shakily through my

hair. For a few brief seconds, I kept my eyes closed in case I was dreaming again. Finally convinced her touch was real, I smiled as I looked up. She was back, and I had my second chance. I'd failed to protect her once, but hell would freeze over before that happened again.

Right now, getting her well was my only priority, but Frank's time was coming. My vengeance would wait . . . but not forever.

ACKNOWLEDGMENTS

To Lee, my husband and best friend in the whole world. Thank you for always believing in me, more than I believe in myself, and for loving me even when I abandon you for a world of fiction. I love you more than you will ever know.

To Jack and Gabriel. You are my inspiration, my motivation, and my reward. No matter what, you will both always be the best thing that ever happened to me, and I am so proud to call myself your mum.

Thank you to Mum and Dad for never ever letting me think that there was a dream too big for me if I didn't work hard enough. On your shoulders I could always see the whole world.

Thank you to my amazing friend Marie. I have no doubt that, without you, this book would never have been written. Your faith and encouragement gave me wings, and without you, this crazy dream would never have become a reality.

Thank you to my amazing and wonderful family, Gerry, Faye, Laura, Sarah, Boo, Gareth, David, Daniel, Ben, and Dave. I can't believe that I didn't tell you about my writing for so long, but it was your love and support that helped me make it to the end.

To Vin and Ria, my cryptic friends. Thank you for all of the technical and other advice, for the beta reading, and most importantly for encouraging me to put myself out there and make this happen. Lee and I are so lucky to have you as friends.

A huge debt of gratitude goes to Lauren-Marie who has helped and supported me on this journey in so many ways. I can't tell you how grateful I am for everything.

I cannot thank Louisa Maggio from LM Cover Creations enough. Not only did you create a cover that I love, you became the first friend that I made on this journey, and I can't wait to work with you again.

Many thanks to L.J. from Mayhem Cover Creations for my fabulous website and teasers. You were a total blast to work with and endlessly patient with my lack of technical knowledge.

Thank you so much to my editor Jenny from Editing 4 Indies. To say that you had a mountainous task with my manuscript is a colossal understatement.

To Angel Dust for my wonderful book trailer. I truly love it, thank you so much. Thank you also to Cassy Roop from Pink Ink Designs for taking time away from your own book release to help make my dream a reality.

To Rachel V across the pond, I am so very grateful for the day that you answered my message. At the start of this book, you were my first beta reader. By the end of the book, you were my friend. So much of this story is owed to you and how you saw O'Connell. I am so grateful to you for everything, and I hope one day that we will get to meet in person.

To the amazing Lily M who was never too busy to beta for me at the drop of a hat. I hope that you will stay with me for many more books to come. Thank you to my other beta readers, Sue R, Ariel, and Sarah.

Thanks also to Natascha, without whom this book wouldn't have a single credible location, and Joey, who inspired my prologue. Your thoughts, insights, and, often, words of encouragement have helped me more than you know.

I was so daunted when I first considered publishing, and there are many people in the literary world that I have to thank for keeping me on track. Firstly, to author L. A. Casey who was never too busy on her own journey to help me on mine. I am, and always will be, a fan for life. To author James Oliver French, your technical know-how continues to astound me, and I'm so grateful to have traveled along this road with you. Thanks to author Julia Derek who gave me my first lesson in the basics of shaping a manuscript so that my editor wouldn't throw it at me. Finally, to Whitney from A Literary Perusal, who painstakingly gave of her own time to help me make this into a better story. I have learned so much from all of you, and I can't thank you enough.

To all of my friends in Bristol for all of your support, no matter how long it's been since I saw you last and for so many happy memories that inspired so much of my writing.

A HUGE thank you to all my friends in Pentwyn including Cerianne, Ruth, Cynthia, Kerry, Kevin, and Amanda. I can't tell you how much all of your support has meant to me.

Thank you to Ashleigh and Andrew for listening for months about every endless detail of my adventure without complaint. And for not stapling anything to me in all that time.

A MASSIVE thank you to each and every blogger who has helped me get *The Hurricane* out there. So many of you give your own time and money to help and promote authors. You are, without doubt, the unsung heroes of the literary world. I can't thank you individually, for fear that I will forget someone, but know that I am truly grateful for every one of you that has helped me along the way.

Last, but not least, my biggest thanks go to you, the reader, for taking a chance on this book by an unknown author. Just to know that you have read it is a dream come true.

ABOUT THE AUTHOR

R. J. Prescott was born in Cardiff, South Wales, and studied law at the University of Bristol, England. Four weeks before graduation, she fell in love, and stayed. Ten years later she convinced her crazy, wonderful firefighter husband to move back to Cardiff where they now live with their two equally crazy sons. Juggling work, writing, and family doesn't leave a lot of time, but curling up on the sofa with a cup of tea and a bar of chocolate for family movie night is definitely the best part of R. J. Prescott's week. *The Hurricane* is her debut New Adult Novel.

Facebook: www.facebook.com/rjprescottauthor
Twitter: @rjprescottauth
Website: http://rjprescott.com
Email: r.j.prescott@hotmail.com